The new Zebra Regency Romance logo that you see on the cover is a photograph of an actual regency "tuzzy-muzzy." The fashionable regency lady often wore a tuzzy-muzzy tied with a satin or velvet riband around her wrist to carry a fragrant nosegay. Usually made of gold or silver, tuzzy-muzzies varied in design from the elegantly simple to the exquisitely ornate. The Zebra Regency Romance tuzzy-muzzy is made of alabaster with a silver filigree edging.

A STOLEN KISS

"Now kindly release me."

"Give me a kiss, and I shall," Peter said.

"One kiss?" Kate asked.

"For now."

She stepped closer, her arms slipping about his shoulders as she smiled up at him. "Very well," she said softly, stroking the back of his neck with her fingertips. "One kiss, and then I must really insist you leave. I have my reputation to think of, you know."

Peter's breath caught in his throat at the invitation of her upturned face and moist, parted lips. Against his will his arms slid around her waist, drawing her closer to his body. All thought of duty and deception fled as pure sensation filled his head, and he lowered his mouth to hers in a kiss of burning passion . . .

D1444107

THE TIMELESS CHARM OF ZEBRA'S REGENCY ROMANCES

CHANGE OF HEART
(3278, $3.95)

by Julie Caille

For six years, Diana Farington had buried herself in the country, far from the gossip surrounding her ill-fated marriage and her late husband's demise. When she reluctantly returns to London to oversee her sister's debut, she vows to hold her head high. The behavior of the dangerously handsome Lord Lucan, was too much to bear. Diana knew that she could only expect an improper proposal from the rake, and she was determined that *no* man, let alone Lord Lucan, would turn her head again.

The Earl of Lucan knew that second chances were rare, so when he saw the golden-haired Diana again after so many years, he swore he would win her heart this time around. She had lost her innocence over the years, but he swore he could make her trust — and love — again.

THE HEART'S INTRIGUE
(3130, $2.95)

by Evelyn Bond

Lady Clarissa Tregallen preferred the solitude of Cornwall to the ballrooms and noisy routs of the London *ton,* but the future bride of the tediously respectable Duke of Mainwaring would soon be forced to enter Society. To this she was resigned — until her evening walk revealed a handsome, wounded stranger. Bryan Deverell was certainly a spy, but how could she turn over a wounded man to the local authorities?

Deverell planned to take advantage of the beauty's hospitality and be on his way once he recovered, yet he found himself reluctant to leave his charming hostess. He would prove to this very proper lady that she was also a very *passionate* one, and that a scoundrel such as he could win her heart.

SWEET PRETENDER
(3248, $3.95)

by Violet Hamilton

As the belle of Philadelphia, spirited Sarah Ravensham had no fondness for the hateful British. But as a patriotic American, it was her duty to convey a certain document safely into the hands of Britain's prime minister — even if it meant spending weeks aboard ship in the company of the infuriating Britisher of them all, the handsome Col. Lucien Valentine.

Sarah was unduly alarmed when her cabin had been searched. But when she found herself in the embrace of the arrogant Colonel — and responding to his touch — she realized the full extent of the dangers she was facing. Not the least of which was the danger to her own impetuous heart . . .

Available wherever paperbacks are sold, or order direct from the Publisher. Send cover price plus 50¢ per copy for mailing and handling to Zebra Books, Dept. 3546, 475 Park Avenue South, New York, N.Y. 10016. Residents of New York, New Jersey and Pennsylvania must include sales tax. DO NOT SEND CASH.

A Heart's Disguise
Joan Overfield

ZEBRA BOOKS
KENSINGTON PUBLISHING CORP.

This book is most humbly dedicated to the memory of Janet Louise Roberts, whose wonderful Regencies first inspired me to write.

ZEBRA BOOKS

are published by

Kensington Publishing Corp.
475 Park Avenue South
New York, NY 10016

First printing: October, 1991

Printed in the United States of America

lamb three times that week, but she wisely held her tongue. "Perhaps she was only trying to help," she said delicately. "You have been very busy of late, and I'm sure Lucille only wished to ease some of the burden from your shoulders."

"Rot!" Portia dismissed this flummery with the contempt it deserved. "The vixen was trying to usurp my authority with the servants, and I insist you speak to her at once."

The hand Kate had been using to rub her aching head dropped, and her green eyes took on a chilling aspect. "Indeed?" she asked, tilting her head back to study Portia's face. "And pray what would you have me say?"

"Don't take that tone of voice with me, missy," Portia snapped, singularly unimpressed by Kate's response. "I am your aunt, and you will treat me with the respect afforded my station."

"And Lucille is my sister-in-law," Kate responded stiffly, wishing her aunt would go away and leave her in peace. "Would you have me deny her the only home she has ever known merely because the two of you can not get along?"

"Why not?" Portia demanded, folding her arms across her meager bosom and returning Kate's glare with apparent indifference. "It would do her a world of good, if you ask me. It's not healthy, the way she clings to your skirts."

"She does not cling to my skirts!" Kate denied hotly, if somewhat untruthfully. Lucille *did* cling, and with a limpet-like determination that was nothing short of amazing. Cossetted and spoiled first by her parents and then by her indulgent younger brother, the petulant woman never let a single day pass without making mention of Charles's death and the promise he had extracted from Kate to always grant her refuge.

"Pooh, the woman could put a leech to the blush," Portia grumbled, refusing to abandon her attack. "To

6

Chapter One

"This is it; I have reached the end of my endurance!" Mrs. Portia Stone exclaimed, her brown eyes sparkling with fury as she burst into the small book-lined study. "Either that hen-witted female goes, or I do!"

Mrs. Katherine Delecourt glanced up from the ledger she had been studying, her heart plummeting to the soles of her leather slippers at the sour expression on Portia's face. Evidently it was too much to hope her stubborn aunt and her equally quarrelsome sister-in-law could make it through an entire afternoon without coming to daggers drawn, she thought, closing the book and pushing it away from her with a weary sigh.

"What is it this time, Aunt?" she asked, pinching the bridge of her nose. She'd been working on the accounts since nuncheon, and her head was throbbing with pain.

The resigned question was all it took to loosen Portia's tongue, and she launched into a litany of complaints that was all too familiar to Kate. "And if that wasn't enough to give a saint the vapors, the sly wench went behind my back and told Cook she was not to fix lamb for dinner!" she concluded in the tone of one reporting some heinous crime. "Can you imagine such cheek?"

Indeed Kate could, considering they'd already had

5

say nothing of the way she is forever weeping and wailing like one of those Irish ghosts. Isn't there some way you can think of to be shed of her?"

Before Kate could give vent to her impatience, the door opened. A plump woman with graying blond hair scrapped back in a prim bun came striding in. At the sight of Portia sitting on one of the striped chairs, she came to an abrupt halt, her lips thinning with displeasure. "Well," she said, pulling her shawl tight about her, "I can see you wasted no time in running to Katherine with your tale of woe."

" 'He who hesitates is sometimes lost'," Portia responded with a provoking smile. "And I suppose you are here to discuss the latest political *on-dit* with her?"

"Aunt Portia, please—"

"Trust *you* to attribute your motives to another," Miss Lucille Delecourt returned with a loud sniff. "But as it happens, I was going to ask dearest Katherine if she would like to accompany me to town. The lending library has a copy of Miss Burney's latest work, and I am sure she is longing to read it."

"That is very kind of you Lucille, but I really don't think—"

"My niece thinks far too much of her mind to read that fool woman's scribblings!" Portia snapped, shooting her enemy an angry scowl. "She is accompanying me to the squire's for a lecture on the latest scientific advances. A far more *intellectual* way of passing one's afternoon."

"Scientific advances!" Lucille responded, outraged. "I should say not! Charles would never have approved. The women of our family have never concerned themselves with anything that smacks of learning!"

"That much is readily apparent," Portia reposted silkily. "All the more reason why I insist she attend the lecture. The women in *our* family do value their minds, you see, and I shouldn't wish her to develop any . . . unfortunate habits."

7

Lucille was quick to pick up the cudgels her small chin thrusting out in defiance. "She is going to read Burney."

"She is going to the lecture," Portia insisted, and the fight began, with both ladies determined to emerge victorious.

While they squabbled, the object of their disagreement listened in stony silence, her sense of ill-use increasing with each passing moment. In the sixteen months since Charles's death she had remained acquiescent as the two older women decided her every move. At first she was too dazed with grief to notice, and later, as the grief eased, it seemed easier to continue placating them rather than trying to assert her independence.

In the last few weeks, however, she had grown increasingly impatient with their incessant quarreling, and with the dull routine she had somehow fallen into. She was only five and twenty, she reminded herself indignantly, and surely there was more to life than sitting and listening to two aged females haggling over her like a pair of dogs with but one bone.

"If you belonged to the *ton* as I do, you would know no one reads those dull-as-ditchwater tracts," Portia said, regarding the other woman with a superior smile. "But then, you've never been to London, have you?"

"How dare you!" Tears glistened in Lucille's blue eyes. "My family is in every way superior to yours, and we care nothing for fast London ways! Katherine is a Delecourt now, and it is her duty to honor her husband's wishes."

"Superior! Why, of all the moonshine—"

"Will you be silent!" Kate's palm came slamming down on the desk tops startling both combatants into silence. They turned and gaped at her, the shock on their faces so great one would have thought the chair itself had spoken.

"Why, Katherine, dearest, whatever is it?" Lucille asked in the solicitous tones she always adopted towards

8

her sister-in-law. "Is your poor head bothering you?"

"It's your stomach, I'll wager" Portia nodded her head wisely. "Pity we're not having lamb for dinner; mutton's just the thing for a spot of indigestion."

"It's not my stomach or my head," Kate retorted, a surge of emotion dispelling the last of the lingering indifference.

"Then what is it?" Portia was gazing at her anxiously.

"Do you want something?" Lucille pressed closer.

Kate was silent a long moment as she considered the question. What did she want? She said the first thing to pop into her head. "I want to go to the beach."

Lucille and Portia exchanged puzzled looks, the animosity of a few seconds ago quite forgotten. "I beg your pardon?" Portia asked in disbelief.

"I want to go to the beach," Kate repeated, her cheeks flushing with excitement.

"The beach!" There was another exchange of horrified glances.

"You can not mean to go there," Lucille managed at last, clasping one hand to her throat in a dramatic gesture. "Why, whatever would the neighbors think?"

"That I am taking the fresh airs I should imagine" Kate said, warming rapidly to her impromptu outburst. A quick glance at the clock on her desk showed it to be a little after three. If she hurried, she could change into her walking clothes and be on the beach within the hour. It was too late for her to go exploring, but if the light held she could walk as far as the old dock. She might even have Cook pack her a small snack to take with her. . . .

"Pray, don't be impertinent, Katherine," Portia said, bending a frown on her niece. "You can not go there; it's not safe. You don't know, because you have been much too distracted, but the Owlers have been rather active of late, and 'tis common knowledge they use the beach for their rendezvous. I quite shudder to think of what should befall you were you to stumble upon them."

The mention of the smugglers who plied their trade along this side of the Romney Marsh gave Kate pause, but only for a moment. "Oh come, Aunt," she said, refusing to be dissuaded, "surely you are exaggerating the danger. Charles warned me about the Owlers, but he also said so long as one doesn't interfere with them they are perfectly harmless."

"Harmless? A group of armed men who go about defying their King?" Lucille's tone was scathing. "No, my dear, I think I must agree with your aunt. You can not go to the beach; those ruffians would carry you off in the blink of an eye. Now, do be a good girl and go put on your new bonnet. I don't want the last copy to be gone before we get there."

"I thought it was understood she was accompanying me to the squire's," Portia reentered the fray with a vengeance. "And that bonnet is a perfect abomination. It looks like a garden gone all to weeds."

"What nonsense! It's quite the loveliest chapeau and if you had an ounce of taste you . . . why, Katherine, where are you going?"

Kate paused at the door, her fingers curling around the cool brass. "I told you where I am going" she said, striving for an even tone. "The beach."

"But the smugglers—"

"You shall be carried off, missy, you mark my words!"

"Good!" Kate's exclamation once again silenced both women. "Good," she repeated, shooting them a satisfied smile over her shoulder. "I hope they may indeed carry me off, because at least then I should have some peace and quiet!" And with that she opened the door and slammed it behind her, leaving the others to gape after her in open-mouthed astonishment.

* * *

Half an hour later Kate stood on the fog-shrouded beach; her eyes closing as she savored the sharp tang of the ocean. Above the muted roar of the waves crashing against the rocks, she could hear the lonely cries of seagulls. The sound brought a wistful smile to her lips. If only she could fly away from her earthly cares, she thought, opening her eyes to gaze across the white-capped waves.

In defiance of convention she'd left off the starched cap she usually wore, and the brisk wind soon made short work of her tidy chignon. She brushed a lock of bright blond hair back from her cheeks, taking a perverse delight as she envisioned her aunt's and sister-in-law's horror were they to see her comporting herself with so little regard for the proprieties. Aunt Portia and Lucille might disagree on everything else, but they appeared united when it came to how a widow should and should not behave.

The thought of her quarelling relations brought to mind the scene in her study. What on earth was she going to do, she brooded, turning to walk along the shoreline. She could hardly toss both women out into the cold; however tempting that solution might seem, but neither could she choose between the two of them. She sincerely loved her irascible aunt, and odd as it seemed, she'd also grown attached to Lucille, despite the other woman's dramatic airs and unfortunate tendency towards loquacity. Besides, as she was always reminding Aunt Portia, Lucille *was* Charles's sister, and she simply couldn't ask her to leave. Perhaps she should be the one to go, she decided, her eyes dancing with the wry sense of humor that had been stilled for so long.

She continued walking, and although she was no closer to resolving her dilemma, she was relieved to find her spirits much improved. She was just about to turn back when something further down the beach caught her eye. At first she thought it was a clump of seaweed or a log that had washed ashore; then she saw a flash of red, and the terrible truth struck her full in the chest. It was a *man!*

For an agonizing moment she was frozen with indecision; a dozen different possibilities running through her head. Her aunt's dire warnings were uppermost in her mind, and she wondered if it could be some sort of trap designed to lure her to her doom. Or worse yet, it could be just what it appeared to be—the body of a drowned man. She'd once seen them pull the remains of a fisherman from the quay near her home in Brighton, and the memory was enough to make her stomach roll with nausea. She was debating whether to investigate further or go back for help when a low groan reached her ears.

The faint sound ended her paralysis and she began running towards the figure, all concern for her own safety forgotten. Her flight was hampered by the wet sand and her full skirts, and she was breathing unevenly as she collapsed on her knees beside him. Limbs trembling, she laid her hand on his shoulder, and the slight movement beneath her fingertips assured her that she hadn't imagined the low groan. She murmured a brief prayer of relief and sat back on her heels; her teeth sinking into her bottom lip as she surveyed the unconscious man.

He was lying facedown on the sand, dressed in the dark, rough-spun clothing Charles told her the smugglers often affected. One arm was flung out over his head, as if he had been dragging himself along, while the other lay at an awkward angle at his side. The flash of color that had attracted her attention turned out to be a sash of red silk wrapped tightly above his elbow, and she wondered that a simple fisherman should sport so expensive an armband. The possibility he was other than a simple fisherman occurred, but she dismissed it as unimportant. First she would see how badly he was hurt, and then she would worry about his choice of occupations. Praying she wasn't doing him any additional injury, she carefully rolled him onto his back.

The first thing that struck her about him was his relative youth. She'd somehow formed the notion that smugglers were ancient, grizzled men, while the man at her feet looked scarce to be in his thirties. He was also far more handsome than she thought he would be with high cheekbones and a slender, well-shaped nose that lent him a surprisingly aristocratic air. Even with the lower half of his face covered with a dark beard there was something about him that made her gaze linger on his strong features longer than was proper.

She next turned her attention to tenuously examining his arm, struggling to recall the bit of medical knowledge her mother had taught her. She didn't think the bone had been broken, but it was obvious he would need immediate attention. His rasping breath also concerned her and she ran a cautious hand over his chest, her fingers hesitating as she felt the thick padding above his left shoulder. A bandage? she wondered, refusing to speculate how he may have come by such a wound.

When she was satisfied she had done all that she could, she turned her mind to what she should do next. Clearly she couldn't leave him here, but taking him up to her house entailed more than a little risk. Not from the man himself, she felt certain. Rather it was the authorities she feared. Aiding a smuggler was a crime punishable by transportation, and she was intelligent enough to know that that was probably what he was. She stood and gazed down into his face, and for some reason she thought of Charles.

Had he lain on some beach, alone and hurt with no one to aid him? Perhaps if they had, he might still be alive. The thought galvanized her, and her hand flew to the front of her cape, her fingers unfastening it with lightning speed. Ignoring the damp chill that struck her almost at once, she quickly spread it over the man.

When she was satisfied he was completely covered,

she brushed a lock of dark hair back from his forehead. "I'll be back," she whispered, her tone quietly determined. "I shall not let you die, do you hear me? I shall not let you die!" And then she leapt to her feet, running back towards the house as if the devil himself was in hot pursuit.

The house was all but deserted as she burst through the front door; her wild eyes and flushed countenance mute evidence of her agitation. The footman gaped openly to see his quiet mistress so disheveled, and he took a faltering step forward.

"Be there something wrong, Mrs. Delecourt?" he asked hesitantly, envisioning a platoon of French dragoons even now making their way towards the house.

"Where are my aunt and sister-in-law?" Kate ignored the hesitant question. During her mad rush up the cliff it occurred to her that the two older women could provide a greater impediment to her plans than the authorities, and she'd prayed they were gone.

"They-they be out, ma'am," the footman stammered, wondering if he should send for the butler or attempt to hold off the French horde himself. Well, he squared his boney shoulders resolutely, the Gauls would not find getting past *him* so easy! "What is it you want, ma'am?" he asked, prepared to sacrifice his all in her defense.

"I want you to fetch a litter and then gather the other footmen," she instructed briskly. "And blankets; we will need blankets. Oh, and send someone for Nurse Mason. We shall have need of her services."

"But — " The footman was far from reassured by these requests.

"And I want the room Charles's uncle used prepared for a guest," Kate continued briskly, her mind spinning with a myriad of details. "It is far enough from the rest of the house to be safe. Well, why are you just standing there?" She glared at him angrily. "Hurry!" And she dashed up to her room to grab another cape.

When she came scurrying down the stairs a few minutes later she found the footmen waiting for her. Richards, the Delecourt's formidable butler was with them, his expression faintly disapproving as he stepped forward to greet her.

"James indicated there was some sort of difficulty, madam," he intoned in the languid accents he considered suitable for one of his exalted position. "May I inquire as to what that difficulty might be, or whether or not it will be necessary to send for the constable?"

"No constable!" Kate replied, shuddering at the thought of turning the unconscious man over to the doubtful care of the drunken lout who served as the local representative of the law. "That is the last thing we need!"

"Indeed?" One of Richards's brows raised itself in an elegant arch over his eye.

Kate sighed, knowing she would be forced to explain. "Richards, an injured man has washed ashore. Judging by the way he was dressed, I should think a King's man would be the last person he would care to see. I trust you take my meaning?"

"Unquestionably, madam," Richards bowed majestically before turning back to the footmen. "Shake a leg, lads," he advised, all pretenses of a cultured accent vanishing. "It be one o' the Owlers!"

The trip back up the path carrying the injured man was accomplished with relative ease, and less than an hour later Kate was able to see him settled safely in the large bed. Nurse Mason, the ancient woman who had acted as her late husband's nanny, was already there, with a basin of warm water and fresh bandages at the ready.

"We'll see to this, madam," she said, shooting Kate a stern look. "Mind ye get back to yer rooms and change out o' that damp dress a' fore ye takes a chill."

"Nonsense," Kate answered briskly, guessing the real

15

reason why the servant wanted her out of the room. "I'm hardly an innocent maid who will swoon at her first sight of a man, you know. I can help."

"That may as be," Nurse Mason grumbled darkly, already turning her skills towards her patient, "but what'll ye do when ye sees blood, hm? There'll be plenty; I'm warnin' ye."

"I won't swoon," Kate assured her, her small chin coming up with pride. She stepped closer to the bed and held out her hand for some bandages. "What is it you want me to do?"

The nurse's dark eyes narrowed speculatively, and then she broke into a gap-toothed smile. "Have some spirit, do ye?" she murmured with obvious appreciation. "Good. I might o' knowed my Charles would have no use for some milk and water miss. Now, pay attention, and mind ye don't get in the way," and she began rattling off a list of grisly instructions.

With the help of the little man who'd served as Charles's valet they soon had the man stripped of his sodden clothing. With the dark jacket peeled away it quickly became obvious he had been shot — twice, according to Nurse, who began digging for the musket-balls with a ruthless efficiency that set Kate's senses reeling. When she was satisfied she'd retrieved all the fragments, Nurse stepped back, wiping her blood-stained hands on a fresh towel.

"He'll live, provided the fever don't carry him off, but he'll be weak as a babe for at least a fortnight," she predicted, slanting Kate a hard look. "Are ye sure ye want him here?"

"I'm sure," Kate replied, brushing back a lock of hair that had fallen across his broad forehead. She'd already performed the gesture a dozen times, but the thick, soft hair seemed to have a will of its own. She was vaguely amazed that a man's hair could be so delicately textured. It reminded her of black silk.

"Ye knows what 'twill mean if ye're caught?" Nurse

16

pressed, frowning at the gentle smile on the younger woman's face.

"I know."

"Then why are ye doing it?"

The smile faded from Kate's face as she considered the blunt demand. Why indeed, she mused, her fingers trailing over the man's peaceful features. It was a question she'd been asking herself, and the answer, she realized, was amazingly simple. Her hand dropped to her side, and she raised her eyes to meet the other woman's troubled gaze.

"There has already been enough death," she said quietly.

Nurse was silent for a moment, and then nodded. "Thought it must be something like that. Well, what's to do, then? Ye'll not want yer aunt and Miss Lucille to know about this, I'm thinkin'."

"Heaven forbid," Kate responded with a shudder. "Aunt would demand that he be transported to the nearest roundhouse, and Lucille—"

"Would screech like a scalded cat and then swoon dead away," Nurse concluded, well aware of her former charge's dramatic propensities. "Reckon we'll just have to keep 'em from the door, then, won't we?"

"How?" Kate was open to suggestion.

Nurse shot her an evil smile. "Ye're a bright lass," she said with a conspiratorial wink. "I'll wager ye'll think of a way."

"Cow Pox!" Portia gaped at her in amazement. "In *our* house?"

"Or something very much like it," Kate replied vaguely, wishing she could have come up with some other method of keeping the two women away from the north wing. She detested prevarications of any kind and hated lying to her aunt, regardless of the reason.

"Really, Katherine, must you be so obtuse?" Portia shot her an angry scowl. "One either has a disease, or

17

one has not. It is rather like being with child; there is no shilly-shallying about it."

"Mrs. Stone!" Lucille's pasty cheeks flamed scarlet with mortification. "Must you be so indelicate? I will thank you to remember I am an unmarried lady!"

"Rot," Portia said succinctly, casting the other woman a supercilious look. "You may be unwed, but you aren't some green girl to be put to the blush by a bit of plain speaking. Besides, we were discussing the stableboy's spots" she turned back to Kate. "Now, has the poor wretch cow pox, or has he not?"

"Nurse is convinced that he has," Kate answered, mentally appealing to God for forgiveness. "Jems has a fever, and his body and face are covered with lesions. Nurse doesn't think he is *terribly* contagious, but she thought it might be best to keep him shut away . . . just to be safe."

"Hmph. Seems to me it would have made better sense to keep him locked away in the servants' quarters rather than putting us all at risk," Portia grumbled, then laid a thoughtful finger on her lips. "Are the lesions oozing?"

Too late Kate remembered her aunt's fascination with illness. She'd have to think fast if she didn't want the older woman stalking up the stairs and demanding to be admitted to the sickroom. "Oh yes, they oozed something awful," she said quickly, praying that if she painted a disgusting enough picture her aunt would lose all interest. "The bandages stuck to them, and when we pried them off the poor lad moaned from the pain."

"Katherine!" Lucille clapped her hand over her mouth and shot Kate a desperate look. *"Please!"*

"I am sorry, Lucille," Kate murmured, casting down her eyes with every indication of remorse. "But you can see Aunt Portia, why it would be best if we leave Nurse to tend the boy. We wouldn't wish to risk infection . . . would we?"

18

"Hmph" Portia gave another sniff but mercifully allowed the topic to drop. They continued eating dinner in a leisurely fashion until Portia remarked, "And how was your walk, my dear? I trust you didn't encounter any smugglers along the way?"

Kate promptly choked on the sip of wine she had just taken. "Smugglers?" She wheezed, fumbling for her napkin.

"Or Owlers, or gentlemen, or whatever the beasts are calling themselves these days," Portia explained, frowning to see her sensible niece being so missish. "Katherine, are you feeling quite the thing? I vow, you are behaving most strangely."

"Oh no, not at all, that is, I am fine," Kate managed a shaky smile. "Never better, as a matter of fact. And I found my walk most invigorating. I shall probably be going out tomorrow."

"I really don't think that is advisable, dearest," Lucille said, grateful the conversation had moved on to the more genteel topic of smugglers. "I happened to speak with Reverend Boothe while in the village, and he told me the Owlers have grown most shockingly bold. Why, last evening a group of them attempted to smuggle in some barrels of brandy under the very noses of the Excise men!"

"Trust the good vicar to know about smuggled brandy," Portia offered with a malicious laugh. " 'Tis common knowledge he has a decided predilection for spirits . . . and I don't mean the holy kind."

Other than pursing her mouth Lucille ignored the other woman's spiteful comment. "Well, needless to say, they did not get away with it," she continued dramatically. "Reverend Boothe said the guards were able to draw their weapons, and were even able to get off a few shots before they made their escape."

The wine in Kate's glass sloshed dangerously close to the rim, and she set the glass down before she could spill any more of it. "Were . . . were any of them hit?"

19

she asked, moistening her lips with a nervous tongue.

"Probably." Lucille blinked at her reaction. "At least, Reverend Boothe said there was a great deal of blood all over the docks. The soldiers are searching the town, although it is supposed the wounded man either drowned or escaped to the marsh."

Kate paled with horror. If the man abovestairs was the man shot by the Excise men then he was in even greater danger than she had first supposed. Were they to suspect he was anywhere in the vicinity, it was likely they would institute a thorough search, and she doubted if her gentle birth would prevent her own house from being forcibly entered. He would have to be hidden. Perhaps a note could be sent to his confederates in the marsh, and—

"Oh, Katherine, my wretched tongue!" Lucille's penitent cry made Kate glance up in surprise. Lucille was gazing at her with tear-drenched eyes, her bottom lip quivering with remorse.

"I am so sorry, my dearest," she said, dabbing at her eyes with a black-edged handkerchief. "I hadn't meant to remind you of poor Charles's untimely death. Can you ever forgive me?"

Kate stared at her, unable to reply. She hadn't even been thinking of her late husband, she realized dully. For the first time in over a year his tragic loss had been the farthest thing from her mind. Her only concern had been the wounded man lying in the guest bedroom. The knowledge filled her with an overwhelming sense of guilt.

Chapter Two

His first thought was that he was dead. The last thing he could remember clearly was the wave that overturned his boat, casting him into the icy water. He'd been over a quarter of a mile out, and with two bullets in him, he knew there was no chance he would reach shore alive. But it was not in his nature to give up and so he had struck out for land; ignoring the pain and exhaustion as he swam through the darkness towards the distant point of light.

His next cognizant thought was that he hurt — badly. The realization brought his brows together in a puzzled frown. Although not a religious man he'd always thought of death as peaceful, an end to all physical suffering. That he could still feel was either a very good sign or a very bad one. Steeling himself for whatever he might find, he opened one eye and glanced cautiously about him.

He was in a bed chamber, not a luxurious one by some standards, but certainly nicer than those he had been accustomed to of late. The walls were covered with a thick floral pattern in greens and blues, and he could see several portraits prominently displayed. The few pieces of furniture he could see without turning his head were carved of rich mahogany and had a decidedly English air about them. This was a real home and not some fine cell, he realized, releasing the breath he'd been unconsciously holding. One of his deepest fears was that he had somehow been taken captive.

Feeling slightly reassured he continued studying his new surroundings, noting the cheerful fire that blazed in the hearth with annoyance. Why were they bothering with a fire, he wondered fretfully. It was already hot as Hades in here . . .

"Awake are ye?" The gruff voice beside the bed made him start, and he turned his head sharply, glaring up at the speaker.

"None o'that, mind," the old woman scolded, frowning down at him like a disapproving parent. "I'll not have ye tearin' out all my fine work with yer thrashin'."

He continued gazing up into her wizened features, struggling against the return of the swirling blackness. His primary concern was to determine where he was. Later he would decide what to tell the woman . . . if anything. For her own safety, it was best that she knew as little as possible. He moistened his lips with his tongue.

"Where . . . where am I?"

"Safe," the woman answered just as his eyes drifted closed. "Ye're safe now, lad . . ."

The room was in shadows when next he woke; save for the red glow from the fire and the faint light of the candle flickering on his bedside table. He glared at the fire, wondering if they were trying to roast him alive. If so, they were doing a damned good job of it. He'd never felt hotter in his life. He moved restlessly beneath the bedcovers, wondering where the old woman had gone and whether he'd be able to charm her into giving him a glass of water. Once he'd done that he'd set about wheedling some badly needed information from her; beginning with where he was. "Safe" was not so precise a location as he would like. He turned his head on the pillow and that was when he saw the woman sitting in the chair.

He could tell at first glance that she was not his nurse, for she was far too young and comely, but that was all he could discern for the moment. As his situation could be described as precarious at best, he decided it would be wisest to lie quietly until he had more information. Her eyes were intent on the book she held in her hands and she did not seem to notice his perusal, so he took the opportunity to study her with narrowed eyes.

He placed her age as somewhere in her mid-twenties, and she was blessed with a delicate beauty that made the breath catch in his throat. In profile her face was perfection, with a high forehead, gently rounded chin and a soft, full mouth. Her nose was small but decidedly aristocratic, and he wondered what color her eyes would be. Blue, perhaps, to complement the curls of guinea gold he could see peeking from beneath the brim of her prim cap, or maybe the soft gray of a foggy morning. One of his mistresses had had such eyes, and he'd considered them one of her more attractive features.

As if aware of his scrutiny the woman suddenly looked up, and when she saw he was awake she hurried gracefully to his side.

"How are you feeling?" she asked, her tone soft with concern as she bent over him.

Her eyes were a gentle misty green every bit as attractive as her oval face. He allowed himself the brief luxury of admiring them before summoning up his most charming smile.

"Like I've died and gone to heaven, ma'am, and you're surely the prettiest angel as ever I've seen," he said, falling easily into the lilting brogue that had been a vital part of him for these past two months. Until he knew more of his location and his lovely benefactress he decided it wisest to cling to the identity he'd so painstakingly established for himself.

Kate blinked, momentarily nonplussed by his teasing words and the roguish smile that accompanied them. When Nurse told her he'd awakened she expected to find him weak and confused; or at the very least she'd assumed he would be suspicious. He'd just been shot, after all, and it was only natural that he should be a little wary. But the bearded man grinning up at her looked as if he hadn't a care in the world, and her own suspicions stirred to life.

"I hate to disappoint you, sir, but you are most definitely *not* in heaven" she responded tartly, moving away from the bed. "You are in my home, just outside of Rye. I found you washed up on shore not very far from here."

Rye! He quickly masked his shock. Good lord, was he *that* close to Payton? He'd have to tread lightly then, lest he be discovered by the very man he'd been pursuing all these weeks. Keeping his smile as broad as ever he hastened to answer his hostess.

"Rye, is it? Well, if 'tis England that I now find myself, then I know I am still alive. No self-respecting Irishman would ever consider England to be heaven. The other place, mayhap," he added, risking a daring wink.

Kate tried not to smile, but it proved impossible. The man was probably a smuggler and heaven only knew what else, but she was helpless to resist his boyish appeal. "And you consider yourself to be a self-respecting Irishman?" she asked, tilting her head to one side as she studied him.

Before he could answer the door opened and the older woman he'd seen earlier bustled in, a slightly-built man carrying a tray trailing at her heels. Upon seeing him awake she broke into a pleased smile.

"Thought ye'd be awake," she said, eyeing him thoughtfully. "How are ye feelin'? Hot?" A gnarled hand was placed on his forehead.

"As the very devil, ma'am" he answered, his eyes flicking hopefully towards the carafe of water on the tray. "You English keep your rooms much too warm for my liking."

" 'Tis not the room that's heating your blood," she responded grimly, pouring some water into a glass. Kate moved closer to help her, but the valet stepped in front of her, blocking her path.

"We shall see to the . . . gentleman, Mrs. Delecourt," he said, his tone respectful, but determined. "It would be best if you left."

Kate frowned, not caring for the summary way she was being dismissed. She knew her staff only had her best interests at heart, but she still found it irksome. Her eyes flashed to the bed where the man was drinking thirstily from the glass Nurse held for him, and the protest she was about to utter withered on her lips. The flush on his cheekbones and the glitter in his eyes told its own story, and she realized that now was not the time to assert her authority.

"Very well, Peters," she said, casting one final glance towards the bed. "But I expect to be kept fully informed of our guest's health."

"Yes, Mrs. Delecourt," he assured her, guiding her inexorably from the room. "We shall notify you immediately should there be any change. Good night." And he closed the door in her face.

Kate scowled at the expanse of wood, and for a moment she was strongly tempted to give it a hard kick. But only for a moment. Given her limited experience in the sickroom it was probably just as well that she'd left; should their guest become seriously ill, she was likely to be more of a hinderance than a help.

She returned to the east wing to prepare for bed. She'd moved there shortly after receiving word of Charles's death, unable to bear the memories the master suite held for her. The room was done in shades of gold and pink, and decorated with the daintily carved cherrywood furniture she had brought from her old house. She knew her aunt and sister-in-law found her preference for the simple room puzzling, but she didn't care. They had governed so many other aspects of her life this past year that she'd needed to assert herself somehow; even if it was only in so small a matter as her room.

After bidding her maid good night she climbed into the canopied bed, exhausted by the day's events. She was just drifting off to sleep when she realized that she still knew next to nothing about their mysterious guest. Not his name, nor his direction, nor how he'd come to wash ashore on her beach—all but dead from two gunshot wounds. The thought brought her eyes flying open again.

Was he the smuggler shot in Rye? she wondered, nibbling worriedly on her bottom lip. Logic dictated that he was. And yet there was something about him that made her doubt the evidence. Granted her discourse with him was limited to that brief exchange, but she still found it hard to believe that he was a smuggler.

He seemed much too charming for one thing, and despite his rough appearance there was a decided air of quality about him. She thought about the well-defined planes of his face, and the cultured texture of his voice that even his brogue could not disguise. Yes, there was a great deal about the man that bore closer inspection, and she was determined to do just that. The moment she knew he was up to it, she would have another talk with him. And this time, she was determined to come away with some answers.

She rose early the following morning; eager to check on her guest. After donning a gown of gray merino trimmed with black ribbons, she tucked her hair under a freshly starched cap, and hurried to the sick room. Nurse Mason was still tending their mysterious guest, and at Kate's insistence she admitted her.

"But only for a moment, mind," she grumbled, mov-

26

ing back to the bed. "He's finally asleep, and I'll not have ye wakin' him."

"I won't," Kate promised, stepping closer to gaze down into the man's peaceful features with unabashed curiosity. In repose he was even more attractive than ever, and again she was struck by the aura of power that emanated from him. She glanced up at the nurse. "Has his fever broken?"

"Early this mornin', God be praised. 'Twas fearsome while it lasted, but he's a strong lad; given time and plenty of rest and he'll soon be back plyin' his trade."

"Has he told you his name?" Kate asked, deciding it was wisest not to dwell on what his "trade" might be.

"Mickey," Nurse supplied obligingly. "Leastways that was the name he kept givin' when we asked him."

"And his surname?"

Nurse's shoulders moved in an eloquent shrug. "Just Mickey. When we pressed for more he grew restive." She sent Kate a puzzled look. "Does it matter?"

"Not really," Kate admitted, aware of a vague sense of unease. She'd feel better if she at least knew the name of the man she was harboring. "Although I can not help but wonder how we shall contact his friends. They must surely be concerned by now."

"Don't be worryin' about that, Ma'am," Nurse informed her with a knowing smirk. "If he's what I think him to be, his 'friends' will know soon enough how to find him."

"Then you have heard what happened in town?" Kate asked, her green eyes wide with surprise.

The older woman gave a contemptuous snort. "The whole county knows of it! News travels fast in these marshes. How else do ye think they'll know where to find him once they start lookin'?"

Kate stirred uneasily, not caring for the thought that the whole countryside may already know of her actions.

"Although" Nurse was continuing in a thoughtful tone, "the more I think on it, the more I wonder

27

if he was one o' them shot by the Excise men."

"But his wounds . . ."

"I'm not denyin' he was shot," Nurse assured her quickly, "I'm just sayin' I doubt it was the spoilers what shot him. A Brown Bess leaves a devil of a hole in a man, and the musketball I dug from him was too small for that. More n' likely he was shot with a pistol," she added with a decisive nod.

How the older woman had come by such gruesome knowledge was another thing Kate thought it wise not to explore. Charles had once told her that the smugglers were so successful because they enjoyed the support of the common folk. Nurse lived alone in a tiny cottage no more than a stone's throw from the infamous marsh, and it wouldn't be surprising if she was involved in some way.

"When do you think he'll awaken?" she asked instead.

"When he's had enough of sleepin'," Nurse answered with the experience of many years. "And like as not he'll be hungry as a lion when he does. I've got a pot of veal broth cookin' for him; that'll put the roses back in his cheeks soon enough."

Roses in a smuggler's cheeks sounded somewhat incongruous to Kate, and she smiled at the image it invoked. The smile faded as she thought of what else would have to be dealt with once Mickey had regained his senses. "I want to be informed the moment he is awake," she said, turning from the bed without a backwards glance. "There are several questions I should like to ask him."

Nurse stirred uneasily. "I don't think that t'would be wise, Mrs. Delecourt. We know naught of this fellow, and for all we know of him he could well slit yer throat a'fore ye could say boo. Or do worse," she added darkly, her eyes flicking towards the muscular figure lying unmoving on the bed.

That was a possibility Kate had already considered, and it was the main reason she was so anxious to learn

28

more of him. As mistress of the house it was her duty to safeguard its inhabitants, and it was a duty she took very seriously. She did not think the man meant her ill, but until she knew for certain she would take whatever precautions she deemed necessary.

"Send for me" she stressed, sending Nurse a look which brooked no argument.

"Very well, Ma'am," Nurse said with a loud sniff. "But Mr. Charles would not be approvin'."

The mention of her husband brought a sad smile to Kate's lips. "No," she said softly, "I think he would have."

"Well, 'tis about time you chose to honor us with your presence" Portia greeted Kate as she entered the morning room. "What has kept you so long? We have been waiting breakfast for you!"

"I'm sorry, Aunt, I fear I overslept," Kate replied, wincing inwardly at how easily the lie came to her lips. "You should have started without me."

"That is what I said," Lucille said, shooting Portia a smug look. "But some people would not listen."

"Some people think more of their manners than their bellies," Portia responded with a poisonous smile. "Not that you would know about that, of course."

Kate stifled a small sigh and signalled for the footman to start pouring the tea. It looked like the beginning of another long day, she decided glumly, wondering if she could convince Mickey to take her aunt and sister-in-law with him when he left.

Portia and Lucille continued squabbling through the rest of the meal, arguing over everything from whether the marmalade had turned to sugar, to the way the war was being fought on the peninsula. Neither seemed to notice Kate's air of distraction, having grown accustomed to her long silences. They were finishing the last of the tea when Portia snapped her fingers.

"That reminds me, Katherine, I just had a note from

Gussie, and she wants to know when you will be coming to the city."

"The city?" Kate looked up from her plate in confusion.

"London," Portia enunciated, rolling her eyes heavenward. "The capital of our country, the center of our little world, the—"

"I know what London is, Aunt," Kate interrupted, not up to the older woman's potent brand of sarcasm. "I meant I don't recall telling Augusta that I would be coming this year."

"Well, of course you shall," Portia's scowl grew fierce. "It is to be Louisa's coming out, and you must know we are depending upon you to show her how to go about. Heaven knows that goosecap Gussie would only make a hash of it." She gave a contemptuous sniff at the thought of the timorous woman her only son had so ill advisedly married.

Kate set her fork down in alarm. "But I can't leave Kent," she exclaimed, paling at the thought of leaving the safety of her comfortable home.

"Katherine, we have already discussed this," Portia said with an obvious attempt at patience, "and I thought it was agreed that it was past time you were casting off your widow weeds and reentering the social whirl. You are still in your prime, and it would be beyond all that is foolish for you to continue shutting yourself away. Even Lucille agrees with me on this, don't you?" she cast the other woman a look that dared her to object.

"Yes, Katherine, Charles would not wish you to mourn him forever," she supplied dutifully. "And as your aunt has said, we have discussed the matter and decided it was all for the best."

"When was this discussed?" Kate demanded suspiciously, striving to recall the conversation. She had a vague memory of Aunt Portia mentioning it was almost time for her granddaughter to make her bows, but that was all. Surely her two warring relations hadn't cast aside their differences long enough to scheme against her, she thought, studying them beneath her lashes. Or had they?

There was a covert exchange of glances between the two. "Actually," Lucille cleared her throat, "actually you were not exactly present when the conversation took place . . ."

"But you did agree with me that a London season sounded delightful," Portia interjected quickly. "You even mentioned that you wouldn't mind seeing the city again."

"I meant in the future; not now!"

"The Season won't begin for a month yet," Portia pointed out with the cunning of a Machiavelli. "That *is* the future."

"But—"

"Nothing need be decided just yet," Lucille said, taking pity on Kate's distress. "Only promise us that you'll think about it. Please?"

"Very well, I will consider it," Kate said, surrendering to the inevitable with a heavy sigh. Besides, she admitted with innate honesty; they were right. It was time she was getting on with her life. The realization made her smile.

Only yesterday she'd walked along the beach dissatisfied with her life and wishing for some nameless change. Given the events in the last twenty-four hours, it would seem she had gotten that wish.

At the sound of the door closing behind the two women Lord Peter Wyndham, earl of Tregarren, opened one blue eye to peek cautiously about him. Alone, thank God. Since regaining his senses he'd noted that someone—the nurse, the valet, or a footman—was always with him; leaving' him to wonder if he was being kept prisoner after all. But after the conversation he'd just overheard he understood the reason behind their caution. So they thought him a smuggler, did they? He smiled grimly. The irony of the situation was not lost on him.

He lay quietly a few moments, absorbing his surroundings with a greater sense of awareness. The room was much as he remembered it, small but comfortable, with the door providing the only entrance and exit. His eyes flicked towards the tall, wide windows and he considered their value as an escape route should the need arise. Judging from the slant of the sun streaming through the opened drapes he estimated he was on the second or possibly third floor. Not an insurmountable distance under ordinary circumstances, but the circumstances were now far from ordinary.

How the devil had his disguise been penetrated, he wondered, his jaw hardening with fury. He'd spent the better part of two months establishing his identity as "Mickey," a fisherman of Irish descent who was not adverse to smuggling a load or two past the ever-vigilant British navy. He'd thought he'd succeeded, but apparently he had underestimated his enemy. On what was to have been his last run he'd been met on the beach by a squad of French regulars. He was only here now because he'd been desperate enough to make a run for it, taking his captors completely by surprise.

He managed to reach his small boat and was about to cast off when a young sentry confronted him; pistol drawn, ordering him to surrender in halting English. He had pretended to comply, and then at the last moment made a grab for the pistol. He succeeded in wresting it from the lad's hand, but not before earning two bullets for his pains. And not before leaving the young man lying dead on the wet sand. After that came the long, painful journey in the blackness as he struggled to tend his wounds and sail his craft through the stormy waters.

A dozen different times his agonized body urged him

32

to simply give up and let death take him, and a dozen different times his proud spirit refused. He was a Wyndham — an earl — and the very notion of surrender was an anathema to him. He'd been bred to know his duty, and if he was to die, then he would die in the commission of that duty. No other course was possible. And if his deep patriotism was not sufficient motivation, there was still his brother to be considered.

Peter's lips thinned as he remembered his last meeting with James. He'd returned home from his club to find his half brother sprawled in a chair, a glass of his best brandy cradled in his hand.

"When are you going to swallow your fine English pride and let me bring you some *real* brandy, eh?" he demanded, his green eyes dancing with mischief as he'd grinned up at Peter. "And don't be telling me you gentlemen don't buy smuggled brandy, for I've the guineas in my pocket to prove otherwise."

"That may be, but this gentleman still doesn't buy French goods," he'd responded, untying his cravat and throwing himself on a chair facing James. "Now cut line and tell me why you've come. Have you reconsidered my offer to set you up in business?"

James had thrust a hand through his dark hair, and for a moment there was a coldness in his usually laughing eyes. "As I'm always telling you, brother, I've no use for Tregarren gold. Our esteemed father had his chance to do right by mother and me and he did naught but leave us to starve. I appreciate your generosity, but I'll have none of it."

"Then why are you here?" Peter had accepted James's decision, and admired him the more for it.

"I've some news that might be of interest to your fine friends in Whitehall."

Peter had stiffened with caution. His image as a dilettante lord interested in little but gaming and ladybirds had hid his secret involvement with the Home Office for over three years, and he wondered how

James had learned of it. When he asked him, his half brother had shot him a lazy smile.

"Our mutual parent may have been many things, lad, but he loved his country, and I can not imagine his son being any different. If you aren't in the thick of things, then you know someone who is."

"What is it you have learned?"

"There's a lord. Payton is his name, and I think he bears close watching. The gentlemen say he is not to be trusted."

Peter knew Payton; socially at least, and what he did know of the man led him to doubt James's oblique warning. "What is that supposed to mean?"

"Merely that it 'tisn't just brandy and silk his Nibs brings back in those fine boats of his," James had responded bluntly. "The word is the earl has turned traitor and is selling information to the blasted French."

Peter had managed to hide his shock at the news that not only was the fastidious lord personally involved in smuggling, but that he was betraying his country as well. "Can you prove this?"

"Not just now," James had rolled his muscular shoulders indifferently. "But I will. I've met some of his men, honorable men for all they're smugglers, and I think they'll be of a mind to help. The gentry's not the only ones who love their country, you know."

"I'm well aware of that," he responded grimly. "But you must know how careful we will need to be. Payton is a member of the Privy Council, and an intimate of the Prince's. The thought of him passing such high intelligence to the enemy is too horrifying to contemplate. When will you have the proof?"

"I've arranged to go on a run with some of the Owlers by way of the Marsh," James explained. "I won't say I'll learn much, but it will be a start. Given time I'll build you a strong enough gibbet for his lordship, and then may the devil take his black soul."

"You'll be careful?" Peter had asked, knowing James's flamboyant ways only all too well.

"Aren't I always?" James's eyes were wide with innocence. "Don't worry, little brother. I'll be back within a week, and then we'll decide how to best trap the bastard."

But James hadn't come back in a week. He had disappeared so completely it was as if he had never existed. Peter had made a few, cautious inquiries, but was unable to uncover anything. Finally he had gone to his superiors and presented them with a daring plan. They would still use the gentlemen to gather evidence on Payton, but with a slight difference. He would be the one to pose as a smuggler, moving freely among them until he had the proof necessary to arrest Payton.

He'd set up a "carriage accident" to explain his absence from London and then slipped quietly away, disappearing into the nether world of smuggling. He'd been so good at his craft that he was soon accepted by the others, and made to feel welcome among them. He had just made tentative contact with a band of Owlers operating out of Dymchurch when he'd set out on a run two nights ago.

Somewhere, somehow—he had been betrayed. The questions were how and by whom? Had he been viewed as competition, and removed by smugglers unwilling to share their prosperous trade with anyone? Or had his careful disguise been penetrated? There was also the small matter of his temporary lodgings to be considered.

His hostess and her servants thought him a smuggler, and yet they continued harboring him, despite the dreadful risk they were running. Why? Were they involved with the local Owlers? The old nurse certainly knew more about wounds than was the usual, and his hostess seemed far too acquiescent for his liking. He'd seen the gold band on her finger and heard the servants refer to her as Mrs. Delecourt, so it was obvious she was married. But if this was the case, where the deuce was her husband? What kind of man would allow his gently bred wife to tend personally the wounds of a potential criminal? It was all quite mysterious, and another mystery was the last thing he needed right now.

Until he had more information he had no choice but to remain where he was, continuing with the charade he had already established. Meanwhile he would work on regaining his strength, and with any luck, learn the answers to some of his questions. He thought again of his hostess and a very masculine smile touched his lips. Given the fact he might even now be languishing in some pesthole of a French prison, he did not think he would find the situation so very difficult.

was married. But if this was the lady, why
was her brother? ... What kind of ...
gently bred wife to bed personally to, when

Chapter Three

It was two days before Kate was able to maneuver
her way back into the guest bedchamber. Nurse had
long since pronounced Mickey to be out of danger, but
she remained adamant on the subject of Kate visiting
him.

" 'Tis not done, Madam," she said, fixing Kate with a
cold look. "And that's an end to it."

In the past Kate would have allowed herself to be
guided by the conventions, but not any longer. Since
making the decision to live again she had regained
much of her old spirit, and she refused to be dictated
to. She waited until Nurse had returned to her cottage
for more herbs, and then slipped quietly up the stairs.
The footman proved somewhat recalcitrant at first but
she was soon able to dislodge him; insisting that he return to his other duties. After he had gone she turned to
her guest with a hesitant smile.

"Good day to you, sir," she said, noting his improved
color with relief. They had found an old nightshirt that
belonged to Charles's father, and her guest looked quite
at home in the big bed. "I trust you are feeling much
more the thing."

"That I am, my lady," Peter answered, hiding his suspicions behind his most winning smile. He'd seen the
small byplay between her and the footman, and he
wondered what the devil she was up to. No lady of his

wide acquaintance would even think of visiting a wounded smuggler. Not only would they not wish to risk their reputation, but he sincerely doubted that they would even be interested.

"I am not a lady," Kate replied, then winced at her foolish answer. "That is," she added hastily, blushing at the way he raised his dark eyebrows, "I am not a member of the peerage. I am Mrs. Delecourt."

"You'll be forgiving me, I'm sure, Mrs. Delecourt, for what is an honest mistake," he said, amused by her rosy blush. "For a more genteel—like lady I've yet to be meeting. You could put the proudest duchess to shame, I'll wager."

"Thank you." Kate was not overly impressed by such praise. She suspected he was flattering her to put her at ease and to avoid any questions. She'd already learned from Nurse that he was amazingly adroit when it came to sidestepping direct questions. Well, he would soon learn that she would not be put off by such machinations, she thought, folding her arms across her bosom and regarding him with an assaying look.

"Now that you know my name, I think it only fair that I know yours," she said without preamble. "I know that your given name is Mickey, but I'm afraid I do not know your surname. What is it?"

The blunt question made Peter instantly wary. The nurse had also asked, but he'd put her off by moaning in pain; something told him such a ploy would not work again. His hostess was glaring at him like a patroness at Almacks confronted by an interloper, and he knew he would have to tread a fine line if he meant to appease her and still keep the fiction of his disguise.

"Well now, Mrs. Delecourt, that is what you might call a delicate matter," he answered, thinking quickly. "My mother's name, may God rest her soul, was Smith, and my father's name was Quentin . . . or so she was always claiming. You can appreciate the difficulty, I am sure."

Kate's blush deepened as his meaning dawned. "Then you are a . . . a . . ." her voice faltered as she found herself unable to utter the terrible word.

"A by-blow, ma'am," he said, mimicking the surprisingly cheerful way James often described himself. "Born on the wrong side of the blanket, if you'll forgive me for being so bold."

Kate cringed at his blunt response. Although sheltered by her parents she wasn't wholly insensible to the ways of the world. She knew men often kept mistresses, and that the results of those illegal liaisons were often left to fend for themselves as best they may.

Peter cast her a covert glance, measuring her response with interest. Rather than being embarrassed as he expected she would be, she seemed indignant. Doubtlessly she was one of those females easily given to sentiment, he decided with a flash of complacency. Good. He would only have to portray himself as a poor, put—upon orphan, and he would soon have her eating out of his hand. Her next question, however, shattered his smugness.

"How did you come to be shot, Mr. Quentin?"

"What?" He gaped at her in astonishment.

"How did you come to be shot?" she repeated, amused by his obvious dismay. "You were shot, were you not?" she added when he continued staring at her.

"Indeed, ma'am, I'm sure I don't know what you mean," he said, desperately stalling for time. He hadn't had time to concoct some plausible explanation for his wounds, and he didn't want to answer too hastily lest he entangle himself in a hopeless web of lies. "I'm but a simple fisherman, and—"

"Cut line, sir!" Kate interrupted, her green eyes flashing with annoyance. "I was present when my nurse dug the bullets out of your shoulder, so kindly do not lie to me. Unless the fish have taken to arming themselves, the nature of your injuries is patently obvious!"

Her flare of temper made Peter's lips thin with impatience. "Just so, ma'am," he answered, striving to appear amused. "The clever beasties go swimming about armed like brigands. Why, I had a whole school of them trapped in my net, and what did they do but shoot their way out. I tried to stop them, but what is one man against an army of fish?"

Kate glared at him for a moment, and then gave a weary sigh. "You aren't going to tell me what happened, are you?" she asked with quiet resignation.

The laughter died in Peter's eyes. "There are some things, Mrs. Delecourt 'tis better not knowing. I can not tell you what you want to know."

Kate considered his answer and then slowly nodded her head. "Very well," she said, meeting his gaze, "I will accept that . . . for now. All I ask is that you be honest with me when you can. I can not abide deception in any form."

"Then I may stay here?" He was vaguely surprised by her response.

"Until you are recovered. Unless there is somewhere else you would rather stay?" She glanced at him questioningly. "I am sure my footman could carry a message to your friends."

Peter knew what she meant, and shook his head. "My friends are out to sea just now," he said, reluctant to contact his newfound acquaintances. Until he discovered who had betrayed him and why, it was simply too dangerous. But there was someone he did wish to contact. Before leaving he had taken the precaution of setting certain safeguards into place, and he decided it was time to alert the Home Office as to his location.

"There is, however, someone I should like to write to, if you don't mind my asking, ma'am," he said cautiously. "You might call him something of a family friend."

"All right," she agreed, quickly masking her surprise. "Are you up to writing the letter, or should I do it for you?"

Peter glanced down at his bandaged arm. "I think it had best be you, ma'am. With my poor arm trussed up like this, I fear my penmanship would be even more indecipherable than ever."

"When would you like me to send the letter?"

Peter considered his response carefully before replying. "Oh, there's no hurry just now. Perhaps if you'd be so good as to stop by tomorrow afternoon, I could dictate it to you."

"As you wish," Kate agreed coolly, puzzled by his request. She would have thought he would wish his comrades notified as soon as it could be arranged.

"Mrs. Delecourt, do you mind if I ask you a question?" Mr. Quentin's hesitant query broke Kate's reverie, and she glanced up to find him regarding her with a shuttered expression.

"Certainly, Mr. Quentin," she replied, striving for a cool possession she was far from feeling. "What is it?"

Peter cleared his throat. This was something that had been troubling him since she had walked into his room, and he felt he could not rest until he had the answer. "Well, if you don't mind my asking, ma'am, may I inquire as to where your husband might be?" At her look of alarm he added, "I'm only asking, you see, because I should like to meet the gentleman, and offer him my thanks for his kind hospitality."

Now it was Kate who squirmed uncomfortably. She trusted Mr. Quentin, but that trust only extended so far, and prudent caution kept her from blurting out the truth. She lowered her eyes to her lap, her slender fingers clenching in the soft gray of her gown. "He—he is away from home just now," she stammered, unable to meet his eyes. "But I—I expect him momentarily."

"I see," Peter replied, sensing the lie behind her words. He wondered if her husband had abandoned her, or was off chasing light skirts, and then gave a mental shrug. Either way, he supposed it did not signify, so long as he did not have to worry about the man

41

returning and blowing a hole in him.

"Are you sure he won't mind my being here?" he asked after a careful pause. "I wouldn't want there to be any . . . unfortunate misunderstandings."

The wary glint in his eyes brought a reluctant smile to Kate's lips. "And have you had other unfortunate misunderstandings with husbands?" she asked, greatly daring.

"Oh, a few, here and there," he stirred himself enough to send her a sly wink. "And after all the trouble you've gone to to save my poor miserable hide, I'd not want to be repaying you by getting shot again."

"I appreciate your thoughtfulness," she answered with a soft chuckle. "But you needn't worry. Charles," her voice quavered for a moment, "Charles is the most understanding of men."

"That is good to know," Peter said, hearing the hesitancy in her voice.

Kate rose to her feet, suddenly anxious to be gone. "If you will excuse me, Mr. Quentin, I fear I must be returning to my other duties," she said in a soft rush. "If you want for anything, you have only to ring for the valet."

"Thank you, Mrs. Delecourt," he said, aware of her desire to be gone. "And a rare treat it will be for me, too. I'll feel just like one of those fine pashas in their harems."

A brief smile touched her lips, and then was gone. "Goodbye, Mr. Quentin. I shall see you tomorrow." Peter inclined his head, his melodic accent ever in evidence as he said, "I'll be looking forward to it, Mrs. Delecourt. Until the morrow, then."

After leaving Mickey's rooms Kate returned to her study where she buried herself in her accounts. She'd let a great deal slide over the past year, and she was astonished at the shape they were in. It would take her a good week to straighten them all out, she decided, frowning as she puzzled over an entry from the grocers. She was laboring on another set of accounts when the butler appeared with the morning post. A letter lying on top caught her attention, and she grimaced as she recognized the spidery scrawl.

Wonderful, she thought gloomily, picking up the letter and breaking the wax seal with her finger. She needed only a missive from her cousin-in-law to ruin an already unpleasant day. She sighed and began reading, her heart beginning to race with each passing word. By the time she finished she was fairly quivering with excitement. A plan was forming in her mind, and she picked up her skirts and raced into the small parlor where Aunt Portia and Lucille often spent their afternoons. She paused only long enough to compose her features before striding purposefully into the room.

"Good afternoon, Aunt, Lucille," she greeted them each with a kiss before taking her chair before the fire. "How are you feeling this day?"

"We are well," Aunt Portia answered, gray brows lowering in a skeptical glare as she studied her niece's downcast face. "Why do you ask? Has the stableboy's cow pox spread to the others?"

"Oh no, that is, it is days too early to be certain," she said with a hasty smile. "But you will be happy, Aunt Portia, to know that he is much recovered. With luck, Nurse says he will be about his duties in no time at all."

"That is good to hear," Portia said with a vigorous nod. "It does no good to coddle servants when they're ailing. It gives them pretensions above their station. But that does not answer my question, Katherine. Why do you inquire after our health and in such a mysterious tone?"

Kate allowed a faintly hurt expression to cross her face. "Your pardon, I am sure, Aunt," she said softly. "I did not mean to sound 'mysterious.' It is just that after reading Cousin Caro's letter I am naturally concerned about your well-being."

43

"Caro?" Lucille glanced up from the book she had been reading. "How is the dear lady? We've not had a word from her in at least a month. I trust all is well?"

"Unfortunately not," Kate sighed, and removed the letter from the pocket of her gown. "The poor thing has fallen and broken her ankle."

"And she's writing to say that she wishes to batten herself upon us," Portia grumbled, thrusting aside the Gothic she had been secretly perusing. "I was wondering when she would finally come right out and admit as much. She is forever hinting about it."

"What cheek!" Lucille glared at her. "*She* is a Delecourt, she need not 'hint' to be welcome in our home!"

"Actually," Kate interposed hoping to avoid another skirmish, "travel is quite impossible just now, with her leg all trussed up the way it is. No, she only writes out of loneliness. Her family is all grown, you know, and she is much alone in her house. She writes,

> *How lucky you are, Katherine, to have dear Lucille in constant attendance. Her presence must be a great comfort to you, and I am sure poor Charles must rest easier knowing you will never be alone as I am now alone. If only she could come to Surrey and visit me, but naturally I must not be so selfish as to deprive you of her companionship. After all, you would then have only your elderly aunt to bear you company. I shall manage, somehow.*

"Oh, the poor dear lady," Lucille cried, much affected by the plight of her distant relation. "How terrible for her!"

"Elderly aunt, indeed!" Portia looked ready to spit nails. "I am but a decade older than her, and well she knows it! And as for managing without Lucille, what rot! Why, she as good as demanded you send her to Surrey post haste!"

"And what if she has?" Lucille turned a militant gaze on Portia. "I am her cousin! To whom else should she turn in her hour of need?"

"Hour of need!" Portia gave a contemptuous snort. "The wretch has naught but a sore ankle. Trust you to be taken in by such a Cheltenham Tragedy!"

"Aunt Portia, you mustn't be so harsh," Kate admonished in a gentle voice. Secretly, she was delighted by her aunt's baiting words. She could not have done any better even if she was an actress reciting lines written expressly for her. "Lucille is but expressing a natural concern for her cousin."

"Don't be such a goose, Katherine!" Portia snapped, much put out by Kate's scold. "Why, 'tis as plain as the nose on your face that the selfish creature wants Lucille to act as her unpaid lackey. How the pair of you can be so gullible is beyond all understanding, I vow!"

"Indeed?" Lucille exclaimed, fairly bristling with indignation. "And what has any of this to do with you, might I ask? Caroline is *my* cousin, and if I wish to go to her, then I shall!" She turned to Kate. "Katherine, my dear, you must surely know that under normal circumstances I should never think of abandoning you. But the very thought of poor Caro languishing in pain with no one but a lot of indifferent servants to attend her quite tears at my heart! You must see that I have to go."

"Of course, Lucille," Kate lowered her eyes to hide their triumphant sparkle. "Naturally I shall miss you, but you are right. Caro's needs are what must be considered now."

"I shall go and pack at once!" Lucille said decisively, leaping to her feet. "I'll also speak to the coachman. We haven't had the travelling coach out since before Charles's service and so it will doubtlessly need cleaning. Oh, and I must visit the dressmaker! I can not go to Cousin Caro's looking like a country mouse; I shall require a new wardrobe." She hurried from the room, talk and plans spilling from her with eager abandon.

The moment the door closed behind her Portia

turned to Kate with a smile. "Very well done, my dear," she said approvingly. "You are a bright little minx, to be sure."

Kate gave a guilty start. "I beg your pardon, ma'am, but I'm sure I have no notion what you are referring to," she muttered, feeling vaguely trapped. That was the problem with deceit, she decided; one lived forever in fear of discovery.

Portia leaned back in her chair and fixed Kate with a measuring look. "I am referring to that little drama concerning Cousin Caro's broken ankle," she said bluntly. "It was quite clever of you to have solved our problem so neatly. Although," she added, cocking her head to one side, "I must admit I wouldn't have thought you to be so cunning. You are usually so depressingly honest."

"Do you mean to say you knew?" Kate gasped, staring at her aunt in dismay. "But how? I only just thought of it myself!"

Portia regarded her sagaciously. "Really, child, I am not in my dotage, you know. I only wish you might have let me know what was afoot. I might have been able to help you sooner had I any inkling what you were about."

Kate had no idea how to respond to this and so retreated into a strategic silence. When she'd first read Caro's letter her initial response was irritation. Caro was forever writing to complain of something, and, as Aunt Portia had pointed out so smugly, to hint for an invitation for a prolonged visit. It was only when she reached the paragraph concerning Lucille that she realized the situation could be turned to her own advantage.

The confrontations between her sister-in-law and aunt were growing increasingly acrimonious, and the thought of a few weeks of blessed peace was too tempting to resist. It would do no harm for Lucille to see a bit more of the world, she'd decided piously, and it would also serve to keep Caro from hounding her. There was also another, very compelling reason why she wanted her sister-in-law out of the way for a few weeks. *Mr. Quentin.*

Although she had decided to trust him for the moment, there were still a great many things about him which puzzled her. She was fairly certain he was harmless, but in the event she was mistaken she still had Lucille's safety to consider. Another consideration was his health. True, he was much recovered, but he was still quite weak, and she knew it would be several days yet before he would be up and about.

The fiction that he was the stableboy recovering from the cow pox could not continue indefinitely, and the possibility of discovery increased with each passing day. She didn't think her sister-in-law would take it in her head to visit the sickroom, but with Lucille there was no telling. It was just the odd sort of start she would take; especially if she even suspected it would annoy Portia. Portia—Kate's dark gold brows puckered in a troubled frown. There was another problem to be solved.

"Naturally you may rely upon my discretion," Portia continued happily; unaware of the direction of her niece's thoughts. "I shan't so much as hint that I shall do other than miss the wretch. Though we must be careful not to do it *too* brown," she cautioned. "A few tears will more than suffice, I should think."

Kate gave a noncommittal grunt, her mind spinning with possibilities. There had to be something she could do, she brooded, gazing off into space. Having rid herself of one potential problem, she would not rest until she had disposed of the other.

"I shall write dear Mrs. Givens at once," Portia said, ignoring Kate's silence. "She has never cared overly much for Lucille, and I'm sure once she knows she is gone she will be more than happy to join me for tea. Why, I might even have my literary group in!" she added with a bright smile of satisfaction. "Yes, things will be much more agreeable in the future. "Do you not agree, my love?"

Kate stirred slowly, her eyes narrowing as she gazed at her aunt. "Yes, Aunt," she said demurely, her smile widening with evil intent. "Very agreeable, indeed."

Chapter Four

Peter spent a restful evening recovering his strength and planning his strategy. Since most of the servants accepted him as a smuggler he carefully cultivated their misconceptions, and in the process was able to pick up some valuable information. From the taciturn valet he learned that the Owlers had heard of him and were already making inquiries, while the young footman informed him that his uncle had a fast boat available and was willing to set sail for Ireland . . . for a price. Even the old nurse unbent enough to mention that she knew of several locations in the Marsh where a man could stay well-hidden for weeks. He thanked everyone with a wink and a smile, but made no promises one way or another. He would contact the Home Office first, and await their instructions. But it eased his mind somewhat to know that he had several options available to him, should the need arise.

He wondered if his hostess was aware most of her household was involved in the smuggling trade, and then decided that she did. For all her pretty blond looks, Mrs. Delecourt struck him as a strong, intelligent woman, and as he had already learned, it wasn't easy getting anything past her too-seeing green eyes.

The next morning he submitted to the valet's ministrations, although he refused to allow his beard to be shaved. It wasn't likely he would be recognized so far from London and his own estates, but it was a risk he preferred not to take. Besides, he'd grown rather attached to the thing, and wanted to keep it as long as possible. The other thing he balked at was the robe the nurse laid out for him, but he proved less successful in avoiding it.

"Blast it, ma'am, I'll not be wearing that gaudy thing!" he protested, glaring up at her from the pillows, the sheets clasped protectively to his chest. "I'll look like a Covent Garden Abbess!"

"This belonged to Mr. Delecourt's uncle, and if 'twas good enough for a gentleman, then 'tis good enough for the likes of ye!" Nurse shot back, the robe held out before her as she approached his bed with a purposeful gleam in her dark eyes. "I'll not have ye talkin' to my mistress in naught but yer bedclothes, and that's all there's left to be said. Now, do ye put it on yerself, or will ye require assistance?" And she smiled with such cold menace that Peter grudgingly complied. He was still brooding over the matter when Mrs. Delecourt joined him shortly after breakfast.

"Good morning Mr. Quentin," she said, her green eyes moving over him as she settled on the chair beside his bed. "You are looking well today."

"I'm looking like a curst fool, you mean" Peter grumbled, shooting her a resentful glare from beneath his thick lashes. "That witch of a nurse insisted upon it. She said 'tis what a gentleman would wear in a lady's presence, and there was no talking her out of it."

Kate's eyes rested on the bright purple and red robe, her smile growing more pronounced at the gold braid adorning the deep cuffs and wide lapels. "It is rather grand," she agreed, dimples flashing in her soft cheeks. "It makes you look quite . . . dashing."

Peter's scowl deepened at the amusement evident in her soft voice. "That may as be, ma'am, but I take leave to tell you that it is dashed uncomfortable. I feel like a Christmas goose trussed up for the roasting! Ah well," he allowed a triumphant smile to touch his lips, "at least I was able to keep her from sticking that bloody cap on my head as well! *That* I would not allow; threaten me how she would."

"Then you are indeed to be congratulated, sir," Kate replied, much amused by his smug tones. "Nurse is a most formidable woman, and once her mind is made up on something she can be quite stubborn."

"Aye, so I noticed," Peter said, covertly studying her averted face. " 'Twould seem to be a trait she shares with you, ma'am. Any lady who would take a poor, injured stranger into her home as you have is a lady to be reckoned with. Your husband is a lucky man."

Kate's smile wavered, but did not collapse. "Thank you, Mr. Quentin," she murmured softly, her eyes falling to the portable writing desk she brought with her. She ran her hand across the rose-splashed satin, struggling to control the inexplicable sense of guilt she felt at continuing the deception. In the next moment, however, her common sense was asserting itself.

The man was a criminal, she scolded herself sternly. He was probably so accustomed to lying that he wouldn't recognize the truth if it bit him on the nose. Why, for all she knew, he could be lying to her even now! Her eyes narrowed at the realization, and she flicked him a suspicious glance.

"Is there something amiss, Mrs. Delecourt?" Peter asked, stirring uneasily beneath her speculative gaze.

"Not at all, Mr. Quentin," she returned coolly, flicking open the desk and withdrawing a sheet of parchment. "I have my writing supplies with me, as you can see, and I would be more than happy to write a letter to your friend for you. Provided you are feeling up to it, that is?" she added, her tone challenging as she raised her head.

"More than up to it, ma'am," he assured her, quickly flashing her his widest smile. "It's to Lord Peter Wyndham the earl of Tregarren."

"Tregarren!" Kate's eyes widened in surprise. "You know him?"

"Only very slightly," Peter answered with studied carelessness. "As I said, he's something of an old family friend. Er . . . have you had the honor of meeting him, ma'am? He's much in the social round, or so I am told," and he watched her closely.

"Indeed," Kate responded in arctic accents, her golden brows gathering in a disapproving frown at the thought of the sardonic Corinthian who had been Society's darling the year she had made her coming out. She'd never met him, of course, although she had once caught a brief glance of him at the theater. He'd been quite handsome, as she recalled, but the stories about his gaming and his wenching that had reached even her tender ears had been enough to set her mind firmly against him. How any man could wager a thousand pounds on the turn of a card when half the country was in want was far beyond her comprehension.

"Indeed, what, ma'am?" Peter pressed, an incipient feeling of indignation stirring in his breast. He saw the icy disdain on her face, and it angered him as he was fair certain they had never met.

"Indeed he is much in the social round," Kate responded, taking a nub from the desk's pocket and checking its sharpness on the pad of her thumb. "He is also rumored to be quite the dandy, although I would not know as I have never been introduced to the man. Now, what is it you would like me to write?" She looked up at him, her green eyes cool.

Peter's eyes flashed in annoyance. *Dandy!* He fumed, struggling to control his expression. He'd been accused of many things in his day; indeed, he deliberately cultivated his image as a care-for-nothing rake, but the charge of dandyism flicked him raw on his pride. He was strongly tempted to remind her of the danger of casting stones; especially against a man who wasn't there to defend himself, but he managed to control the impulse.

"Write him that I have suffered a slight accident, and will be unable to complete the race" he said tersely, his voice losing some of its musical cadence.

"Accident?" Kate's eyebrows arched in surprise. "Do you mean you shan't try to fob him off with tales of shooting fish, as you did me?"

"Ah, but it was an accident, Mrs. Delecourt, in a roundabout manner of speaking," he answered, still wary.

"Very roundabout, but then, that seems to be the only way you do speak" Kate observed archly. "Now, what is this about a race? I thought you were fishing."

"Aye, but a man can't fish all the day long. The race is an unofficial one, you might say. A hypothetical question of how long it would take to sail from Lyme Regis to Calais . . . if one was of a mind to."

Kate sat back in her chair. "To Calais . . . but we are at war with France!" she exclaimed, her dislike of the young earl increasing along with her indignation. "Whyever should his lordship wish to race there?"

"I didn't say he did, ma'am," he said quickly, annoyed by her self-righteous tone of voice.

"No, *he* did not, but it is obvious *you* did," Kate snapped, her eyes bright with fury. "That is how you came to be shot, isn't it?"

"Mrs. Delecourt, I have told you—"

"No! Not another word about shooting fish, I warn you!" Kate interrupted, her chin coming up proudly. "I've already said that if I can not have the truth from you, then I prefer not to hear your lies, and I meant it." She picked up the quill, her fingers shaking slightly. "Is there anything else you wish to tell his lordship?"

"Only that I am well and recovering at an inn" Peter replied, his tone guarded. "You do see, do you not, why I can not tell him more than that?"

Kate nodded, grateful for his sensitivity. The

53

thought of the rich and haughty Tregarren knowing she had offered refuge to a strange man was too uncomfortable to be borne. She shuddered to think of the speculation it would cause were the *ton* to learn of her activities. To say nothing of how the authorities would react, she added mentally, feeling a cold shiver of fright stealing down her spine.

"I am sure you are right" she said quietly. "But is there nothing else you wish to add? Surely your . . . friend will want to know more than these few facts."

"A few facts is all he'll be needing, Mrs. Delecourt," Peter replied, thinking of the young lord who was assisting him. "For all his racketing ways, his lordship is hardly a slowtop. He'll know what to do."

Yes, hire some other poor fool to sail his race for him, Kate thought, wisely keeping her opinions to herself. Even though he had said nothing, she'd noted how he had tensed when she'd called Lord Tregarren a dandy. His loyalty to the earl touched her and she hoped the wretch appreciated it, although she strongly doubted it. From what she had heard, the man cared for little save the cut of his jacket and the beauty of his newest ladybird.

"Very well then, Mr. Quentin," she said, setting the quill down. "If that is all, then I will send this out in the morning post."

Peter hesitated, wondering if he should add something more informative. He thought a minute and then said, "You might tell him that the boat we purchased in Portsmouth was not so great a bargain as first we thought."

"It wasn't?"

"No," Peter's lips thinned in a grim smile. "In fact, it developed a rather serious leak and was lost. You must tell him he is not to use that boatwright again. His work is not trustworthy."

"Very well," Kate nodded. "I only hope that his lordship didn't pay a great deal for the craft. It would be a pity if he lost his money and his boat as well. Do you think he will be reimbursed for his loss?"

Peter's eyes shimmered with blue ice. "Aye," he said in a deceptively flat voice. "I think I can assure you his lordship will be fully reimbursed. He is a man who always collects what's owed him, Mrs. Delecourt, and a man who always pays his debts; upon that you may depend."

Kate's plans to spend the rest of the day in solitary pursuits were dashed when she came down to luncheon and found Lucille waiting for her; her cloak draped over one arm and her thin face set in an aggrieved expression.

"Really, Katherine, it was quite thoughtless of you to keep me dangling like this," she chided sternly. "I have been waiting for hours!"

Kate stared at her in confusion. "I beg your pardon, Lucille," she said, searching her mind for any engagements she may have forgotten. "I can't recall our having any appointments today. Were we supposed to go calling?"

"Of course not!" Lucille shot her an outraged look. "Today is Thursday; you must know we never go out on Thursday."

"Then what the deuce are you talking about?" Kate demanded, more confused than ever.

"Katherine! Such language!" Lucille clasped her hands to her heart. "Charles would surely swoon to hear you speak so!"

"Charles would have said something even stronger," Kate returned, rubbing a weary hand across her forehead. "Now, kindly tell me what this is all about. I truly can't recall agreeing to go out today."

Lucille gave a sigh which indicated she considered herself to be much put upon, and then said "You didn't precisely agree to accompany me to the modiste's, but you must have known I would want you to come. You have always advised me on my wardrobe."

Kate dropped her hand, understanding slowly dawning. "You want me to go with you to Rye?"

"Of course, if you have other plans, I will understand," Lucille continued in tones of long-suffering. "I could always ask your aunt to accompany me. Despite her dubious tastes she is of the *ton;* I am sure she would not allow me to disgrace myself."

"I didn't say I wouldn't go with you," Kate interposed quickly, horrified at the havoc Aunt Portia could wreak were she to be placed in charge of Lucille's wardrobe. "A trip into Rye sounds the very thing."

"Then what are we waiting for?" Lucille gave her another scowl. "I vow, Katherine, there are times when you are so slow!"

Lucille did unbend enough to give Kate enough time to change her gown, and then they were on their way. Kate had also taken the time to slip the letter she had written into her pocket, and she was hoping for a few minutes of privacy in which to mail it. Having given Mickey her promise, she was determined to keep her word. Somehow, she would manage to slip away.

In the end, however, slipping away from Lucille proved to be absurdly easy. The modiste — Mrs. Tedrow — had been dressing the quality of the neighborhood for the better part of a quarter century, and she took greatest exception to the suggestion her client might require anyone's opinion other than her own.

"I'm sure you must have much to occupy you, Mrs. Delecourt," she said, nudging Kate steadily towards the door. "It shouldn't take more than two or three hours to fit Miss Lucille. Why don't you come back then, hm?"

"Yes, Katherine, why don't you come back then?" Lucille said, holding a length of puce silk to her face and judging the effects in the glass. "I shall be fine in Mrs. Tedrow's capable hands."

Kate was more than happy to comply, although a lingering sense of obligation made her pause by the door.

"Well, if you are certain" she said, her eyes flicking towards her sister-in-law. "I did want to stop at the linen drapers while we were in town."

"That will be fine, dearest," Lucille had abandoned the silk for a bolt of brown velvet. "Stop by once you have completed your errands. There's a good girl." She seemed to forget completely that she had insisted Kate accompany her; a fact which displeased Kate to no end.

The town of Rye slumbered under the wet March skies as Kate left the modiste's shop. Once the letter had been posted she decided to go for a walk; a suggestion which horrified the elderly coachman, until she grudgingly consented to allow the footman to trail after her. Leaving High Street she made her way towards the harbor, pausing every now and then to peek into the elegant shops that lined the cobblestoned streets, their bowed windows lavishly decorated with the goods that could be found inside. She was just about to turn around and start back when a weathered sign hanging in front of an old inn caught her eye.

"James, what is that place?" she asked, indicating the ancient building with a gloved hand. "I don't believe I've ever seen it before."

"Don't reckon ye have, ma'am," the young footman said, the tips of his ears going quite red. "And ye should not be seein' it now. We'd best be gettin' away from here a'fore someone sees us. Come now," and he laid a solicitous hand on her elbow.

She pulled away, her chin firming with resolution. "Not until you tell me about that inn," she said, growing more intrigued by the second. "I can see it is called the Mermaid, but what sort of an establishment is it? A brothel?" She thought that might account for his odd behavior.

"Mrs. Delecourt!" The footman's face turned as red as his hair. "A lady ought not to know of such places!"

"Then it *is* a brothel," Kate cast the inn another look and then shrugged her shoulders. "Well, I must say I am disappointed. It doesn't look nearly as decadent as I supposed such a place would look. Well, perhaps it isn't a very prosperous establishment." She turned to go.

" 'Tis not a . . . a bawdy house, ma'am," James corrected, stammering over the indelicate word. "Leastways, not a proper bawdy house. It's an inn, all right, but ye'd not be knowin' the likes of the folks what stay there." He cast a nervous look up and down the bustling street before leaning towards her.

"Smugglers, ma'am," he whispered conspiratorially. "They say they sits out in the open, bold as ye please, their pistols on the table and their loot spread out before 'em. Even the Excise men won't go in there; it be that dangerous."

Kate cast the shabby looking inn another glance. "Really?" she asked, feeling vaguely surprised that the news didn't shock her as much as it once would have. Even a week ago the notion that smugglers should thrive so openly would have horrified her, now she took it as a matter of course. A slight smile lifted the corners of her mouth. She didn't know if that was a good sign or a bad one.

They were just about to leave as the door to the inn burst open, and two men, their arms draped about each other's shoulders, came stumbling out into the street. They were calling out raucous challenges in loud voices, and when they saw Kate they came to an abrupt halt.

"Well, will you look what we have here," the first man said, breaking loose from his friend and staggering over to stand in front of Kate. He pulled the cap from his head and bowed mockingly. "Good day to you, me lady," he said, his eyes sliding over her in a menacing manner. "How nice to be makin' your acquaintance, me lady."

Beside her James swallowed nervously. The other man was hanging back, but he knew he would rush to his friend's aid at the first sign of trouble. Still, he could not stand by and allow his mistress to be insulted by riffraff. He took a deep breath and squared his bony shoulders.

"Come, ma'am," he said, grasping her elbow in a protective grip. " 'Tis time we was gettin' back."

Kate was only too happy to comply. The filthy man blocking her path fairly radiated menace, and she wanted nothing more than to be gone. Not only did she fear for her own safety, but she was worried about James. She knew he would try to defend her, and what chance would a lad have against two armed men?

"As you say, James," she replied, lifting her jaw proudly and laying her hand on his shaking arm. They took a step forward but the heavyset man remained where he was, his drunken leer growing even more pronounced. Kate tilted her head back and fixed him with an icy look.

"Sir, would you be so good as to step aside," she requested, praying she would be able to brazen her way out of the dangerous situation. "You are blocking our path."

"Oh, am I now?" The man's dark eyes widened in mock horror. "Well, I'll tell you what, me lady, give me a kiss, and I'll give a thought to steppin' back for you."

James gave a loud gasp, his thin face flushing with outrage. "How' dare ye speak to Mrs. Delecourt like that!" he cried, his hands clenching into fists. "She's not some doxy to be kissing the likes of you! Stand aside!"

At the mention of her name, the other man gave a sudden start. His cold gray eyes widened and then narrowed as he studied her. He hesitated a moment and then started forward, his beefy hand closing over the pistol stuck in the waistband of his trousers.

Kate was so busy restraining James and keeping a sharp eye on their assailant, that she didn't notice the other man had moved until he appeared beside her. The sight of his large, muscular frame made her pale with horror. She was considering the wisdom of screaming for help when the man interposed himself between her and the other man.

"Shove off, mate," he advised, slapping his hand on the drunk's shoulder. "There's better sport to be found elsewhere."

"And leave this sweeting to you?" The drunk's eyes narrowed belligerently. "I think not, Cap'n. I have to take your orders when we're at sea, but we're on dry land now." He made a grab for Kate.

The tall man easily blocked his move, shoving the man back with such force that he went sprawling into the dirt. "I said shove off, Pruitt, and I meant it," he growled, his fists clenching and unclenching. "Leave while you still can."

Had he been sober the tone of deadly menace in his captain's voice would have given him pause, but as it was, he had imbibed just enough rum to make him incautious. He glared up angrily, lust turning to murderous fury. "Give me one good reason why I should," he muttered, wiping the back of his hand across his mouth.

In answer, the captain pulled his pistol from his waistband and trained it on the man's forehead. There was a click as he cocked the trigger. "Get yourself back to the boat," he said softly. "Now. A'fore I forgets you're a good man when you ain't drunk."

Kate's heart leapt so wildly that for a moment she feared she would disgrace herself by swooning. The prospect of seeing a man shot down before her eyes, however much he might deserve such a fate, was enough to make her sick with horror. She tightened her hold on James's arm, struggling for the courage to intervene when the man on the ground gave a casual shrug.

"Aye aye, Cap'n" he said, breaking into a lazy smile. "No gentry be worth a bullet. I'll just be gettin' back to the Sea Horse, then."

The captain kept the pistol trained on him, although

he did ease up the pressure on the trigger. When the man rolled to his feet and began walking away, he turned back to a wide-eyed Kate.

"A thousand pardons to you, Mrs. Delecourt," he said in a surprisingly gentle voice. "I hope you'll not be judging us all by the likes of—"

"Captain, look out!" Kate called out just as the other man aimed a blow at the back of the captain's head.

He ducked, and the blow fell harmlessly on his hunched shoulders. Before the other man could recover, he brought his own fist up in a punishing uppercut that made the man's head snap back. He followed it with a round house punch to the side of the head, and a jab to the midsection, and the man fell back in the dirt. When he did not rise, the captain turned to Kate with a wide grin.

"My thanks to you, ma'am. I should have known better than to present my back to a mad dog like Pruitt. You wasn't hurt, was you?" His eyes moved over her with concern.

Kate shook her head. "I-I am fine, Captain" she said, feeling decidedly bemused by the turn of events.

"That's good then." He knelt over and grabbed the other man by the jacket, slinging him over his shoulder as if he was a mere lad. "Well, we'd best be getting back to the ship. Mind you hurry back to the more respectable part of town. Pruitt's not the only rascal hereabouts."

"We shall do that," Kate assured him, much struck by the irony of his warning. "And my thanks to you for your assistance."

The captain shifted his burden so that he could doff his hat. "My pleasure, Mrs. Delecourt. 'Twas the least I could do seeing that you was kind enough to take in a friend of mine."

Kate stiffened with interest. "You know Mr. Quentin?" she asked warily.

The captain shrugged negligently. "Can't say as I do,

ma'am. But names don't mean much to such as us. The fact you helped one of us is more than enough. We are in your debt, Mrs. Delecourt."

"As I am in yours, Captain," Kate accepted his reply with a cool nod. "And seeing that you are in my debt, would you mind answering a question for me?"

"What's that?"

"What is your name?"

The captain hesitated. "O'Rourake," he said at last, "though I'll thank you not to be bandying it about. There's certain people I'd just as soon not know I was here."

She smiled in understanding. "Of course, Captain O'Rourake, you may count upon my discretion. Good-bye," she grabbed a silent James by the arm and began dragging him away.

"Mrs. Delecourt!" Captain O'Rourake called out.

"Yes?" she cast him a questioning look.

"You might tell your Mr. Quentin to be looking sharp. Those people I spoke of be sniffing around and asking all manner of questions about him."

"I see" Kate replied, her brows gathering in a worried frown. "Thank you for the information, Captain."

"You're welcome, Mrs. Delecourt," his wide smile revealed several missing teeth. "And should your guest have need of a new bunk, send word to the Mermaid. They'll know how to find me."

"I shall remember that, sir," she promised, a soft smile curving her lips. "And I shall remember you. Good day, Captain."

"Good day, Mrs. Delecourt," the captain inclined his head respectfully and then left, still carrying the unconscious Pruitt over one beefy shoulder.

Leaving the Mermaid Inn far behind, Kate and James hurried back to the modiste's. "Not a word of this to Miss Lucille, mind," she cautioned as they neared their destination. "I fear she would never understand."

"*She* wouldn't understand!" the footman muttered feelingly, his hands still damp with fear. "I don't reckon I'll ever understand what happened. We was lucky not to have had our throats slit!"

Kate considered this to be a melodramatic exaggeration. To be sure, things were decidedly uncomfortable for a while, but they were never in any real danger of being murdered. At least, she amended anxiously, she didn't *think* they were. It did not bear reflection, and so she put the incident firmly from her mind.

Lucille was enjoying a companionable cup of tea with Mrs. Tedrow when Kate arrived, and it didn't take much prodding for her to join them. Over an enjoyable feast of cream buns and sandwiches, the topic turned easily to clothing and the fashion atrocities currently being committed in London.

"Miss Delecourt informs me you will be journeying to the city for the coming Season," Mrs. Tedrow remarked, eyeing Kate with professional avarice. "Naturally you will be requiring a new wardrobe now that you are out of mourning. I have some patterns I would be more than happy to show you; all in the latest of fashion, I assure you."

Kate stared down at her dress of gray cambric trimmed with lace and black ribbons. "I didn't realize my gown was so out of mode as to put me in danger of being a fossil," she replied, her tone cool as she glanced up at the dressmaker. "Nor am I yet out of mourning. It's been scarce a year, after all."

"Sixteen months," Lucille provided, without the usual flow of tears that accompanied the statement. "And a year is all that is required, you know. Anything else would be empty show."

Kate was so stunned by her sister-in-law's casual pronouncement that she almost dropped her teacup. Only yesterday Lucille had dissolved into tears when Cook served a bowl of mutton soup. It was Charles's favorite

63

dish, she had sobbed into her black-edged handkerchief, and she could not bear to eat it without thinking of her beloved brother.

"I meant no insult, Mrs. Delecourt," Mrs. Tedrow interposed quickly, seeing her chances for a fat bill slipping through her fingers. "I only meant that you will be wanting some new gowns. Fashions change so quickly, you know, and you wouldn't wish to appear countrified. And as your sister says, a year is more than long enough to go about draped all in black."

"My gown is gray."

"All your gowns are gray" Lucille pointed out in a surprisingly firm voice. Ever since Mrs. Tedrow had put the idea into her head that it was past time to get her sister-in-law out of mourning, she had become determined to do just that. "You need some lively colors, to cheer you up, dearest," she added in a wheedling tone. "And you know how much Charles loved seeing you in bright colors, especially blue."

That was so, Kate conceded silently, recalling how much he enjoyed helping her with her wardrobe. He'd even designed a peignoir for her, and she'd worn it the night before he left to join his regiment. The memory brought a soft smile to her lips. "I suppose a few new gowns would not go amiss," she said at last. "Nothing grand, of course. I am much too old for frills."

Pattern books were immediately produced, along with several ells of richly hued fabric. In the end she chose two day dresses of blue and yellow striped cambric and deep rose gauze, and a riding habit of sapphire blue velvet. At Lucille's insistence she also bought an evening gown of emerald satin, trimmed at the neckline and full sleeves with blonde lace. Several hats and bonnets were also selected, and these were to be made up by Mrs. Tedrow's niece, who ran a millinery shop on the next street. A rather convenient happenstance, Kate thought with a newfound sense of cynicism.

After arranging for the purchases to be delivered to

the house, Kate and Lucille left Mrs. Tedrow's and made their way to the bootmakers. "If you are going to do a thing, Katherine, then you had best do it thoroughly," Lucille said when Kate objected to the extravagance. "Old shoes with new clothes is an absurdity. A few pairs of dancing slippers and some new boots won't beggar you."

It was also decided that some new gloves, a parasol and some plumes for a turban (yet to be purchased) would also prove not beyond her means, and so a bemused Kate found herself back at the drapery shops standing mutely to one side as Lucille sent the clerk scurrying to fill her order. It was rather like watching a kitten turning into a tiger, she mused, torn between admiration and amusement. She was so accustomed to thinking of Lucille as a useless watering pot, that it was quite an eye-opening experience to see her in this light.

She was contemplating the ramifications of this revelation when the door opened, and a portly man in a black greatcoat entered the shop. At the sight of the two ladies he doffed his hat politely.

"Mrs. Delecourt, Miss Delecourt," he said, bowing to each one in turn. "Such a pleasure to see you again."

"Reverend Boothe," Kate acknowledged him with a civil nod. She'd never liked the man above half, and considered him the worst sort of hypocrite; condemning the evils of smuggling from his lofty pulpit when the whole countryside knew he kept his cellars filled with French brandy. Still, she was reluctant to give him the cut directly, and forced herself to inquire after his health.

"Quite well, quite well, thank you," he answered in his pompous way. "Although my poor nerves have yet to recover. One may only wonder what is coming of this world when a man of God is subjected to such indignities. I am of a good mind to write my MP and complain, although I doubt much good would come of it."

"Complain about what?" Lucille asked, studying the vicar with wide eyes. "What has happened?"

"Ah, that is right, I had forgotten you had not heard," he said, shaking his head at them like a disappointed parent. "It is dangerous, you know, for you ladies to live so isolated as you do. These are uncertain times, and communications with one's neighbors can be vital. If you—"

"Reverend Boothe," Kate interrupted, unwilling to listen to another sermon on the subject, "kindly answer my sister-in-law's question. What has happened?" If anything, she added with silent exasperation. She'd never met anyone more capable of creating a tempest out of a raindrop in all her life.

"Why, the soldiers who searched my house, of course."

What?" Kate and Lucille exclaimed together.

"They're searching everyone's house," Reverend Boothe said, delighted at finally having their undivided attention. "They're looking for the smuggler who was shot on the docks. You recall, Miss Delecourt," his watery eyes flicked to Lucille, "I mentioned it the last time you were in town."

"But-but I thought it was assumed he was killed," Kate protested, recalling Captain O'Rourake's warning. "And even if he is still alive, surely he would want to put as much distance between himself and the authorities as possible!"

"One would think so," he agreed with a wise nod, "but that is because you do not know these arrogant fellows, Mrs. Delecourt. Why, they would like nothing better than to stay right under the noses of the Excise men while they recover from their wounds! It makes them feel superior, one may only suppose. But as it happens, the authorities have had word from an informer that the villain is being hidden right here in Rye."

"That is dreadful!" Lucille gasped, her hands fluttering to her chest. "But that still does not excuse the soldiers from searching *your* home! They would be better to concentrate their efforts among the lower classes. They are always consorting with the Owlers."

"But that is just it!" Reverend Boothe exclaimed, his voice dropping to a confidential whisper as he leaned towards them. "The informant claims the rascal is being hidden by a member of *our* class! A person of some importance, I believe he called him, and the soldiers said that if need be they will search every house between here and Dover until they catch him."

Chapter Five

The sound of shattering glass exploded into the tension filled silence as the bottle of scent Kate had been examining slipped from her nerveless fingers. She gave a convulsive start, her green eyes blinking rapidly as she sought to regain her composure.

"Oh dear, how very clumsy of me," she said, turning a parody of her usually warm smile on the elderly shopkeeper. "My apologies, Mr. Welles, you must be sure to put it on my bill."

"Are you all right, ma'am?" Reverend Boothe asked, waddling forward to study her with anxious eyes. "I did not mean to alarm you; upon my soul I did not."

"I'm not alarmed," Kate denied, then added, "That is, naturally I am concerned; the thought of a dangerous criminal hiding somewhere in the neighborhood is enough to give anyone pause. But I would not go so far as to say I am frightened."

"Well, I am!" Lucille cried, her eyes darting nervously about her as if she expected the smuggler to leap out at her any moment. "Oh, do hurry. Katherine! It will be dark soon, and would just as lief not be abroad after sunset."

Considering it was scarce three o'clock there seemed to be little likelihood of this, but Kate was only too happy to comply. The sooner she returned home to warn Mickey of the danger, the better. "You are right,

Lucille," she said, adopting the same dutiful manner she had affected in the past few months. "We had best leave at once."

They took a hasty leave of the vicar, who insisted upon walking them to their carriage. Several minutes were lost listening to his list of instructions; including the rather ridiculous suggestion that they check beneath their beds . . . just in case. "For one never knows with these fellows," he concluded with a solemn nod. "It would be just like one of them to lurk beneath some helpless lady's bed. You must take every precaution."

Lucille spent the return trip to Delecourt House in near hysterics, certain they would all be brutalized in their sleep. At first Kate halfheartedly attempted to soothe her, but when she began insisting that the bedchambers be thoroughly searched she became alarmed enough to snap.

"Oh, for pity's sake, Lucille, do be sensible! There are over ten beds in the house, not counting the servants' quarters, and I for one do not intend to go creeping about peeking beneath each and everyone of them! Besides, what would we do if we found him? Invite him to tea?"

"You may scoff if you wish," Lucille returned with a loud sniff, "but I intend to check my room the moment we are home! And I will write Uncle Alfred. He is with the Admiralty, and I am sure he will know what to do. Perhaps he might even send a detachment of soldiers to guard us," she added hopefully.

The possibility so horrified Kate that she gave another start. "Don't be a goose, he would never do that! And what do you care? You will soon be safely tucked away at Cousin Caro's."

"You don't think I mean to go *now?*" Lucille gasped in outrage. "Why, I should never be so lacking in courage as to desert you in your hour of need!"

"I thought this was Cousin Caro's hour of need," Kate answered, desperately attempting to salvage the situation. She was counting on Lucille being gone, and was not about to be denied. "She is the one laying helpless on a bed of pain, not I."

"Yes, but—"

"Really, Lucille, I quite wonder at you!" Kate continued, knowing that guilt could often achieve what cool reason could not. "To raise poor Caro's hopes only to dash them again seems beyond cruelty to me. You must know she is counting upon you coming to visit her! Oh well," she turned her head and pretended to study the passing scenery, "you must do as you see fit."

It took very little time for her ploy to take effect. Lucille fidgeted on her bench, her teeth nibbling her bottom lip as she worked the matter out in her mind. The prospect of staying to nobly defend her sister-in-law from a vicious smuggler was almost as tantalizing as sacrificing herself to the needs of an invalid cousin. In the end, however, common sense prevailed, and she gave a dejected sigh.

"You are right, Katherine," she said, looking properly downcast. "Having agreed to go to Caro's, I can scarce cry off now. But you must promise me you will take every care while I am gone. I shan't be able to sleep a wink for worrying about you!"

"I'll be fine," Kate felt the smallest twinge for her manipulating ways. "And don't forget I shall have Aunt Portia to protect me."

The mention of her rival brought a spark to Lucille's eyes. "Hmph I'd forgotten about that harpy. But you are right, with that tongue of hers she would prove more than enough protection against a legion of smugglers! Why, one could almost feel sorry for the fellow were she to get her hands on him. She'd nag him to death in a minute, mark my words."

Kate murmured something appropriately soothing, and then lapsed into a troubled silence. If the garrison posted nearby was involved in the search, then things were serious indeed. She hoped her distance from the town as well as her impeccable reputation would keep the soldiers from her door, but what if it did not? Mickey was recovering faster than she would have believed possible, but he was not so well as to be able to risk an escape. And if the houses were being searched, she thought it stood to reason that the roads would also be closely watched. A strange man would most certainly be stopped. And once stopped . . . she shivered at the grim outcome of such a possibility.

She remembered Captain O'Rourake and his offer of assistance. She had thought of mentioning it to Mickey at some later date, when he was stronger and in better condition to travel. Now it appeared she would have to tell him at once. It would be interesting to see how he reacted, she decided with a slow smile. He would no doubt find it amusing to learn she had made the acquaintance of yet another "fisherman."

"What?"

"Yes, the soldiers are searching the town even now, and if no trace of you . . . of the smuggler . . . is found, they'll carry the search further afield. I doubt they will venture this far out, but—"

"No, I didn't mean that," he interrupted, waving his good hand impatiently. "I meant the brawl at the Mermaid." He shot her a suspicious glare. "You didn't actually go inside that pesthole, did you?"

"Of course not!" Kate exclaimed, indignant that he should think her so lacking in good sense.

"Well, thank heavens for that," he muttered, his shoulders slumping in relief.

"I was outside, and that is where the fight started."

Peter's words of thanksgiving withered on his lips and he could only stare at her in speechless fury. His mouth opened, but it was several seconds before sound emerged. "Please tell me you are joking," he said at last, his voice sounding harsh even to his own ears.

"Whyever should I joke about such a thing?" she demanded, her brows puckering with annoyance. "Really, Mr. Quentin, were you not attending? The vicar—"

"I don't give a tinker's curse what that great rasher of wind said!" Peter exclaimed angrily, his dark blue eyes flashing with fury. "I want to know what the devil you thought you were doing hanging about such a place! In fact, you had no right to be in that part of town without proper escort."

Kate stared at him in wordless amazement; scarce believing the evidence of her own ears. A *smuggler* was taking *her* to task for her behavior? It was too ludicrous to be borne. She raised her chin, her eyes defiant as she glared at him. "I beg your pardon," she said slowly, her voice frosting over with displeasure, "but the last I heard Rye was a free town where people might wander where they please.

"And for your information," she added when he opened his lips in protest, "I was not without escort. I had a footman with me."

"Aye, a stripling of a lad scarce out of short breeches!" Peter shot back, his temper flaring to meet hers. When he'd first begun this mission he'd paid the Mermaid a visit, and the vice and corruption he'd seen there had been enough to shock even his jaded sensibilities. The thought of her anywhere near that place was enough to make his blood run cold, and it was all he could do not to give her a sound shaking.

"James gave a very good accounting of himself," Kate protested, defending the young footman's honor. "He stood right up to that ruffian, and told him to mind his manners! It was most heroic of him."

"Foolish is what you mean," Peter muttered darkly, vowing to have a word with the footman. "He should have been dragging you out of there as fast as he could."

"He was." Kate's chin came up another notch. "That is when the fight started."

Peter's jaw clenched as he silently cursed the restraints placed upon him by his masquerade. If he were able to appear as his true self she'd listen to him soon enough, he thought sulkily. Or would she? He somehow doubted she would be much impressed by his rank.

"Tell me more about the vicar," he said, deciding to abandon the matter of the Mermaid for the moment. "Did he say the soldiers were searching all the houses in town, or just his?"

"He said they were conducting a thorough search," Kate said, resisting the temptation to remind him she had already offered him the information. "Apparently his house was among the first they searched."

Peter frowned as he considered the information. "But what sense is there in that?" he asked, thrusting his hand through his thick hair. "A vicar would seem the last person I would suspect of harboring a smuggler. Unless he is of a particularly sympathetic nature?" He glanced questioningly at Kate.

Kate's lips quirked in a wry smile at the thought of anyone accusing the plump vicar of possessing such human frailties. "More likely he has a fondness for French brandy," she said, seeing no need to be polite. " 'Tis well known that he is among the Owlers' best customers. I'm surprised *you've* not made his acquaintance," she added, sending him a knowing look. "Unless your shooting fish are of good English stock?"

Peter ignored her digs recalling that he had heard something of the good vicar just before his ill-fated voyage. "Has he a hidden room beneath the altar?" he asked, struggling to remember what he had heard.

"You would know the answer to that better than I," she said with another taunting smile. "But I fear it was more than Reverend Boothe's tippling that made the soldiers search his house."

"Oh?" He raised a dark eyebrow inquiringly.

"Yes," she nodded, "according to Reverend Boothe, the soldiers are acting on the word of an informant who says that the smuggler they are seeking is being harbored by a member of the gentry."

Peter paled at the information. "My God," he whispered hoarsely, his eyes dark with shock as he gazed up at her. "Is he certain?"

"He seemed fair sure of it," Kate answered, recalling the vicar's indignation. "He said the person . . . whoever he or she may be . . . is of some importance, and naturally he thought that applied to him. He is threatening to write his MP about it," she added, hoping to lighten the bleak atmosphere that had descended upon the small room.

Peter bit back a furious oath, turning his head to gaze out the window. "I shall leave at once," he said at last, so lost in thought that he dropped his lilting accent. "I'll have to wait until it is dark, and then—"

"But you can't go now!" Kate protested, not noticing the change in his voice. "You're far too weak to even attempt such a thing!"

"I will manage," Peter replied, every inch the haughty lord. "One of your footmen mentioned he has an uncle with a boat, and—"

"If you are referring to Andrew, then I think it only fair to warn you that his uncle is naught but a common drunkard whose poor seamanship is only surpassed by his love for the bottle!" Kate retorted, furious that he should prove to be so obstinate. "You would be far safer to turn yourself into the watch than to place yourself in his hands!"

"Then I shall think of something else!" Peter snapped, pushing himself away from the pillows and glaring at her for all he was worth. "Damn it, madam, don't you understand? I will not have you placed in jeopardy because of me! I would sooner die."

Kate remained silent, her anger dissolving as she realized he meant every word of what he was saying. He would give up his own life to protect hers, and the depth of such a commitment made her stare at him in mounting confusion. Even in the gaudy robe, his lean jaw bristling with a neat beard, there was something decidedly regal about him, and not for the first time she began questioning the true identity of the man she was sheltering.

"There is no need to go to such extremes," she said coolly, struggling to hide her perturbation. "If you are so determined to leave, then by all means go. All I ask is that you wait until you are stronger, or until more secure arrangements can be made."

"What sort of arrangements?" he asked warily, unwilling to believe in her easy capitulation.

"Captain O'Rourake indicated he was willing to assist you," she replied, forcing herself to think logically. "If you like, I could arrange for a message to be sent to him at the Mermaid."

Peter laid back against the pillows, turning the plan over in his mind. It did have merit, he decided grudgingly, and certainly placing his safety in the hands of a smuggler could be no less dangerous than remaining where he was. He'd heard of O'Rourake, and knew him to be a man of honor . . . for a smuggler. 'Twas said that while he was willing to run a load of brandy or silk past the cutters, he drew the line at aiding the enemy. He'd even been known to slip the Navy information about French troop movements.

Another consideration was his health. Much as it stung his pride to admit it, he knew he was in no shape to attempt an escape. The bleeding had stopped and he was no longer plagued by the fever, but the slightest activity exhausted him; leaving him as weak as a damned kitten. Even now he was beginning to shake, and he could feel the perspiration trickling down his back. In this condition, he would be lucky to reach the door without collapsing.

"Very well," he muttered, temporarily admitting defeat. "But I will be the one to send the letter. The less contact you have with O'Rourake, the better I shall like it."

Kate bristled at the imperious command, but managed to swallow her indignation when she noted the lines of pain and weariness on his face. What did it matter who contacted the captain? she asked herself silently. The important thing was that he was notified, and the proper arrangements were made.

"As you wish, Mr. Quentin," she said, her expression controlled as she rose to her feet. "I'll have a footman bring you whatever writing supplies you require."

"Thank you, ma'am," Peter replied, his eyes closing as he gave in to the heavy exhaustion that pulled at him. He heard the door closing when he suddenly remembered something.

"Mrs. Delecourt?"

"Yes?" She glanced over her shoulder at him.

"Did you post my letter to London?"

"Yes, of course," she replied, puzzled by the note of urgency in his voice.

"Good." His eyes closed again, and with the suddenness of a candle being extinguished, he was asleep.

Kate shook her head and closed the door, irritated by his stubborn and intractable nature. She was halfway to her room when she realized his voice had sounded more than urgent. It had sounded completely different, the inflections more cultured and imperative. The Irish accent she'd grown accustomed to had been quite gone, and its absence filled her with confusion.

They were having guests for dinner that evening, and as could be expected, the search for the smuggler was the main topic of conversation.

"Well, it's all a hum if you want my opinion," Mrs. Elizabeth Turner, one of Lucille's oldest friends, offered with a disdainful sniff. "As if one of us would stoop to helping a common criminal! I can't believe our soldiers would allow themselves to be taken in by this 'informant.' It is obvious he is only trying to put them off the scent so that the real villain can escape."

Her husband, a stoop-shouldered gentleman in his sixties, patted her hand soothingly. "Very true, my love, and I would agree with you, but for the fact that the information was only extracted after a certain amount of . . . er . . . persuasion was applied. I think we may rely upon the veracity of the man's confession."

Kate, who had been idly toying with her food glanced up at this, her eyes widening with comprehension. "Do you mean to say the man was *tortured?*" she demanded, dropping her fork with a loud clang. "But that is barbaric!"

"Not barbaric; common sense," the other guest, Dr. Markham opined with a casual shrug. "And I would hardly call cuffing a fellow about a few times 'torture.' This is England, you know," he shot her a reproachful look.

"I sincerely doubt you would be so sanguine if you were the one being 'cuffed about'!" Kate snapped, thoroughly incensed by his callous disregard for his fellow man.

"It is necessary, ma'am," Dr. Markham informed her bluntly, his face purpling with rage. "We are at war, and while our gallant soldiers are spilling their blood on foreign soil, these ruffians grow fat in the pocket trading with our enemy! Treason, that's what it is, and if a bit of rough handling helps put a speedy end to it, then I say bravo!"

"If the smugglers grow wealthy, then it is because so many 'loyal' Englishmen are so willing to purchase their goods!" Kate cried, stumbling to her feet. "If you want to stop the smuggling, Dr. Markham, then you had best start by arresting the members of Parliament who toast their King's health with smuggled brandy!"

"Now see here, Mrs. Delecourt—"

"And as for our brave soldiers," she interrupted, her

eyes sparkling with fury, "do you think you need remind *me* of what they have sacrificed? My husband died fighting Napoleon's tyranny, but he did not die so that his fellow countrymen could be brutalized by their own government!"

There was a moment of charged silence as Kate resumed her seat. She did not regret her words, but she did regret the vehemence with which she spoke them. The last thing she needed now was to draw attention to herself, and if the dark glances being cast in her direction by the irate doctor were any indication, that was precisely what she had done.

"Oh, I have a bit of news," Mrs. Turner said after several uncomfortable minutes had passed. "Lord Payton has returned, and is taking up residence at the Priory."

"Really?" Lucille's smile was as falsely bright as the pained smile she turned on her friend. "How interesting! I vow I can not recall the last time he was here. Did you know him, Katherine?"

"I can not say the name is familiar," Kate replied, properly grateful for her sister-in-law's help in glossing over her faux pas. "Is he an old neighbor?"

"In a manner of speaking," Lucille continued with the same determined cheerfulness. "He was married to poor Anne Carrington, and he inherited the estate when she died. That must have been . . . what, five years ago now."

"Four," Dr. Markham corrected, stuffing a forkful of baked fish into his mouth. "Hunting accident."

"Oh yes, I remember now," Portia said, as eager as Lucille to salvage something of the evening. "I remember thinking what a dreadful mishap it was, and she scarcely into her twenties."

"What happened?" Kate asked, more out of a sense of guilt than out of any real curiosity. Although now that she thought of it, she seemed to remember hearing something of a tragic accident while she was in London. She'd just made her bows, and was much too busy

78

worrying over whether or not she would have a partner for the next dance to pay any mind to gossip.

"She and Lord Payton were out hunting with friends when Anne's horse bolted, carrying her directly into the line of fire," Mrs. Turner said eagerly her eyes gleaming with the enthusiasm of the dedicated gossiper. "She was shot right through the heart and died in her husband's arms."

"How terrible!" Kate cried, her indifference lost as a wave of warm sympathy washed over her. "Poor man, I can understand then why he would choose to absent himself for so long! What bitter memories the place must bring him!"

"Yes, but that's all in the past now, and best not spoken of," Portia said in her most bracing manner. "Although I must confess that I am surprised Payton would wish to absent himself from London so close to the start of the Season. He is hardly the type to enjoy rusticating; bit of a fop, I thought him," she added with a flash of her customary malice.

"Daresay he's making sure the place is up to scratch before he puts it on the block," Mr. Turner offered suddenly. "Heard he's been sailing in some rather deep waters of late."

This caused no end of alarm amongst his listeners, and the speculation as to what the marquess would or would not do saw them safely through the rest of the meal. As they were keeping country hours, the guests lingered for less than an hour after they had finished dining before taking their leave. Lucille was warmly embraced by her friend and implored to write often, and even Kate was allowed a tiny peck on the cheek by the tolerant Mrs. Turner.

"And mind you don't forget to drop us a line every now and then," she added, giving Kate's hand an admonishing pat. "Your aunt and Lucille have said you are returning to London for the Season, and I would not wish you to forget all your old friends."

Kate cast her aunt a rueful glance over the older woman's turbaned head. Evidently her promise to consider Aunt Portia's offer had been taken for granted, she thought, turning a soft smile on Mrs. Turner. "So it would appear, ma'am," she said pleasantly. "And you have my word I shall keep you *au courant* of the events in London."

"When shall you leave?"

"Next week."

"Soon."

Portia and Kate answered in unison, and Kate sent her aunt another speaking glance. "That has yet to be decided," Kate said before Portia could formulate a reply. "With Lucille leaving as well, there are several arrangements yet to be made. May I hope to call upon you before I go?"

"Of course, my dear, of course," Mrs. Turner assured her with another pat. She and her husband lingered another few minutes and then departed, taking the doctor with them. The moment their aged carriage was out of sight Portia rounded on Kate.

"Well, miss?" she demanded, thrusting both hands on her hips. "I trust you have an explanation for such a sad want of behavior? I vow, I have never been more embarrassed in all my life!"

Considering some of the dust her aunt had been known to raise in her day, this seemed a rather harsh condemnation to Kate. Although she was wise enough to keep such thoughts to herself. "Really, Aunt, you make too much of the matter," she said languidly making her way back into the cozy parlor. "Dr. Markham and I had but a minor disagreement. 'Tis nothing of import."

"Nothing of import?" Portia echoed, shocked to the marrow of her old bones to hear her niece speaking so flippantly. "Upon my word, Katherine, I shall consider us beyond lucky if we aren't all clapped into irons by the next sunset! How could you speak so to Dr. Markham

80

of all people? You must know he is a staunch Tory."

"I know that daughter of his is never without a piece of French silk on her back!" Kate shot back, then quickly bit her tongue.

"Katherine Josephine," Portia said, making use of Kate's full name, "if you hope to get along in Society without ruining all our chances, I must urge you to guard that tongue of yours. Everyone wears French silks, to refine upon it as you have is simply not done. I should have thought you were aware of that," she added with a cross shake of her head.

"I am," Kate answered honestly, "it is just that it doesn't seem right that the authorities are tearing the countryside apart looking for a man who is only supplying commodities everyone wants. If smuggling is a crime, then why is buying smuggling goods not also illegal?"

"It is, but one can not arrest the entire countryside," Portia muttered, rubbing her aching head with a weary hand.

And to think less than a week ago she was bemoaning Katherine's lack of spirit, she mused wryly.

"But—"

"Oh please, Katherine, I have heard quite enough!" Portia exclaimed impatiently, shooting Lucille an angry scowl. "I blame this preoccupation about smugglers on you!" she said. "If you hadn't taken her into town, she would never have heard about this wretched Owler!"

"Me!" Lucille clasped a hand to her bosom, the very image of outraged innocence. *"You* are the one who warned her not to walk on the beach lest she be carried off by the wretches!"

"And you are the one who told us about the fellow who had been shot in town!" Portia returned, unwilling to accept any blame in the matter. "But that is neither here nor there, I suppose. As I have said, we have all heard quite enough on the subject for the evening. Katherine," here she gave her smirking niece a quelling look, "I trust we may rely upon your good sense to keep your rather revolutionary thoughts to yourself once we are in London?"

"Yes, Aunt," Kate answered decorously, although there was a hint of mischief in her bright green eyes. "Nor shall I say a single word on the Luddites, I assure you."

Portia actually paled, the thought of Katherine blossoming into a radical filling her with horror. Clearly her prolonged grief was oversetting her usually sensible mind, she decided, vowing to remove her niece to London the moment she was able.

"Now, what is this nonsense that we shall not be leaving for London for another week?" she demanded, bristling with the impatience to be gone. "It won't take above a few days to pack and close up the house."

Kate's amusement vanished as she thought of Mr. Quentin. She could never leave until she knew he was safely out of harm's way. "There is a great deal more to it than that, Aunt Portia," she said, searching her mind for acceptable delays. "There is the wardrobe I have ordered from the villages and of course I will want to remain here to see Lucille safely off."

"Oh, you needn't worry about me," Lucille said with a self-sacrificing sigh. "I don't mind setting off all alone with only the servants to wave good-bye."

"And then there is the stable boy to consider," Kate added, feeling somewhat desperate. "I can not leave while he is ill."

"What?" Portia scowled at her. "Never say that wretch is still malingering! Really, Katherine, the way you cosset these servants of yours is nothing short of disgusting. Tell him to get back to the stables, spots and all."

"But he's a mere lad," Kate protested, regretting her impetuous decision to mention the fictitious invalid. "I would never forgive myself if he were to die while I was away."

"If you are so concerned for his health, then why didn't you ask Dr. Markham to have a look at him while he was here?" Portia asked impatiently. "The man is a pompous prig, I grant you, but he is also a damned fine sawbones! I daresay he could have cured the boy in a thrice if you had let him."

The thought of the doctor coming anywhere near the "stable boy" was enough to make Kate start with horror. "I do not mean he is quite so ill as all that," she said hastily, wishing there was some way to end this bizarre conversation. "I simply meant I don't wish to leave just yet. Perhaps in a fortnight—"

"Five days," Portia bargained, willing to haggle over the matter if it would get her niece to London any sooner.

Kate considered that, then rejected it. She was sure she could arrange for his departure before then, but she could not be certain. "A sennight," she said, deciding that would give her more than enough time to achieve her goals.

"A sennight!" Portia's gray brows met in a straight line over her nose. "Katherine, you must be jesting! We can not wait a—"

"A sennight" Kate repeated, folding her arms across her chest and meeting her aunt glare for glare. "And not a moment sooner. And," she raised a slender finger warningly, "if you persist in pressing me on the matter, I vow I shall not leave at all! Agreed?"

Portia scowled at her niece. She hated losing in anything, but she was wise enough to know when she was bested. "Oh very well," she said with an angry sigh. "If you insist. I only hope the dratted lad is worth all this fuss and bother."

"He is," Kate replied quietly, her shoulders slumping with relief. "He is."

Chapter Six

In between helping Lucille with her packing and seeing to her own belongings, Kate was unable to visit Mr. Quentin . . . or Mickey, as she privately called him . . . until some two days later. She was finally able to shake Lucille off by laying claim to a headache, and then slipped off to enjoy her freedom with little sense of remorse. She found him sitting up in a chair in front of the fireplace and moved towards him with a polite smile.

"Good evening, Mr. Quentin," she said, hurrying to his side. "How wonderful to see you up and about!"

Peter looked up from the crude map he had been studying, his dark brows gathering in a troubled frown as he gazed up at her. There was something different about her appearance and for a moment he could not think of what it was, and then it came to him.

"You aren't wearing a cap!" he exclaimed, speaking the first words to come into his mind.

Kate flushed, running a nervous hand over her hair. "It was my sister-in-law's idea," she muttered, feeling absurdly embarrassed. "She said I was much too young to continue wearing them."

"She was right," Peter's eyes lingered on the wispy curls that had escaped the elegant chignon. "You look most attractive, ma'am, if you don't mind my saying so."

"Not at all," she responded shyly, although she knew she should be setting him down for such effrontery. Her aunt and many of her friends would doubtlessly be shocked that she allowed a strange man, and a common smuggler at that, to treat her with such marked familiarity.

"You mentioned your sister-in-law," he said, seizing upon the information she had let slip. "Am I to take it that she resides with you?"

Kate gave a wary nod, already regretting her impetuous slip of the tongue. "My sister-in-law, Lucille, and my Aunt Portia both live with me" she said, wondering why the information should be of such interest to him.

"That must be a great comfort to you" he answered with genuine relief. He had been concerned for her safety, but he was also curious as to how many people were living in the house and why they had yet to so much as poke their noses in the door. Granted he was hardly an invited guest, but he knew enough of country life to know that any visitor was a subject of great interest. That two elderly ladies hadn't come snooping about was indeed odd; unless his presence in the house was being kept a secret, he realized with a sudden frown.

"Not really," Kate replied to his remark with a rueful smile. "They can not abide each other and are forever quarreling. The day I found you on the beach I had slipped away in order to escape their childish squabbling."

"Ah, then it would seem I am in the dear ladies' debt," he replied, thinking of his own battling relations. At any given time half the family wasn't speaking to the other, and he was always being asked to choose sides.

"Indeed, and you may also thank Lucille for my being in Rye the other day," Kate continued, sensing the sudden lightness of his mood. "We went in so that she might visit the modiste, and that is when I met the captain . . . and Reverend Boothe, of course."

"I'll thank her for the vicar, although I'm sure you won't mind if I don't say the same of the captain. I'd just as lief you'd never met the gentleman; especially given the circumstances of that meeting," he added, fixing her with a stern look.

Kate gave a cool sniff, but managed to refrain from comment. The less said of the matter, the better, she decided, plucking an imaginary thread from the skirt of her gown. It was also gray, but since her other gowns were out of fashion she decided it would have to suffice until she had more time to refurbish her wardrobe.

"Speaking of Captain O'Rourake, have you had time to contact him?" she asked, opting for what she hoped was a safe topic of conversation.

"Not as yet," Peter answered warily, recalling the decision he had reached after careful consideration.

"But that makes no sense!" she cried, forgetting her vow to avoid a confrontation. "The countryside is thick with soldiers searching for you!"

"That is precisely why I decided not to take the risk," he replied, annoyed that she would dare question him. "I doubt your newfound friend would be thanking me for bringing the soldiers down about his head. You must know the Mermaid is being watched," he added when she frowned at him. "As you learned to your cost, it is a notorious haven for smugglers."

"I hadn't thought of that," Kate confessed, feeling more than a little foolish. "I assumed that since the authorities were concentrating their search among the upper class that the Mermaid would be safe from scrutiny. Especially after the other evening."

"Why? What happened the other evening?" Peter demanded, not caring for her tone of voice.

She hesitated, wondering how much she should tell him, then with a casual shrug confessed all. By the time she had finished he was thin-lipped with displeasure.

"I must agree with your aunt, Mrs. Delecourt. Publicly defending the smuggling trade at such a time was probably not the wisest thing you might have done. 'Tis sure to cause the most unpleasant sort of speculation."

"I was not defending the smuggling trade!" Kate answered indignantly. "I quite agree with Dr. Markham that it is treason to trade with our enemy while we are at war. I merely meant that those who buy such goods are equally to blame. More so in fact. Were it not for them, there would be no smuggling!"

"An interesting point, ma'am" Peter conceded, "but not altogether a true one. Since the days of the Romans there have been smugglers in these waters, and I daresay there will be more when we are all dust. But I repeat, ma'am, you chose a devil of a time to air your views."

"I know, but I can take some consolation in the fact that my tongue wagging seems to have gone unremarked. My poor manners are not nearly so interesting as Lord Payton's return. From what Aunt Portia has said, it is the talk of the neighborhood."

The mention of the marquess made Peter stiffen with alarm. What the devil was the bastard doing in Kent, he wondered, struggling to hide his reaction. He was supposed to be safely tucked in his London townhouse. He scratched his beard idly, a look of supreme indifference on his face.

"A lord is it, now?" he said, his accent more obvious than ever. "Well, 'tis honored I'm sure you must be. Will you be having him to tea like a proper country hostess?"

Kate gave him a reproving look at his cutting words. "As I have never had the honor of making his lordship's acquaintance, I should think it most unlikely," she said coolly. "And you mustn't be so harsh on the poor man. He suffered a dreadful tragedy, you know," and she proceeded to tell him the sad tale.

Peter listened with every indication of interest, although he was more than familiar with the story. Familiar enough, in fact, to know that word was the shooting was far from "accidental." Payton had been deep in the suds when his wife's death released the bulk of her fortune into his greedy hands. He wondered why he had returned to the estates he had virtually ignored for the past five years. When he asked as much, Kate shrugged her shoulders.

"No one knows. Although Mr. Turner thinks it is because Lord Payton may be thinking of selling the estate."

"Is he now?" Peter filed the information away. "Well, I suppose I don't blame him. The whole place must be filled with sad memories for him."

"Yes," Kate agreed, thinking of her own tragic loss. "But there are doubtlessly happy ones as well. When a marriage is good, a whole house can be filled with love."

They continued chatting for another half hour, and Kate was struck by his incisive intelligence. It was obvious he'd received some education, and she wondered why he'd chosen the life he had. With his looks and quick mind he would have been a success in whatever endeavor he chose, and she was appalled that he should squander his life so.

She was no closer to resolving the puzzle when Mickey said, "I was wondering, Mrs. Delecourt, if there was something you might do for me."

Kate stirred in her chair, somewhat embarrassed by the direction of her thoughts. "Certainly, Mr. Quentin, if I can," she said briskly, fixing a pleasant smile to her face. "What is it?"

"Well," his blue eyes grew merry, " 'tis not that I would have you think me ungrateful, but I fear this robe, fashionable as it might be, is hardly a fitting garment to be wearing outside this room. I wouldn't want to be offending the maid's sensibilities," he added, assuming a pious mien.

Kate took his meaning at once. Now that he was recovering it was only natural he should wish to be up and about, and with the soldiers actively seeking him, having a change of clothes at the ready might prove to be expedient. "That is very thoughtful of you, sir," she said, her lips curving in a teasing smile. "And on behalf of my maids, I thank you. I will have the footmen check my husband's trunks to see what they can find. You are slightly taller, but I am sure we will be able to improvise something."

Peter fingered the brilliant robe. "Just one more thing, ma'am," he added, the teasing light in his eyes growing more pronounced as he grinned up at her. "Are your husband's tastes in any way similar to his uncle's?"

Kate's smile widened in understanding. "I think you may rely upon Charles's discretion and his good taste," she told him, her nose coming up in mock hauteur. "Although not a dandy, he is considered by his friends to be a gentleman of impeccable taste."

Peter tilted his head back. "Having met you, Mrs. Delecourt, I surely do not dispute the first," he told her with a provocative drawl, "although I shall reserve judgement on the latter until I've seen a sample of his wardrobe. So long as he hasn't a passion for clothes more befitting a Persian prince, I daresay I will be more than satisfied."

"And if he does?"

"Then I'll have to be borrowing the footman's coat and trousers," came the prompt reply. "Given a choice of looking like a servant or a delicate tulip of the *ton*, I know what my choice will be."

Lucille departed two days later amidst a copious flow of tears and recriminations. "Are you quite sure you will be all right, my dear?" she asked, dabbing at her eyes with a new embroidered handkerchief. "I feel like the greatest coward abandoning you at such a time!"

"I shall be fine," Kate assured her, giving one of the pink plumes dangling from Lucille's bonnet a teasing flick. "Just mind you don't get carried off by some highwayman who shall take one look at you and fall madly in love! Your new clothes make you look as fine as a sixpence."

Lucille preened, running a gloved hand across the dark rose velvet of her new travelling pelisse. "They do? I wasn't at all certain when the parcels first arrived. Rose, for a lady of my advanced years . . ." She shot Kate a hopeful look.

"You look scarce out of the schoolroom," Kate did not disappoint her, but was fulsome in her praise. "Now, don't forget to write us the moment you arrive at Cousin Caro's, otherwise we shall be distracted with worry. Won't we, Aunt?" she turned a stern look on Portia who had come outside to bid the traveller farewell.

"Distracted," Portia echoed dutifully, bustling over to deposit a quick kiss on Lucille's cheek. "Take care, mind, and don't allow that harridan to bully you about. You are not a servant, you know."

"You needn't concern yourself with me, Mrs. Stone," Lucille replied silkily. "In this past year I have become rather adept at handling harridans. Good-bye." And with that she boarded the coach, disappearing down the lane in a great cloud of dust.

"Well!" Portia turned on Kate, her eyes gleaming with a martial light. "Upon my soul, I have never been so insulted in all my days! And you, miss, how dare you laugh at me! Did you not hear what that pea goose just called me?"

"Indeed I did," Kate replied, wiping the tears of laughter from her cheeks. "I had no idea Lucille could be so witty!"

"Hmph" Portia pretended to be indignant another few moments, and then broke into a low chuckle. "It was a rather clever set down, wasn't it?" she acknowledged with reluctant admiration. "Well, I wish the wretch joy in her new occupation of drudge. I make no doubt that Caroline will run her ragged within the week."

"Do you really think so?" Kate asked, frowning with concern as they made their way back to the house. Now that she had achieved her objective of removing Lucille from the house before she learned of Mickey's existence, she was beset with guilt. She would never forgive herself if Lucille was mistreated because of her.

"Yes, and you needn't look so guilt stricken," Portia replied, correctly reading her niece's troubled expression. "You may take it from me that the only thing that will make that female happier than ordering someone about, is to be ordered about herself. She will adore playing the martyr every bit as much as she enjoyed playing the bereaved sister. More so, for you shall not be there to compete with her."

"Aunt, that is a terrible thing to say!" Kate gasped, shocked to her toes by Portia's blunt statement. "Lucille loved Charles!"

"I'm not saying she didn't," Portia said coolly. "I'm just saying she is more fond of feigning emotion than she is in the emotion itself. Charles's death was an excuse to drape herself in black and go about mourning like some tragic heroine out of a novel. I am sure she did genuinely grieve for her brother, but most of it was a game to her."

"You make her sound so . . . so shallow," Kate answered, decidedly shaken by her aunt's brutal summation.

"Most people are shallow, my love," Portia said with a shrug. "I am four and sixty, and I have found that digging beneath a person's exterior is a useless endeavor at best. Few people one meets are worthy of the effort."

Kate said nothing, her thoughts turning to Mickey, as they often did. He was far from shallow, and something told her that it would be more than worth her while to dig beneath the careless facade he presented to the world. But the question was, would she learn anything?

It dawned on her that even after all this time she still

knew next to nothing about him. She'd done her best to respect his privacy, but it had been hard. The few questions she had asked were either ignored, or answered with such errant foolishness as to be patently false. She recalled his wild tale of shooting fish. But what did she really know? The realization occupied her thoughts long after she returned to the house.

With the help of Nurse and two of the other maids who had been sworn to secrecy, Kate altered several of Charles's old coats and trousers to fit Mickey's more muscular frame. It was not a project the older woman approved of, if her grumbles and complaints were any indication, but it was a project which filled Kate with satisfaction nonetheless. She'd been wrapped in grief and indifference for so long, she'd forgotten the pleasure to be found in simple work.

Three days after Lucille's departure she sat quietly in the parlor, a pile of mending beside her. Aunt Portia was at her literary group, and she was making use of the sunshine streaming through the mullioned windows to add the finishing touches to the shirt she was sewing. She'd just finished tucking back the cuffs when a maid burst in, her eyes bulging with fright.

"S-soldiers, ma'am," she stammered, wringing her hands with agitation. "A w-whole platoon of 'em comin' down the road!"

The shirt Kate was mending went flying as she leapt to her feet. "Are they coming here?" she demanded sharply.

The maid's head bobbed rapidly. "Yes, ma'am. Ol' Twiggs from the Mortimers came up the sea path to warn us. He said the soldiers just left there, and that they're searching the woods as well."

The Mortimers were her nearest neighbors to the north, which meant she had less than fifteen minutes, provided they stuck to the road. She pushed her anxiety firmly to one side and forced herself to consider all the alternatives. There was no time to rush Mickey to the safety of the caves, she decided coolly, which meant they would have to hide him inside. But where?

For a wild moment she wished her aunt was there. The old woman was an autocratic old witch at times, but she was also crafty as a fox. She would know what to do. Or even Lucille, she thought, a wisp of hysteria filtering into her calm. If nothing else she could keep the soldiers distracted peeking beneath the beds while she hustled Mickey out the—Kate froze suddenly.

No, her logical mind told her sternly. It was a wild plan. Preposterous. It would never work. But it was also the only chance they had, she realized with mounting excitement. With luck her scheme would succeed, if not. . . . She refused to consider that possibility.

"Pick this up" she instructed, turning on the maid with a determined gleam in her eye. "No, wait," she contradicted as the maid bent to retrieve the shirt. "Hide the shirt, but leave the rest of it out. Then I want you and the others to go back into the kitchens and wait there."

"But Mrs. Delecourt—"

"Do as I say, Mary!" There was no time for politeness. "And tell the rest of the staff that they are to cooperate with the soldiers; no matter what. Do you understand?"

"But—"

"Do you understand?"

The maid mentally raised her hands in defeat. Whatever scheme her employer had in her head she prayed it would work; otherwise 'twould be the gallows for the handsome smuggler hiding upstairs. "As you say, ma'am" she muttered at last. "But I'm fair certain Mr. Richards will not be likin' this," and she slunk off to carry out her orders.

Kate wasted no time but dashed upstairs, bursting into Mickey's room. "The soldiers are coming" she said without preamble. "You have to hide."

Peter turned from the window, the color fading from his face at the news. "How far away?" he asked tersely.

"Fifteen minutes," Kate replied somewhat breathlessly, stepping forward to gaze up into his stormy blue eyes. "They're coming by the road and through the woods. We shall have to hide you in the house."

Peter's lips thinned as he considered the dangers involved. Not to himself, but to her. The penalty for harboring a smuggler was almost as great as that for smuggling itself, and he could not bear the image of her locked in a filthy cell. He would eventually be freed, but in the meantime what of her? Her reputation would be in shreds, and he doubted her useless wastrel of a husband would be of much aid to her.

"No," he said, his shoulders squaring as he reached the only conclusion available to a man of honor. "They would only find me and that would make all of you guilty. I will surrender myself."

"What?" Kate gaped at him in horror. "Mickey, you can not be serious! They *hang* smugglers! And what difference does it make if you surrender or not? They will still know I was hiding you."

"I will tell them I forced you to help me," Peter replied, thinking quickly. "I'll tell them I threatened to have your husband killed if you did not cooperate."

"Don't be a goose, they should never believe you," Kate snapped, grabbing him by the sleeve and dragging him towards the bed. "Now quickly, hide."

"Where?" Peter retorted, stung by the casual way she had brushed his noble offer aside.

"Here." Kate bent and lifted the bedcovers. "Well?" she demanded when he made no move to comply with her orders. "What are you waiting for? The soldiers will be here any moment now!"

"Are you seriously suggesting I hide beneath a bed?" Peter's voice rose several octaves. "You are mad!"

"Mad enough to think it will work," she replied, still prodding at him. "Hurry!"

"But—" Peter began protesting hotly, only to be interrupted by a loud pounding at the door. They both froze, exchanging grim looks.

"There's no time now," Kate cried in desperation. "Please, Mickey, this is no time to play at being a gentleman! This will work. I know it will. Get under the bed before they find you!"

"I am surrendering." It was among the hardest things he had ever done in his life, but Peter proudly stood his ground.

"And you'll tell them that moonshine about threatening my husband?" Kate demanded, aware that the noises were drawing ever closer.

"Yes." Peter's chin came up in determination.

"They would never believe you."

"Why the devil not?" he asked, his eyes narrowing at the conviction in her voice.

"Because he is already dead, you idiot! Now for God's sake, get beneath the bed!" And with that she all but stuffed him under the ancient canopied bed.

Chapter Seven

The soldiers were in the front hall arguing with Richards when Kate made her appearance. Glancing over the heads of the brightly uniformed men she spied the hard-eyed officer commanding them, and fixed him with her most forbidding expression.

"Well?" she demanded in Aunt Portia's most haughty accents. "And pray what is the meaning of this? How dare you come bursting into my home without so much as a by your leave!"

"I beg your pardon, ma'am," Captain Allen Parker said, studying the woman before him with a mixture of wariness and admiration. "But we are here on the King's business, and I must ask you to step aside while we search your house."

"Search my house?" Kate continued down the stairs, her chin held proudly. "I should say not! Do you know to whom you are speaking?"

The captain who had heard this same protest many times in the past week, gave a weary sigh. "I would say that you are a subject of his majesty, King George," he said, his face expressionless. "And if you count yourself a loyal subject, you will not interfere." He turned to the pimply faced lieutenant standing beside him.

"'Take half the men and search the cellars," he instructed in clipped tones. "I will take the other half and start in the attic."

"Just one moment," Kate said, her eyes frosty with displeasure as she confronted the captain. "I am Mrs. Charles Delecourt, my uncle just happens to be Sir Alfred Dunshead of the Admiralty. Perhaps you have heard of him?" She infused just enough condescension in the request to make his jaw harden with annoyance.

"No, Mrs. Delecourt, I can not say that I have," he told her bluntly. "But as we are here on crown business, I can not see that it signifies. We are looking for the smuggler shot in Rye some days ago, and have reason to believe he is somewhere in this area."

"Smugglers!" The shriek Kate uttered could have come straight from Lucille's lips. She clasped her hand to her breast, an expression of horror twisting her features. "Dear God! Never say you think he has taken refuge *here* in my own house!"

"We are not accusing you," the captain said quickly, mistaking her terror for indignation. "We are searching every house in the neighborhood, and as you are so close to the sea we —"

"What are you doing just standing there?" Kate interrupted, grabbing him by the arm and dragging him towards the kitchens. "I insist you search my house from top to bottom!"

"But that is what we are trying to do," the captain began, only to be interrupted again.

"A smuggler, lurking about my house, why, the thought is enough to give me the vapors," Kate continued in Lucille's shrill tones. "We shall all be murdered in our sleep, I just know it! You must leave us some soldiers, Captain, to guard us. My aged aunt and I live here all alone, and it is your duty to protect us."

Captain Parker exchanged a speaking glance with his junior officer as they shouldered their way into the kitchen. "I shouldn't think that necessary, ma'am. The fellow is not likely to hang about very long once he knows we are on to him!" *Especially as he has already heard you nag,* he thought silently.

Kate gave one of Aunt Portia's loud sniffs but said nothing, standing to one side as she watched the soldiers poke about the large room. When they turned in the direction of the cellar doors she moved to block them. "You call this a search?" she demanded indignantly. "You didn't even look in any of the cupboards! Why, a shipload of smugglers could be hidden in there for all you know."

One of the soldiers gave a loud snicker, only to be silenced by a cutting glare from his captain. "I don't think that very likely, Mrs. Delecourt," he managed through clenched teeth. "They are much too small to hide one man, let alone a dozen. Now kindly stand aside."

She scuttled to one side like a disgruntled crab. "Well, you might at least check the flour barrel," she grumbled. "It *is* large enough to hide a man, and you didn't so much as give it a poke. You may make sure I shall mention such dereliction of duty to Uncle Alfred the very next time I see him; see if I do not."

The captain choked back a blistering oath, silently cursing the fates that had handed him this assignment. It would be just like the tart-tongued bitch to do it, he thought disgruntedly and if he ever wished a battle command, he could not afford to offend anyone even remotely connected to the Admiralty. He turned to his sergeant. "Check it," he rapped out in a curt voice.

The sergeant's pale eyes bulged with surprise. "But Captain—"

"Search it!"

The old soldier did as ordered, and with the help of a giggling corporal the barrel was most thoroughly searched. A great deal of flour was displaced in the meanwhile, and by the time they were done the two soldiers were coated with a fine layer of flour.

"There, madam, I trust your fears have been put to rest," Captain Parker said, shooting Kate a triumphant look. "No smugglers have secreted themselves in your grainery."

Kate gave another sniff. "If you say so," she conceded with an arrogant lift of her chin. "But I am still far from satisfied. This is a large house, and he could be hiding anywhere. Now do hurry; you have wasted enough time in here already."

And so it continued; the soldiers searching each level of the house and Kate dogging them every step of the way. She ignored the captain's increasingly vociferous demands that she stand back and allow them to do their duty; insisting they search the most unlikely places she could conceive of. She had them peeking up chimneys, peering into wardrobes, and poking into trunks with their bayonets, all to no avail.

When she tired of hectoring them as she was certain Aunt Portia would have done, she turned into Lucille, sobbing that the entire population of Romney Marsh was only waiting until they marched away before leaping out of the wainscotting and slitting their throats. By the time they reached the west wing it was a task and captain and most of his men would willingly have performed themselves, if only for a few moments of uninterrupted peace. But it was when she demanded they search beneath the beds that she finally managed to break them.

"Mrs. Delecourt," the captain began, all pretense of politeness gone "you may take it from me, smugglers do not hide beneath beds!"

"How do you know?" Kate demanded, delighted she had achieved her objective at long last. She had begun to run out of things to check, and was growing quite desperate. "Are *you* a smuggler?"

"Of course not!"

"Then how do you know where they hide?" she asked, pausing in front of the room across the hall from Mickey's room. The rest of the wing had already been searched, and she was praying she could stop them

99

from searching any further. She had told them the wing was unoccupied; a falsehood that would become readily apparent were they to glance inside Mickey's room.

"It is my job to know, ma'am!" Captain Parker snapped, bereft of patience and tact. "We are not going to bend over and peep beneath the beds like a lot of nervous old maids!"

In a twinkling Kate metamorphosed into Aunt Portia. "Well!" she gasped, her eyes snapping with righteous fury, "I have never been so insulted in all my life! How dare you speak to me so! I shall write my uncle of your insolence at once! He is with—"

"The Admiralty," he finished disgustedly deciding no command was worth enduring another moment of this mad woman's company. "I know. You have told us a dozen times already." He cast a glance at his weary lieutenant and jerked his head towards the staircase. "Gather up the men, we're leaving."

"Leaving? Why, you've barely begun to search!" Kate protested, trailing after them like a determined terrier. "What of the rest of the house and the outer buildings? Surely you mean to check them!"

"We have already checked your stable," the captain informed her, striding purposefully towards the front door. "I can assure you it was empty save for your animals and your ostler."

"But what about my aunt and me?" She was Lucille again. "You simply can not leave us here alone without protection. I insist you assign some men to stay with us until you have captured this ruffian! Provided you ever do, that is," she allowed a touch of Aunt Portia to come out at the end, to speed him on his way.

"I'll catch him, ma'am, never fear," Captain Parker said, setting his plumed hat firmly on his head. "And as for protection, might I suggest you write your Uncle Alfred of the Admiralty? I am sure he would be more than happy to assist you." And pleased with that final bit of impertinence he left, vowing to his lieutenant that he would invade France on his own before returning to this house again.

The moment the soldiers disappeared Kate dashed back up the stairs. There was no sign of Mickey when she flung open the door and she wondered if he had somehow slipped away. She was about to step out again when she became aware of the sounds coming from beneath the bed. He was laughing!

"Mickey!" She hurried over, dropping to her knees and peeking under the counterpane. "What are you doing beneath there? Come out at once!"

"As you wish, ma'am," Peter chuckled, his eyes gleaming with amusement as he grinned up at her. "But might I remind you, 'twas your idea to stick me here in the first place."

"Well, I didn't mean for you to take up permanent residence," she grumbled, grabbing his arm and pulling carefully. "The soldiers have gone now, and it is safe to come out."

"Safe for whom, ma'am?" he asked, grimacing as he wiggled out from his sanctuary. The action pulled at his injuries, but he ignored the pain. "I heard you bear leading the captain about, and my heart quite went out to the poor lad. From the little I heard, you must have been making his life a sheer misery."

"I tried," Kate admitted, slipping an arm about him and helping him sit up. "But the good captain proved more stubborn than you may suppose. I was growing quite desperate at the end."

"No more than was I," Peter brushed the dirt from his jacket and trousers. "The notion of being found cowering beneath the furniture like a rat was not at all to my liking. Congratulations on your quick thinking, ma'am. However did you think of such a thing?"

Kate blushed as she remembered the inspiration for her idea. She doubted either her aunt or Lucille would be pleased that she had made use of them in such a fashion. "It was just an idea," she said, shrugging her

101

shoulders and refusing to meet his eyes, "but I thought if I were to appear . . . cooperative I could put the soldiers off their guard. It worked."

"Mmm," Peter murmured, studying her profile with reluctant admiration. Sitting this close to her he could see the amber lights gleaming in the blond depths of her hair, and smell the delicate rose of her perfume. Learning she was widowed was both a relief and a complication he could have well done with out. He reached out and cupped her chin with his hand, turning her head towards his.

"Kate, why did you let me think your husband was still alive?" he asked quietly, his blue eyes serious as they met hers.

The color deepened in Kate's cheeks as much from the shock of hearing her Christian name on his lips as from the intimacy of his touch. She gazed into his eyes, her heart pounding with an emotion she dared not acknowledge.

"I thought it best," she said simply, seeing no reason to prevaricate. "A woman alone learns to be cautious."

"Especially a woman who takes wounded strangers into her house," he agreed, unable to resist the temptation of touching her; however briefly. "My thanks again for that," he added in a husky voice, his finger trailing across the gentle curve of her cheek. "I should have died out there had it not been for you."

Kate trembled at the caress. "You — you're welcome," she stammered, ignoring the voice of reason that cried out to her to pull back and leave the room at once.

"Why did you do it?" he pressed, longing to learn more of the beautiful woman who had rescued him. She was a puzzle to him; a sweet enigma whose mysteries he ached to solve. "Was it because of your husband?"

Kate nodded her head, her eyes lowering to study her clenched hands. "He fell in battle over a year ago," she said softly, the tearing pain now a dull, familiar ache.

"For a long while it was as if part of me had died with him; the part that felt, and laughed, and loved. I was so empty inside . . ."

"And then?" he asked when her voice trailed off.

"Then I slowly started coming back to life," she continued, her tone thoughtful as she relived those dark days. "It was like waking from a heavy sleep; my senses seemed to return one by one. I remember the first time I lost my temper with my aunt I was actually relieved! I was so certain I would never feel anything again, even anger."

"And it shamed you?" he guessed, his finger moving from her cheek to the shiny gold of her hair.

"At first," she admitted, risking a quick glance at his gentle expression. "But then I realized Charles would not have wanted me to grieve forever. He loved life so much, he would have been angry to see me squander mine." Her fingers closed tightly around the dark blue merino of her gown. "I—I wish you might have met him."

"As do I. He must have been a wonderful man."

"He was."

There was another uncomfortable silence and then Peter shook his head with a wry chuckle. "I ought to have tumbled to the fact that you were a widow," he said, rising to his feet and then helping her to hers. "The gray gowns you wore, the way the staff acted when I mentioned your husband. It quite shames me that I was so lack witted! In my occupation, being unobservant is the very next thing to being dead."

"Fishing is such a dangerous occupation, then?" Kate teased, wiping the dust from her skirt.

Peter had not been thinking of fishing, but he decided that answer would serve as well as the truth. "The sea is a harsh mistress, and she'll not tolerate being ignored," he said simply. "Any man who doesn't pay close attention to her ever changeable moods will soon find himself in serious straits."

103

Kate wanted very much to ask if that was what happened to him, but she managed to hold her tongue. She doubted he would tell her the truth, and in any case, she already knew how he had come to be injured. She became aware that she was still standing close to Mickey, and moved reluctantly away. "I had best check on the servants," she said with a hasty smile. "This is certain to have upset them, and I'm sure they'll need advice setting the house to rights again."

"As you say, ma'am," Peter inclined his head politely. "And once again, thank you for my life. You are as resourceful as you are lovely."

Kate blushed at his warm words and hurried towards the door. She had just reached it when she remembered something Mickey had said. She paused and shot him an apologetic look over her shoulder. "I'm sorry I didn't tell you about Charles," she said with quiet dignity. "I detest lies more than anything, but I was afraid to tell you the truth."

"Pray don't refine on it, ma'am," he replied swiftly, keenly aware of his own sense of guilt. "I understand completely."

"Good." She moistened her lips and smiled weakly. "Well, good-bye, then."

Peter watched her leave, his hands clenching in angry fists as he considered the irony of the situation. She was a woman who could not abide a lie, and he was a man who dared not tell the truth.

"Well, upon my soul, it certainly sounds as if you had an interesting afternoon," Portia said, her thin lips pursing with displeasure as she glared at her niece. "And to think I missed it all to hear a dreary lecture on Coleridge!"

"You'd not have thought it so amusing if you'd been here, I assure you," Kate muttered, taking a restorative sip of madeira to calm her badly frazzled nerves.

"Those wretched men all but tore the house to shreds, and that young captain was most rude to me as well. I've half a notion to write a letter of complaint to his superior about his behavior!"

"Wouldn't do you much good," Portia answered, helping herself to another glass of the sweet wine. "He was only doing his duty, after all."

"Well, if his *duty* includes terrifying servants and insulting defenseless ladies then I may only conclude that he has a long and illustrious career ahead of him," Kate continued with a grumble. Her ill humor had begun as a defense against her aunt's probing questions, but the more she thought about the invasion of her house the angrier she became. Much as she hated giving Reverend Boothe credit for anything she had to admit he was right about one thing; having one's house searched by armed troops was an insult not to be meekly endured! Perhaps she *would* write to Uncle Alfred, she decided. Certainly the Admiralty couldn't condone such behavior on the part of its officers.

Portia spent the rest of the meal telling Kate about the lecture and filling her in on the latest neighborhood gossip. "Of course with most of our friends gone to London there was really very little to discuss," she concluded with a sigh. "Thank heavens we shall also be leaving in a few other days, otherwise I am certain I should expire from boredom! I vow, I am quite starved for some really delicious bit of scandal to sink my teeth into."

"What about Lord Payton? Surely his arrival must have sparked some talk," Kate said, wincing at the thought of leaving her home and Mickey behind.

"That is so," Portia brightened at once. "I had no idea he was so thoroughly repellent, but you would not believe the stories that are whispered about him! It was almost enough to shock these ancient ears."

"Then perhaps it is just as well he means to sell his wife's estate," Kate said, not really interested in the shady past of her notorious neighbor. "He does not sound like the sort of person I should care to meet."

"Oh pooh, Katherine, you have grown positively prudish these days!" Portia protested with an angry scowl. "A bit of scandal gives a man dash. The earl is most handsome, and a prime catch on the Marriage Mart. You could do much worse for yourself."

"You're not seriously suggesting I set my cap for this man?" Her aunt's comment jolted Kate out of her reverie. "Aunt Portia! You heard what Mr. Turner said; the man's pockets are to let!"

"Posh, the man is as wealthy as a Cresus. Mr. Turner had no right to say such things, and even if they were true it still doesn't signify. The man is titled, well-born, and not without some charms to recommend him," Portia listed each virtue on her gnarled fingers.

"You just called him thoroughly repellent!"

Portia gave her a sagacious look. "I quite wonder about this younger generation," she said with a heartfelt sigh. "We were never so nice in our notions in my day."

"But—"

"Idiot, has it not occurred to you that even if you consider Payton to be beneath your notice there are still his friends to be considered?"

"Friends?" Kate frowned at her aunt in confusion.

"Friends," came the succinct reply. "And if the gossip I heard today is to be believed some of the most eligible *partis* in England may be found in their numbers. Including," there was a dramatic pause, "the earl of Tregarren."

"Aunt, I have already told you that I have no interest in . . . who did you say?"

"Aha, that got your attention, didn't it?" Portia fairly gloated. "Well, that's a relief, then. I was beginning to think you had lost all sense of proportion."

"The earl is a friend of Lord Payton's?" Kate demanded, ignoring her aunt's last comment.

"Bosom beaus, if Lillian Baldrick is to be believed. According to her Payton and Tregarren were close as two inkleweavers until the earl ran his curricle into a tree while racing in Hyde Park."

"Is he here? The earl I mean?" Kate asked, her heart pounding as she considered what this news could mean to Mickey. Surely his patron . . . if such Tregarren was, would be willing to help him slip safely away. Perhaps she could write him a note and . . .

"Tregarren? Here? I should say not," Portia regarded Kate with marked impatience. "Were you not listening? The foolish lad ran his curricle into a tree less than three months ago! He's hardly in any shape to go racketing about the countryside, you know. Although . . ."

"Although what?" Kate prodded when her aunt didn't continue.

"Well, when I first heard the story I must admit I had my suspicions," Portia continued in a confiding manner. "The earl is a known whipster and a member of the Four in Hand Club. For such a man to suffer a carriage accident is somewhat hard to believe."

"Perhaps he was boskey," Kate suggested, wishing her aunt would get to the point.

"Undoubtedly, he is an earl, after all, and all these young lords drink like proverbial fishes. But that is not what I meant."

"Then what do you mean?"

"Really? Katherine, how can you be such a slowtop?" Portia demanded in exasperation. "I am referring to a scandal, or a duel, or both. Why else would a handsome and wealthy bachelor quit the city at the height of the season?"

Kate hardly considered the end of December to be the "height of the season," but knew better than to correct her aunt. Besides, she realized, her lips twisting, in a moue of disapproval, she was right. The earl had undoubtedly involved himself in something so unsavory his only choice was to flee London. She wondered if it had anything to do with his bet and Mickey's part in it.

"It was gaming, I'll wager," Portia speculated happily. "Or ladybirds. The Tregarrens are known for their predilection for the muslin set. The earl's father was said to have enough mistresses to keep a pasha happy, and enough bastards to make him a Royal Duke! Although I suppose I ought not to say such things," she added with a belated sense of propriety.

"He sounds as repellent as Lord Payton," Kate said, losing all interest in the matter. "I should be just as happy never to make his acquaintance."

"Katherine," Portia sent her another frown, "if you are going to raise your pretty little nose at every man who has even a slightly tainted past, then I fear you will run the risk of being labeled a prude."

"I see nothing wrong with that," Kate responded, stung by the criticism in her aunt's voice. "I can think of far worse things to be called."

"That may as be," Portia consented grudgingly, "but it is still a sobriquet I would as lief not bear applied to you." She studied Kate another moment and then shook her head. "You used to be such a lively gel, Katherine! It quite vexes me to see you grown serious and solemn before your time. Next you'll start reading Hannah Moore and performing good works, I don't wonder."

"You make virtue sound like a failing!"

"And so it is, in our world."

"But I thought you told me I ought to be mindful of my reputation!" Kate exclaimed, recalling any number of lectures on that very subject.

"Mindful yes," Portia replied with a loud sniff, cursing her niece's prodigious memory and her own scolding tongue. "But I certainly did not mean to imply that you should become fanatical on the subject. It is my opinion, and I am sure most gentlemen would agree with me, that the only thing a man finds more distressful than lack of virtue in a woman, is a surfeit of it. You must take care, else you will become as odiously prim as that sister-in-law of yours."

Kate thought suddenly of Mickey, and wondered what her aunt would say if she knew that even as they spoke, she was keeping a smuggler hidden in the house. Doubtlessly the old tartar would approve, she decided, her eyes dancing with devilish amusement. "Oh, I daresay there are some who would feel I have already achieved that sad state," she mumured, dimples flashing as she remembered Captain Parker's utter frustration.

"Well there, you see?" Portia looked triumphant. "This trip to London could not have come at a more fortuitous time! The sennight's reprieve you wrangled out of me is all but at an end, and once we are in the city I'll soon have you merry as a cricket; see if I do not." She gave a solemn nod and picked up her wine glass. "What's for dessert?"

Chapter Eight

Upstairs in his room Peter paced restlessly back and forth, his agitation increasing with each step he took. Now that he'd had time to consider the afternoon's events, he realized how very close they had come to disaster. Had Kate not succeeded in distracting the soldiers when she had, they would doubtlessly have been in the official's custody by now.

Despite the grim nature of his thoughts, he could not help but smile as he remembered the clever way she'd dealt with the hapless soldiers. Little devil, he thought, pausing in front of the blue tiled fireplace. Her understanding of human nature was indeed prodigious if she knew that the best way to get someone to do one thing, was to tell them to do exactly the opposite.

His smile faded abruptly as he thought of the future. There was no hope for it, he decided grimly, staring down into the flames flickering in the grate. He would have to leave. He should have left upon first hearing of the soldiers' search, but he'd allowed himself to be persuaded otherwise by his hostess. The realization was not a pleasant one, but he was not the kind of man to avoid something merely because it was unpleasant. He freely accepted his own guilt for allowing things to continue as they had, and resolved to set things right as soon as it could be safely arranged.

Feeling somewhat better for having finally reached a decision, he crossed the room to the window. His letter should have reached London by now, and with luck, Westley would soon be contacting him. He would give it another forty-eight hours, and then he would begin making plans of his own. Two days, he brooded, staring out the window into the darkness, two days, and then he would never see his lovely hostess again.

"And once you have taken all the rugs out, I think you should start on the furniture," Kate decided, laying a thoughtful finger on her lips as she studied the list in her hand. "Also, I think it is time the parlor had some new wallpaper. I will send you some samples from London."

"Very goods Mrs. Delecourt," Mrs. Parks, the housekeeper nodded her head in approval. "And you might give some thought to the library as well. The rug what's in there now ain't fit for a stable dog to lie on!"

Kate made a face as she thought of the ancient, faded rug with its frayed edges and ugly stains. She and Charles had talked about replacing it many times, but somehow they had never gotten around to it. "You are right, Mrs. Parks," she said with a sigh. "That rug is beyond all hopes of redemption. I'll see about purchasing us a new one."

"And some new drapes for the dining room" the housekeeper added, pleased to see her mistress's interest in the household returning. The poor thing had been cast so low this past year, Mrs. Parks doubted if she would have noticed the whole house falling in about her pretty ears. Evidently this trip to London was just what the dear lady needed, she decided with a smug feeling of contentment.

"All right" Kate agreed, more out of a sense of dis-interest than out of any concern for the dining room's appearance. Since rising that morning she had pur-posefully buried herself in the mundane demands of housework, hoping the distractions would keep her from thinking of Mickey and the odd feelings he stirred in her. So far, she had been less than successful in that endeavor.

They spent the rest of the morning going over vari-ous lists and discussing other improvements to be car-ried out during her prolonged absence. Kate was about to suggest they call a halt for luncheon when one of the maids came in to tell her she had a visitor.

"Who is it?" she asked worriedly, visions of Captain Parker returning to search her house haunting her.

"The Viscount Westley ma'am," the maid provided, bristling with self-importance. "Mr. Richards put him in the drawing room, and said I was to come fetch you."

Westley, the name was unfamiliar to Kate. "Did he say what he wanted?"

The young maid shook her head vigorously. "No. ma'am. Just asked if he could please have a word with you."

Kate's eyebrows arched with interest. "Well, we shall have to see what he wants," she said, much in-trigued. "Kindly tell him I shall be with him shortly."

The maid bobbed a quick curtsey and then hurried out, leaving Kate and Mrs. Parks alone. "Shall I have Cook prepare some tea?" The housekeeper asked, shooting Kate a speculative look. "That will give you time to change into something more . . . fashionable."

Kate looked down at her plain black frock and grimaced. She'd donned the gown, one of her oldest, in anticipation of a hard day's work, and while it was more than suitable for rummaging about dusty rooms, it was hardly suitable for receiving guests.

"That will be fine, Mrs. Parks," she said, already thinking of what she would wear. "You might also tell Aunt of our visitor. She knows everyone in Society, and may be acquainted with our mysterious caller."

"An excellent suggestion, Mrs. Delecourt," Mrs. Parks nodded her approval. "And I shall send Betsy to your room as well. I am sure you won't wish to greet his lordship in your caps."

When Kate entered the drawing room some twenty minutes later, she looked every inch the country lady at her leisure. She wore her new gown of rose gauze, her hair arranged in a charming pile of curls at the nape of her neck. Portia looked up at her entrance, her lined face breaking into a pleased smile as she took in Kate's appearance.

"Here is my niece now," she said to the young man who was already rising to his feet. "Kate, my dear, allow me to make you known to Lord Giles Henry Richardson, Viscount Westley. My lord, this is my niece, Mrs. Katherine Delecourt."

"Mrs. Delecourt," the viscount bowed politely over her hand. "It is a pleasure to make your acquaintance."

"Thank you, my lord," Kate responded, studying the handsome young man before her through modestly lowered lashes. She placed his age as somewhere in his late twenties, and she found his appearance pleasing, if somewhat dandified for her tastes. Good heavens, were all the gentlemen in London adorning themselves with a dozen or more fobs, she wondered, her face expressionless as she retrieved her hand from his weak grasp. It was a wonder he didn't clank and jingle as he walked!

"I was just renewing my family's connection to your aunt, Mrs. Delecourt," the viscount said, flipping back the tails of his coat of blue superfine as he resumed his seat. "You would not credit it, ma'am but

113

my mother and your aunt were bosom beaus in their salad days. Is that not amazing?"

"Amazing" Kate agreed dryly, secretly amused by his delicate mannerisms.

"I'd forgotten Sybil had bagged a peer" Portia said, thoroughly enjoying herself. "Not that I should be surprised, I suppose. She was a true diamond of the first water."

"Yes, physical perfection is something of a family trait," his lordship agreed, running a slender hand through his carefully arranged blond locks. "But I shall be sure to tell her you remembered her, Mrs. Stone. I am sure it will please her."

Another ten minutes were spent discussing various family members, and laughing over the latest scandal from London. Kate played the dutiful hostess, plying her guest with tea and laughing at all the proper places, all the while wondering why the foppish young lord had honored them with his presence. She was about to throw good breeding to the wind and ask him, when he set his cup down on the tea tray.

"Mrs. Delecourt, I was wondering if it might be possible to ask a favor of you."

"A favor?" she repeated, her brows puckering slightly.

"I know I am presuming a great deal on so short an acquaintance, but I assure you the matter is most important."

"Indeed?" Kate grew even more curious. "And what might this favor be, my lord?"

"Well," he leaned as far forward as the exaggerated height of his collar would allow, "you must know I am something of an artist; strictly an amateur, I assure you, and I would very much like to sketch your charming cove."

"My cove?" Kate blinked at him in surprise.

"I adore seascapes, you see, and I am presumptuous enough to think I have something of a talent for them," he simpered like a young miss. "Well, I was walking about your lovely countryside looking for the right sort of place to set my easel when I saw your beach. It is exactly what I have been looking for, and I shall be quite crushed if you do not let me immortalize it with oil and canvas. Do say yes, I implore you."

Kate was hard-pressed not to burst into laughter. Immortalize it indeed, she thought, her lips twitching with amusement. If his lordship's sartorial splendor was any indication of his artistic ability, the painting would doubtlessly be a garish horror. "I suppose that would be all right," she said politely, seeing no reason why she should object. "The tide is out just now, but you are more than welcome to . . . er . . . set up your easel, if that is what you want." She sent him a weak smile.

He clapped his hands together in a gesture of delight. "Dear Mrs. Delecourt, you are too generous! I shall dedicate my work to you!"

"That is not necessary," she assured him hastily. "All I ask is that you watch your step on the path as it is somewhat slippery because of the rain."

"I shall be as nimble footed as a sprite," he pledged, laying a bejeweled hand over his heart. "And my thanks to you once again for your kind support of the arts! Your good deed shall not go unrewarded, I promise you."

He took his leave a few minutes later, speculating as to whether a pearl gray or a dove gray would best capture the essence of the sea. When the door closed behind him, Kate turned to her aunt with a laugh.

"If that is the sort of man I may expect to encounter in London, Aunt, I take leave to tell you you are wasting your time! I'd as lief wed Richards as a man-milner like the viscount!"

Portia was equally as disgusted by the foppish

young lord, although she was too wise to say as much to Katherine. The blasted girl would probably use that as an excuse to remain buried in this wilderness. "Society has any number of interesting gentlemen," she replied, seeking refuge in her tea cup. "If you don't like dandies, there are still the rakes and Corinthians to be considered."

"Like Lord Tregarren do you mean?" Kate asked, naming the only rake she could think of. "No thank you, ma'am, I would prefer a gentleman with some sense of honor to call his own."

"In London?" Portia's lips twisted in a knowing sneer. "You'd have better luck finding a Papist in the House of Lords!" She reached out and gave Kate's hand a loving pat. "But don't worry, my sweet, your clever aunt shall be there to see you don't come up a cropper. I have a plan, you see."

Kate picked up her own tea cup with a resigned sigh. "That," she said in the tones of a criminal sentenced to the gallows, "is precisely what I was afraid of."

"Where the devil have you been?" Peter demanded, his face set with anger as he stepped out from behind the large boulder where he'd been hiding. "I've been waiting out here for the last quarter of an hour!"

"Taking my leave of your hostess, dear boy," Giles replied good-naturedly, carefully setting his easel and box of paints on the wet sand. "Not the easiest of tasks, as I am sure you are aware."

Peter stiffened at the teasing words. "And what is that supposed to mean?" he asked, the brittle tones in his voice bringing the viscount's head snapping up.

"Nothing untoward, I promise you" he replied quickly, well-aware of Tregarren's dangerous reputation. "I merely meant that having met your lovely hostess I can understand your reluctance to be parted from her. She is quite beautiful."

"Yes, she is," Peter agreed, leaning his back against the large rock and fixing the viscount with an icy look. "Would you care to explain why you were so long contacting me? I was about to try for Dover on my own."

The rebuke stung, but Westley accepted it with a casual shrug of his shoulders. "The message you sent us was hardly brimming with information, my lord. We knew where you were and that you were still in disguise, but that is all. Had it not been for one of your local gentlemen, I might have been even longer in contacting you."

"O'Rourake?" Peter guessed.

Giles nodded, his handsome face breaking into a grin as he thought of the loquacious smuggler. "A most remarkable gentleman, and a veritable fountain of useful information. It was his idea that I smuggle a note up to you on your luncheon tray."

Peter grunted his approval of the plan. He'd found the note hidden under his tankard of ale, and the sight of the familiar handwriting had filled him with relief. He'd already made tentative arrangements to contact O'Rourake, and was grateful he wouldn't have to place his life in the hands of a man he'd never met. "What else did he say?"

"That the good widow had taken you in and was hiding you from the revenue men; which we already knew. He also said you'd had a narrow escape from a detachment of rather inept regulars."

Peter flushed at the memory of his lying beneath the bed. He prayed Westley never learned of it; nor anyone else for that matter. "What other news have you?" he asked gruffly anxious to change the subject. "What about our contact in Portsmouth?"

"You were right" Giles said, flipping open a sketch

pad and setting it on the easel. "The man was not as trustworthy as we had been led to believe."

"Was?" Peter seized on the word at once.

"A boating accident," Peter expanded, selecting a piece of charcoal from the box and applying it to the blank paper. "Theirs, not ours, I would hasten to add. We would have preferred taking the fellow alive. Dead men are seldom of any use to anyone."

Peter accepted the news without so much as a blink. The spy had known the rules going in, and he had violated them with full realization of what he risked. His only regret was that the man hadn't survived to be interrogated. He still didn't know why his mission had gone awry.

"I have some other news that may interest you," Giles said, his skillful hand flying over the paper as a sketch of the cove rapidly took shape. "A frigate docked in Jamaica some five weeks ago with a rather irate gentleman aboard. Seems the fellow claims he was kidnapped from a Folkestone tavern."

"That is news? I thought that was his Majesty's customary way of recruiting sailors."

"Undoubtedly, but the man in question claims to be your brother."

Peter straightened at once, his face paling with shock. "James?" he whispered, a faint flame of hope flickering to life. "Are you certain?"

"He matches the description you gave us of your half brother," Giles replied cautiously, "but naturally there is no way we can be certain until his ship arrives."

"When?" Peter demanded, half-afraid to believe the good news. He'd all but given James up for dead.

"The Chelsea set sail from Kingston the third of this month, and with fair weather should be arriving within eight weeks."

"Eight weeks!" Peter exclaimed indignantly, "but

a good ship can make that crossing in less—"

"We thought it best that the ship not alter its original course so as to avoid suspicion," Giles soothed. "She'll stop first in Charleston and New York to take on cargo before setting sail for Plymouth. Meanwhile your brother . . . or whoever he may be is receiving the best of care, you have my word on it."

Peter relaxed again, a smile forming on his lips as he thought of James chafing under "the best of care." He'd not like being kept confined to his cabin while the ship was under full sail.

"Is there nothing else you wish to tell me?" he asked, turning his thoughts to the matter at hand. "I have been incommunicado for the past three months, you know. You must have something of import to relate."

"Well, now that the Regency Bill has been approved Prinny has become puffed up beyond all bearing, and is busy selling offices to anyone with a fortune to spend. The ladies have abandoned Madame Trullier on Bond Street in favor of a self-styled Polish countess with an impossible last name who has set up shop in—"

"Westley!"

"Well, I thought you should wish to know the latest *on dits,* m'lord," Giles replied, his brown eyes merry with laughter. "You would not wish to be thought hopelessly out of step when you return to the city."

Peter knew the viscount well enough to see past his teasing words. "I have been recalled?"

Giles nodded, the sparkle fading from his eyes. "It has been decided that we have been chasing mare's nests, and you are ordered to present yourself at Whitehall without delay. That is why I have come."

Peter's hands clenched in silent anger. "Payton's influence reaches far," he said softly. "I would not have thought the Home Office capable of such duplicity."

119

"You have been gone for a long while, my lord, so you do not know how uncertain things have become," Giles said, shooting Peter a warning look. "I joked about Prinny, but the truth of the matter is that we are all at a dangerous impasse just now. If the Prince should fail to form a government it could easily trigger a constitutional crisis, and God above knows what advantage Boney might make of that. Spencer is being cautious, yes, but so must we all be. Payton's time will come, I promise you."

Peter would have liked to debate the matter, but he realized this was neither the time nor the place. His investigation had proven little against the marquess, and without further information there was nothing they could do. He would simply have to bide his time until James returned to see what he had learned. In the meanwhile Payton would have to be kept under close observation, and his best chance of doing that was as Lord Tregarren, dilettante and womanizer.

"When do we leave?" he asked, his eyes flicking towards the manor house high on the cliffs.

"Tonight," Giles ignored the direction of Peter's wistful stare. "Return to the beach at precisely two this morning and you will find a boat waiting for you. You will be taken first to Dover for a briefing, and then on to London. The Prince has been asking about you," he added, sending Peter a tentative smile. "He and the beau are quarreling again, and he insists you are the only other man in London who knows how to properly tie his cravat."

"I should have thought that is an honor you would wish to claim," Peter returned, grateful for the young man's tact. "You look every inch the dandy to me."

"Thank you," Giles inclined his head graciously. "I do try. And if the reaction of Mrs. Delecourt and her fearsome aunt are any indication, I have succeeded

120

beyond all expectations. They gaped at me like I was the man in the moon."

Peter smiled again, envisioning Kate's reaction to Giles's excessive mode of dress. "Is there anything else?" he asked, stuffing his hands into the pockets of his ill-fitting coat as he turned to watch the white-capped waves.

Giles hesitated, his attention apparently on his sketch. "There is one more small thing to be considered. Mrs. Delecourt."

"What of her?" Peter turned from his angry contemplation of the sea to stare at the viscount.

"I am sure I need hardly tell you that you must not tell her of our plans," he said, aware of Tregarren's every move despite his apparent unconcern. "There is too much at stake to risk disclosure to anyone."

"Of course I know that, damn it! Do you take me for a raw recruit?" Peter was furious.

"There is also some concern she may recognize you once you return to London," Giles ignored the outburst. "Do you think that may be a problem?"

Peter forced himself to relax. "I should consider that highly unlikely," he said, fingering his beard. "I have been careful to keep my true identity well-hidden the entire time I have been here, and I am convinced she accepts me as Mickey Quentin."

"A smuggler?"

Peter shrugged. "She has never come out and called me that to my face, but yes, that is what she takes me for."

"Hmm, then one may only wonder at her reasons for hiding you from the Excise men." The look Giles sent him was frankly speculative. "Is she . . . er . . . in the trade?"

"No!" Peter was enraged by the suggestion. "She was only doing what she considered her Christian duty."

"Odd that she would regard helping a criminal as a Christian duty, but I must bow to your superior knowledge of the lady" Giles took Peter's explanation in stride. "And you're certain she won't tumble to the whole thing once she claps eyes on you at Almack's?"

"I am positive" Peter scowled, "and in any case I consider it most unlikely that we shall ever see each other again. From what I have gathered she has not been to London since her marriage."

"That is a relief," Giles gave a loud sigh, "I must own I was quaking in my boots at the thought she would inadvertently expose our charade to the world. And I could hardly throw such a charming lady into gaol on the outside chance she could betray us."

"Kate would die sooner than betray anyone!" Peter snapped, his blue eyes narrowing on Giles. "And if you think for one moment I would tolerate your hurting her after all she has done for me . . ."

"Perish the thought," Giles held both hands up in a gesture of surrender. "I was merely speculating, that is all. But if you claim the lady will not be a threat to us then that is an end to it. Although," he tilted his head to one side and shot Peter a knowing look, "you must own it would be a deuced coil if she *was* to recognize you. The news would be all over London within a day, and if Payton was to get wind of it . . ." He drew a finger across his throat in a graphic gesture.

"He'll not get wind of anything" Peter replied, his voice coldly insistent. "I told you, Kate is not in the social round, and even if she was I think we may rely upon her discretion on the off chance she should recognize me . . . which she won't."

Giles looked thoughtful and then brightened. "Of course, my lord, you are right. I hadn't thought of it in quite that light before."

"What light?" Peter wasn't sure if he trusted the pleased look on the viscount's face.

"Her reputation." Giles added a final touch to his drawing and then sat back to admire it. "You have been living beneath her roof these past two weeks after all, and with *your* reputation there is no way she could announce that fact without branding herself your mistress. Certainly she is lovely enough to be taken for one of your flirts."

"But it was nothing like that!" Peter was genuinely appalled. "Good God, I was near death when she found me!"

"Of course, but we can not admit that without first explaining how you came to be in such a state, *n' est-ce-pas?*" Giles asked with a haughty lift of his dark blond eyebrows. "Believe me, my lord, in the event Mrs. Delecourt should recognize you upon some chance meeting our best hope of silencing her is to threaten her with social ruin. Not the actions of a gentleman, I grant you, but then what choice have we?"

There was no answer for that, and Peter quietly admitted the bitter truth. Despite his gratitude, despite the unwilling admiration he felt for Kate, he knew that if it need be, he would have no choice but to betray her. He only prayed that that day would never come; for when it did, something deep inside him would surely die.

Chapter Nine

Kate spent the remainder of the afternoon going over her lists and listening to Portia's excited prattling. As she had feared, the viscount's unexpected appearance had set the older lady off, and she bubbled over with schemes and plans for the coming season.

"Naturally we shall make our first public appearance at Almack's," she said with a happy sigh, following Kate from the drawing room into the study. "Your voucher arrived in this morning's post, thank God. I was beginning to grow quite frantic."

"Why? Did you think they would reject my application?" Kate paused long enough in her duties to shoot her aunt a teasing look.

"With all I know about those creatures?" Her aunt gave a derisive snort. "I should say not! I merely meant that I hadn't expected they would be so quick in replying to my letter. It is so near to the start of the Season, after all." Here she bent a meaningful frown upon her niece.

Kate ignored her, having long since learned the futility of arguing with her willful aunt. Portia, of course, expected no reply, and continued her rambling monologue. Kate kept her head bent over her work, interjecting an occasional "how interesting" or "that sounds delightful" whenever her aunt paused for breath. They continued in this fashion for another quarter hour when something Portia said penetrated Kate's concentration, and her head came snapping back up with sudden wariness.

"I beg your pardon," she said, trying desperately to remember her aunt's last remark. "What did you say?"

"I knew you weren't listening," Portia smirked in triumph. "You really ought to pay me more mind, you know. You just agreed to appear at court dressed as a turnip."

"I did not!"

"Indeed you did! You also agreed that having Prinny shot at the next showing at the Royal Academy sounded just the thing. That sounds delightful, I believe you said."

Kate pinked with embarrassment at having been caught at a lie. "I am sorry, Aunt Portia," she muttered, setting her list aside with a weary sigh. "But you must know I am rushing to set things to right before we leave. I can hardly go dashing off and leave the servants with no direction!"

"Heaven forbid you should be so derelict in your duties!" Portia retorted with a shake of her head. "The way you fret over that staff of yours is nothing short of amazing, and I only wonder that you aren't bundling them off to London with you. That reminds me," she gave a sudden frown. "What about that wretched stable boy? I'm assuming he has recovered completely since you appear so willing to leave him."

"Oh, he is already back at his duties," Kate replied swiftly, uttering that particular lie without so much as a blink. "Nurse has assured me he will be as good as new in a week or two."

"Well, considering the care you lavished on the creature it would have been dashed ungrateful of him to die," Portia snapped, already dismissing the matter from her mind. "But enough of that now, I think we must next discuss my granddaughter's coming out ball. The invitations have all been sent out and Gussie is looking to me to oversee the whole of it, and I am looking to you to help me."

"Your faith in me is deeply touching, Aunt," Kate answered, relieved her aunt had abandoned the rather delicate subject of the fictitious stableboy.

"Nonsense. What is there to careful planning but making lists; a skill at which you appear to be quite adept. Now pay attention child, for I've no wish for my granddaughter to make her bows in sackcloth." Then she launched into an eager discussion of the latest styles.

After bidding Giles a terse adieu Peter made his way back to the house. The rain which had been threatening all morning began falling, and by the time he reached the servants' entrance he had become thoroughly soaked. Richards opened the door for him, his eyebrows lifting as he took in his sodden condition.

"A cup of Nurse's special tea, I think," he said, stepping aside as Peter brushed past him. "And I do not think a bath would go amiss. I shall have the footman bring you some warm water."

"Thank you, Richards," Peter was so weary he unconsciously used the superior form of address, a slip of the tongue that brought a speculative gleam to the butler's dark eyes. "That sounds delightful."

"Very good, sir," Richards executed a deep, formal bow. "Will there be anything else?"

Peter was already half way through the door, his only thought to reach his own room before collapsing. "No," he replied wearily, "that will be all."

"As you wish, Mr. Quentin," Richards murmured, keeping a sharp eye on the younger man until the door swung shut behind him. The moment he was out of sight he turned to Mrs. Parks with a knowing wink. "An Owler, my arse!" he chortled, rubbing his hands together with obvious delight. "Half a crown says he's been having us on! The lad's a marquise at the very least, you mark my words!"

In his room Peter managed to strip off his wet clothes before collapsing on his bed. The walk back from the beach had exhausted him; an admission that had his lips thinning in anger. Fine shape he was in to attempt an escape, he thought, his eyelids closing wearily. He'd thought he'd all but recovered from the French soldier's bullet, but apparently he had overestimated his strength.

He must have dozed off, for when he next opened his eyes it was to find the footman had brought up a hip bath and was filling it with water heated over the fireplace. He was so accustomed to this luxury that it was only as the footman was pouring water over his head that the incongruity of the situation struck him.

Until now the servants had treated him as an equal; willing to help him when he was too weak to help himself, but not so willing they would have gone to the trouble of bathing him. What the devil was going on here, he wondered, casting the footman a wary glance over his bare shoulder.

"My thanks for the assistance, lad," he said, falling belatedly into his lilting brogue. "But I'm not some weak slip of a lord to need such coddling. I've been bathing myself these past five and twenty years or more, and I think I can be trusted to do a proper job of it on my own. Get along with you, now."

"Are–are ye certain, Mr. Quentin?" The footman's voice quavered slightly as he remembered the talk in the kitchen. If the muscular man before him was really a lord in disguise, then he wanted his share of whatever gratuity that might be left behind. " 'Tis no bother, I assure ye."

Mr. Quentin; Peter winced at the young man's respectful tones. "Maybe not to you, lad, but as for myself, I'd as lief not be baring my . . . er . . . treasures to a young boy. Now, if 'twas one of the maids asking to scrub my back, well, that would be a different thing entirely," and he gave the boy a sly wink, praying a bit of judicious ribaldry would restore him to his status as a smuggler and ne'er do well.

The footman gave an appreciative chuckle and then departed, much to Peter's great relief. Thank God they were pulling him out tonight, he decided, slumping against the curved back of the tub. It was obvious his disguise had been penetrated; in another moment the footman would have been bowing and calling him "my lord."

After soaking for a few minutes Peter rubbed the bar of soap across his chest, his thoughts turning to the coming interview in Dover. His superiors would be expecting a full report of his activities over the past three months, and there was precious little he could tell them. He hadn't uncovered a single shred of evidence that verified James's accusations. In fact, the only person he'd discovered who had any contact with the smugglers at all was his hostess, but he wasn't about to hand her over to the authorities!

Peters' expression grew grim at the thought of leaving Kate without so much as a word of thanks. To behave so churlishly after all she had done for him went against everything he held dear, but the need for secrecy ruled out any other possibility. Perhaps at some point in the distant future he would be able to repay her for her kindness; until then, it would be better for all if he simply vanished. Let her think him an ungrateful lout. It was better than her discovering she'd been harboring a liar all this time.

He continued bathing, idly soaping his face as he planned how best to slip out of the house unobserved.

He'd wait until well after midnight, he decided, and he'd also make use of the servant's entrance. That way, if anyone should hear him leaving they would think him a footman slipping out to dally with . . .

"Oh!"

The soft, feminine cry of distress brought his eyes flying open, and he sat up with a noisy splash. In the next moment he was cursing, his eyes burning with pain as they filled with soap. "Damnation!" he exclaimed, covering them with his hands and scrubbing furiously, "I can't see a bloody thing!"

He splashed more water on his face, and was fumbling for the cloth when he felt a towel land on his shoulder. He snatched it up and began drying his face. When he could open his eyes without pain he cast a bleary glance over his shoulder, his heart leaping in his chest at the sight of a red-faced Kate backing slowly towards the door.

"I–I was wondering how you were feeling," she stammered, her green eyes wide in her face as she gazed raptly at him. "I–I haven't seen you since yesterday and I . . ." Her voice trailed off, another wave of color washing over her delicate features as the impropriety of the situation dawned on her.

Peter saw the embarrassment in her face and was torn between laughter and honor. The humor of their position appealed to him, but as a gentleman, he knew he could not pause to enjoy it. He politely lowered the towel.

"I'm feeling fine, Mrs. Delecourt," he said, inclining his head mockingly. "And I thank you for your concern. Is there anything else you would care to be asking?"

She shook her head vigorously, her hand fumbling for the doorknob. "No! That is . . . good-bye!" She succeeded in wrenching the door open and stumbled out, slamming the door closed behind her.

Peter stared after her, his lips quivering as he struggled manfully to contain himself. In the end it proved too great a task and he burst out laughing, the sound of his merriment echoing loudly in the firelit chamber.

Kate fled to the sanctuary of her rooms, the sound of Mickey's laughter ringing in her ears. The devil! she fumed, flinging herself onto the bed and covering her head with a pillow. How dare he laugh at her! She told herself that she hated him for his mocking arrogance, but even as she made the silent vow the image of him lounging in the hip bath rose to taunt her. Muttering a decidedly unladylike word she rolled on to her back and stared up at her ceiling.

She hadn't meant to go to his room. Indeed, since the incident with the soldiers she'd done her best to avoid him. But when she had gone up the stairs to rest, her feet had somehow turned towards the west wing until she had found herself standing outside his door. She'd knocked timidly, and when there'd been no answer she had peeked inside, meaning only to assure herself that he was all right. Then she'd seen the hip bath set before the fireplace, and some nameless compulsion had urged her on until she was standing inside, watching the dance of the firelight on his gleaming back.

Her cheeks grew warm at the memory, and she cursed herself for such missish behavior. It wasn't as if the male form held any great mysteries for her, she thought with increasing agitation. She was a widow, after all, and she had seen a man in a state of undress before. She and Charles had shared many intimacies during their brief marriage, and she had helped nurse Mickey after finding him on the beach. Therefore, she should be able to put the incident from her mind and continue on as if nothing had happened.

But something *had* happened, she admitted with a heavy sigh. In those brief moments when she had watched Mickey in his bath, feelings she thought buried with Charles had stirred to life, leaving her torn with confusion. That she could feel such things now for a man she neither truly knew nor fully trusted was a devastating realization.

Perhaps her aunt was right and it was time she remarried, she decided with another sigh. She was in the very prime of her life, and as both Lucille and Portia had often told her, Charles would have wanted her to find happiness again. In London she would doubtlessly meet many men; surely among all the dandies, dilettantes, and ne'er do wells, she could find some man worthy of her love. Some man who would sweep her off her feet and carry her off like some wonderful hero out of the gothics her aunt secretly read. The only problem was, instead of some tilted blond paragon, it was Mickey's face that first sprang to mind when she began envisioning possible candidates.

"My goodness, don't you look fine as a sixpence this evening!" Portia exclaimed some four hours later as Kate hurried to take her seat at the dining table. "I had no idea we were dressing for dinner; you should have said something!"

"I am sorry, Aunt," Kate replied, the skirts of her green silk gown rustling as she sat on the chair the footman held for her. "I hadn't meant to dress so elegantly, but when the gown arrived it looked so lovely I simply couldn't wait. It seems forever since I last dressed to the nines."

"Months," Portia agreed, her expression smug as she studied her niece's ethereal beauty. The gal would knock the London men off their pins, she thought, all but rubbing her hands together in eager anticipation.

Aloud she said, "Aren't those the emeralds Charles gave you for your engagement? Don't think I've seen you wear them since your wedding."

Kate's hand closed around the tear-shaped pendant hanging between her breasts. "There never seemed to be an occasion," she said, fingering the glittering stones and wondering again what had made her don the tangible sign of Charles's love. "They always seemed too grand for the country," and her hand fell back to her side.

"Fine jewelry is always in the best of taste," Portia declared, dipping her spoon into the mutton broth and taking a noisy sip. "Speaking of Charles, you never did show Lucille's letter to me. How is the wretch faring? Already complaining about Caro's incessant demands, I suppose. I warned her how it would be."

"Indeed not, she writes that all is well and that she has been reading novels to Caro while she recuperates," Kate replied, picking up her own spoon and taking a small sip of the flavorful broth. "They've just finished *The Fairchild Family,* which Lucille described as a most edifying tale."

"Prosy as a sermon is what she means," Portia grumbled, reaching for a roll. "Gussie read that horror to her youngest, and the poor mite had bad dreams for the next week! Well, what else has she to say? She'll be wanting to come home any day now, I expect."

"Actually," a playful smile touched Kate's mouth as she watched her aunt lift another spoonful of soup to her lips, "she mentioned something about the two of them joining us in London."

"What?" Portia sputtered soup everywhere, her spoon clattering to the table as she stared at Kate. "Do you mean to say she is threatening to land on us again?" she demanded indignantly. "But what of that

miser's damned leg? I thought she was all but at death's door!"

"Oh, Caro's ankle is much better," Kate assured her, taking a wicked pleasure at the sight of her formidable aunt reduced to such a state. After her emotionally wrenching afternoon she thought she deserved a bit of a diversion. "It was hardly more than a bad sprain, really, but Lucille feels a trip to the city is just the thing to lift the poor lady out of the sulks."

"It would take more than a trip to the city to accomplish that," Portia muttered, signaling for the footman to refill her wineglass. "It would take a miracle! And if she thinks I will allow them to stay with me, then she is even more dull witted than I first thought her to be. I will accept Lucille under protest, but there is nothing in this world that will persuade me to open my home to that clutch-fisted female!"

"You may rest at ease, ma'am," Kate said, finally taking pity on her aunt. "Caroline has a son who lives in London, and they will be staying in his home on Harley Street."

"Well, thank God for that," Portia answered with a heartfelt sigh. "And as Harley Street is not so fashionable a location, we should not have to worry about tripping over them every time we poke our noses out the door. You must take care not to cultivate the association, Katherine. It will do you little good to have your name linked too closely with theirs."

"Lucille is my sister-in-law, Aunt Portia," Kate pointed out gently, sitting back as the first course was removed and the next course set before her. "I can hardly ignore her existence."

"Perhaps not, but neither do you need to live in her pocket," Portia returned with a brisk nod. "You are far too nice for your own good, Katherine; that is your problem. You must develop a thicker skin if you are to survive a London Season."

Kate's amusement vanished along with her appetite. "I'll try, Aunt," she promised, recalling her earlier decision to submit to her aunt's matchmaking schemes. "Just as I will try to follow your lead in other matters."

"Eh?" Portia blinked at her in confusion, her wineglass poised halfway to her lips. "What other matters?"

Kate moistened her lips with a nervous tongue, trying to remember the reasons for her hard won decision. "I have been thinking," she began, her fingers clenching around her napkin, "and I have decided you are right. It is high time I was giving some thought to remarrying."

"It is?" Portia blinked again, wondering if perhaps she had indulged in too much sherry while waiting for Katherine to join her. She pulled her hand back from the wineglass and gazed at her niece suspiciously. "Since when?"

"Since this afternoon," Kate admitted honestly. "I—I have thought about it before, of course, but after the viscount's visit I remembered what you said about my remarrying someday and I—"

"Westley?" Portia was certain she was bosky, either that, or the deceitful creature was twigging her. "But you called him a man-milner!" She shook a threatening finger at Kate as the certainty she was being played for a fool grew ever stronger. "And don't try cozening me into believing you have developed a tendre for that preening dandy either, missy, because I am not that senile!"

"Of course, I haven't developed a tendre for him!" Kate gasped, indignant at the very accusation.

"Then what the deuce are you gabbling about?" Portia demanded, her expression as pugnacious as ever.

"I want another husband!" Kate exclaimed, driven past all restraint with frustration. "And I want you to help me find one!"

Portia stared at her for several seconds in open-mouthed astonishment, and then a cunning look spread slowly over her face. She picked up her wine-glass again. "Well, well," she drawled, lifting the glass as if in a toast, "this has certainly turned out to be a most interesting evening after all. And here I was worried about being bored."

"Now, Aunt Portia," Kate began hastily, anxious to regain precious ground she had already lost, "I did not mean to imply that I wish to get leg shackled to the first man I meet. I merely meant that I'm not as . . . as adverse to the prospect of a second marriage as I once was. There's no need to rush this, I promise you."

"If you say so, dearest."

"I mean it," not for one moment did Kate trust the sweet tone in her aunt's voice. "We shall have the whole season before us, and I am certain we shall be able to find some charming gentleman to suit me. There is no need to go to any extremes."

"Yes, Katherine."

"And if I don't find anyone this season, then there is always next year; agreed?"

"Hmm." Portia nibbled on the salmon which had been set before her. "You might have a word with Cook before we leave, Katherine. There is far too much dill in this fish, don't you think?"

"Aunt Portia!"

"Yes?" The innocent look Portia sent Kate would have done Mrs. Siddons proud. "What is it?"

"I want your word that you won't do anything outrageous once we are in London," Kate said sternly, regretting her impetuous outburst. "I won't have you setting obvious traps for me."

"What sort of traps?" Portia asked, intrigued.

"Never mind," Kate answered, not about to provide

135

her scheming aunt with any further ammunition. "Just give me your word that you shan't make a cake of us all, and I will be content."

Portia pouted childishly. "You are being very hard on your poor aged aunt," she said with a sigh.

"I am merely developing some of that thick skin you were speaking of," Kate returned. "Now, do I have your word?"

"Hmph, your skin is already sufficiently thick if you want my opinion," Portia muttered, her cheeks pinking. "You'd best have a care that it doesn't get *too* thick, lest you be taken as hard."

"Aunt . . ."

"Oh very well, you ungrateful chit, I shall not attack any defenseless men or knock them on the head with a club! There? Are you satisfied?"

"Marginally," Kate's lips quivered at the images conjured by her aunt's words. "But I suppose it will have to suffice; for now."

Portia gave the poached salmon on her plate a vicious jab with her fork. "I have whelped a rhinoceros," she complained to no one in particular. "If this is any indication of how the season shall go, then I am sorry I mentioned the matter at all!"

"Believe me, Aunt," Kate responded with a gusty sigh, "you can not be any sorrier than I am."

Following dinner they retired to the drawing room where Portia quickly became engrossed in her latest scientific journal. Kate sat in her favorite chair feigning interest in a volume of poetry, but her thoughts were firmly centered on Mickey and what had happened in his bedchamber. Or rather, what hadn't happened.

Now that she'd had time to reflect on the matter, she decided there was nothing so terrible about her reactions. She was only human, after all, and Mickey was a very handsome man. It was not totally unthinkable that she should respond to him. And what had she seen, really? The bath's high, curving sides had hidden anything which might have been deemed shocking. She'd caught a glimpse of nothing more than a bit of back and a set of shoulders; that was all. A set of broad, muscular shoulders that gleamed like mahogany in the . . .

"Katherine, did you hear me?" Portia's voice cut into her thoughts, and she raised her head to find Portia staring at her with a quizzing look. "I have called your name twice!"

"I am sorry," although she hadn't read so much as a single stanza, Kate was careful to mark her place before closing the book. "What is it?"

"Are we still leaving for London the day after tomorrow?" Portia asked, wondering what the deuce Katherine had been thinking of to bring that look to her face.

"Of course," Kate replied, faintly surprised. "Did you think we would not?"

"The way things have been changing around here, one never knows," Portia answered, closing her journal and setting it on the table. "Well, if that is the case, I suppose I had ought to be getting these old bones into bed. What about you?"

Kate was quiet a long moment, the realization that she'd yet to inform Mickey of her plans weighing heavily on her mind. "You go up, Aunt," she replied quietly, reaching a swift decision. "I–I wish to finish my book."

"Yes, I can see how fascinating you must find it," Portia responded dryly, her eyes flicking from the book to Kate's face. "You haven't turned a single page in the past hour."

Kate blushed at her acuity. "Coleridge can't be rushed," she muttered, unable to meet her aunt's sharp gaze. "He must be savored to be understood fully."

"I see," Portia answered, rising to brush a kiss across Kate's cheek. "Just mind you don't stay up all night savoring him, hmm? There is a great deal left to be done if we mean to leave on time. Good night, my dear."

Kate waited another twenty minutes plotting the best way of breaking her news, but in the end she decided only the truth would serve. He was her guest . . . in a manner of speaking, and it was only common courtesy that she inform him of her plans. She would make it clear that he was welcome to stay if he wished, and then she would bid him adieu.

The thought brought a swift pain which she sternly repressed, determined to do what she considered the proper thing. Her more pragmatic self argued that it might be advisable to wait until morning, but she wanted to do it now, tonight, before she lost her nerve. She would simply knock on his door, inform him of her plans, wish him well, and then she would retire to her room to sleep the sleep of the just. What could possibly be wrong with that?

Once she'd worked things out to her satisfaction she set her book down and left the room. As they kept country hours the servants had all long since retired, and the house felt oddly deserted as she crept up the stairs. Most of the candles in the hallway had been extinguished, and the shadows on the walls leapt and writhed like specters in a nightmare. Mickey's room lay at the far end of the long hall, and by the time she reached his door Kate had worked herself into a state of nervous agitation.

Mentally scolding herself for being no better than some schoolroom miss, Kate took a deep breath and knocked on the door. There was no answer. She frowned and knocked again, this time louder. It was scarcely past eleven in the evening, and she was certain Mickey hadn't retired. When again there was no answer she reached out and touched the brass doorknob, her fingers closing about the cold metal. She gave it a cautious twist, and the door swung silently open.

"Mickey? Mr. Quentin? Are you awake?" Kate peeked cautiously about the darkened room. "It is Mrs. Delecourt, I must speak to you, it is very important."

Silence.

"Mr. Quentin," she ventured further inside, her heart beating rapidly as she remembered what had happened the last time she'd been in this room. Much to her relief the hip bath had been removed, and the shapes of the remaining pieces of furniture could be clearly seen in the faint light spilling in from the hallway. She skirted her way around a table and a large chair, edging ever closer to the large bed in the corner.

She could see a lumpy shape hidden in the covers, and ventured closer to give it a cautious poke. "Mr. Quentin?" she began, "please, I must speak with . . ."

The man on the bed exploded into motion at the light touch of her hand, rolling off the bed without a sound. Before Kate could give more than a frightened gasp he grabbed her roughly, clamping a hand over her mouth as he threw her on to the covers. She struggled against his suffocating hold when the feel of the cold, sharp blade against her throat stopped her. She froze with fear, her eyes wide as she stared up into the dark angry eyes glaring down into hers.

...ly. At the fingers tightened around his throat. Un-
...edly, though, the shock was so great that his head
...red a bit, and he blinked down at the woman be-
... clutched in anguish, and ...
... Kate.

Chapter Ten

It was the sound of the door opening that first penetrated Peter's sleep. He'd been resting fitfully, his
dreams filled with memories of his desperate escape
from France, when his senses warned him someone else
was in the room. He'd barely had time to absorb this
when he felt the light touch on his arm, and all of his
training came rushing to the fore. He came flying off
the bed fully prepared to kill whoever had attacked
him.

His fingers tightened over his enemy's mouth as he
fought to throw off the last vestiges of sleep. "One
word," he warned coldly, still not quite awake, "and I
will slit your throat."

Kate's terror increased at the deadly words. It was
Mickey's voice, but without the soft, Irish lilt she had
become accustomed to. With a fatalistic calm she realized it wasn't the first time she had heard him lose his
accent, and she wondered if she was about to be killed
by a man she didn't even know.

Peter shook his head, and as full consciousness returned he became aware of several things simultane-
ously. First, he realized that he was in a bedchamber
and not a leaky boat, and secondly he knew without
questioning the matter that he was in no immediate
physical danger. The next thing he became aware of

was that the figure lying beneath him was female. Decidedly female. The shock was so great that his head cleared at once, and he blinked down at the woman he was crushing on the bed.

"Kate?"

The sound of her given name reassured Kate somewhat, and she gave a cautious nod. He was still holding a knife to her throat, but he no longer seemed so menacing and the cold aura of danger that had emanated from him ceased with each passing second. Perhaps, she thought with rising hope, she might live after all.

Peter was so stunned that for a moment he could not think. Then the familiar feel of the knife's handle in his hand brought reality crashing down and he quickly tossed the knife away, lifting his hand from her mouth at the same time.

"Are you all right?" he asked hoarsely his blue eyes darkening as he anxiously searched her for any sign of injury. "I didn't hurt you?"

She shook her head again and drew in a deep lungful of air. "I . . . I am fine," she said, albeit in a weak voice. Now that the danger had passed her heart was slowing to its normal beat. As her terror slowly ebbed, anger was rising to take its place.

"Are you certain?" Peter asked, shaking as he realized how close he had come to killing her. "The knife didn't cut you?"

"I told you, I am fine," Kate interrupted, her fear turning to sheer fury. "You beast!" she exclaimed, temper turning to action as she swung her fist at his unprotected jaw. "How dare you threaten me!"

Peter was taken aback by her sudden anger, and barely managed to dodge the blow. He grabbed her fist and wrestled it down to the bedcovers. "What the devil is wrong with you?" he demanded, his own temper flaring to life as he fought to hold her down. He winced as her knee slashed up, striking his thigh. "Ouch! Stop fighting me, you little hellion!"

141

"I will not stop fighting you!" she retorted hotly, struggling to throw off his hateful weight. "If you think I shall meekly submit while you rape me, you—"

"Rape you?" Peter snarled, enraged by her accusation. "How can you accuse me of such a thing?" He had never been so insulted in all his life, and his wounded pride cried out for satisfaction.

"When you throw me to a bed and hold a knife to my throat, what else am I to think?" she pointed out through clenched teeth, meeting his furious glare with proud defiance. "Or is it your custom to attack everyone who has the misfortune to awaken you?"

Her stinging words brought to mind the awkwardness of their positions and Peter rolled cautiously to one side, keeping a wary eye on her knee. "I did not attack you," he denied in a huffy tone, helping her to her feet. "I thought I was defending myself."

"Against what?" She continued glaring at him as she restored her gown to order. "And pray do not give me that moonshine about shooting fish; 'tis as false a story as your stupid accent!"

Peter stiffened at once, wariness replacing his anger. "I don't know what you mean," he hedged, running a hand through his rumpled hair.

Kate saw the caution on his harsh face, and it filled her with a grim sense of satisfaction. Since meeting Mickey—or whoever the devil he was—she had been in a constant state of confusion, and it rather pleased her to have him at such a disadvantage. Instead of dashing to safety as she should have done, she folded her arms across her chest and faced him with a lift of chin.

"I mean," she began in a dulcet tone as patently false as his lilting accent, "that you have a brogue that appears to come and go with the tide. Oh, it was most affecting at first, I assure you, but I'm not so big a gudgeon as to be fooled by it now. You are no more Irish than . . . than Napoleon!"

Peter's jaw clenched at the thought of his disguise un-

142

raveling before his eyes. That he was hours away from rescue was of no importance; for her own good as well as for the good of the mission, he had to stick to his story. "I am Irish," he replied, stalling for time. "I did not lie to you."

"And I am Princess Charlotte!" Kate wasn't the least bit taken in by such flummery. "Would you care to hear my German accent? It is far more credible than that silly lilt *you* affect whenever the mood strikes you."

Peter said nothing, mentally cursing her for her sharp tongue and equally sharp mind. Despite what the servants knew—or thought they knew—he could not afford to let her guess the truth. He had to say something, anything that would distract her. Hating himself for what he was about to do he allowed his eyes to rake over her in a thoroughly insulting manner.

"Are you familiar with Shakespeare, Mrs. Dele-court?" he asked, his tone mocking.

"Shakespeare?" Her frown deepened at his non se-quitur. "What has he to do with anything? You are try-ing to distract me, and—"

"Methinks the lady doth protest too much," he quoted, reaching out to stroke the line of her jaw. "Care to tell me what brought you creeping into my room, or would you like me to draw my own conclusions?"

Kate went still as the implications of his words struck her. "You-you can not be serious," she stammered, shocked and enraged by turns. "I would never—"

"You must have liked what you saw this afternoon," he continued, determined to play the scene through to its bitter end. "Did you come back for a closer peek? You should have said something, my sweet, or I wouldn't have been so rough with you. Unless that is the way you prefer it? You must let me know, so that I can best please you."

Kate went white and then red with fury, her hand lashing out across his face. "You-you bastard!" she spat, choosing the one word she felt would cut the deepest.

"You are no gentleman to say such things to me!"

Peter took the blow stoically, deciding it was the least he deserved for what he had said and for what he was about to say. He continued staring down at her, his lips twisting in a derisive smile. "Aye, but I've never pretended to be a gentleman, have I? And as for the other, you are right, I *am* a bastard. And a smuggler, and a few other things that would make a proper lady like you swoon if she was to learn of them. Isn't that why you're here?"

"It is not!" Kate gasped, vowing hell would surely freeze over before she ever revealed the real reason why she had come to his room. "I-I came to tell you that I want you to leave my house."

"Now?" His finger stroked down the slender column of her throat. In the flickering light from the hallway she looked like an ethereal angel, and he could feel his body responding to her nearness. "This very moment?"

"Of course not this very moment," she answered, resolutely ignoring the affect his touch was having on her resolve. " 'Tis dark outside."

"Tomorrow morning, then?" he pressed, his heart pounding as passion heated his blood. The next few minutes would be critical, and he prayed his duty would rule his desire. Although he wanted nothing more than to follow through with his seductive play he knew he could never betray her or his sense of honor. Circumstances might have forced him to play the libertine, but that did not mean he had to live the role.

"Tomorrow would be f-fine," Kate replied, hating the weakness in her voice. She cleared her throat and tried again. "Yes, I would definitely prefer that you leave on the morrow" she said, raising her eyes to meet his sapphire blue gaze with an equanimity she was far from feeling. "Now kindly release me."

"Give me a kiss, and I shall," he said, deciding he had nothing to lose by alienating her even further. "Come, my love," he added when she gaped up at him in

144

shocked disbelief, "you know it is what you really want . . ."

"Why, you . . ." Kate could think of no epithet strong enough to convey her fury and her disdain. Nor would she dignify his outrageous comments with a struggle. He would probably delight in that, she thought with a flash of feminine insight; doubtlessly he would look upon it as proof she welcomed his disgusting advances. Still, she couldn't stand there quietly and allow him to get away with such arrogant behavior . . .

"One kiss?" she asked, an evil plan forming in her mind.

"For now," he answered, scarce believing she was actually acquiescing to his insulting proposition. Perhaps he had misjudged her after all; the thought filled him with an odd sense of outrage.

She forced herself to step closer, her arms slipping about his shoulders as she smiled up at him. "Very well," she said softly stroking the back of his neck with her fingertips. "One kiss, and then I must really insist you leave. I have my reputation to think of, you know."

Peter's breath caught in his throat at the invitation of her upturned face and moist, parted lips. Against his will his arms slid around her waist, drawing her closer to his rapidly hardening body. All thought of duty and deception fled as pure sensation filled his head, and he lowered his mouth to hers in a kiss of burning passion.

The touch of his lips shattered Kate's resolve, and for a brief moment she found herself responding in helpless abandon. The insistent probing of his tongue made her gasp with desire and she arched closer, revelling in his heady taste. She heard him groan in pleasure, and the sound filled her with feminine pride. When his hand closed over her breast, the thumb teasing her hardened nipple to life she gave a soft cry.

"Kate," Peter moaned, his mouth avidly seeking the soft flesh of her neck. "That's it. Melt for me, my love."

The husky words penetrated the sensual mists filling

145

Kate's head, and shame washed over her in humiliating waves. She went rigid in his arms, and when he attempted to draw her closer she saw her opportunity and took it; her knee lashing upwards with deadly accuracy.

Peter gave a harsh cry as pain exploded through him. He released her at once, crumpling to the floor and cupping himself protectively.

Kate danced away the moment she was freed, fleeing towards the door without a backwards glance. She wrenched open the door and started through, pausing only long enough to send him a triumphant look. "Tomorrow" she said, her breath coming out in broken gasps. "If you are still here when I awaken, I swear to heaven I shall hand you over to that miserable little captain myself!" And with that she turned and fled to the safety of her rooms as if all the demons in hell were pursuing her.

After a restless night she rose early and made her way to Mickey's rooms. In the cool, gray light of morning her fiery temper had cooled somewhat, but she was still determined that he should go. The man was a liar and a rake, and his presence in the house was clearly having a detrimental effect upon her. Only look at how she had behaved last evening, screeching at him like an archshrew one moment, and then melting in his arms the very next.

Another memory from last night stirred to life, bringing her brows together in a scowl. He had been dressed. At the time she'd been too overset with emotion to note his appearance consciously, but now she had no difficulty conjuring up his image. He'd been wearing a shirt; the very shirt she'd been altering the day the soldiers had come, and his legs had been encased in an old pair of Charles's riding breeches. He'd even had on *boots* she realized, shoving open the door to his rooms without knocking. As she expected, it was quite empty.

"Are you going to sulk for the entire journey?" Portia demanded as the coach set out for London. "If so, I am going to regret sending my maid ahead with the luggage. At least she has some conversation; limited though it may be."

"I am sorry, Aunt Portia," Kate apologized dully, turning from the window to give the older lady a vague smile. "I do not mean to be rude; it is just that I am so very tired."

"Hmph I don't doubt that for a moment," Portia grumbled, shooting her niece a worried look. "Really, Katherine, one would think you hadn't a servant to your name the way you've been driving yourself these last days. Surely it wasn't necessary for you to oversee every detail of our packing!"

Kate thought of the backbreaking work she had performed in an effort to drive all memory of Mickey from her mind. "Yes, Aunt," she replied quietly, her eyes drifting towards the windows, "it was quite necessary."

While Portia scolded her for her unladylike zeal, Kate continued brooding over Mickey's departure. She tried telling herself she was glad he was gone but it wasn't long before her conscience got the better of her. Much as it vexed her she began fretting about his wounds, wondering if he would make it to Captain O'Rourake's before the Excise men captured him. In the end she'd gone to Richards, reluctantly asking him if he knew what had happened to the wretch.

"The young gentleman must have left some time in the night, Mrs. Delecourt," she was informed with a sly wink. "But I've no doubt we shall soon be hearing from him."

At first Kate feared the wiley butler had somehow learned of what had transpired in the moonlit chamber, and the very notion was enough to send her scurrying back to the parlor. But now that she'd had time to consider the matter, she wasn't so certain. Ricahrds, for all his pompous posing, was devoted to her, and she doubted he would consider her making love to a complete stranger suitable matter for a jest. Not that she and Mickey had actually made love, she amended quickly, wincing at the burning memory.

"Of course Gussie is setting up a dreadful wail because we aren't putting up with her," Portia had abandoned Kate's behavior and was now taking her daughter-in-law to task. "But as I told her, I have a perfectly good house on Richmond Street that is just sitting there, and I see no reason why we should all be squeezed in together. Besides, she and I would be at caps-pulling within the hour of my arrival."

"I remember that house," Kate said, stirring herself to join in the conversation. "I made my bows from there."

"So you did," Portia agreed, remembering the shy eighteen year old who had spent most of the evening hiding behind the floral arrangements. "And had your engagement party there too, as I recall. Your papa had wanted to hold it at his estate, but I told him no one would want to travel clear to Devon at the height of the Season. Men!" And she shook her head in exasperation.

The rest of the journey was spent reminiscing over past seasons and planning for the coming one. Since they had set out so early they arrived in London late that afternoon, and after stopping at Portia's house long enough to change they hurried to St. James Park where Portia's son Arthur resided with his family.

His wife, Augusta, was as big a fool as Portia had claimed, and it didn't take Kate longer than five minutes in her company to know that her help was indeed sorely needed.

"No, Augusta," she said in the same patient tones she usually reserved for Lucille, "Louisa can not be presented in a cherry silk gown, she must be dressed in white the same as all the other unmarried ladies."

"Oh, but white is such an insipid color, don't you think?" Gussie sighed, sending her plump offspring a look of maternal pride. "And my little angel is such a diamond of the first water that she really deserves a more exotic setting.

"Diamonds show well regardless of the setting," Kate returned in a dampening manner that was reminiscent of Portia at her best. "She will wear white, Augusta."

Gussie sighed again. "If you say so, Katherine. Naturally as a widow you are far more worldly than I, and I shall bow to your superior knowledge of the matter. We will be happy to be guided by you, won't we, poppet?" And she gave her daughter another smile.

"Yes, Mama," Louisa replied with the bored look that only seventeen-year-old girls can affect. She'd had her heart set on the red gown and did not look kindly upon the pretty blonde who had snatched it out of her grasp.

"Have you any friends making their bows with you, Louisa?" Kate asked, ignoring the young girl's obvious lack of enthusiasm. "Perhaps we might have them all over for tea."

"I am too old for tea parties," Louisa informed her with a toss of her pale brown curls. "I want a masquerade ball."

Kate and Portia exchanged speaking glances before Kate said, "A masquerade sounds just the thing . . . once you have been properly introduced. In the meanwhile, I believe a small tea will be quite charming. I am looking forward to meeting your friends." *Provided that you have any,* she added silently.

Another hour was spent in the same fashion, with Kate proposing outings that had Louisa either rolling her eyes or shrugging her plump shoulders in indifference. Finally Kate had endured all that she could and stood to go.

"I shall be back on the morrow," she said with a determinedly bright smile. "We shall go to the modiste's shop first thing so that we might check on the latest styles. I am longing to refurbish my wardrobe."

"Yes," Louisa put in with a buttery smile, "I thought that gown rather had the look of the country about it. It is good to see you are aware of such things, Cousin Kate."

"The little minx," Portia grumbled as they made their way back to her home on Richmond Street. "She has a disposition that could curdle cream, and we have the task of making her a match!"

"We shall be lucky if we can manage to get her a partner for whist," Kate replied, rubbing her weary head. "Goodness, she is almost as unpleasant as Lady Vickerson, and at least she had the lure of money and beauty to sweeten the pot! Louisa has neither."

"Well, Arthur is not exactly a beggar, you know," Portia said, looking somewhat indignant. "And the girl is not without some attraction; she does have nice eyes."

"Yes, when she's not casting them about like a second-rate actress in a third-rate play," Kate replied with feeling, turning on her seat to give Portia a considering look. "Aunt, are you seriously suggesting that we *can* find a match for Louisa?"

"Certainly," Portia nodded briskly. "London is full of men willing to overlook a great deal more than a bit of eye rolling for a portion of two thousand pounds per anum. I'm not saying it will be easy, mind, but it can be done."

"Two thousand pounds?"

"Can't have it said my only granddaughter's a spinster," Portia grumbled, not meeting Kate's incredulous gaze. "I'm prepared to come down sweet if she makes a match I approve of."

"Sweet indeed," Kate answered ruefully, remembering her own small bridal portion. Fortunately for her Charles fell in love with her on first sight, or so he had always claimed. Thinking of Charles made her remember Gussie's cryptic comment, and she turned to Portia with a puzzled frown.

"Aunt, what on earth did Gussie mean by that odd remark about my being a worldly widow? Surely she can not think I am *fast?*"

"Knowing Gussie, it is impossible to tell precisely what she means about anything," Portia answered with a shrug. "I can only assure you she meant no direct insult."

"What about an indirect one?"

"Really, Katherine, you are giving the creature more credit than she deserves! Catty remarks require malice, and malice requires intelligence; a commodity, I am sure you will agreed that Gussie singularly lacks."

"That is so," Kate agreed at last. "But still, I can not like that she thinks me a merry widow who can not wait to cast off her weeds. It is insulting."

"It is also the way of the world," Portia said sagely. "Not all couples love one another as you and Charles did, you know. Only look at Lord Payton; his wife not cold in her grave a month and he was off chasing lightskirts. Nor is such behavior limited to the men. Many a lady has been known to take a lover before the death knell has even been rung over her husband! You mustn't be such an innocent, Katherine."

"I am not an innocent, Aunt," Kate answered, visions of herself locked in a passionate embrace with Mickey rising to taunt her. "It is just I would prefer not to be thought of as fast."

"Believe me, my dear, if anyone knew how long and hard I have fought to get you to London they would never think such a thing!" Portia exclaimed, giving her hand a loving pat. "And if you will but recall, I have already warned you on the dangers of being regarded as *too* proper."

"Yes, I believe you said it was certain to give the gentleman a horror of me," Kate said, infusing a light note in her voice. "And heaven knows we can not have that."

"Especially now that you've decided to do the right

151

thing and allow me to choose a new husband for you," Portia agreed, rubbing her gloved hands together eagerly. "With your looks and the income you will have from Charles's estate, it shouldn't be very difficult at all. With luck, I shall have you safely shackled before the season is even half over."

"I never said I would allow you to select a husband for me!" Kate protested, greatly regretting her impetuous tongue.

"What nonsense; you all but got down on your hands and knees and begged me to do it," Portia replied with an aggrieved sniff.

"But—"

"No, Katherine," Portia shook a finger at her sternly, "it is too late to cry off now. I have given the matter of your future husband a great deal of thought, and although I have no specific *parti* in mind, I think I know just the type of man you require."

"Do you?" Kate asked, the throbbing in her head becoming a full-fledged headache. "And pray, what kind is that?"

"Why, the kind of man you can love, of course," Portia answered, giving her a beatific smile. "You married once for love, and I can not think you will be happy unless you do so again. And he is out there, Katherine, never fear. I shall leave no stone unturned until I find him. I give you my word on it!"

Chapter Eleven

Peter's first days in London were spent secreted away in his house being interviewed by officials of the Home Office. As Giles had warned him they were not the least bit interested in his "suspicions," and when he grudgingly admitted he had no solid evidence to offer against Payton it was decided that the matter would be "dropped."

"Not that the whole mission was a total loss, mind," one of his superiors informed with a patronizing pat on the arm. "The information you gave us on those smuggler johnnies ought to put a quick end to their games soon enough, eh?"

"You'd be better advised, sir, to put an end to the **buying** of contraband rather than being so concerned **with** the selling of it," Peter replied coldly, goaded beyond all endurance by the man's maniacal blindness. "The smugglers would stop soon enough once they had no one left to buy their brandy and silks."

The elderly lord merely shook his head, chuckling at the misguided idealism of youth. "Then who would be left to run the country, eh?" He laughed, retrieving his hat and cane from the butler. "No, once we hang a few more of those scoundrels they'll soon find more lawful forms of employment. Count upon it."

"Pompous old windbag," Peter muttered the moment the door had closed behind his visitors. "God, I shudder to think of my country's fate being left to such men!"

"Yes, it is enough to give one the vapors," Giles agreed, pouring himself a generous helping of brandy from the cellarette. "And might I commend you for your rather interesting comments on how best to curtail the smuggling trade? You have rather Whiggish sentiments for such a notable Tory."

"The only thing I am notable for is my devotion to the muslin set," Peter replied, a feeling of bitterness washing over him. Three months, he thought with increasing frustration, three months of pain and suffering, and for what? To be patted on his head by an overfed buffoon and told to go outside and play like a good boy. He had wasted all that time for nothing.

"Well, at least it is better than being noted as a fashionable fribble," Giles said, brown eyes intent as he watched the emotions playing across Tregarren's face.

"Ah, but at least you enjoy being a fashionable fribble," Peter returned, his thoughts still bitter.

"No more than you enjoy your reputation as a rake," Giles responded in kind, lifting his glass in a mocking toast. "Which reminds me, you would not believe the tales being spread about you during your brief . . . er . . . hiatus."

"I know it was speculated that my injuries were really caused by a duel," Peter answered, remembering the tale his butler had faithfully repeated to him. "Do you mean it gets worse?"

"Infinitely," Giles poured Peter a snifter of brandy and handed it to him. "Which one would you care to hear first? The one involving you and a certain lady of high rank and low morals, or the one concerning you and the actresses?"

"Actresses, as in plural?" Peter took a deep draught of the fiery liquor.

154

"Actresses as in a trio of delightful beauties who had the misfortune of being absented from town at the same time you were gone. Naturally, the . . . er . . . ladies in question deny everything."

Peter choked on the sip he had just taken, and Giles obligingly pounded him on the back. "Good God," he wheezed when he could breathe again. "That is what they are saying of me? I had no notion my reputation was so black! Surely no one actually believes such fustian?"

"Only the gossipmongers and half the matchmaking mamas in town," Giles shrugged indifferently. "There was also some talk of having you banned from Almack's, but it was never seriously considered. Earls, even those whose reputations are not all that they should be, are at a premium these days, and the Patronesses weren't about to let you slip through their fat fingers. Might have been better if they had."

"Yes, it is a bloody bore at the best of times," Peter said, shaking his head at the foibles of the *ton*. "I only visit it to keep an eye on certain persons, and to keep my female relations from ringing a peal over my head. It is a dangerous place for a confirmed bachelor."

"So it is, but as it happens, I was not referring to the Marriage Mart."

"What were you referring to?"

"Payton."

Peter glanced up at Giles's clipped response. "What about Payton?" He asked warily, setting his snifter on the cherry-wood side table. "Do you mean to say the Patronesses have finally come to their collective senses and banished him from that holiest of the holies?"

"Not precisely," Giles answered, pausing to flick a loose string from the arm of his claret velvet jacket. "But it is no secret that they are less than pleased with the good marquess of late. No, I was referring to the fact that had you been banished from Almack's it would have colored you a sufficient shade of black to put you in Payton's good graces. 'Tis well-known that he only accepts out and out reprobates in his inner circle."

"That is so," Peter agreed, much struck. In the next moment he was cursing softly. "I do not see that it matters one way or another," he said, making no attempt to hide his disgust. "You forget the investigation against him has been ordered dropped."

"Officially."

"What?"

"I believe Wentworth's precise words were that he was 'officially' ordering you to drop the investigation," Giles expanded with a cunning smile. "Nothing was said about an 'unofficial' investigation."

Peter froze, a matching grin spreading across his face as he swung around to Giles. "The Home Office would never approve," he said slowly, his mind already spinning with possibilities.

"The Home Office," Giles pointed out with a courtly bow, "need never know."

Peter regarded Giles silently. "Do you know, Westley, I fear I may have misjudged you," he said, his blue eyes sparkling with renewed determination. "You are a devious bastard without equal."

"Thank you, my lord," Giles bowed again, his smile widening. "It is nice to know we fashionable fribbles have our uses. But enough of this useless flattery, what do you think our first move should be? We'll have to act fast if we mean to have him safely netted before The Chelsea reaches Portsmouth."

After a leisurely breakfast Kate and Portia set out for St. James Square where they found Gussie still abed with a sick headache. But if they thought this

156

would excuse them from the proposed shopping expedition their hopes were soon dashed when they met a Miss Compton, whom Louisa introduced as her companion.

"She was my governess," that young lady informed them with a worldly sigh. "But now that I am all grown Mama says I may hire her as my companion; otherwise the poor thing would be without a position. Isn't that so, Elizabeth?" And she shot the diminutive brunette a superior smile.

"Quite so, Louisa," Elizabeth returned, unaffected by her former charge's casual cruelty. She turned to the other women with a singiularly sweet smile, her light hazel eyes sparkling with amusement as she offered them her hand. "Mrs. Stone, Mrs. Delecourt, it is a pleasure to meet you. I have often heard my employer speak of you, and I have been looking forward to making your acquaintance."

"Hmph, well, if it was Gussie describing me, I daresay you were expecting me to be sprouting two horns and a tail," Portia said, her wrinkled face breaking into a warm smile of approval. "Sorry to disappoint you."

"Oh, I'm not the least bit disappointed, ma'am, I assure you," Elizabeth answered, delighted the elderly woman was every bit as irascible as Mrs. Stone had warned she would be. Louisa would require firm handling if they were to scrape through the season without a scandal.

The first stop on their itinerary was Countess Valenska's on Strand Street, which, according to a surprisingly knowledgeable Elizabeth, was the most fashionable shop in London. The prices were certainly fashionable, and Kate did her best not to gasp at the exorbitantly priced silk and velvets. Louisa, on the other hand, took the extravagance in stride, ordering ballgowns and other items with such abandon that

Kate was finally compelled to put down her foot.

"No, Louisa, you do not need five new ballgowns so early in the season," she said firmly, plucking the pattern book from her hands and giving it to the young assistant who had been waiting on them. "And certainly you don't need one in such an outlandish color. As a debutante you must know you are restricted to white or some other pastel."

"But I abhor white!" Louisa protested, her bottom lip thrusting forward in a mulish pout. "And pastels are for insipid girls. Why can't I have the peacock blue? 'Tis all the crack amongst the London ladies!"

Kate opened her lips to administer a sharp set down only to be interrupted by Elizabeth, who heretofore had maintained a prudent silence. "Well, naturally elderly ladies have need of such artifice, Louisa," she said, sending Kate a teasing wink. "And if you wish to emulate them, I suppose it is your affair. But as for me, I know *I* would not wish to be taken as so aged."

Louisa's pout cleared at once. "Aged?" she asked, sticking a thick finger in her mouth.

"Sadly aged," Elizabeth corrected with a mournful sigh. "I shouldn't be at all surprised if people were to think you all of one and twenty . . . if not older." She turned to Kate, all wide-eyed innocence. "You wear blue on occasions do you not, ma'am?"

"Always," Kate agreed, falling into line at once. "And you are quite right, Miss Compton, bright colors are just the thing to draw attention away from the ravages of age." She retrieved the pattern book from the smirking assistant and studied the disputed illustration, thoughtfully.

"Very well, Louisa, if your heart is truly set on having this done up in blue, I suppose we might make an exception."

"No, that is quite all right, Cousin!" Louisa exclaimed, shuddering at how close she had come to committing such a solecism. "And as you say, I have more than enough gowns for the moment."

"Well," Kate pretended to hesitate, "if you're certain . . ."

"Oh, I am!"

"If you don't want the blue you might wish to try a nice bright red," Portia advised, not wishing to miss out on the fun. "I know it is one of *my* favorite colors."

Louisa assured them that she adored all things pastel and would not hear of wearing any other color, and the small group soon departed for the other shops on their list. After visiting the milner's shop they stopped at a book shop where Portia hoped to find the newest book on hot air balloons.

While the others were busy browsing, Kate wandered to the front of the shop to study a book she had seen in the window. The book, *Sense And Sensibility,* had caught her eye because of the intriguing title, but it wasn't long before she was completely engrossed in the well-written novel; chuckling in delight over the telling prose. She was turning the page when something made her glance up, the blood draining from her face as she stared at the man who was hurrying past the window. *Mickey!*

The book fell from her lifeless hands, and for a moment she was too shocked to move. In the next moment she picked up her skirts, dashing from the store and calling out in a frantic voice, "Mickey! Mr. Quentin! Stop!"

"Katherine, what on earth are you doing?" Portia ran up beside her, gasping from the unfamiliar exertion. "Come back in the shop at once; you are making a spectacle of yourself!"

"But-but I saw . . . I saw . . ."

"Who?" Portia demanded when Kate stuttered to a halt. "Who did you think you saw?"

Kate's shoulders slumped at the realization that her mind must have been playing tricks on her. Of course Mickey wasn't in London, she decided glumly. He was doubtlessly off running the blockades, or engaging in even more nefarious conduct.

"No one, Aunt Portia," she said quietly, turning back towards the book shop. "I didn't see anyone."

"Well, the next time you don't see anyone, I'd appreciate it if you didn't go dashing after them," Portia grumbled, leading her back to the others. "You looked like a damn Bedlamite."

The rest of the day passed without incident, and after enjoying a quiet luncheon at Gussie's, Kate and Portia returned to their own home.

"It went rather well, don't you think?" Portia asked, settling back in her favorite chair with a sigh. "That Louisa is a trial to be sure, but I must say her companion is delightful. How old would you say she was?"

"Miss Compton?" Kate glanced up from her novel; she had bought the book after returning to the shop. "I'm not sure; my age, I suppose, perhaps older. Why?"

"She's not bad looking," Portia continued as if Kate hadn't spoken. "And one can tell she is a lady. I wonder how she came to be a governess, especially in that household."

"You must ask her," Kate said, a suspicion dawning slowly in her mind. She recognized that expression on her aunt's face, and knew it boded no good for the charming Miss Compton. "Aunt, you are not scheming anything . . . are you?" she asked, not really expecting the older woman to tell her the truth.

Portia took offense at once. "And what sort of question is that?" she bristled. "Scheming, indeed! I was but making polite conversation!"

"If you say so," Kate wasn't the least bit taken in by her aunt's look of reproach. "Just mind you don't im-

160

pose overly much on Miss Compton's kind nature. I rather like her."

"So do I," Portia agreed, abandoning all pretense of innocence. "That is why I think we should find her a husband, a second son, perhaps, or a rich Cit who has need of a well-bred wife."

"Aunt . . ."

"Or we might consider a nice widower," Portia laid a thoughtful finger on her lip. "Someone who already has established his nursery and is looking for someone to give him succor in his declining years . . ."

"Aunt Portia!" Kate interrupted, her voice stern. "I really do not think this is any of our concern! Miss Compton is a very attractive lady, and if she is still unmarried then we can only conclude that is her choice. Stay out of it."

Portia gave a loud sniff, not deigning to answer Kate's firm demand. Instead she picked up her new book and began reading, grumbling all the while about impertinent nieces who had yet to learn their place.

Kate let her grumble, turning her attention back to her book. She began reading again, but her fickle mind would not concentrate on the neatly printed words. What on earth had made her think she'd seen Mickey? she brooded, the book falling limply from her hands. She hadn't even been thinking of the lying beast. Her thoughts had been on the book in her hands, and what she and the others would do that afternoon. She'd been debating whether or not to buy the book or try to obtain it from a lending library when she suddenly looked up to see him strolling past the window.

He'd been wearing a black redingote; a beaver hat set jauntily on his dark head. There was a gold-tipped cane clasped in his hand, and his hard jaw was . . . her thoughts skittered to an abrupt halt. His jaw, she thought, an image of the man she'd glimpsed so briefly forming in her mind: his jaw was clean-shaven. There was no short, dark beard adorning his face.

She gave a soft sigh, relief making her giddy. She hadn't seen Mickey, nor had she lost her mind as she was beginning to think she had. She had simply seen a man who looked like him; that was all. London must be full of men with his dark, good looks, she rationalized, and she could hardly go dashing down the street after every man with curly black hair and wide-set shoulders. Not that she cared a whit if she ever saw him again, of course.

Portia saw the brooding expression on her niece's face and stirred with sudden interest. "By the by, my dear, I meant to ask you earlier but it must have slipped my mind; how do you feel about going to a musicale?"

"A musicale?" Kate looked up warily.

"A *small* musicale," Portia stressed. "One of my old friends, Lady Honoria Chapman, is having a few friends over for refreshments and the like, and we are invited. Since we have no other plans for the evening I thought it might be fun to attend . . . if you have no objection, that is?"

Kate's first inclination was to say no, but Portia looked so hopeful she couldn't say no; even though she strongly suspected her of play acting. Besides, she'd always been rather fond of music, and an intimate party sounded the perfect way of getting her feet wet again.

"What time would we need to be there?" she asked, her eyes going to the ornately carved clock setting on the mantel.

"Not until nine; Honoria believes in keeping country hours, even in the city."

Nine o'clock sounded rather late to Kate, although she knew that most London parties didn't even begin until well after midnight. "Where does her ladyship live?"

"In Mayfair, not far from Arthur and Gussie; although I'm sure we needn't call on them," Portia provided hurriedly. "They're certain to be out."

"Undoubtedly," Kate agreed, no more eager than Portia to endure a moment more of Lousia's company than was necessary.

"Then you'll go?" Portia could scarcely believe her niece was being so amenable. She was certain she would have to spend the greater part of the evening wheedling and scheming before she could ever get her to agree.

"Why not?" Kate gave a girlish laugh, feeling younger than she had in years. "By all means let us go."

"You're certain?" Portia could still not believe her luck. "Most people would find such entertainment dull beyond all bearing."

"That is because they haven't been buried in the country for the past three years as I have," Kate replied, her thoughts already turning to what she would wear. "Believe me, a nice, uneventful musicale sounds a delightful way to pass an evening."

"All right," Portia gave a pleased smile. "We shall go, then. And who knows? Perhaps the musicale shall not prove to be so uneventful after all. Why, anything might happen."

"No! Absolutely not!"

"But, my lord . . ."

"I said, no, damn it!" Peter shot Giles an angry look, his jaw thrusting forward pugnaciously. "I am more than willing to lay down my life for my country, Westley but I positively draw the line at attending musicales. I refuse to spend an entire evening listening to amateur musicians pounding away on the pianoforte and screeching like a bagful of cats! And nothing you say will ever convince me otherwise."

He turned from the window and stalked across the room to stand before the fireplace, his expression shuttered as he stared down at the dancing flames. He'd spent the better part of the afternoon attempting to get one of Payton's cronies bosky so that he could pump him for information, and his head still hadn't cleared. In fact, he'd imbibed so much that as he was walking down Strand Street he thought he'd heard Kate calling out to him. He'd even stopped and turned around; his eyes frantically searching the teeming streets, but he hadn't seen anything. How could he? She was still safely tucked away in Kent.

Which just went to show how sadly out of shape he was, he decided with a self-deprecating smile. Six months ago it would have taken more than half a bottle of indifferent brandy to get him so distinguished. He'd have to develop a harder head if he meant to run with the pack of jackals that surrounded the marquess.

"Payton." Westley's drawling tones cut into Peter's thoughts and he frowned at him in confusion.

"I beg your pardon?"

"Payton," Giles repeated, his thin lips lifting in a knowing smirk. "You said there was nothing I could say that would make you change your mind, but I say there is."

"Payton is attending Lady Honoria's musicale?"

Giles mockingly applauded Peter's grasp of the obvious. "And quite looking forward to it, might I add. Rumor even has it he may be persuaded to perform a song or two."

"Are you certain?" Peter's frown grew more pronounced at this startling bit of information. "It's hardly his usual mode of entertainment."

"True, but one can not remain in a bawdy house

twenty-four hours a day, as I have already learned to my cost," Giles responded with a languid yawn. "But in Payton's case, there is a method to his madness; Lady Honoria's niece, who is as wealthy as she is slow witted. Unfortunately for him, Lady Honoria is not so lacking in gray matter, and would never consent to the girl marrying a fortune hunter."

"Where the devil do you get your information?" Peter asked, admiration and disgust obvious in his deep voice.

"Sources."

"Mmm," Peter tapped a thoughtful finger on the mantel. "Some day you must explain these sources of yours to me. They seem remarkably well-informed." His expression grew troubled. "You're certain about Payton?"

"Positive. My man has it from his man that his lordship means to put in an appearance around ten this evening."

Peter's head came snapping around. "Your information comes from a *servant?*" he demanded.

"Well, you needn't look so outraged, my lord," Westley replied amused by Peter's expression. "Surely you know the impossibility of hiding anything from your servants. They know everything, and if the price is high enough, they will repeat it to anyone who cares to listen."

"What price did Payton's valet demand?"

"The correct way to starch a neckcloth," Giles gave his wrists a flick, causing the lace to cascade over the cuffs in an artful fall. "The marquess threatened to take a horsewhip to him if he ruined another one."

"Bullying bastard," Peter grumbled without heat.

"You'll get no argument from me," Giles said, his habitually bored expression hardening imperceptibly. "In fact, the more I learn of Payton the more I long to put a bullet through his heart; provided, of course, that he even possess such an organ. One wonders."

"What time does the torture begin?" Peter asked, pulling his watch from his pocket and studying it with a frown. It was a little past seven now, with luck he would have time for dinner before shaving and dressing for the evening.

"Nine o'clock, but you needn't arrive until the fashionably late hour of half past ten, if you wish," Giles assured him. "And naturally you will leave before Payton. We wouldn't wish him to think you were following him."

"Indeed not." Peter cocked his head to one side as a sudden thought occurred to him. "There is just one small problem."

"What is it?"

"I don't know Lady Honoria, at least, not personally," he said, studying Giles with a challenging smile. "How can I pop in to her little soirée when I haven't even been invited?"

"Is that all?" The look Giles sent him indicated he considered him to be the slowest top alive. "Really, my lord, your sense of humility is indeed to be commended. You are the Earl of Tregarren, and a wealthy bachelor in the bargain. If you but poke your nose through the drawing room door, I can assure you you will be greeted like a long lost son."

"I will? Why?"

"Lady Honoria might object to Payton as a suitor for her niece's hand, but she suffers no such reservations with you. In fact, she is rather hoping you and the chit will make a match of it."

"My God," Peter paled at the thought of being leg shackled to some dim witted debutante. "How do you know?"

Giles smiled again. "Sources."

Chapter Twelve

The street in front of Lady Honoria's house was clogged with carriages, necessitating a brief wait as liveried footmen scurried about assisting the arriving guests. In their carriage Kate turned to Portia, her expression rueful in the flickering lamp light.

"A *small* musicale?" she drawled, her eyebrows lifting in wry suspicion.

"Small by London standards," Portia replied unperturbed at having being caught in a lie. "Shouldn't be more than thirty or forty people here. Once the Season starts, there will be at least double that at any party of note. Well, you must remember what it is like."

Indeed Kate did, and she suppressed a tiny shudder. She'd always had a horror of crowds, and the awful squeezes that were all the rage in London had often left her quaking with anxiety. She never felt as if she could breathe packed into the overheated rooms, and she usually spent the greater part of the evening out on the balcony in search of fresh air. She smiled slightly as she remembered that was how she met Charles.

They were soon ushered inside the imposing Palladium-styled mansion, and after surrendering their wraps to the hovering maids, they set out to find their hostess.

"Good heavens," Kate said, her green eyes wide as she glanced around the wide, statue-littered hallways. "It looks like a Greek Temple!"

"Roman," Portia corrected, averting her gaze as they went past the statue of a scowling man wearing a fierce expression and little else. "Honoria and her husband went there on their bridal trip, and she went mad for all things Latin."

Kate eyed the bust of a man; Caesar, if his hooked nose was any indication, and gave a small sigh. "Mad," she said succinctly, "is a very good word for it."

They found Lady Honoria in a black and gold salon, receiving her guests in an imperious manner that showed she was still every inch the duke's daughter. "Welcome to my home," she boomed in a stentorian voiced thrusting a bejeweled hand under Kate's nose.

"My lady," for a moment Kate wondered if she was expected to shake the older lady's hand or kiss it. She did neither, but dropped a low curtsey instead. "I am most pleased to meet you."

Lady Honoria nodded briskly, causing the three large plumes adorning her turban to shift to one side. "Of course you are, my dear. Dare say you don't meet many duke's daughters stuck up there in the marshes, eh?"

Kate allowed that she did not, and Lady Honoria dismissed them by pointing her fan in the direction of a gold and white striped settee and ordering them to sit still until the music began.

"I'd forgotten what a quizz she has grown to be," Portia said as they took their seats. "Ah well, as you say, it is better than spending a dull evening at home."

"I'm not so sure," Kate replied, discreetly rubbing one slipper-clad foot against the other. "At least at home we wouldn't be courting pneumonia. It is like ice in here!"

"Marble." Portia tapped her foot against the shiny, black stone that stretched the length of the sparsely decorated room. "It gives off a dreadful chill."

"Now I know why ghosts are forever moaning," Kate muttered, wishing she'd worn her thick woolen socks instead of gossamer silk-stockings. And brought her Norwich shawl, she added, crossing her bare arms across her chest in an effort to warm herself. It looked to be a long, uncomfortable evening.

Several of the older guests recognized Portia and drifted over to welcome her back to London. Much to Kate's relief she was also recognized, and she spent a pleasant half hour reminiscing past seasons. Among the small group clustered about her was Anthony Blackburn, a young officer who had been one of Charles's old friends.

"I was very sorry to hear of Charles's death," he told her, his dark eyes filled with sympathy. "He was a dashed fine chap."

"Yes," Kate replied with a sad smile, "he was. And what of you Mr. Blackburn? Still in the . . . Rifles, was it not?"

"Yes, but I sold out last year. Bad leg." He tapped his thigh meaningfully.

"I am very sorry to hear that," she murmured softly, remembering how proud he had been of his uniform.

"Yes, well, it can't be helped, I suppose," he shrugged awkwardly and then assumed a bright expression. "Still, it's not all that bad. I have an older brother, William, who is in the India Company, and he assures me I shall have no trouble finding a position. He is in Calcutta, and I will be sailing out to join him in a few months."

The subject of India saw them safely over the awkwardness of his injury, and when he asked her to accompany him into the drawing room she was quick to

169

accept. "Anything to escape this mausoleum," she muttered, taking his arm as they skirted a group of women ogling the scowling statue. "I do not see how her ladyship can endure it. It's a wonder she hasn't turned to stone along with the rest of the antiquities."

Mr. Blackburn remained silent, and she had the odd feeling that he disapproved of her small jest. Ah well, she gave a mental shrug, there was no accounting for tastes. Charles would have shaken his head at her and pretended to be shocked, while Mickey would have laughed with her and made some ribald remark in return. She frowned in sudden irritation as she realized the direction her thoughts had taken.

Blast it all, she chastised herself sternly, she was not going to give that lying, phony Irishman another thought! He was a scoundrel, and a lecher, and a . . .

"I wonder how the devil he got in here." Mr. Blackburn's whispered comment brought Kate's harangue to a halt, and she glanced wildly around her.

"Who?" She demanded, wondering if her thoughts had managed to conjure up Mickey like the evil ghost in a fairy tale.

"Lord Payton," Mr. Blackburn nodded at the beefy man who was making his bows to an elderly lady in black silk. "His reputation isn't at all good, you know, and I quite wonder that Lady Honoria should invite him."

"That is Lord Payton?" Kate gave the man a searching look; intrigued at having finally clapped eyes on her infamous neighbor.

"Yes, I met him once years ago, and I can not say that I cared for him," Mr. Blackburn's lips thinned with disapproval. He turned to Kate. "Do you know him? I believe he is a neighbor of yours."

Kate shook her head. "He wasn't in residence when Charles and I arrived in the neighborhood, and . . .

and afterwards I was in mourning. I had heard he was visiting his estates recently, but we never had the occasion to meet."

Mr. Blackburn bit his lips, clearly torn between the dictates of society and a reluctance to approach a man he considered beneath his notice. In the end good breeding won out, and he gave a resigned sigh. "Would you care to meet him now?"

"I really should," she said after a moment's consideration. "He is my neighbor, even though we have never met."

"That is so," Mr. Blackburn agreed with visible reluctance. "He is a marquess, after all, and it would not do for you to slight him. Very well, then," and he guided her over to Payton to perform the stiff introductions.

"Mrs. Delecourt," the marquess drawled, bowing over her hand with a natural grace. "It is a pleasure to meet you."

"Thank you, my lord," Kate answered, thinking that for a rake, he really wasn't so very bad. Certainly he looked every inch the perfect gentlemen in his cream satin evening breeches and his black velvet coat; his dark hair brushed back from his high forehead. In fact, the only thing about his appearance she found the least bit objectionable were his eyes. They were a pale ice-blue, and they moved over her with predatory intent. She could not help but compare them to another pair of blue eyes; eyes that sparkled with life and laughter. . . .

"So you are the tragically widowed beauty I heard so much of the last time I was in Rye," Payton continued, still retaining possession of her hand. "I meant to call upon you and offer you my condolences, but alas, there was no time. Do say you forgive me," and he gave her a smile that was as false as it was wide.

171

"There is nothing to forgive, my lord," Kate replied, hastily revising her earlier good opinion of him as she extracted her hand from his too familiar hold. "And I understand that you, too, have suffered a sad loss. Pray accept my deepest sympathies."

His heavy shoulders moved up and down in an indifferent shrug. "It was years ago," he said, his eyes resting on the gentle swell of white flesh visible above the modest neckline of her ruby silk dress. "And life does go on, as I am sure you have already discovered."

Kate stiffened; her indifference turning rapidly to distaste. "For some of us, perhaps," she said, her chin lifting with haughty pride. "I pray you will excuse us, my lord, but the music is about to start and I must be returning to my aunt. Good-bye."

"Good night, Mrs. Delecourt," rather than taking offense at her attempt to snub him, the marquess seemed amused. "I shall look forward to seeing you again. It is always a good thing to be on good terms with one's neighbors, do you not agree?"

"If you say so, Lord Payton," Kate replied, laying her hand on Mr. Blackburn's arm. "Good evening."

"Good lord, but the fellow is an out and out bounder," Mr. Blackburn complained as he led Kate back to the funereal salon. "My apologies, Mrs. Delecourt, for inflicting him upon you."

"I was the one who sought the introduction," Kate reminded him with a reassuring smile. "I had heard much of him when he was in Rye, and I suppose my curiosity was piqued."

"You know the old adage about curiosity, ma'am" Mr. Blackburn was emboldened by her warm smile to give her hand an admonishing pat. "I should hate to see anything untoward happen to you."

For some reason Kate thought again of Mickey. It was her curiosity to investigate the odd shape on the

172

beach that had first brought him into her life. "Don't worry, Mr. Blackburn," she told him fervently, "I have already learned that particular lesson, and in the future I shall endeavor to curb such impulses. They seem to bring me nothing but misfortune."

It was approaching eleven o'clock before Peter made his appearance at Lady Honoria's. As Giles had assured him his lack of invitation proved no impediment, and he was soon ushered into the music room with all due ceremony. He paused long enough to do the pretty with his hostess and her simpering niece and listened to the indifferent performing, and then set out to find Payton. He finally located his quarry in the drawing room, and strolled over to offer a sardonic greeting.

"Payton, old fellow, it is you! What the devil are you doing here? I thought this was a respectable gathering."

"And so it was, Tregarren until *you* arrived," Payton returned, his blue eyes gleaming with speculation as they studied Peter's face. "I'd heard you were back in town, but I never thought to look for you here. Lost?"

"I am like the proverbial bad penny," Peter said, falling easily into the sardonic drawl he affected in his persona as the rakish Lord Tregarren. "One never knows where I may next appear."

"That is so, but one can not help but wonder what moved you to appear here. God knows it can not be the wine," and he set down his glass with a grimace.

"Ratafia?" Peter shuddered with mock horror. "No, thank you. I would as soon drink milk or some equally loathsome beverage. But as for why I am here in the bosom of respectability, I suppose you might lay the blame on my mother's plate. Since my . . . er . . . accident she has been nagging at me to marry and set up my nursery before, and I quote, 'it is too late.' She

173

is threatening to arrange a match herself if I do not attend to matters post haste."

"Have you a prospective bride in mind?"

Peter gave an indifferent shrug and cast a derisive glance about him. "Does it matter? One well-bred virgin will do as well as the next, I suppose. Now, what about you? Why are you here? Do not tell me you have turned virtuous and are abandoning your evil ways. My poor heart could never withstand such a shock."

Payton's lips lifted in a bitter smile. "Hardly. My reasons for attending this wake are much the same as yours, only in my case it is inopportuning creditors nagging me on. I have been advised by a man of business to make an advantageous match as quickly as possible."

"Ah, like that is it?" Peter nodded in understanding. "Well, allow me the first to wish you happiness. Who is the lucky bride?"

"Like you I have decided that any chit will do," Payton gave a cold laugh. "Only in my case, it is the depths of her pockets rather than the blue of her blood that interests me. I am even not particularly concerned if she is a virgin."

"You would take soiled goods?" Peter was surprised. In their world even a man considering a marriage of convenience would hesitate before offering his name to a woman who had given herself outside of marriage. That Payton was willing to do so was an indication of just how desperate he was. Peter smiled in cold anticipation of how he would put that knowledge to use in his favor.

"No, but I was willing to consider a nubile widow whose husband left her a rather comfortable living. Unfortunately the bitch would have naught to do with me. Pity, she was rather comely."

"Oh?" Peter tried to sound interested, but he had already tired of the conversation. Now that he knew Payton was deep in dun territory he was anxious to get back to his home. He'd contact a friend of his; a money lender, and see if he could buy up Payton's most pressing notes. Perhaps if a bit of judicious pressure were brought to bear on him he would grow reckless enough to make a mistake, and once he made that mistake . . . Peter's smile widened at the possibilities.

"Yes," Payton was too lost in own lascivious musings to note Peter's preoccupation. "A pretty little blond with soft green eyes and a body made for loving. Yes indeed, my Mrs. Delecourt has much to offer a man were she not so damned proper in her notions."

Peter had heard the expression "his heart stopped" a hundred different times in his life, but it was the first time he had ever experienced the phenomenon himself. He was literally frozen; unable to think or move as he struggled to absorb what Payton had said. It was like being in a dream, or a nightmare; only far, far worse, because he knew himself to be wide awake. He took a deep breath to compose himself and then turned to Payton.

"Who did you say?" he asked carefully.

"Mrs. Delecourt," Payton repeated. "Can't think of her first name at the moment. Her house isn't far from my estates in Rye; not so large, but profitable, and as I said, her late husband left her rather well-heeled. I could have done worse," and he gave a shrug to indicate that he considered the matter of no real import.

"How well do you know her?" Peter asked, struggling to remember everything Kate had said of Payton. She'd claimed not to know him, as he recalled, but how could he trust her? He'd always assumed her an innocent in all this, but now he wasn't so certain. Why the hell hadn't the little witch told him she was coming to London? She could ruin everything!

"We met for the first time this evening," Payton finally took note of Peter's odd behavior, and was regarding him quizzically. "Why do you ask? Do *you* know her?"

Peter quickly controlled himself. "Not at all," he said, assuming a wolfish smile. "But if she is half so lovely as you claim, that is a situation I am anxious to remedy. Where is she? Point her out to me at once," and he began glancing about the crowded room in eager anticipation.

"I shouldn't waste my time, old boy," Payton advised him with a mocking sneer. "The lady is almost depressingly virtuous; she all but cut me dead because I held her hand overly long.

The thought of Payton touching Kate in any way at all made Peter stiffen with murderous fury, and he struggled for composure. "Well, in that case you may spare me the introductions," he managed at last, striving for a light tone. "Virtuous widows, comely or otherwise are hardly in my line. You are welcome to her."

"Thank you," Payton bowed mockingly. "But as I said, she has made it more than obvious that we would not suit. Now if you will excuse me, I promised Miss Chapman I would play a small selection for the guests. Hayden," he rolled his eyes in disgust.

Peter nodded in sympathy. "Say no more," he said soothingly. "I understand completely. A man must do what a man must do, and all that. Lady Honoria's niece will make a charming marchioness."

"She is a delightful widgeon with more hair than wit," Lord Payton returned bluntly, "but she will do. Besides, I have often found intelligence in a female to be a less than desirable thing. Another flaw of Mrs.

176

Delecourt's; she struck me as far too sharp by half."

"Please enough of this feminine paragon, I beg you," Peter implored, holding his hands up in mock surrender. The subject of Kate was far too volatile for his liking, and he was anxious to change the conversation before he inadvertently betrayed himself. "All this talk of virtue and marriage is giving me a headache. I'm off to White's for a game of hazzard and some decent wine. Enjoy your evening, Payton." He turned to go.

"Tregarren wait."

"Yes?" He gave Payton a reluctant look over his shoulder.

"It shouldn't take me above a quarter hour to placate Miss Chapman. Why don't you wait for me, and we shall go to your club together? I feel rather in the mood for a game of chance myself."

Peter hesitated, weighing the danger of discovery against the chance to learn more about his prey. This was the first time Payton had actively sought his company, and he did not wish to rebuff him. Perhaps if he stayed out of the music room he might manage to avoid detection, he thought with growing optimism.

"Very well, Payton," he said, shooting the other man a languid smile. "I'll wait; so long as I'm not expected to be part of your audience. Hayden is a particular favorite of mine, and I have no wish to hear his work butchered at your hands. I will remain in here until you are ready to go."

"All right," Payton nodded briskly. "But to be safe, give me at least half an hour. One mustn't play and run, you know."

"Ah yes, the never ending demands of an audience," Peter murmured. "Forty-five minutes, then. But not one second more, Payton, or else I shall leave you to walk! Mind you are not late."

* * *

"Katherine, if you do not sit still, I vow I shall pinch you!" Portia whispered, her lips set in a stiff smile as she bent towards her niece's ear. "You are being rude."

"I can't help it," Kate shot back, shifting again as the horsehide chair found a new way to torment her. "This chair *itches!*"

"You are a lady, Katherine," Portia returned severely. "You are expected to ignore such minor discomforts."

Kate muttered something decidedly unladylike beneath her breath, wondering if her aunt would consider the discomfort so minor if it was her posterior that was being used as a pin cushion. Nor was the chair the only distraction. For the last fifteen minutes or so the back of her neck had been prickling like mad, and she'd had the oddest sensation someone was staring at her. It was so strong she'd actually turned around, but outside of catching the glimpse of some man's back as he slipped out on to the balcony to blow a cloud, she hadn't seen a thing.

Men were lucky, she decided glumly, turning her attention to the front of the room where the odious marquess she had met earlier was hammering away at the pianoforte. They could step outside any time they pleased, and no one thought more of it. Perhaps she ought to take up smoking, she thought with a flash of whimsy, grinning at the thought of how her aunt would react to such shocking dissipation. For all Portia pretended to be so sanguine and sophisticated, she was really delightfully provincial.

"Ouch!" She leapt as a particularly sharp hair came in contact with her sensitive skin.

"Katherine!" Portia gave a warning hiss.

"I am sorry Aunt, but I can not endure another minute of this torture," Kate answered, rising to her feet. "I will be in the drawing room when you are ready to go."

Murmuring apologies to those whose feet she tripped over in her haste to slip unobtrusively from the room, Kate made her way to the door. Her precipitous departure earned her an angry glare from her hostess, but she was beyond caring. She merely smiled prettily and kept walking, not stopping until she reached the relative safety of the drawing room.

It was surprisingly full; several of the guests who had already performed or were waiting to perform were all milling about, and drinking the sweet fruit-laden wine which was all Lady Honoria was offering by way of refreshment. Kate helped herself to a glass from a passing tray and was settling back to enjoy her drink when her neck began prickling again. What on earth . . . she glanced around in confusion. Nothing. Then she saw a flash of black as another man slipped out the door.

What in Hades was going on? she wondered, setting her glass down with an aggrieved frown. Were all the men in society secret tobacco fiends? Charles had certainly never indulged in that particular vice, at least, she didn't think he had, nor had Mickey shown any inclination to. . . . She picked up her glass again and took a deep draught.

Why couldn't she get that man out of her mind? she brooded with a feeling close to despair. It was almost as if he was haunting her, and the thought filled her with helpless fury. What good was it to come to London if he only followed her like some vengeful ghost, she asked herself rhetorically.

She might as well have stayed at home! At least there she might have had some measure of peace, and

179

not been subjected to the hazards of a London season. Hazards like brattish cousins and insulting lords, she tallied with a half-smile; to say nothing of instruments of torture devised as furniture, and the feeling that she was being watched that never went away. Her neck gave another warning prickle.

Damn it to hell why the devil hadn't she stayed in the music room, Peter cursed silently, rubbing his arms in an effort to warm himself. He'd slipped into the music room shortly after Payton had taken his seat at the pianoforte unable to resist the urge to get even a glimpse of her. The sight of her, her soft blond hair bound back in a stylish arrangement of curls and her slender body draped in shimmering ruby silk, had made him catch his breath in wonder.

His blood grew warm at the memory of the last time he'd seen her. God, she had been so warm, so soft; her lips eager beneath his as he'd tasted her honeyed sweetness. He swore again, this time out loud at the inevitable effect his memories had upon him.

The woman was half-witch, he decided defensively, shifting uncomfortably as the cold night air made his wounds throb. He'd spent a little over a fortnight in her company, and yet her very image was seared deep into his soul. He could remember everything about her. The way she looked, the way she smelled, the way she moved . . . he closed his eyes and groaned in frustration.

He didn't have time for this nonsense, he told himself savagely. His country's safety as well as the safety of his brother depended upon his every action, and he would not, he *would not* allow himself to be distracted. He opened his eyes on that thought and peered through the window into the drawing room.

She was still there, blast it, sitting there and drinking ratafia as if she hadn't a care in the world. The room was crowded, but not so crowded he could hope to avoid detection. What the devil was he going to do now? His eyes strayed to the balcony on the other side of him, and he wondered if he should make a try for it. He was only a story or so above the ground, and even if he fell he didn't think he'd be hurt too badly.

He was about to jump when something made him glance through the window again, and the sight of Payton entering the room in search of him set him to cursing again. He had no choice now, he realized grimly. He would have to risk it and hope and pray Kate would not see him. Although he did not hold out much hope for such a miracle; not the way his luck had been running. He took one final breath for luck and opened the door; stepping into the room with a pained smile pinned to his lips.

"There you are," Payton gave Peter a relieved smile as he approached. "I was beginning to think you'd grown bored and left."

"I almost did," Peter said, laying a familiar hand on Payton's shoulder and turning him towards the door. "Shall we go? I sent word to my groom to have my team waiting, and I don't want them growing restless."

"Wait, don't you wish to say goodbye to our hostess?" Payton was faintly surprised by Tregarren's lack of manners. "She's certain to take offense if you don't."

"Let her, I'm not trying to get into her good graces," Peter snapped, noting to his horror that Kate and an older woman in a maroon-colored turban were heading in his direction. If she looked up, he was a dead man.

"Well, I am," Payton was now staring at Peter, his expression thoroughly annoyed. "I told you I was playing up sweet for the niece, and I won't slip out of the house like some light-handed servant. Won't take but a minute, she's in that Roman horror of hers."

Peter cursed Payton's sudden burst of good breeding but there was nothing he could do without risking drawing even more notice. "Very well, then," he said curtly, "but mind you don't be all night about it." He adroitly turned the marquess around and began leading him away from the approaching women.

"Aren't bosky, are you?" Payton's shorter legs had a harder time keeping up with Peter's quick strides. "The old gal's like to cut up stiff if she smells brandy on you. Miss Chapman says she's as stern as a Methodist on the subject."

"Then I shall not breathe on her. For God's sake, Payton would you hurry—"

"Oh look, there's Mrs. Delecourt," Payton dug his heels in, dragging Peter to a halt. "Regular vision, isn't she?"

"An incomparable." Sweat beaded Peter's forehead as he fought against the urge to say to hell with honor and bolt for the door. "Now come, Payton we really must—"

"Would you like to meet her?"

"God, no!" Peter exclaimed, furious at the way things were spinning out of control. It was like the time he was captured, he thought wildly, and there was nothing he could do to halt the inexorable march of events. "That is," he added, amending his tone, "I have already said that she is not in my usual style, and in any case we have to find Lady Honoria, remember?"

"The old tartar isn't going anywhere," Payton was already signaling Kate with a lift of his hand. "Besides, I want to see if my widow takes as great a dislike to you as she did to me. But I warn you, if she falls madly in love with you I shall be most hipped. I

182

saw her first."

"That is what you think," Peter muttered beneath his breath. There was no escape, he realized dully. His only choice was to stand his ground with as much grace as he could muster, and pray he would still have a reputation left when the screaming was over. He squared his shoulders, his chin coming up as he faced the approaching ladies with all the resigned dignity of a condemned man facing a firing squad.

disagreeable as Payton; otherwise she would cut them
...h dead on the spot.
...he saw Payton at once; his hand upraised in greet-
...and she gave a cool nod of acknowledgement. Odi-
...road, she thought her gaze shifting to ... beside him
...probably one of those that ... thrown ... but ... the
...e him, a ... be ... she ...
...t ... something ... should ... her ...
...e couldn't ... she told her ... would ... since of

Chapter Thirteen

"Look, there is Lord Payton trying to get our attention," Portia exclaimed as she and Kate began thread-
ing their way through the crowd. "Let's go over and
offer him our congratulations for his fine playing."

Kate had seen the marquess entering the room a few
moments ago, and she was less than thrilled with the
prospect of meeting him again. She'd mentioned their
earlier meeting to her aunt but had kept the details deliberately vague, not wishing another lecture on her
"overly nice" sensibilities. "One doesn't compliment a
man for such ham-fisted pounding, Aunt," she informed Portia haughtily, refusing to look in Payton's direction, "one condemns him to perdition. Now come, it
is quite late and I want to go home."

"What do you mean it is late? It is scarcely past midnight!" Portia protested, shooting her niece an angry
scowl. "And as for Lord Payton's playing, what would
you know about it, missy? You went sneaking out of
there before he was half done; something I mean to discuss with you once we are.. . . Good heavens! Is that
the earl of Tregarren standing beside Payton?"

Against her will Kate glanced in the direction Portia
indicated. She'd heard so much about the earl of late
she felt as if she knew him, and despite her earlier vow
to Mr. Blackburn, she was anxious to satisfy her curiosity on the matter. She hoped he didn't prove to be as

disagreeable as Payton; otherwise she would cut them both dead on the spot.

She saw Payton at once; his hand upraised in greeting, and she gave a cool nod of acknowledgement. Odious toad, she thought her eyes drifting to his left. He was probably one of those men who thought his title gave him carte . . . her thoughts slammed to a halt at the sight of the tall dark haired man standing beside Payton, his blue eyes cold as he watched them approach.

It couldn't be, she told herself weakly, her stomach lurching as she struggled to keep from fainting. It was like this afternoon, when she thought she'd seen him walking down Strand Street. It wasn't Mickey. It couldn't be. Could it?

"Ah, Mrs. Delecourt, what a delightful surprise!" Payton exclaimed as Kate and Portia joined them. "Did I not say we would be seeing more of each other?"

Kate didn't respond to his sally, her eyes riveted to the earl's face. She *knew* that face, she told herself with something approaching hysteria. She knew those finely chiseled cheekbones, that hawkish nose, the arched eyebrows that betrayed his every thought with a lift or a twitch. Her eyes rested on the lower half of his face. And she knew that mouth. Even without the soft curling beard surrounding it, she knew she'd never forget the firm lips that had covered hers with blatant mastery.

Payton noted the pole-axed way she was staring at Tregarren, and some of his pleasure with the little scene he'd managed vanished. He turned to the earl. "Mrs. Delecourt, allow me to make you known to my old friend, Lord Peter Wyndham, earl of Tregarren," he said somewhat stiffly. "My lord, this lovely lady is my neighbor from Kent, Mrs. Delecourt."

"Mrs. Delecourt," Peter bowed coolly, studying Kate's stunned expression with concern. She was white from shock, her green eyes glittering like emeralds as she studied him with a sort of dazed horror. He hoped she didn't faint. He'd never be able to maintain the fiction that they'd never met if she collapsed into his arms like a character out of a French farce.

Kate continued staring at the earl, searching his aristocratic features for . . . for what? A flash of recognition, a flush of shame, something, anything—that indicated he recognized her. Instead he merely looked at her; his eyes those of a stranger as he returned her perusal with an expression of sardonic amusement.

A sharp poke in the ribs brought her jolting back to reality, and she gave a small jerk. She turned to Portia who was glaring at her with obvious impatience. "I . . . this is my aunt, Mrs. Portia Stone," she stammered, her cheeks pinking as she realized she was making a cake of herself. "Aunt Portia, I believe you said you are already acquainted with their lordships."

"We have met," Portia replied languidly hiding her annoyance at her niece's freakish behavior. "Not that I expect either of you gentlemen to remember, of course. It was a number of years ago." She gave Lord Tregarren a particularly bright smile.

"And may I say how pleased I am that you have recovered from your accident, my lord?" she asked, anxious to make up for Kate's muteness. "Although I suppose I really had ought to be ringing a peal over your head for so foolish behavior. Carriage racing at your age!" She waggled a playful finger at him. "Naughty, naughty."

Peter could have kissed the delightful old dragon. Not only had her teasing provided a badly needed levity, but it also offered him the perfect excuse to extract himself from this bizarre situation. Kate was in shock now, but when she recovered he knew it wasn't long before she began demanding answers to the questions he could read in her eyes. Answers he dared not give her.

"Curricle racing, ma'am," he corrected, favoring Portia with a brilliant smile. "I was curricle racing. And as for the accident, it really amounted to nothing more than a few broken bones and a badly bruised sense of pride. Hardly enough to warrant such universal speculation, I assure you."

"Ah, but universal speculation is bread and life to our set," Portia riposted delighted that the earl was not so high in the instep as she had heard. "And you must admit the circumstances of your . . ." she paused delicately, "accident caused a great deal of speculation and concern. We have so few eligible earls, it would be a great pity to lose one through simple carelessness."

"Then in the future I shall take better care of myself, if only to spare you ladies a moment's worry," he returned with an urbane bow. "Now if you will excuse Payton and myself, we really had ought to be going. All this talk of curricles reminds me I have left my team waiting out front, and my cattle are certain to be frozen. Mrs. Stone, Mrs. Delecourt, it has been a pleasure. Come Payton."

Less than fifteen minutes later the two were in Peter's best carriage, rumbling down the congested streets. Peter collapsed against the velvet squabs, his eyes closing as he considered how close he had come to disaster. Even now, he could scarcely believe that he had managed to escape the explosive situation unscathed. Perhaps his luck was changing after all, he thought with a flash of gallows humor. God knew it couldn't get worse.

"Well, what did you think of Mrs. Delecourt?" Payton asked, partaking of a deep sip from his silver hip flask. "Lovely as an angel, isn't she?"

"As I said, an incomparable," Peter replied, opening his eyes to study the marquess thoughtfully. He didn't often indulge in strong spirits while on duty, but then, he had seldom endured an evening like tonight, either. He held out his hand imperiously.

"She seemed taken with you," Payton wiped his

mouth on the back of his hand before passing the flask to Peter. "Couldn't take her eyes off you, in fact."

Peter shrugged then tilted the flask back, savoring the unmistakable smoothness of French brandy before he swallowed. "She looked like a simpleton," he said as brutally as he could manage. "I thought you said she was a bluestocking, but she stood there gaping at me as if she was a moonling. It was damned embarrassing."

Payton laughed suddenly. "Aye, she did look a start, didn't she?" he said with a wide grin. "Mayhap she's unused to such exalted company, hmm?"

"Maybe," Peter shrugged again, wishing Payton would change the subject. It made him far too nervous, and nerves were one thing he could ill afford just now. He raised the flask to his lips for another sip and then slanted the marquess a questioning look. "Do you still wish to go to Whites, or have you some other destination in mind?" he asked, deliberately changing the subject.

Payton's eyes lit up at once. "Such as?"

"I shall leave that up to you," he replied, relieved Payton had taken the bait. He would deal with the ramifications of Kate's presence in London later, but for now he meant to concentrate all his energies on trapping the marquess.

"Belle Terre?"

Peter thought about the infamous gaming hell as well-known for its beautiful cyprians as for the depth of play to be found at its green baize tables. "Very well," he said, doing his best to sound enthused. "Belle Terre it shall be, and after that, we shall have to see. The night is still young, after all. Let it take us where it will."

In her own carriage Kate wasn't faring nearly so well. The footman had barely closed the door behind them before her aunt was ringing a peal over her head.

"All right, missy and pray what is the meaning of *that?*"

Kate shifted uneasily on her bench. "Meaning of what, Aunt?" she asked, striving to assume a properly innocent expression.

Portia, however, was not so easily gulled. "Kindly do not be flippant, Katherine," she told her niece in her most severe tones. "It ill becomes you. You know full well what I mean. How could you stand there gaping at Lord Tregarren like . . . like one of those damned statues come to life?"

Despite the chaos of her own emotions Kate could not help but smile at the image her aunt's words invoked. "I couldn't possibly be mistaken for one of Lady Honoria's statues," she informed Portia, flippantly. "I have on far too many clothes."

"Katherine Josephine!"

"I'm sorry, Aunt Portia," Kate apologized, searching for the words that would explain her actions not only to her aunt, but to herself at last. "But the simple truth is, I am not at all certain why I acted as I did. It is just that . . . for a moment . . . I–I thought I recognized Lord Tregarren."

"I am sure you did," Portia responded with a frown, struggling to comprehend Kate's explanation. "Our world is not so very large, and I daresay you must have clapped eyes on his lordship any number of times. But that still doesn't justify your—"

"No," Kate interrupted,waving her hand impatiently. "I meant, I *recognized* him; as if he were an old friend, someone I knew quite well but hadn't seen in a very long time."

"Who?" Portia was fascinated.

"That's just it, I don't know!" Kate exclaimed, her distress obvious even in the dim light of the carriage lamp. More than anything she wanted to confess the truth to her aunt, but she dared not. Not only was it far

189

too risky, but at the moment she wasn't even certain what the truth was.

"I only know the feeling was quite strong," she continued, determined to be as honest as she could. "That is why I kept staring at him. I thought that if I looked at him long enough and hard enough it would come to me, but it never did."

Portia was quiet a long moment, much struck by Kate's impassioned declaration. "How singularly odd," she said at last, tapping her chin with her plumed fan. "And you say you have no idea why he should seem so familiar to you?"

"None," Kate verified, rubbing her forehead with her gloved hand. She should have followed her original instincts and stayed at home, she thought unhappily; at least then she wouldn't be wondering if she had run mad.

"Do you think it might be because he resembles Charles?" Portia persisted, anxious to understand Kate's actions. "He also had brown hair, as I recall."

"No, Charles's hair was a soft brown," Kate corrected, her expression softening as she remembered her husband's boyish good looks. "And he had hazel eyes. He looked nothing like the earl."

"Well, there must be some plausible explanation we can make!" Portia exclaimed, highly vexed.

"Why?"

Portia blinked at Kate's blunt question. "Why?" she echoed, feeling somewhat confused. "Well, because tongues are sure to be wagging tomorrow, and . . ."

"Why?" Kate repeated, her resolve slowly asserting itself. "Really, Aunt, you act as if I lifted my skirts to my knees and danced a jig! What did I do that was so terrible? I stared at the earl of Tregarren; that is all. I sincerely doubt if anyone even noticed."

"Lord Tregarren noticed," Portia reminded her with a sniff. "He looked most embarrassed, in fact."

190

"Yes, well, I am sure we may count upon his lordship's sense of discretion," Kate muttered, wishing her aunt would simply let the matter drop. She wanted a few minutes of blissful silence so that she could come to terms to the evening's bizarre events.

"Hmph! Now I know you are not well acquainted with his lordship, else you would not utter such fustian," Portia replied, her nose coming up several notches. "Everyone knows his reputation is more than a trifle tarnished." She was quiet for a moment and then said, "Still, I suppose you are right and I am reflecting far too much on the matter. As you say, you did nothing so very awful. It will all be forgotten come morning."

"Thank you," Kate replied with an ironic smile. "It is reassuring to know I am not totally ruined." They continued on in silence for several minutes, and then Kate's curiosity got the better of her.

"What did the earl do to so tarnish his reputation?" she asked, thinking of Mickey and the wager he had mentioned. Certainly if anyone even suspected the earl of attempting to sail to France at such a time his reputation would most certainly suffer.

"Ladybirds," Portia was fiddling with the fastenings of her new cloak. "It is something of a family failing, as his late father had a decided predilection for the Muslin Set." She sent Kate an annoyed frown. "Didn't I already tell you all this?"

"So you did," Kate agreed with alacrity, "but I still do not see why such a . . . er . . . common failing should make him an outcast. I thought it de rigueur for most men of his class to keep a mistress or an opera singer."

"The earl of Tregarren is hardly an outcast," Portia corrected dryly. "I will admit that there are a few who would like to see him censored for some of his more . . . shall we say . . . flamboyant escapades. But by and large the lad is well-liked. Or at least he was, until this latest scandal."

"What scandal?"

"The duel, of course."

Kate was hopelessly confused, until she remembered her aunt had mentioned something about the earl being injured in a duel shortly after Christmas. "But I thought you said he was injured in a curricle accident!" she protested. "You even teased him about it!"

"Really, Katherine, don't be such a gudgeon!" Portia snapped. "Duelling is against the law! He could hardly confess to such a thing, now could he?"

"I suppose not," Kate conceded, her scalp prickling as a sudden thought occurred to her. "Was his lordship injured in this duel?"

"Of course," Portia frowned at her. "You heard him; he had several broken bones."

"He also inferred they were the result of a carriage accident, so you will forgive me if I doubt his veracity," she answered dryly, possibilities racing through her head. "But how, precisely was he injured? Was he shot?"

"Good God, Katherine, what sort of morbid question is that?" Portia was scandalized.

"Was he?"

"How should I know? I am not the Oracle at Delphi, you know!"

"But aren't most duels conducted with pistols?" Kate pressed, excitement growing within her. "And if his lordship was injured as a result of this duel, then it stands to reason he was shot . . . doesn't it?"

"I suppose that it does," Portia agreed slowly. "Although I hardly see that it signifies. Why should it matter one way or another if Tregarren was shot, run through with a sword, or bashed over the head with a battle axe?"

Kate's lips thinned with anger. "Oh it matters, Aunt Portia," she said softly. "It matters very, very much!"

* * *

"We've got problems," Giles announced, his expression grim as he strode into Peter's dressing rooms the following morning. "This could ruin everything!"

Peter turned from his mirror, dismissing his valet with a flick of his hand. Once the door had closed behind the servant he settled himself on the comfortable Sheraton chair and regarded Westley through narrowed eyes. He supposed he should be surprised the viscount already knew of Kate's presence in London, but as he had already observed, the younger man's sources were nothing if not highly efficient. He crossed one booted foot across the other and fixed him with a somber look.

"What do you think we ought to do?"

Giles shrugged, crossing the room to stand before the window. "There's nothing we can do but hold our breath and pray it doesn't all explode in our face," he said, lifting the heavy crimson velvet drape with one finger. "It's risky, I'll grant you, but not nearly so risky as acting too precipitously."

"That is what I thought; the less said the better," Peter replied, thinking of the hours he'd spent staring at the ceiling and wrangling with the question of what he should do about Kate. In the end he'd decided it was safest to play a waiting game; safer for her, and infinitely safer for him.

"I could not agree with you more," Giles continued staring out the window, a rueful smile softening the hard edges of his mouth. "Although it may not be so easy getting Admiral Heatherton to hold his tongue. The old boy is quite cast up into the boughs over this, and is prattling to anyone who will listen how it *really* isn't his fault."

"How could it be his fault?" Peter asked, his brow wrinkling in confusion. He wondered if the navy had placed Kate under close observation, and the thought filled him with a cold anger. He'd be damned if he would allow her to be so harassed when she had done nothing to warrant such treatment. Someone, he vowed, would learn of his displeasure.

"Because he was in charge of the whole affair," Giles left the window to stand in the center of the room. "Not the wisest of choices, I'll admit, but you know how the Admiralty positively dotes on its old sea dogs; even unworthy curs such as Heatherton."

"The Admiralty is involved?" Peter's leg dropped to the floor as he sat up. Good God, things were even worse than he dared imagine! He would have to contact Kate's Uncle Alfred something-or-other at once. Something would have to be done and soon, before her reputation was totally in shreds.

"Well, of course they are involved; how else could we get him home?" Giles's amusement was slowly giving way to bafflement.

"Get who home?" Peter was staring at Giles as if he'd taken leave of his senses.

"Your half brother!"

"The Admiralty is sending James home?" Peter asked, wondering what one possibly had to do with the other.

"Well, they were until the wretch jumped ship in Charleston!" Giles exclaimed, his hands resting on his hips as he glared at Peter. "Do you mean this is the first you have heard of it?"

Peter nodded, his thoughts shifting abruptly from Kate to James. "How do they know he jumped ship?" he demanded, fearing Payton may have learned of James's return and intercepted him. "He could have been kidnapped for all we know!"

"We know because after escaping from his cabin your brother ran up on deck, climbed up on the railing, saluted the captain and his crew, and then dove off into the river. The last they saw of him he was making for an American frigate anchored nearby."

Peter was silent for a long moment, a slow grin spreading across his face. "The ship must have been going too slow for his liking," he said, easily envisioning the scene Giles had just described. "He has always been of an impatient nature."

"Well, you may laugh if you like," Giles retorted, fighting not to smile, "but I can assure you the Admiralty is far from amused. And as for us, you must surely realize this knocks our plans cock-a-hoop. We were counting on James's testimony to help us tighten the noose around Payton. Now we don't even know where the wretch is!"

"Knowing James, I'd say he was on the fastest ship bound for England; after a brief visit to the nearest brothel, that is."

"Ah, a man after my own heart," Giles did smile then. "Perhaps I shall not draw his cork after all. I must own I was tempted to do so when Lord Marris called me to his office to inform me of this latest contretemps."

Lord Marris was undersecretary to Castlereagh, and Peter knew he was deeply involved in the nether world of espionage. "James must have indeed ruffled a few feathers if he managed to attract his grace's notice," he drawled, in amusement. "He would be delighted if he but knew. He has little use for the English nobility."

"Except you." Giles was watching him closely.

"Except me," Peter agreed softly, remembering that first awkward meeting some two years earlier. He'd finally tracked James down after learning of his half brother's existence quite by accident. In a fit of noblesse oblige he now blushed to remember he had offered to set James up in his own shipping business. James had thrown the offer back in his face and then knocked him flat. Not the most auspicious of beginnings, but despite that he and James had become fast friends, and he loved his audacious older brother without question.

"And you're certain he is making for England?"

Peter glanced up to find Giles watching him, and the frank skepticism he saw made him bristle with anger. "I would stake my life on it," he said, rising slowly to his feet. "He is as loyal a subject as either you or me, and I will not allow you to stain his honor by implying otherwise!"

"I wasn't implying anything," Giles returned, unaffected by Peter's obvious anger. "I was merely wondering when we might expect him."

Peter relaxed at once. "When did he jump ship?"

"A little under five weeks ago, according to the dispatches."

"Then we may expect him any day now," Peter said after some swift calculations. "I'll alert my staff to look for him."

"Do that," Giles nodded, still watching Peter, "and then kindly tell me what the devil you were talking about when we began this absurd conversation."

Peter stilled at once. "I'm not sure I take your meaning," he prevaricated, unwilling to expose Kate until it was absolutely necessary.

" 'What do you think we should do, the less said the better,' " Giles quoted, his eyes never leaving Peter's face. "At first I thought you were referring to that troublesome brother of yours, but now that I know such is not the case I am left to wonder who or possibly what you were talking about. Has it aught to do with Payton?"

"Not precisely," Peter answered, feeling like a schoolboy caught in some naughty act. "That is, he was there, but I would not say he is directly involved. Oh, by the by, he let it slip that he is so deep in the suds that he must make a marriage of convenience. I thought we might turn that knowledge to our own advantage; especially if we were to buy up all his notes."

"A commendable suggestion," Giles replied, "but that still doesn't answer my question. Who were you talking about?"

Peter glared at him. "Devil take it, Westley, I am your superior officer! 'Tis *you* who ought to be making explanations to *me!*"

"We are not in the army," he returned mildly, his eyes taking on a teasing sparkle. "But if it will please you, I can offer an explanation for any number of things. Where shall I start?"

Peter uttered an oath that only made Giles grin wider. He knew he was being petulant and wrong headed, and knew also that he had no option but to tell the viscount the truth. They were working together, after all, and if their circumstances were reversed, he would not thank the other man for keeping such vital information to himself. He gave a heavy sigh and crossed the room to stand before the window as Giles had done earlier.

"Mrs. Delecourt is back in London."

The teasing smile turned into a worried frown. "Are you certain?" he asked slowly. "You've seen her?"

"I was introduced to her last night at Lady Honoria's," Peter said, shooting Giles a speaking glance over his shoulder. "By Payton."

"They know each other?"

Peter shook his head, easily guessing the direction of Giles's thoughts. "They met for the first time last night, and according to the marquess, she took to him in strong dislike. The bastard had the unmitigated gall to kiss her hand."

"A hanging offense, I agree," Giles said, looking thoughtful. "I take it the lady recognized you?"

"I don't know," Peter admitted, recalling the dazed look on Kate's face. "She stared at me as if she did, but she didn't say anything. Thank God. I am hoping to avoid her as best I can in the meanwhile."

"A wise decision. But how can you say she did not recognize you? You were a guest in her home for over

197

two weeks."

"Yes, but I had a beard then," Peter reminded him, touching his clean shaven cheek lightly. "And I was posing as a smuggler. She was suspicious, I think, but just uncertain enough to hold her tongue."

"But what if you meet her again?" Giles asked, his mouth growing hard. "Payton is too important to let slip through our fingers because of a pretty widow. Steps may have to be taken."

Peter's blue eyes narrowed dangerously. He knew what those "steps" could include, and he was not about to let Kate be clapped into gaol as a threat to king and country. Although he and Giles were acting without official sanction they were still acting in the name of the crown, and in an emergency they could call upon the full weight of English law to back them.

"She is not to be touched," he said, his cold voice brooking no opposition. "The woman saved my life."

"And her loose tongue could take it, and James's life as well," Giles pointed out with merciless logic. "Have you thought of that?"

"Of course I have!" Peter exclaimed, bringing his fist down on the window's oak frame. "I've thought about nothing else since first seeing her, but damn it, I won't have her harmed! I'll think of something."

"What?"

"I don't know!" Peter made an effort to control his temper. "I'll think of something," he repeated, his shoulders squaring as he faced Giles. "Mrs. Delecourt won't endanger our mission," he said steadily. "I give you my word on it."

"All right," Giles inclined his head. "But in the meanwhile I shall have to make contingency plans. Nothing harmful," he added, holding up both hands as Peter took a menacing step forward, "just something that will safely remove her should she prove a threat."

Peter was quiet as he considered Giles's words. "I

could always tell her who I am," he said, naming one of the many possibilities that had occurred to him during the long night. "Who I *really* am, that is. Her husband died fighting for England, and I know she is loyal as well. She would never betray us."

"Too dangerous," Giles rejected the plan with a firm shake of his head. "You have been at this far longer than I, and you must know that once an agent has been exposed he is worse than useless. It would take only one word, one whisper, and you would be a dead man."

Peter could not in all honesty contradict Westley's dire prediction, but another thought did occur to him. If he could not go to Kate as he truly was, then he could always go to her as the man society took him for. A rake. A libertine. Even, he winced, as the dandy she had once named him. He would make himself so thoroughly repellent, that she would have no desire to claim even a passing acquaintance with him.

He thought of the damage this could well do to his already shaky reputation, and then he considered the alternative. He would do it, he decided stoically. He would risk his own good name rather than endanger hers. It was the least he could do to repay her for his life. At least, that was the explanation he gave himself.

Chapter Fourteen

Kate stumbled down to the breakfast table the following morning, bleary-eyed and out of sorts after an almost sleepless night. She collapsed onto the chair the footman held for her, gulping down her scalding coffee without so much as glancing in Portia's direction. Needless to say, the older woman was highly incensed by such poor manners.

"Well, you are certainly a sight to brighten an otherwise dreary morning!" she said, glaring at Kate down the length of her nose. "What on earth ails you? Not jug-bit, are you?"

"Of course not," Kate held out her cup for more coffee. "I am merely tired, that is all."

"Ha! You look just as my Albert used to look after a night at his club!" Portia was singularly unsympathetic. "I did not see you imbibe so much, but you must have drunk like a lord to end up like this. You'd best take care, my dear. We would not wish it bandied about that you are a tippler."

"I do not tipple!" Kate denied hotly. "I told you, I am tired. I scarcely slept a wink all night."

"Oh." Rather than being reassured Portia was more suspicious than ever. "Why couldn't you sleep?"

Kate groaned inelegantly and closed her eyes. Just once, she thought wistfully, she wished her aunt would go away and leave her to suffer in blissful silence. She pried open one eye and regarded the older woman with resignation. "I was thinking" she said bluntly refusing to elaborate.

"About Lord Tregarren?"

Kate's head came up in amazement. "How did you know?"

Portia lifted her cup to her lips for a dainty sip. "Stands to reason," she said in the smug tones that usually set Kate's teeth on edge. "You was struck dumb at the very sight of him, and last night coming home in the carriage he was all you would talk about."

"He is all you would talk about!" Kate protested, appalled by her aunt's convoluted, if accurate, thought processes. She had been brooding over the earl, but not for the romantic reasons her aunt suspected. She wasn't developing a tendre for the handsome rake, but she was considering killing him.

She'd spent an endless night tossing and turning, her mind doing a squirrel's race as she compared the image of the earl to her memory of Mickey. They were identical; she'd decided with growing indignation; two peas from the very same pod. She'd once heard that most people had a double; someone so like them in appearance they could be twins, but she refused to believe it. Take away Mickey's short beard, and you would have the earl of Tregarren; she was almost certain of it. The question was, what could she do about it?

"Well, given your extraordinary behavior last evening I do not see that I had another choice," Portia defended herself with a good-natured grumble. "Which reminds me; have you come any closer to discerning why his lordship seemed so familiar to you?"

"No," Kate was so accustomed to lying to her poor aunt she barely felt a twinge of guilt. "It was probably just one of those odd things one hears about."

"Probably," Portia agreed, nibbling on a piece of toast she had just dunked in her coffee. "I remember my mama once had a very similar experience. She was visiting a distant cousin, and she said that just as they were turning off the road she had a sudden vision of the house that was so vivid she knew how the rooms would be laid out. Then when they actually reached the house, it was just as it was in her vision. Fancy that!"

Kate mumbled something appropriate, although she was far from mollified. This was no flash of feyness, she thought, jabbing her eggs with her fork. This was a case of a woman duped, or at least, a woman who strongly suspected she had been duped. That was the worst part, not knowing. Either Mickey was Tregarren, or she was losing her mind. She did not know which possibility alarmed her more . . . another worrisome development.

She kept brooding on the matter; worrying over it as one would a sore tooth. Tregarren had been shot; Mickey had been shot. They both had the same black hair and vivid blue eyes. They moved alike, sounded alike. And then there was the fact that Mickey claimed to know Tregarren. He'd even sent him a letter when he had been injured. But if he was Tregarren, why would he send himself a letter? It made no sense. Unless . . .

". . . my cousin Elinore," Portia reminisced happily. "She always knew when someone was going to die. She'd be off buying crepe before the rest of us even knew the poor soul was sick!"

"Aunt, does Tregarren have a brother?" Kate interrupted, her green eyes gleaming with sudden excitement. "Someone near his age?"

"My heavens, are you still mooning over that man?" Portia shook her head with obvious disapproval. "Really, child, he is quite above your touch! Rich as a nabob *and* possessed of a title that is numbered as one of the oldest in England."

"Does he?"

"How would I —" Portia stopped abruptly. "Wait a moment; I do seem to recall hearing he was the only male. I remember because at the time he was racketing about like a madman, and there was a great deal of speculation as to who would inherit should he die without issue. There was only a very distant cousin, if I remember correctly."

"Does this cousin much resemble him?" Kate pressed, deciding that in a pinch, a cousin would do as well as a brother.

"Having never met the man I can not say," Portia responded with a thoughtful frown. "But I remember hearing he was well into his fifties without so much as a baby in the basket to inherit the title." She shook her head and gave a disapproving sigh. "The earl really ought to give more thought to the succession. But that's a rake for you; no thought for anything or anyone, save their own pleasure."

Kate fell silent once more. So much for that theory; she thought glumly. And it had seemed so promising too.

"Don't forget we are promised at Gussie's for tea," Portia said, ignoring Kate's brown study. "And afterwards we are to escort Louisa to Soames Gallery so that we might view the latest exhibition of watercolors."

Kate stirred reluctantly, and gave her aunt a vague smile. "I had no idea Louisa had an interest in the arts," she said, thrusting her confusing doubts to the back of her mind.

"She doesn't, but she does have an interest in young men, and there are always plenty of them to be found cluttering up galleries and exhibitions. They go there looking for young women," she added with a wink.

Kate smiled wanly. She supposed she might as well take Louisa about; her mood was already so thoroughly black she doubted she would suffer from the younger girl's dampening presence.

"The place is certain to be a madhouse," Portia added with mounting enthusiasm. "Lady Putnum assures me *everyone* will be there. It will be just the place for Louisa to be seen by all the right people."

"A horrifying possibility," Kate muttered beneath her breath.

"Katherine!"

"I'm sorry," Kate had the good manners to blush. "I was only funning. Escorting Louisa to the gallery sounds delightful; when shall we be leaving?"

Portia gave her a stern look. "Don't be sarcastic, missy. In any case, I should think you should be chomping at the bit to go."

"Why?" Kate helped herself to some of the kippers.

"Because Lord Tregarren is certain to be there."

Kate just managed not to drop her fork. She hadn't considered that possibility, she realized, a plan forming slowly in her mind. If she was convinced Tregarren was Mickey—and she wasn't certain that he was—then it was up to her to discover it. Even if she was never able to prove a thing at least she'd have the satisfaction of knowing the truth, and what better place to learn that truth than from the earl himself?

"I am surprised his lordship should bother," she said, striving for an indifferent tone. "Attending an art exhibition sounds rather tame for such a noted whipster and womanizer."

"Perhaps, but I'm willing to wager a monkey he will be there," Portia answered knowingly. "Ought to make for a rather interesting afternoon, don't you think?"

Kate gave a slow smile. "Aunt," she said, raising her fork to her lips, "you have no idea how interesting."

Gussie had recovered enough from her headache to join them for tea, although she declared a trip to the gallery to be above her meager powers. Miss Compton was once again pressed into service, a circumstance which delighted Kate.

"Do you like art, Miss Compton?" she asked as they

strolled through the stately gallery, brochures in hand.

"Very much so," Elizabeth admitted in her soft voice, her hazel eyes resting wistfully on a brooding landscape. "I particularly enjoy Turner's work. My papa used to have one of his canvases in our home, and I always loved it."

The admission intrigued Kate, confirming what she always suspected about the lovely companion; that she was a gentlewoman fallen on hard times. Turner's works were hardly inexpensive, and the fact her father could afford one was mute testimony to the girl's monied background. "You are lucky your father had such elegant tastes," she said, hoping to learn more. "I fear my father was addicted to hunting scenes; the gorier the better. I recall one showing hounds tearing a deer to pieces. It gave me nightmares when I was a child."

"I can imagine," Elizabeth smiled slightly. "I used to be terrified of a stuffed owl in papa's study. I made the footman cover it with a sheet whenever he was at sea."

"Your father was in the navy?" Kate noted her use of the past tense, and wondered if her father had died, leaving her penniless.

An odd, shuttered look stole over Elizabeth's face. "He was," she admitted softly. "But he is dead now." She bent her dark head over her brochure and pretended to study it. "Oh look, they have a copy of 'The Nightwatch,' do let us go and look at it. I have always longed to see it."

Kate took the hint and allowed herself to be distracted. She knew from painful experience that prodding questions were seldom welcome, and she respectfully held her tongue. Perhaps in time Miss Compton might choose to tell her more, but until that time she was resolved not to pressure her. The girl was entitled to her secrets, after all.

They continued about the gallery, admiring the many paintings and stopping to visit with friends. Louisa behaved far better than Kate had dared hope, only acting up a little when she demanded Miss Compton return to the coach to fetch her shawl.

"Here, Louisa you may have mine," Kate said, removing the rich paisley shawl from her own shoulders and draping it about Louisa's plump form. "There is no need to trouble Miss Compton."

"But she is my companion," Louisa protested, her bottom lip thrusting forward in a manner that was becoming depressingly familiar. "It should be no trouble at all for her to see to my wants!"

"That is so," Kate returned silkily, her green eyes taking on a hard cast that made the younger woman squirm. "And if you are so chilled that you must have your shawl and none other, then perhaps it might be better if we all returned to the carriage. I would not wish you to catch cold. The decision is yours."

Louisa's muddy brown eyes narrowed as she realized she had been bested. "I shall be all right," she said sullenly, her fingers closing around the shawl's delicate material. "Thank you."

"You are welcome," Kate replied, grateful the chit was not without some sensibility. Not that she intended to let the incident pass without comment, of course. At the earliest possibility she meant to read the little minx a lecture she would not soon forget.

"Thank you, Mrs. Delecourt," Elizabeth said as they continued their stroll. "But truly, I should not have minded fetching Louisa's shawl. I am a servant, after all."

"Nonsense, you are a lady, and—"

"No," Elizabeth interrupted with a shake of her head, "I am a servant. An upper one, perhaps, but a servant nonetheless. I am quite content with my position, and see no reason to wrap it in fine linen. Besides," an impish smile lit her features, "as I said, I have no objection to fetching for Louisa. It is a great deal easier than attempting to teach her Italian, I assure you."

Across the room Peter and Giles watched the unfolding drama with increasing grimness. "So much for your avoiding the lady," Giles sighed, shooting Peter a rueful look. "Don't suppose I could convince you to crawl out of here on your hands and knees before she sees you?"

"Do you really think it would do any good?" Peter responded, his eyes never leaving Kate's face. He'd seen the little exchange, and he was glad Kate had put the ill-mannered chit in her place.

"No, but one may always hope." Giles was also studying Kate. "Well, if you won't turn tail and run like the veriest coward, what would you suggest? I shall willingly follow your lead."

Peter was silent as he reviewed his options. Avoiding her was chancy at best, and after last night, he sincerely doubted his nerves would withstand the strain. That left him only one other choice.

"Well?" Giles was looking at him askance. "What is it to be? Glorious death or an ignominious retreat?"

"Ah, you Infantrymen," he answered, smiling as his plan formed quickly in his mind. "When will you learn that sometimes the only way to take the citadel is by a frontal assault? Have you any brandy with you?"

"Yes . . ." he could hear the confusion in Giles's voice.

"Good, give it to me, then listen carefully. This is what I want you to do."

"I can imagine the difficulties you must have encountered," Kate said in response to Elizabeth's droll comment; smiling to think of the sulky Louisa being put through her verbs. "I daresay she must have spent a great deal of the time sighing and rolling her eyes in disgust."

Elizabeth smiled, although she was far too polite to agree. Instead she said, "Languages are often difficult for most people. I am fortunate in that I seem to have an affinity for them. In addition to Italian I also speak French, German, and a spattering of Spanish."

"You speak French?" Kate was delighted, and instantly lapsed into the musical language, her accent flawless as she complimented Elizabeth on her intelligence.

"You are also a gifted linguist," Elizabeth returned in the same language. "One might take you for a Parisienne."

Before Kate could reply she heard her name called out, and turned to see an elegantly dressed dandy with waving blond hair making his way towards her. Her eyes widened in recognition.

"Lord Westley?" she asked hesitantly.

"Mrs. Delecourt!" he exclaimed, holding his hand out to her with a beaming smile. "How thoroughly splendid to see you once again! I might have known that as a patron of the arts you would be unable to resist the lure of such an exhibition; only look how you encouraged *my* humble efforts." He turned towards Elizabeth, who was regarding him with a mixture of disgust and delight evident in her hazel eyes.

"But who is the exquisite creature?" he demanded, lifting his quizzing glass to his eyes in an affected gesture. "I must meet her at once!"

Kate exchanged a speaking glance with Elizabeth and then performed the requested introductions, trying not to laugh at the expression on the other woman's face.

"I pray you will forgive me for gaping at you, Miss Compton," he said, raising her hand to his lips. "But as an artist I am naturally sensitive to works of great beauty. Such skin tones! Titian would have cut off his right arm to paint you."

"In which case he would have had a great deal of difficulty in painting anything," Elizabeth retorted, extracting her hand from his.

"Intelligence and beauty!" One hand was clutched

dramatically to his chest. "Truly this is my lucky day."

His antics drew several curious stares. When Louisa and Portia joined them, Giles was quick to include them in his performance.

"I might have guessed Miss Louisa was your granddaughter," he told Portia once the second round of introductions had been made. "I should have known those eyes anywhere; like brown diamonds. I wonder how one would go about creating such an effect," he tapped his quizzing glass against his cheek and then shrugged.

"Well, no matter, you ladies must walk with me and tell me which paintings you admire. Then I shall tell you why my work is infinitely better."

"That is very kind of you," Kate began, only to be interrupted by Louisa, who had crowded between her and the viscount.

"That sounds utterly delightful," she said, preening and batting her lashes in a display that made Kate squirm with shame.

While the other three ladies tagged behind them Giles escorted them through the various rooms, flirting and making disparaging remarks about every painting they viewed.

"Gainsborough," he sniffed, holding his glass up to study the canvas. "So awfully flat, do you not agree? His subjects all look as if they have just been fed a healthy dose of laudanum! The Dutch Masters now, they truly understood portraiture. Rembrandt, for example. . . ." And he rattled on until Kate's head began to throb.

They were making their way back to the main portion of the gallery when Kate was suddenly jostled from behind and would have fallen had Elizabeth not been quick to grab her. Once she was steady on her feet she whirled around to give whoever had bumped her a piece of her mind. The sight of Lord Tregarren, his black hair rumpled and his blue eyes glittering in his flushed face, withered the stinging retort she was about to utter. She could only stare at him; too shocked to speak.

"A thousand pardons, my lady," he said, sweeping his hat from his head and bowing so deeply that he listed dangerously forward. He straightened slowly, his foolish grin fading as he studied her face. "I know you," he said, enunciating his words with painful precision. "You're Payton's little widow, aren't you? Mrs. Dearborne, is it not?"

Good lord, he was drunk, she realized, her nose wrinkling at the strong smell of spirits wafting from him. It was barely three o'clock in the afternoon, and he was already intoxicated! In that moment she found herself praying that she was mistaken and that he was not Mickey. She couldn't bear it if her charming smuggler should turn out to be no better than a dissipated rake.

"Mrs. Delecourt," she corrected, her green eyes reflecting her displeasure. "And I am *not* Lord Payton's little widow!" Had he been sober she might have engaged him in conversation; perhaps even quizzed him as she had planned. But in his present state she wanted only to escape from him. She turned her slender shoulder on him and would have walked off without another word, had Portia not materialized beside her.

"Lord Tregarren, what a delightful surprise," she said, shooting Kate a triumphant look before offering the earl her hand. "This seems to be our day for meeting old acquaintances. I believe you already know Lord Westley? And this is my niece Miss Louisa Stone, and her companion, Miss Compton."

Peter doffed his hat clumsily; silently cursing the older woman for her interference. He was certain Kate had been about to walk away, and he wondered what the devil he should do now. Before he could decide on a specific course, Louisa stepped forward to favor him with a simpering smile.

"What do you think of the exhibition? Lord Westley has been kind enough to show us about."

Encroaching little mushroom, he thought, although he kept his face expressionless. "Art is not my strong suit, Miss Stone," he informed her coolly, his blue eyes moving over Giles in obvious derision. "I leave that to the ladies and . . . others."

Giles merely raised his dark blond eyebrows in astonishment. "In which case, my lord, one may only wonder how you came to stumble in here. Your club, I believe, is some three blocks to the north." He indicated the direction with a languid wave of his quizzing glass.

Even though he knew Giles was but playing a part Peter stiffened, and there was very little acting on his part as he replied, "You'd best have a care, Westley. Jackson's salon is also not so very far from here, and it would be my pleasure to escort you there if you but say another word."

Kate's brows descended as she took the earl's slurred warning. The bully was threatening to beat poor Lord Westley, and for no other reason than the fact the viscount had pointed out . . . and rightly so . . . that he was too drunk to know where he was! Well, her eyes took on a determined sparkle, she would just see about that.

"Come, my lord," she said, brushing aside her distaste as she gave him a strained smile. "You may not care overly much for art, but there is a picture I should much like to show you. This way," and she laid a commanding hand on his arm.

He gazed down at her; appalled by her request. Their objective had been to send her fleeing from him in disgust; not to seek his company actively.

"Now, if you please," she added, digging her nails none too gently into his arm.

Peter met her icy green gaze and noted with relief

that she was furious with him. Perhaps the situation might be salvaged after all, he thought with growing optimism. "I am, of course, yours to command, ma'am," he said in his most insolent manner. "By all means show me this infamous painting."

Kate gritted her teeth and towed him off, waiting until they were safely out of ear shot before lighting into him. "Well, I hope you are proud of yourself, my lord," she began, forgetting her plans to quiz him as she sent him a cutting glare from the corners of her eyes. "That was without doubt one of the poorest shows of manners I have seen in many a day! How dare you insult poor Lord Westley?"

Her scolding tones pleased Peter, although he took pains to appear distinguished. "By the same way you would presume to ring a peal over my head, Mrs. Delecourt," he snapped, his dark eyebrows descending in an unpleasant scowl. "You're neither my mother nor my wife, and I'll be damned if I'll allow you to dictate my behavior!"

It was several seconds before Kate could speak. On the one hand she could concede his point; if he wasn't Mickey then that meant they had met for the first time yesterday, and she would be greatly above herself to presume correcting him. But on the other hand, she told herself, if he was going to go about picking fights in public then he would have to be prepared to deal with the consequences of his brutish actions. She dropped her hand from his arm and whirled around to face him.

"One would think you have had enough of . . . curricle accidents, Lord Tregarren," she said mockingly. "Surely you have more regard for your family's name than to risk it so foolishly?"

She thought he was Lord Tregarren, Peter realized, all but swamped with relief. Perhaps he'd only imagined that flash of recognition in her emerald eyes, he thought, studying her lovely face through half-lowered eyes.

"And what would you know of my 'accident,' Mrs. Delecourt?" he drawled, meeting her gaze challengingly. "Rumors and innuendoes; that is all."

"I know you were injured in a duel," she said, refusing to be intimidated.

"Do you?" he stepped closer.

"Y–yes," despite her resolve her voice trembled. Standing this close to him she was more struck than ever by his resemblance to Mickey. When he had turned on her angrily he looked as Mickey had looked the day he'd learned of her meeting with Captain O'Rourake.

"How?" He caught a strand of hair that had escaped from beneath her bonnet; winding the golden curl about his finger.

"I–I just do," Kate's courage began deserting her as her confusion mounted. Her mind was a whirlwind, tearing her in a dozen different directions at once. He was Mickey; he wasn't Mickey; not knowing was absolutely maddening. There *had* to be some way she could be certain!

Peter trembled as he touched her soft skin, aware he was treading a very fine line between muddying his already sullied reputation and ruining her own. Several people were already watching them with avid interest. The longer he remained in her company, the more the speculation would grow. He closed his eyes briefly, hating himself for what he was about to do. When he opened them they were filled with bleak resolve.

"Such a prim creature you are, Mrs. Delecourt," he said, the brandy on his breath evident as he bent closer. "You say you aren't Payton's widow, but I wonder if you would be mine? You are very lovely, and—" He got no further as her hand lashed out across his face.

213

"How dare you!" she cried softly, beyond caring if she was creating a scene. "If I were a man I should call you out!"

Peter smiled coolly, reaching up to touch his face. "Were you a man, my sweet, I should not have made the offer."

"Oh!" For a moment Kate was speechless with fury. How could she ever have mistaken this beast for Mickey? Her mysterious smuggler might have been many things, but he was first and foremost a gentleman, and she knew he would never have insulted her so publicly! She drew herself up, her cheeks flushing with the force of her anger.

"I have changed my mind, m'lord," she said in frosty accents. "I don't think I shall waste my time showing you the painting. I doubt you have either the wit or the decency to appreciate it." And with that she turned and stalked away, vowing it would be a very cold day in Hades before she gave the drunken lout so much as a civil nod.

Peter watched her walk away, his heart heavy. He had achieved his goal, but the cost was the respect of the woman he admired above all others. For the first time since entering his King's employ, he found himself wondering if the ends did indeed justify the means.

Chapter Fifteen

Peter spent the following morning locked in his study; attending to his correspondence. During the two months he'd spent incognito he'd left the day-to-day running of his estates to his manager, and he was only now assuming the reins. Much had happened during his absence, and he was frowning over the report of a fire in the cottage of one of his tenants when a small frisson of alarm warned him he was no longer alone. He reached for the pistol he kept tucked in his pocket and whirled around in his chair; leveling his pistol at the door that led out onto the balcony.

"Step forward and identify yourself or I will fire," he ordered, cocking the pistol.

"A fine way you have of greeting your brother," a black haired man drawled, hands held to shoulder height as he stepped out from the shadows. "And after all I've endured to get here."

"James?" Peter lowered the pistol, staring at the man in disbelief. "Is that you?"

"Well, it surely isn't your poor, mad King," James responded, his dark green eyes sparkling with mischief as he advanced towards Peter. "Now would you kindly lower your cannon? I've developed a healthy respect for such weapons of late."

"James, it is you!" Peter returned the pistol to his pocket before rising from his chair to embrace his brother. "I'd all but given you up for dead!"

"Believe me, when I woke up in the smelly hold of that ship, I thought I was dead," James answered, returning Peter's embrace with a resounding laugh. "And a more black and dreadful place I hope never to be seeing."

"What happened?" Peter asked, his hands resting on James's shoulders as he searched his brother's face for any sign of injury. "Were you kidnapped?"

"Aye," James responded moving to sit on the chair facing Peter's desk. "There's the word for it. One moment I was sitting in the Queen of Hearts in Folkestone enjoying a pleasant talk with an old friend, and the next thing I know I'm on a packet ship bound for the Indies." His lips turned up in a mocking smile before he added, "You've no idea how relieved I was to learn I'd merely been kidnapped. For a moment I greatly feared his majesty's men had gotten their bloody hands on me."

Peter smiled slightly. "And the old friend?"

"Dead," James shrugged, the laughter dying in his eyes. "That's why I was so late in coming to London. I thought to pay a visit to my old mates, and learned he'd been found in the quay the morning after I was taken." He drew a finger across his throat.

Peter cursed beneath his breath. "Do you think Payton is involved?"

"Up to his pink and white elbows," James said bluntly, his jaw hardening in a manner that was identical to Peter's. " 'Twas him who gave the order for Hill's murder . . . and my own as well. It seems his lordship has no liking for Irish bastards who asked too many questions about his precious ships."

"You were to have been killed?"

"Aye. But according to another old friend Hill couldn't bring himself to cutting my throat and tossing me in the bay, so he settled for drugging me and shipping me off to Jamaica. Poor sot; he probably never knew what hit him."

Peter was silent as he considered what his brother had just told him. "Have you any proof it was Payton who gave the order?"

"Not the kind of proof that would hold up in a court where the judge and all the jurors have 'Lord' in front of their names," James replied with a bitter laugh. "My friends are prostitutes and smugglers; not the type your world gives a tinker's damn about. We'd be laughed out of court."

Peter would have liked to deny James's charge, but he could not. He was painfully aware of Payton's influence and knew his brother was all too correct. "But you have proof?" he pressed.

James's eyes regained their sparkle. "I have proof," he said, extracting a folded piece of paper from his pocket and handing it to Peter.

"What's this?"

"The manifest for the marquess's next run," James informed him with a grin. "It was what you might call borrowed from his ship's captain when the lad wasn't looking."

"You picked his pocket?" Peter was amused.

"Guilty as charged, your lordship. Though it really wasn't much of a challenge; him not wearing them at the time and all."

"You gulled him while he was in a brothel?"

James's eyes widened in mock dismay. "Faith! And how would a fine dandy like yourself know such a word?"

Dandy. Peter winced at the memory the word invoked. "You would be amazed," he said instead, forcing his attention back to the list in his hand. "Won't the captain miss this when he is finished taking his pleasure?"

"Do you take me for a Johnny Raw? I left a very fine copy in its place. Not even his lordship would be able to tell the difference at first glance."

Peter froze as the implication of James words hit

him. He raised his eyes to meet James's gaze. "Then this list is in Payton's own hand?" he asked in disbelief.

"That it is," James informed him with a mocking grin. "Now mind you note the third item on the second page. I'm sure you will agree it will be of some interest to your friends in Whitehall."

Peter flipped the page over, his eyes moving to the item James indicated. The items he saw set down in the flowery script he recognized as Payton's own made him tense with fury.

"The bastard! The blackhearted bastard! He's selling the French our rifles!"

"I thought that would prove a fine coffin nail," James folded his arms across his chest and regarded Peter coolly. "But you'll be needing others . . . won't you?"

Peter glanced up, his blue eyes meeting James's. "We'll need others," he confirmed heavily, "but this at least will give us leverage to force the Home Office into reopening the investigation against Payton."

James's eyebrows rose in surprise. "The investigation?" he repeated. "Do you mean to say there is one already afoot? How?"

"Do you really think I would do nothing when you disappeared?" Some of the cold anger Peter had felt when he'd been unable to find a trace of James was evident in his deep voice.

"Well, in light of what I had told you, I suppose you couldn't sit idly back and twiddle your thumbs, but—"

"The information you brought me concerning Payton had little to do with my reasons for wanting to find you!" Peter snapped, hurt by James's continued rejection of him. "How many times must I tell you that you are my brother? There is nothing I would not have done in order to find you!"

James did not speak at first, an uncomfortable lump forming in his throat. In those first few minutes after awakening in the stinking hold of that ship he had thought himself a dead man, and he realized his one regret was not making a better peace with the rich and powerful man who had claimed him as brother. He'd even prayed to God and whatever saints he could think of that he be granted a second chance, and now he had been handed that chance. He would not fail.

"As I would move earth and heaven to find you" he said, his voice not quite steady. "But tell me more of this investigation of yours. What were you able to learn?"

"Not as much as I would like," Peter was touched by James's words; knowing how hard it must have been for his roguish brother to admit such a thing. He allowed himself the luxury of savoring the gruff confession for a brief moment, and then turned his attention to the more urgent matter of Payton.

"A great deal has happened since you set sail for the warmer climes," he said, and then proceeded to tell James all that had transpired in the last three and a half months.

Kate spent the days following the disastrous visit to the gallery brooding over Lord Tregarren's infamous behavior. The more she considered the matter the more confused she became, until she finally reached the conclusion that the earl couldn't possibly be Mickey. Granted they were much alike in appearance — even to the way they arched their eyebrows — but in the end it was the differences in their characters which decided her. No two men could have been more dissimilar in their behavior.

Mickey was a charming if somewhat, exasperating rogue, given to spinning tales and skipping around the truth with the grace of an opera dancer. Lord Tregarren on the other hand was a top-lofty, ill-mannered lecher, whose apparent fondness for the bottle was only surpassed by his predilection for bullying and violence. He might bear the title, she decided with a grim smile, but it was Mickey who was the *real* gentleman. Only look at the way he'd been prepared to surrender to the soldiers rather than exposing her to any danger; she much doubted a drunken sot like Tregarren would have behaved half so magnaminously.

Another thing which ultimately convinced her was Tregarren's association with Lord Payton. Had Mickey been Tregarren surely he would have sought out the marquess's assistance, rather than hiding out in her modest country home. And, of course, there was the gossip that placed the scandalous earl at his own estate, and in the company of three lightskirts no less. No, Mickey was *not* Tregarren, and she resolved to set both men firmly out of her mind.

Three days later she was in her study going over the accounts when Portia burst in, dramatically waving a piece of paper. "We have done it, my dear!" she crowed, thrusting the paper under Kate's nose. "Do you see this?"

"I should have to be blind not to," Kate grumbled, laying down the book she had been reading. "What is it?"

"It was in this morning's gazette" Portia said, taking the seat facing Kate. "Well? What are you waiting for? Read it!"

Kate bit back a sigh and accepted the article her aunt had apparently clipped out.

An otherwise uneventful exhibition was enlivened by the appearance of Lord T, whose antics are more than living up to those of his late parent, she began, her wheatcolored eyebrows meeting in a frown at the florid prose. *Not content with oversetting the august company with public boastings of his pugilistic prowess, our racketing lord sought out the company of Mrs. D., a lovely widow newly arrived in our city for the season, and proceeded to so enrage the lady that she saw fit to plant the noted sportsman a facer. Despite this grievous insult to his dignity his lordship has yet to name his seconds, and he soon departed from the gathering. Heigh-ho, 'tis just as well; another curricle accident would be certain to have a dampening effect upon the Season.*

The article fluttered from her fingertips. "Oh, my God!"

"Why are you looking like that?" Portia demanded, clearly puzzled. "Do you not know what this means?"

"Yes!" Kate covered her face with her hands, her cheeks heating with shame. "It means everyone in London is laughing at me! Oh, I vow I shall kill that wretched man!"

"Whyever for? Really, Kate, how can you be such a gudgeon?" Portia was thoroughly disgusted. "Do you not know that it is an honor to have your name mentioned in the journals?"

Kate dropped her hands and sent her aunt a knowing scowl. "An *honor?*" she repeated sarcastically.

"Well," Portia hunched her shoulders, "perhaps 'honor' is doing it too brown," she admitted. "But it's not the Cheltenham Tragedy you would make of it! You must know they wouldn't have mentioned the incident at all if they didn't consider you important."

"It is Lord Tregarren who is important, I am merely a lovely widow newly arrived in the city," Kate retorted, picking up the article and rereading it. "Beastly things! I suppose I had ought to be grateful that they didn't put down what he said, word for word!"

"Actually, I should like to know what was said, word for word," Portia responded, cocking her head to one side as she studied her niece. "You never have told me."

Kate's blush grew more pronounced. "Nor shall I," she said, handing the piece of paper back to her aunt. "It was bad enough hearing it the first time; I have no wish to repeat it."

"Really?" Portia's eyes lit up. "It must have been delightfully scandalous, then. Did he offer you *carte blanche?*"

221

"Aunt!"

"Oh, very well," Portia muttered with an aggrieved air. "But I take leave to tell you that you are being monstrously unfair! You must know my friends are dying to learn what really transpired between the two of you."

"Then they shall simply have to expire" Kate retorted, thinking the world could well do without one or more of the malicious gossips who surrounded Portia. "I have told you, the matter is between Lord Tregarren and me."

"If you say so," Portia returned the article to her pocket. "But don't expect the rest of society to honor your privacy as I have. There will be questions a'plenty tonight, and you'd best be prepared to answer them a little more forthrightly if you do not want the world to think the worst of you."

"Tonight?"

"You can not possibly have forgotten that tonight is the night Louisa is to make her bows at Almack's? Katherine!"

"Of course I haven't forgotten" Kate was quick to reassure her aunt, although in truth, the matter had slipped her mind. "I simply didn't think it would signify. Besides," she added when it looked as if Portia would protest, "tonight is Louisa's night, and I shall be keeping very much to the background as befits a chaperone."

"Not too far in the background, mind," Portia cautioned, abandoning one attack in favor of another. "You'll never land yourself another husband by hiding behind the palms, you know."

"Yes, Aunt Portia," Kate replied quietly, berating herself yet again for her impetuous demand for help.

"What gown will you be wearing tonight?" Portia asked curiously. "Not the black, I trust."

Kate gave an indifferent shrug. "I thought to wear the new rose sarsanet the countess sent me."

"The one with the marmaluke sleeves?"

"Yes."

"Too fussy," Portia shook her head decisively. "It would do well enough for a private ball, I suppose, but for Almack's you'll be wanting something with a trifle more dash." She laid a finger on her lips and looked thoughtful; mentally picking her way through her niece's wardrobe.

"I have it!" she cried, flashing Kate a bright smile. "That green silk gown you wore one of our last evenings at home! You remember it, my dear, you wore it with the emeralds Charles gave you."

Kate gave a guilty start, remembering what had happened the last time she'd worn that particular ensemble. The pretty gown was intimately linked to her memories of Mickey, and she knew she'd never be able to wear it without remembering those heated minutes in his arms. She saw Portia was awaiting her answer and managed a credible laugh.

"Really, Aunt, a country gown at Almack's?" she drawled, looking amused. "You can not be serious! Why, the Patronesses would have us drummed out in a heartbeat if they were to suspect us of such a thing! And then where would poor Louisa be, hmm?"

Portia crossed her arms and gave her a dour look. "Pray, do not be impertinent miss," she said coolly. "That is a perfectly lovely gown, and if you wear it with your emeralds no one will ever be the wiser."

"But—"

"There, that is decided," Portia ignored Kate's weak protest and moved on to a new topic. "Now as for your hair, you shall wear it up, with an aigrette of brilliants and feathers just above your ear. All the crack; according to *La Belle Assemblie*."

Kate opened her mouth to protest Portia's high-handed tactics when something stopped her. Perhaps she should wear the gown, she thought, her green eyes growing troubled. She could never hope to exorcise Mickey from her mind as long as she persisted in locking his memory away in the deepest recesses of her heart. As she had done with Charles, her only hope of recovering her equilibrium was to face and master those memories. Only look at the muddle she had already made of things; seeing him through shop windows, and mistaking some drunken oaf for him merely because they had the same coloring.

"Very well, Aunt Portia," she said, giving her aunt a brilliant smile. "The green silk it shall be, and the coiffure you have described sounds delightful. I shall be the belle of the ball!"

"Mayhap not the belle," Portia corrected, wondering what sort of rig Katherine was running. "But I daresay you shall give a good accounting of yourself. Now, enough of this tiresome talk! Let us go in for some tea. We are dining with Gussie tonight, and you know what a miserly table she sets. You'll have to stuff yourself with macaroons if you don't wish to swoon halfway through the evening!"

Peter was dressing for dinner before he finally saw the article in the journals and his colorful oaths brought James dashing into his dressing room.

"Shame on you for your wicked tongue" he scolded playfully, bending to pick the paper up from the floor. "I'll be in church the rest of the evening saying prayers for you. Whatever could you have read to put you in such a temper?"

"That," Peter indicated the offending piece with a fierce jab of his finger. "How dare they print such tripe! I shall bring action against them; see if I do not!"

"For what?" James read the paragraph quickly. "From what you've told me 'tis a truthful enough accounting of what happened."

"But I ruined myself in her eyes in order to spare her this!" Peter cried, feeling particularly ill-used by events. "Damn it, this wasn't supposed to happen!"

James was quiet a long moment, sensing the anguish behind Peter's anger. "What will you do?" he asked, laying a sympathetic hand on his brother's shoulder.

Peter sighed heavily; knowing there was only one honorable thing he could do. "I shall apologize," he said, grateful for James's understanding. "I will grovel at her feet if I need to."

James smiled to think of his proud brother cast so low. "I'm certain there will be no need for such theatrics," he said fondly. "From what you've told me of the lady she's a good enough sort; explain to her that you were too deep in your cups to know what you were about and throw yourself on her tender mercies. Take it from me, there's nothing the ladies like more than reforming a rake; or trying to reform him," he added with a wink.

Peter smiled slightly. "I only wish I could tell her the truth," he said, turning back to the mirror. "She deserves that."

"Aye, that she does," James agreed, sending a silent prayer heavenward that Mrs. Delecourt had acted as she did.

When Peter had first told him his incredible tale he'd been too stunned to think. At first the notion of his wealthy brother passing himself off as an Irish smuggler was highly diverting, but the thought of him being betrayed into enemy hands was less amusing. If it cost him his life he would learn who had sold Peter to the French, and then he would make them pay. He'd already begun making inquiries, and he was fairly certain the trail would eventually lead him to Payton.

"Will your lady be at this fine party you're going to?" he asked, watching as Peter tied his cravat in an intricate knot.

"No, but she will doubtlessly be at Almack's; I will go there first," he said, straightening his shoulders to check the cut of his jacket. Not that he was overly critical of his appearance, but rather because he wanted to make sure the pistol he was carrying in his waistband didn't show. "And how will you be spending your evening?" he queried, casting James a teasing grin in the mirror. "Or do I need to ask?"

James was quick to assume an injured air. "But I've just told you how I mean to spend my nights brother mine; on my hands and knees praying for the deliverance of your Anglican soul."

A bawdy jest occurred to Peter, and when he shared it with James his brother roared with laughter. "Aye, but that will come later; after church. I'd not be wanting to shock the good priest with too much; mind. I'll sin tonight, and confess tomorrow."

"An interesting practice" Peter agreed, chuckling. "Just watch your back while you're out sinning. Payton may have spies watching me, and I don't want him catching you by mistake."

"I'll be as slippery as a Billingsgate eel," James assured him. "Mind you're equally as careful. Don't let the bastard too close to you; lest he bite you like the poisonous snake that he is."

The analogy brought a cold gleam to Peter's eyes. "Ah, but that is the best way to catch an asp," he said softly. "You hold it close, and then you cut off its head."

Almack's was much as Kate envisioned it; hot, overcrowded, and far too pretentious. She found the Patronesses who struck such terror in the hearts of the *ton* be little more than fat, disagreeable old tabbies, though none of these thoughts were evident in the pleasant smile she gave them upon introduction.

When they pronounced themselves "delighted" with her and Louisa, she excused herself and hurried to the corner to partake of the watery orgeat and biscuits for which the establishment was so infamously known. But if she thought she would find any peace in her sanctuary her hopes were quickly dashed by the group of gentlemen who swarmed to her side; surrounding her like a pack of hounds closing in upon the fox.

"Such a delight to meet you, my dear," one ancient roue remarked, eyeing her through his quizzing glass as if she was some exotic animal strayed from the Royal Menagerie. "News of your virtue and beauty are on every set of lips, and I must say that I am relieved to find that at least part of what they say appears to be so," and he pursed his painted lips in a self- satisfied smirk.

"Indeed, Lord Battenham," Kate shot back, her innate sense of pride bringing her chin up with regal hauteur. "And pray what part might that be?"

"Oh, don't mind old Batty," a young man with curly black hair à la Byron laughed, "his gout is playing him up. I, for one, am dashed pleased to meet the lady who placed Tregarren a facer! Daresay the villain deserved it, eh?"

"Thank you, Sir Geoffrey," Kate inclined her head at the languid dandy. He seemed the less objectionable of the lot, and she favored him with a cool smile.

"I say, what did the devil do, ma'am?" another asked, crowding closer. "Must have been dashed awful."

"Oh, it was" Kate turned her green eyes on him, her patience growing decidedly thin. She'd had quite enough of her repellent admirers, and she was determined to send them scurrying after other prey.

"What was it?" Another man inched closer.

"He was annoying me" Kate announced loudly, giving each man in his turn a warning glance. "And I can not bear to be annoyed."

"Neatly done, madam," Sir Geoffrey laughed as the other men scattered like leaves in a whirlwind. "You have them routed and in full flight!"

"Not all of them, I see" she remarked, pleased enough by her easy success to grant him clemency. "You are braver than the rest of them, it would seem."

"Or a trifle more curious" Sir Geoffrey shrugged. "No, don't poker up on me," he warned, when she stiffened warily. "I was only funning. It is the way of our world, you see. We know how foolish we really are, and so we simply laugh at ourselves before anyone else can get the chance."

"I suppose I never thought of it in quite that light," Kate replied, much struck by his words. "And what of you, sir? Do you also laugh at yourself before anyone else?"

"Incessantly" he tucked her hand in the crook of his arm and began leading her about the room. "When one is cursed with the Christian name of Ableheart, one learns early to develop a self-deprecatory wit."

"Good heavens, however did you come to be given such an interesting name?" Kate queried, keeping a sharp eye on Louisa. She was pleased to see the girl had a partner for her first dance, and that Portia and Gussie were also watching her. She had a feeling it would take all three of them to prevent her from behaving too disgracefully.

"A rich old uncle whom my dear mother hoped to endear by naming her second born after him," he said with a light laugh. "I must say I am pleased to say it worked, otherwise I would have been most hipped."

Kate joined in his laughter, pleased the evening was going so well; despite her earlier trepidations. She and Sir Geoffrey continued their stroll and he pointed out various prominent people; adding malicious asides about each one.

"Now, take old Parsey there," he said, indicating a paunchy man in a black satin jacket. "The fellow's reputation is almost as black as Tregarren's, and he hasn't even his lordship's kind heart to fall back upon."

"I did not know that his lordship was possessed of a heart; kind or otherwise," Kate sniffed, her light spirits vanishing at the mention of the man she now considered her nemesis.

"Oh, indeed, although 'tis not so widely known, I'll grant you," Sir Geoffrey replied with another laugh.

"And given the vast numbers of . . . er . . . by-blows in our world, 'twas rare generous of the earl to acknowledge him as he did; to say nothing of going out of his way to actually meet the fellow."

"Lord Tregarren has an illegitimate son?" Kate asked, not the least bit shocked by the news, although she was somewhat surprised that he should trouble to claim the child.

"That he may" Sir Geoffrey shrugged, "but as it happens I was referring to a brother."

Kate stopped abruptly, her earlier speculations returning with a vengeance. "A-a brother?"

"An older brother, and one so like him in appearance they could easily be mistaken for each other. Nor is that the half of it."

"What else?" That she hadn't yet swooned was a testament to her stamina, but Kate was determined to hear him out.

"Well," Sir Geoffrey leaned forward in a confiding manner, "it is said the bloke is Irish, and worse still, a smuggler! Imagine! The high and mighty Tregarren the brother of a common smuggler. Is it not delightful?"

Chapter Sixteen

"His—his brother is a smuggler?" Kate stammered, her heart pounding so hard she was certain it would burst from her chest. In a distant part of her mind she could hear the melodic tinkling of the pianoforte, the low murmur of conversation, and the soft rustling of silk as well-dressed ladies brushed past them. She was aware of all of this, but none of it made any impact on her dazed senses.

Sir Geoffrey was chuckling at her question. "Well, to give the devil his due, I believe he calls himself an 'importer,' although I greatly doubt much of his merchandise ever sees a Custom House."

Yes, that sounds like something Mickey would say, she thought remembering his improbable tale of shooting fish. "How shocking," she murmured, unfurling her fan to hide her shock. "And does this rogue have a name?"

"Something Irish," Sir Geoffrey responded negligently. "As I say, 'tis not something that is widely known. In fact, I should venture to say that I am one of the few in Society who is even aware of the fellow's existence."

"How did you come to learn of it?" she asked, hoping her questions would be taken as idle curiosity.

"Actually, my father and his were classmates at Oxford," he explained sounding rather pleased with the fact. "When the poor chit showed up at their lodgings asking for money it was my pater who gave her the passage home. Lord Quentin seemed singularly disinclined to help."

"Lord *Quentin?*"

Sir Geoffrey nodded. "A family name. He wasn't the earl then, of course, but rather Viscount Quentin; hence the name. Well, you know how it is with these old families; such a confusing jumble of names and titles it quite makes one dizzy! Really, I think the Frenchies have the right of it. Simply do away with all these tiresome titles and call everyone 'Citizen.' Much easier all around, do you not agree?"

"Indeed I do, *Citizen* Geoffrey," she replied, knowing he was expecting some clever comeback. "Although I doubt you should find many here who would share such republican sentiments. In fact, I should think they would disagree most vociferously."

"Too true," he said, looking much taken with the idea. "But at least it would enliven the evening; if only for a little while. I find these little soirees are so depressingly boring. Oh look, speaking of boring there is Lady Jersey. Really, you would not believe who she has taken as her latest lover . . ." He rattled on in his languid fashion until Kate was ready to scream.

The clock on the grand staircase was chiming eleven o'clock as Peter strode into the Assembly Room. He was met near the door by Lady Hertford who fixed him with a frowning look. "Cutting it rather close, aren't you?" she asked in her sharp manner.

"The clock may have tolled, but I've yet to hear the cock's crow," he replied with a sardonic smile; little impressed with her attempts to censure him.

She continued glaring at him for several seconds and then gave a reluctant bark of laughter. "Insolent puppy," she said, holding out a hand for him to kiss. "Don't know why we put up with you. Only promise me you

231

aren't here to make some new scandal with your virtuous widow! Her formidable aunt is also here, and I've no desire to pull caps with that old she-cat."

"I shall be on my best behavior," he promised his eyes already searching the room for some sign of Kate. "Speaking of Mrs. Delecourt, do you know where she might be? There is something I should like to say to her."

Lady Hertford gave him another sharp look and then nodded. "Come to apologize have you? Good. I have always said you have too much of your mother in you to be totally given over to your father's failings. You will find Mrs. Delecourt in the other room. The last I saw of her she was fending off a pack of notorious rakes and rattles."

This news so alarmed Peter that he bid her a hasty good-bye and then set out to rescue his lady love. Damn it, he cursed softly, if he learned anyone had dared insult Kate he would put a bullet through their chest!

His temper was little improved to see her strolling about the room with Sir Geoffrey Horton. Not that he bore the preening dandy any ill will—they were boyhood chums, in fact—but he had a sudden and violent disinclination to see Kate with any man. He noted she was wearing the green dress and emeralds she had worn to his room, and it was all he could do not to storm across the room and pull her away from Horton. But he grimly reminded himself that he was here to rectify an old scandal; not start a new one. He would simply bide his time and wait until she was alone before approaching her. He only hoped she would hear him out before slapping him.

It took some doing, but Kate was finally able to free herself of Sir Geoffrey. She found his cutting wit palled on prolonged contact, and in any case, she wanted to be alone so that she could consider the implications of what she had learned. Mickey was the earl's illegitimate brother! It all fit together so perfectly; like the pieces of an intricate puzzle. Mickey's nationality, his occupation, even his name; it all matched with what Sir Geoffrey had told her. No wonder Mickey had written him after his accident! Who else should he turn to for help but his own brother?

Close upon the heels of that realization came another. If Mickey knew how to contact Tregarren then it logically followed that Tregarren would know how to contact Mickey. But as quickly as the thought arose she banished it from her mind.

What did she care if Tregarren could contact Mickey? He had been but a guest in her home; nothing more. The only reason he'd been on her mind so much of late was because his uncanny resemblance to the earl had been driving her mad. Now that she'd solved that mystery, she could forget all about the wretch.

"Mrs. Delecourt?" A familiar voice shattered her reveries and she whirled around to find the object of her musings standing beside her, his blue eyes wary as she studied her. "I hope I am not disturbing you?"

"Lord Tregarren." Kate stared at him as she struggled for composure. The memory of their last encounter lay between them, and an awkward silence ensued. Much as it would have pleased her to give him the cut direct, she was too aware of the scandal it would cause. But as it was . . . she pinned a tentative smile to her lips.

"You aren't disturbing me, my lord," she said in a painfully polite voice. "I was simply woolgathering; that is all."

"Oh?" Peter was relieved, if slightly wary of her civil manner. He knew Kate to have the devil's own pride and more than a modicum of his temper as well, and he wasn't certain if he trusted that shy smile of hers. "And pray, what were you thinking about?"

"Oh, nothing of import," Kate was annoyed to find she was blushing. He really was extremely handsome, she decided, striving for impartiality. In his cutaway jacket of black velvet and his intricately tied stock he looked every inch the noble lord, and so very like Mickey in appearance she could almost believe it was he who was standing before her. No wonder she had been so confused; but for the beard they would have been indistinguishable!

While she was speaking Peter had been assessing their position. They were standing in a small alcove off to one side, and a pair of ubiquitous potted palms hid them from prying eyes. He knew he would never get a better chance than now, and drew a deep breath.

"I have also been thinking," he said without preamble, "and I should like very much to beg your pardon for my churlish behavior. I know it is asking a great deal, but I would be forever grateful if you could find it in your heart to forgive me."

Kate was stunned as much by his unexpected apology as by the expression on his face. His cheeks and the tips of his ears were stained a dull red, and yet despite his obvious discomfort he met her gaze resolutely rather than shying away from what he had done. Perhaps there was a bit of Mickey in him after all, she mused, her lips curling in a gentle smile.

"Certainly I forgive you, my lord," she said softly. "After such a charming apology, how could I do otherwise?"

"I meant every word of it," he continued, determined to make a clean breast of it. "I can not tell you how much I regret what I said, and I want you to know that you can not despise me any more than I already despise myself."

"I don't despise you," she said, and was surprised to find it was so. It was hard to despise any man who

234

owned up to his mistakes without flinching or making excuses. He reminded her of Mickey on the day the soldiers came and searched her house, and the memory dissolved the last traces of resentment. She held out her hand to him in a gesture of friendship.

"Apology accepted, my lord," she said, her lips lifting in a genuine smile. "Now let us say no more of the matter; it is over and done with as far as I am concerned."

Peter accepted her hand, pressing it between his warm palms. "Thank you," he said, his blue eyes meeting hers as he carried her hand to his lips. "You are being far too kind. I thought I deserved to be horsewhipped."

The touch of his mouth on her hand was having a most disquieting effect upon Kate, and she quickly withdrew it. To cover her sudden confusion she gave a light laugh. "Horsewhip? Well, perhaps that is a *trifle* too severe" she said, not quite meeting his eyes. "Although I must admit I shouldn't have objected if someone had taken you up on your odious boasting."

"Someone did," he reminded her, touching his cheek as if in memory of a kiss. "And allow me to complement you on your science; you pack a devil of a punch."

She flushed at his teasing words; deciding she preferred it when he was being rude. In this mood he reminded her far too much of Mickey.

"I've never struck another person before," she said, pushing the troubling sensation aside. "I–I didn't hurt you, did I?"

"Not at all. But even if you had, I should be the last to admit such a thing. I have a reputation to think of, you know."

The light remark almost made her gasp, it was so close to the type of thing Mickey might have said. To hide her confusion she tilted her head to one side and smiled sweetly. "And which reputation might that be, my lord? Your reputation as a Corinthian, or your reputation as a rake?"

Her playful remark surprised Peter, but before he could think of an appropriate response the faint strains of the waltz caught his ears. Without pausing to weigh the consequences of his actions he took her hand in his and said, "Before I answer, do you think I might persuade you to dance with me?"

At first Kate was tempted to demur, but in the next moment she was scolding herself for her lack of spirit. It was only one dance, after all. What possible harm could it do?

"I should be delighted, my lord," she replied, inclining her head with a gracious smile.

They made their way back to the main room, where a small quartet was supplying the indifferent music. Ignoring the pointed stares of the other guests he caught her in his arms, and was soon whirling her about the floor. For a moment they danced in silence, each lost in their own private musings, but at last Peter spoke.

"You're a most accomplished dancer, Mrs. Delecourt," he said, easily matching his step to hers. "How comes it we have never met? Is this your first visit to the city?"

His question brought her eyes flying open, and she found herself meeting a gaze that was both achingly familiar and yet oddly strange. She flushed again, taking care to hide her confusion behind feigned indignation.

"First visit, indeed!" she exclaimed with mock hauteur. "I will have you know, sir, that I was given my season the same as any young girl! In fact," her green eyes took on a rueful smile, "I had several! My family was beginning to despair of me until I met Charles."

The mention of her young husband brought an unaccustomed stab of jealousy to Peter's heart. Added to that was the deep shame he felt for the cruel way he'd insulted her. "I'm very sorry," he said again, unable to hold back the words. "I know you may not believe me, but I have nothing but respect for our brave soldiers, and knowing your husband died on the peninsula makes me feel doubly ashamed for what I said. I pray that you will forgive me."

"I already have," she reminded him, touched by his genuine remorse. They continued dancing for several more minutes when she said, "How did you know that?"

"Know what?" He was too busy concentrating on dancing to pay much mind to the conversation.

"That Charles died in battle," Kate said, staring up at him in surprise as she remembered the catty article in the gazette. "It wasn't in the paper."

Peter missed a step. "I believe Payton let it slip," he said, silently cursing his own incautious tongue. "You are his neighbor, as I recall."

"Yes, but we met for the first time at Lady Honoria's," Kate retorted, still puzzled. "And his lordship doesn't strike me as the sort who would overly concern himself with his neighbors." Then she made a face.

"Oh dear, how insufferably priggish that sounded! Please pay me no mind, my lord. I'd forgotten the marquess is your particular friend."

"That is all right," Peter said, delighting in her dislike of Payton even as he moved to defend him. "But in all fairness to his lordship I would like to say that he is not nearly so blackhearted as the gossips have painted him."

"Perhaps," Kate agreed coolly. The music had stopped and she allowed him to escort her back to the alcove. "But as it happens, I do not rely totally upon the tattlemongers to form my opinions. We met but the one time I grant you, but it was more than enough to give me his measure. Has he implied otherwise?" she asked in sudden suspicion.

"Indeed he has not," he answered soothingly. "He is well-aware that he is in your black books. Seems quite cast-down about it, in fact," he added with another grin.

"Mmm," Kate dismissed the marquess from her thoughts, her agile mind moving back to his remark about Charles. There was only one way she thought he could have learned of her husband's death; Mickey. Unless . . . She turned to him with a hesitant smile. "My lord, I was wondering if I could ask you a question?"

"Certainly, Mrs. Delecourt, what is it?"

She licked her lips nervously. "I–I was wondering if you have ever been to the Priory," she said, deciding to work up to the point slowly, rather than rushing her fences. "Have you?"

"No, I am afraid that I have not," he answered, wondering if she was merely making idle conversation or if there was some reason behind her question. "The marquess and I have but recently become well-acquainted. The last time he visited his estate I fear I was a trifle . . . indisposed."

"Ah yes, the infamous curricle accident," she felt her heart doing an odd dance as she realized he only could have received his information from one source. She decided the time had come to learn the truth.

"Well, it is a great pity you weren't able to visit the area," she said brightly, sending him a provocative smile. "I own to a certain amount of partiality, but it really is quite lovely; especially with the sea so close at hand. Do you like the sea, my lord?"

"As much as the next man, I suppose," he was more wary than ever. "Why do you ask?"

"No reason," she found his caution amusing: a family trait, it would appear. Mickey had also disliked answering any questions of a personal nature. "I was merely wondering if you enjoyed sailing. Many men do, you know."

Peter stiffened as he realized the minx was flirting

with him. The little devil, he thought, his eyes narrowing with anger. How could she kiss him with such sweet abandon and then turn around and flirt with a notorious rake but a few short weeks later? That he was also this notorious rake in no way lessened his temper. *She* didn't know that . . . at least, he didn't think she did. He gave her a sharp look.

"I can not say that I have ever cared for it, Mrs. Delecourt," he informed her in his most haughty manner. "It seems a most dangerous and foolish sport to me."

"This from a noted Corinthian?" Kate playfully tapped his arm with her fan. "Fie, sir, you would shatter all my poor illusions! Next you will tell me that card playing is the devil's work!"

Peter stared down at her, studying her sparkling eyes and tempting pout with mounting suspicion. He'd seen Kate in every mood imaginable; from compassion to fury, but he'd never seen her behave in such a coquettish fashion. Just what the devil was going on?

"Gaming is many things to many people," he replied guardedly. "And certainly I would never advise anyone to enter into a wager they weren't prepared to lose."

"Really?" Kate's pulses raced as she administered the *coup de grace*. "Then you would never wager on the outcome of a race from Lyme Regis to, say, Calais?"

"Katherine! Where have you been?" Portia exclaimed, her face set in a disapproving frown as she scurried towards them. "I have been searching for you for ages!"

"I am sorry, Aunt Portia," Kate apologized, schooling her features to politeness as the older woman drew nearer. Inside, however, her emotions weren't nearly so controlled. Of all the times for her aunt to remember her existence! she fumed. She'd been so close to learning the truth! Now heaven only knew when she would get another opportunity.

"Ah, good evening, Lord Tregarren," Portia greeted

them, holding her hand out to the earl. "I am happy to see you again."

"Mrs. Stone," Peter managed, feeling as if he had just been plunged into an icy well. His heart pounded with fearful intensity while his senses struggled to deal with the shock that had been dealt to his system. *She knows,* he thought, relief and horror filling him at the same time. What the hell was he going to do now?

"I pray you will excuse us, my lord, but there is someone I should like to introduce to my niece," Portia continued, wondering what on earth ailed the lad. He looked as if he had just swallowed a trout. "I am sure you understand."

"Certainly, Mrs. Stone," he pulled himself together enough to give her a cool bow. He spared Kate a quick glance, inclining his head towards her as well. "Mrs. Delecourt, thank you for the dance. It was most enjoyable."

"Thank you, my lord, I also enjoyed it," she said, noting his withdrawal with frustration. After getting this close to learning the truth she wasn't about to stop now. Throwing decorum and pride to the winds she gave him another smile. "Perhaps we might do it again some evening?"

"Come, Katherine," Portia interrupted before Peter could respond. "We mustn't keep my friends waiting," and she grabbed Kate by the arm, ignoring her protests as she drew her away.

"Well, missy, I hope you are satisfied with the amount of tattle you have caused," she scolded, her tone sharp with disapproval. "The tabbies will be feeding on this little morsel for the next week at the very least!"

"So?" Kate was in no mind to placate her querulous aunt. "I thought a whiff of scandal was necessary in a lady of the *ton*. Heaven knows you have told me so enough times."

Portia flushed to have her own words tossed back in

her face. "That is beside the point," she grumbled, leading Kate to the dowager's bench. "Now, tell me what happened. Did Lord Tregarren apologize? Lady Hertford said he was going to."

"Did she?" Kate sniffed; furious to think her private concerns should be such public knowledge. "And how does she know that?"

The look Portia sent her was eloquent with scorn. "Because he told her as much," she said with an obvious attempt at patience. "Stop being such a goose and tell me all. And you may begin by explaining that last remark to the earl. Really, Katherine, what can you have been thinking of? Begging a man to dance with you . . ."

While a disgruntled Kate was being interrogated by her aunt, Peter was beating an undignified retreat to the door. He'd never known such an emotional turmoil in all his life, and he wanted to be alone so that he could sort through the confusing tangle of fear and fury. But he'd barely reached the staircase when he heard a familiar voice call out his name, and he turned to find Sir Geoffrey bearing down on him.

"Ah, Tregarren I'd hoped I might catch you," Sir Geoffrey drawled, beaming at Peter like a benevolent uncle. "How is it going with your enchanting widow? Everything resolved, I trust?"

Peter's confusion was overridden by a flash of masculine anger at the other man. His blue eyes took on a deadly aspect as he drew himself up to his full height. "Would you care to explain that remark?" he queried, his voice soft with menace.

"Oh, do stop bristling like a hedgehog," Sir Geoffrey drawled, looking not the least bit concerned at the other man's cold anger. "I meant your lady no disrespect, I assure you. Indeed, after watching her route Battenham and his cronies I have nothing but admiration for her."

Peter relaxed marginally, his eyes never leaving the dandy's elegant features. In that moment the baron reminded him of Giles, and he wondered if like Westley there was more to his boyhood friend than first met the eye. "My apology has been accepted and we have danced," he said tersely, unwilling to reveal anything more. "That is all."

"Well, of course she accepted your apology," Sir Geoffrey looked oddly self-satisfied. "There was never any doubt, was there? Especially not after what I told her."

"What did you tell her?" Peter demanded, stiffening in sudden awareness of danger.

"Well, nothing to your detriment, I promise you," Sir Geoffrey sniffed, offended by the suspicion in Peter's voice. "In fact, I daresay you have me to thank for her willingness to overlook your poor conduct. If it had not been for me—"

"Damn you, Geoffrey, what did you tell her?" Peter roared, aching to grab the other man by his lapels and administer a sound shaking.

"Well, I told her about that disreputable brother of yours," Sir Geoffrey replied, mortally offended by the earl's harsh demand. "She thought you the blackest knave alive, and I wished to show her that although you are a rake you—"

"You told her about James?"

"Is that the rascal's name? I couldn't remember. I told her he was an Irish smuggler, and—"

"How the hell do you know about James?" Peter interrupted, thoroughly appalled. This was his worst nightmare come to life, and there was nothing he could do to stop it. The realization filled him with impotent fury.

"You forget my father was privy to *your* father's disgraceful conduct," Geoffrey replied stiffly, regretting his altruistic gesture in aiding his childhood friend. "Had it not been for my father's generosity God above knows what might have happened to that poor girl and her babe. She was threatening to throw herself in the Thames when he arranged her passage back to Limmerick."

"And you told Mrs. Delecourt all this?" Peter asked, a new suspicion dawning. "You told her James was a smuggler?"

"Indeed I did, and it seemed to shock her senseless," he said, shaking his head with amazement. "Truly, I did not mean to upset her. Coming from the country as she does one would think her well-acquainted with the gentleman. The marsh is said to be thick with the ruffians."

Peter said nothing, his expression hardening as he considered the ramifications of Geoffrey's misguided interference. Had it not been for his fear of challenging the furies, he would have wondered what the hell could possibly go wrong next.

Chapter Seventeen

"What?" Giles stared at Peter in horror. "Tell me you are joking. Lie if you must, but please tell me you are joking."

"I won't lie to you, nor am I joking," Peter said, his jaw clenching with the control he was exerting over his emotions. "Sir Geoffrey knows the whole of it, and worse yet, he has told Kate."

A stream of epithets burst from the viscount's lips as he began pacing the spacious confines of his study. "But how did he learn of your brother?" he demanded at last, thrusting an agitated hand through his thick blond hair. "Hell, not even the Home Office knew about your brother until shortly before he disappeared."

Peter sighed, then briefly told him of the baron's father and his connection to his family. "In fact, it was he who first told me about James," he concluded, rubbing a weary hand across his eyes. "He'd kept track of James and his mother all these years; even sending them money so that he might be educated. After I inherited the title Sir Humphrey came to me with the information. He thought that, unlike my father, I should want to do the honorable thing."

"Which you did?"

"Which I did," Peter confirmed, remembering his shock and then his joy at hearing the news. All during his lonely childhood he'd longed for a brother, and

244

learning of James's existence had filled him with happiness. Only his great love for his mother, and James's own adamant refusal, had prevented him from publicly acknowledging him as his brother.

"I suppose I can see why the baron felt he had to inform you about James," Giles grumbled, flinging himself on to the settee. "But why the devil did he see fit to tell his macaroni of a son about it?"

Despite the bleakness of the situation, the scorn in Giles's voice brought a smile to Peter's lips. "Hearing you call Horton a macaroni is not unlike hearing the pot calling the kettle black," he drawled, his eyes resting on the viscount's elegant jacket of emerald and gold satin.

Giles shrugged. "I never said I wasn't a dandy" he grumbled, "but at least I am not a loose-lipped tattler who goes about spilling other people's darkest secrets!"

"Neither is Sir Geoffrey," Peter pointed out with maddening calm. "He has only told Kate, and that was in order to cast me in a better light. Besides," he paused meaningfully, "he doesn't know my darkest secret."

"Or so we fervently hope. But still, this could not have come at a worse time," Giles said, digging a packet out of his coat and offering it to Peter.

His eyebrows climbed at the broken seal on the back of the parchment but he dutifully opened it, a soft curse slipping from his lips as he studied the contents.

"This is a copy of Wellington's orders!"

Giles smiled slightly at Peter's incredulous expression. "So it is, but I prefer to think of it as the Home Office's official sanction to proceed against Payton. You may think of it as bait."

The languid words brought Peter's head snapping up. "They have agreed to my plan?"

"In full."

"It will only work if Payton is desperate enough to make a grab for it himself," Peter cautioned, not allowing himself to grow too hopeful. He'd come this close once before, only to have the rug yanked out from beneath his feet.

"He will be," Giles assured him, his brown eyes taking on a cold gleam that would have surprised many in society. "Your idea to buy up his markers has provided us with the necessary leverage to force the marquess to our will. By tomorrow his new creditors will have served notice that unless he settles his accounts within thirty days, he will be clapped in debtor's prison."

"And you're certain the moneylenders shall not be of use to him?"

"Done. Rothschild is seeing to it."

A wave of relief washed over Peter, and he closed his eyes. "I can't believe it," he said with a heavy sigh. "God, after all these months I can't believe we shall soon have, the badger in our trap."

"Yes, well, don't start celebrating just yet" Giles warned.

"There is still your Mrs. Delecourt to be dealt with."

Peter's eyes flew open. "What of her?" he asked, straightening in his chair. "She knows nothing of this."

"She knows enough to connect James to you," Giles said bluntly. "She knows he is your brother, and from what you have said, she is already fishing for information about him."

Giles's remark brought Peter's brows together in an angry scowl. "I would hardly term a simple question fishing for information," he said frigidly. "I have told you, the woman is harmless."

"Ah, but the answers to that question are neither simple nor harmless," Giles returned, unimpressed by Peter's cold anger. "And one is left to wonder why she asked it in the first place."

"Because she is a woman, damn it!" Peter exploded, not caring for the direction of the marquess's thoughts. "What other reason does she need?"

"A better one than the innate curiosity of her sex," Giles's voice lost its usual sardonic edge as he studied

Peter. "I am sorry, Wyndham, but Whitehall will have to be informed."

Peter's fists clenched in impotent fury. Westley was right; curse him. Kate's actions, however innocently motivated, were placing the mission at risk, and something would have to be done. He heaved a weary sigh.

"Give me a week," he said, his eyes bleak as they met Giles's compassionate gaze. "I will attend to the matter myself."

Giles was silent, then gave a slow nod. "All right," he said with obvious reluctance. "But I can not wait any longer than that. The Secretary wants this resolved by the end of the month."

Peter did some swift calculations. The end of the month; that gave him a little over a fortnight to accomplish his mission. It would be difficult, but he would manage somehow. For reasons he did not fully understand he could not bear the thought of Kate in official custody, and he knew he would do whatever it took to insure her safety. "I shall attend to it," he said, his voice firm. "The Minister shall have his traitor."

"And Mrs. Delecourt?"

Peter retrieved his hat and cape from the side table where he had tossed them shortly after bursting into the viscount's study. "I have told you, she will be dealt with," he said, placing his hat firmly on his head. "Within a few days, a week at the most, she will no longer be a threat to us. I give you my word."

Kate was up early the following morning, filled with a renewed sense of purpose. Now that she knew—or at least strongly suspected—that Mickey was the earl's half brother she was determined to settle the matter once and for all. After spending the past several days doubting her very sanity she decided she was entitled to a few explanations. She would find Mickey and insist he tell her precisely what was going on, and if the devil said even one word about shooting fish, she would box his ears!

While the footman brought her breakfast she plotted what her next move would be. Clearly her first step should be locating Mickey. She didn't even know if he was in London; or even England, for that matter. Since she was still reluctant to contact the earl that meant she would have to proceed on her own, or employ a confederate. In a twinkling, she knew who that confederate would be. She tossed her napkin down and called for her carriage to be brought around.

Thirty minutes later she walked into her aunt's study where she found Elizabeth already hard at work. "No, please, stay where you are," she said as the other woman made to rise. "This is nothing so formal as a social call. In fact, I have come to ask for your assistance."

"Certainly, Mrs. Delecourt," Elizabeth said, setting her quill to one side. "How might I help you?"

Kate grimaced at Elizabeth's words. "Assistance was a poor choice of words. Actually, I am come in search of advice. And please, do call me Kate; I already think of you as Elizabeth."

"Advice on what?" Elizabeth inquired in the cool, practical manner Kate had come to depend upon.

Kate laughed in delight, covering Elizabeth's hand with her own. "Dear Elizabeth! I knew I could count upon you! Now, listen carefully while I tell you a story . . ."

"And you think this Mickey person is Lord Tregarren's half brother," Elizabeth said once Kate concluded her tale. "Are you certain?"

"I'm positive," Kate was amazed at how relieved she felt to share her thoughts with another person. "It all fits so perfectly; what other explanation can there be?"

"That the earl himself is Mickey," Elizabeth answered with alacrity, her finely shaped eyebrows meeting in a scowl. "From what I have heard of his lordship it sounds precisely the sort of rig he would run."

"That is what I thought as well . . . for awhile, at least," Kate agreed, more pleased than ever with her choice of conspirators. Elizabeth was cool and unemotional; looking at a problem from every conceivable angle before arriving at her conclusion.

"What changed your mind?"

"So many things" Kate sighed, listing each reason carefully; including the letter Mickey had written his brother. "So you see, there has to be two of them. If Tregarren was Mickey, then why on earth would he have written himself?"

Elizabeth looked much struck by this, her even teeth nibbling on her full bottom lip before she sighed. "You are right; it makes no sense that he should do such a thing. But an illegitimate half brother who might be his double . . . really, it sounds like something out of a French farce."

"I thought it closer to Shakespeare, myself," Kate said with a laugh, "and I still do not know what I am going to do about it! That wretch! I can not wait to see him again, and when I—"

"Why?"

The blunt question brought Kate to a halt. "What?" she asked, her brows puckering as they met Elizabeth's unwavering stare.

"Why do you wish to see him again?" she asked simply. "Do you want to become lovers?"

"Elizabeth!" Kate was shocked into silence.

"I am sorry, Kate," Elizabeth was contrite but no less resolved. "But what else can come of it? You can not marry him, you know."

The practical words made Kate stare at her in dismay. Until now she'd given very little thought of what would happen once she finally succeeded in locating Mickey; she only knew she had had to, for reasons that were as confusing as they were compelling. She looked away from Elizabeth's steady gaze, her troubled eyes focusing on her clenched hands.

"This has naught to do with-with love," she answered, her voice not as steady as she would have liked. "I only want to find him so that I can finally know the truth."

"And that is the only reason?" Elizabeth pressed.

Kate was silent, remembering the heated kiss he had forced upon her that last evening. It had been an insult, a degradation, but so wonderfully exciting . . . she shook off the sweet memory. "That is the only reason," she repeated stoutly.

Elizabeth studied her a long moment, and then a gentle smile spread slowly across her face. "Then there is nothing left to be said."

"You'll help me?" Kate asked, her shoulders sagging in relief.

"Of course." Elizabeth seemed offended she would even ask. "Now what we need first is a plan of action. I take it you'd rather not approach the earl for information?"

"How do you know that?"

"Because you are here, and not there," Elizabeth answered with a cool shrug. "Do you know where his lordship lives?"

"Curzon Street," Kate replied, remembering the letter she had posted all those weeks ago.

"Mmm. Well, it shouldn't be too difficult to mount a watch on the house," Elizabeth said, busily scratching her plans down on a piece of paper. "Mrs. Stone has over a dozen footmen; I daresay she wouldn't miss a few for a week or so."

"You are going to *spy* on the earl?" Kate gasped in horror.

"Of course." Elizabeth gave her a puzzled look. "How else are we to find your smuggler?"

Kate considered that a moment and then firmly pushed her scruples to one side. "But what if it doesn't work?" she asked, nervously twisting her fingers together. "I told you, I don't even know if he is the country!"

"And you do not know that he is not," Elizabeth returned, ever practical. "We shall try it for a few days and see what happens. Meanwhile you must learn all that you can from Lord Tregarren."

"But I didn't want him to know!" Kate protested, her cheeks growing rosy at the thought of the handsome earl. "I-I am not all that certain he can be trusted."

"A wise decision on your part," Elizabeth nodded her head in approval. "But I didn't mean to imply you should ask him outright for information concerning his brother."

Understanding dawned. "Oh! You want me to *wheedle* it from him!" Kate exclaimed, her eyes sparkling with impish delight.

"Precisely so. Do you think you can do it?"

Suddenly Lucille's image flashed in Kate's mind. "I do not see why not," she said, smiling with cheeky self-confidence. "I have been trained by the very best."

Peter spent the next two days devising a strategy to get Kate out of London. During his stay in her house he had observed her closely, and he knew how very seriously she took her duties as lady of the manor. If there was one thing that would make her return to Kent at the height of the season, it would be a threat to her home or staff. Nothing too serious, he brooded, tapping a slender finger on his inkwell, but critical enough to get her out of the city before the Home Office was forced to move against her.

He was no closer to resolving this dilemma when there was a knock on his door, and James poked his head into the study. His green eyes alight with laughter.

"Are you busy, brother, mine?"

"Not really," Peter tossed his quill down, disgust etched clearly on his features. "What is it?"

James's head disappeared, and a second later he was

walking into the room, shoving an obviously terrified young man ahead of him. "I've brought you a present."

"What the devil . . ." Peter glared at the cowering youth, clad in the black garb of a household servant. "Who is this?"

"That is what I was hoping you might tell me" James answered, throwing himself easily onto the leather chair in front of Peter's desk. "I found him watching your house."

"What?" Peter was on his feet in a flash, his blue eyes narrowing on the strange man.

"I . . . 'tis not what it looks sir . . . me lord," he stammered, his eyes moving nervously between James and Peter. "I was but doin' my duty, is all."

"What duty?" Peter demanded sharply, towering above the servant menacingly. "Who employs you? Speak up, lad, or it will go the worse for you."

"M-Mr. Arthur Stone, me lord, of St. James Square."

"Mr. Stone set you to watching my house?" Peter asked, his brows wrinkling as he tried to put a face to the name.

The servant shook his head quickly. "No, your lordship. 'Twas the young lady, Miss Compton what asked me. She said I was to watch your house and report back to her."

"And what was it you were watching for?" James asked politely.

"A cove with a beard," the footman sent him a quizzing look. "I thought 'twas you at first, but for the color of your eyes."

It took Peter less than a second to make the connection from Miss Compton to Kate. What the devil . . . he wondered. "And did you ask Miss Compton why you should perform this service for her?" he asked, slowly lowering himself to his chair.

The young man gave an outraged sniff and drew himself up proudly. "I'm sure 'tis not me place to be questionin' me betters," he said. "An' for all she's a companion now, 'tis plain as a pikestaff Miss Compton is quality. Sides when me mam was taken with the fever she'd of died for sure if Miss Compton hadn't nursed her. I'd empty the Thames with a teaspoon was she to ask it of me. Any of us would."

"Us?" James seized on the telling word.

"The rest of the footmen," came the explanation. "There be four of us in all."

James and Peter exchanged uneasy looks. "And how long have you had my house under surveillance?" Peter asked at last.

"Me lord?" The footman sent him a confused look.

"How long have you been smacking your peepers on us," James translated with a smile.

"Oh! Since yesterday afternoon, me lord. 'Twas right after Mrs. Delecourt left that Miss Compton called us into the study."

Peter's face remained expressionless, although he felt his stomach tightening with anger. "Mrs. Delecourt?" he asked in a carefully controlled voice.

"Aye," the young man nodded vigorously. "She be the Stones' cousin, and a rare kind thing she is, too. Not at all like that Miss Louisa," he added darkly.

"What is your name, lad?" Peter asked after a long pause.

"You're not callin' the watch on me?" The footman asked fearfully, envisioning himself languishing in the hold of a prison ship. "I was but doin' me duty, an'—"

"No, I'm not sending for the watch" Peter reassured him. "All I want is your name."

"Edward, your lordship, Edward Beech."

"Edward," Peter nodded his head. "I want you to go back to Miss Compton and tell her you have seen the man with the beard. Is that understood?"

"I . . . yes, me lord," Edward mumbled, shifting nervously from one foot to another. "As you say."

"Excellent," Peter dug into his pocket and extracted a

253

crown, which he tossed to the startled footman. "And Edward, not a word about this; hmm? We would not wish to alarm Miss Compton."

Edward quickly pocketed the gold coin. "Yes, me lord," he said, bobbing a hasty bow. "Reckon I know when to keep me trap closed."

"See that you do," Peter replied his voice soft with warning. "Now go. And Edward?"

"Yes, your lordship?" Edward cast him an uneasy look.

"In the future should either Miss Compton or Mrs. Delecourt ask you to do something like this, I want you to come directly to me."

"Yes me lord," Edward bowed and then hastily departed, leaving James to toss Peter a teasing look.

"A rather determined lady, your Mrs. Delecourt" he said, crossing his legs and leaning back in the chair. "Care to tell me why she should be looking for you so industriously?"

"No, I would not."

James chuckled at Peter's sour voice. "Ever the gentleman, eh, little brother?"

"Damn it, James, it's not funny!" Peter exploded, slamming his fist on the desk top as he leapt to his feet.

"Of course it is," James responded, his green eyes bright. "That's the trouble with you English; so stiff and proper you've never learned to laugh at life's absurdities Now stop glowering at me like the wrath of God, and let us decide what is to be done. Have you thought of a way to get her out of London?"

Peter relaxed slightly, his shoulders slumping as he thrust his hand through his thick hair. "That is what I was working on when you and your friend came bursting through my door," he said, giving James a black look.

James ignored his temper. "What about a fire?" he asked. "Nothing too destructive, mind, but enough to send her home to survey the damages. You say you're ready to move on Payton?" Peter nodded. "Good, then she need only be gone a week or so."

Peter considered James's suggestion and he had to admit it had some merits. But fires were dangerous unpredictable things. The smallest blaze could flare out of control into an inferno, and he wasn't about to risk innocent lives and property merely to get one inquisitive widow out of harm's way.

"Blast the woman!" he stormed, feeling thoroughly frustrated. "Doesn't she know what she is risking?"

"No, she doesn't," James said, abruptly serious. "And whose fault might that be?"

The accusation in James's voice brought an angry flush to Peters cheeks. "I've told you" he said through clenched teeth, "if it was left to me I would have told her everything weeks ago! But the decision has already been made. This is a matter of the utmost secrecy, and the fewer who know of it, the better."

"Then you can't screech like an outraged spinster when she acts not out of willfulness but out of ignorance" James said quietly. "If you want her to stay out of your affairs, then you owe it to her to tell her the truth."

Peter closed his eyes as a wave of chilling bitterness washed over him. "I can not."

"Then tell her a new lie."

The simple statement brought his eyes flying open again and he regarded James with renewed interest. "A new lie?" he echoed.

James nodded. "You need her to keep your identity secret and stop asking questions. Correct?"

"Among other things, yes."

"Then give her a good reason to remain silent. The lady was once willing to risk transportation for you. What do you think she would risk now?"

Peter was quiet as he considered that. "For Lord Tregarren, nothing. But for Mickey . . ." his voice trailed off, his eyes turning to purest sapphire as he remembered that last evening.

"Yes?" James was grinning at him.

Peter grinned back, plans and possibilities whirling in his head. "It's one hell of a risk," he said slowly.

"True, but the risk is what makes the game worth playing."

Peter touched his face thoughtfully. "I'll need a beard," he said, "and some proper clothes."

"Improper clothes, is what you mean," James corrected, entering easily into the sport of it. "Leave it to me, and the beard as well. I have an old friend who is an actress; I'm sure I could talk her out of a beard, and some affixant as well. We wouldn't want your whiskers to come off in an inopportune moment now, would we?"

Chapter Eighteen

Kate's cheerful optimism carried her through the next three days as she kept busy with social obligations. Much to her amusement both she and Louisa seemed to have "taken," and each morning's post yielded a flattering assortment of invitations. Evidently petulant, ill-mannered chits were all the rage this season, she mused, wryly astonished that it should be so.

If there were any clouds to darken the halcyon days, it was that she had yet to speak with Lord Tregarren. After days of bumping into him literally every time she turned around, she hadn't managed to catch so much as a glimpse of him, and she was beginning to grow frustrated. How was she to wheedle a man who had suddenly become invisible? She tenuously broached the matter to Portia as they were setting down to breakfast, and earned a sharp rebuke for her efforts.

"You still can not be setting your cap at Tregarren," Portia scolded, her brows meeting in a forbidding scowl. "I have already told you it won't do you a whit of good. You're much too virtuous to be one of his flirts, and you're not high-born enough to be his wife. What could possibly come from such an alliance?"

"I am not setting my cap at his lordship!" Kate denied hotly, her cheeks flaming at her aunt's accusation. "I was merely commenting how odd it was that we haven't seen him these past few days."

"Don't know what's so odd about it," Portia grumbled, helping herself to the buttered scones. "The earl moves in circles far different than the one we occupy. In fact," she looked thoughtful "I think it more odd we've seen as much of him as we have."

Kate gave a start and turned to her aunt. "Why do you say that?" she asked slowly, the suspicion that his lordship had purposefully sought her out leaping to life in her mind.

"Stands to reason," Portia replied around a mouthful of food. "The lad's a rake as I have oft remarked, and his kind don't usually grace Polite Society's more prosaic do's. I overheard Sal Jersey remarking it had been months since Tregarren had been to Almack's, and Lady Honoria's daughter admitted he'd appeared at their musicale without so much as an invitation. Deuced odd, I'd call it."

"As would I," Kate agreed, her mind working furiously as she tried to make sense of what Portia had just related. The earl's presence at Almack's was easily explained as he had come to offer his apologies to her, but what about the other two occasions when they had met? Were they accidents, or was there some other explanation? Did Lord Tregarren know of her involvement with Mickey, and if so, why the devil hadn't he said anything? She shook her head in exasperation.

It was useless speculating on the earl's motives at this point. She would have to bide her time and wait for Elizabeth to contact her. She only hoped her newfound friend did not take overly long. Given the state of her nerves these past few weeks, she doubted she could take the suspense.

"Speaking of odd, there is something I meant to ask you," Portia said, not seeming to notice Kate's distracted air. "It is about Miss Compton."

"What about her?" Kate asked, grateful to put her troublesome thoughts from her mind.

"Well, I was watching her the other day when it suddenly struck me that I ought to know her. It is something about her eyes . . ." Portia chewed on her scone another moment. "Do you know anything of her background? Who her family is; that sort of thing?"

Kate was instantly wary, unwilling to reveal the precious little she did know of her friend. She and Elizabeth had grown quite close of late, and she had no desire to risk their budding friendship. "Only that she is obviously high-born and well-educated," she admitted cautiously, hoping she was not betraying Elizabeth's trust. "I believe she once mentioned her father was in the navy, but that is all."

"Navy . . ." Portia's brows met over her nose as she sought to remember something, but in the end she dismissed it with a shrug of her shoulders. "Oh well, I don't suppose it signifies. Now tell me, what came in this morning's post. Anything of interest?"

"A letter from Lucille," Kate said, knowing nothing could be more certain to divert her aunt's attention. "She writes that her and Caro's trip to London has been put off as Caro's gout is plaguing her.

"Hmph, a glass of sherry before bed each night would soon cure that, but I doubt if a clutch purse like Caro would have a decent bottle in the house," Portia grumbled, looking smugly pleased at the news. "But I asked if anything *interesting* had arrived."

Kate hid a smile at her irascible aunt and turned her attention to the stack of mail piled beside her plate. "Just the usual," she said, sifting through the invitations. "Balls, routs, a tea, and oh, what is this?" She lifted a heavily embossed card from the mound and scanned it quickly.

"Why, it's an invitation from Lord Swansby for a masquerade his sister is holding this Thursday! What a pity we can not attend."

"What do you mean we can not attend?" Portia demanded, setting her cup down with an impatient clatter. "I adore masquerades!"

"You and Louisa both, but that does not change the fact we are promised for cards at the Burkes," Kate returned, tapping the card on the table as her golden eyebrows gathered in a frown. "Besides, I can not like being invited at the last moment like this . . . almost as if we were needed to make up the numbers."

"And what if we were?" Portia's sense of practicality was greater than her pride. "Swansby's a duke, and a wealthy man in the bargain. You ought to be flattered."

"Really, Aunt Portia, I hardly know the man," Kate protested, recalling the dark haired man she had met at a dinner party at the beginning of the Season. He was quite pleasant, if a tad bit dull, and she had no interest in encouraging his suit.

"What nonsense! He danced with you twice at the Blackthorne's, and he was your card partner at the Creshton's only last week."

"I haven't anything to wear," Kate fell back on the oldest of feminine ploys in hopes of discouraging her matchmaking relation. "It takes weeks to have a costume made, and I refuse to disgrace myself by appearing in a rented one."

"Posh, I have trunks filled with old clothes gathering dust in the attic. I'm sure if we looked we could find you something more than suitable," Portia said firmly, her eyes taking on a determined sparkle. "In fact, I have just the costume in mind; 'tis the gown I wore to my engagement ball. It is lovely; all white and gold satin with paniers and an underskirt of embroidered gold brocade. You can wear it with my scarlet domino and a black loo mask."

"Very well, Aunt," Kate capitulated with a sigh, knowing it would be useless to argue. Besides, the ensemble did sound charming. She would wear it with the delicate set of topaz and diamonds she'd inherited from Charles's mother.

"Louisa might be a problem," Portia continued, rightfully assuming her granddaughter had been included in the invitation. "She is far too . . . er . . . tall to wear any of my things, and in any case she is certain to have her own ideas. We shall discuss it with her when we take tea with them this afternoon."

As it turned out Louisa had several ideas, and while she and Portia were wrangling over the matter Elizabeth drew Kate to the other side of the room for a private coze."

"I have news," she said, her bronze-colored eyes sparkling with excitement. "Edward has seen your smuggler!"

"Who is Edward?" Kate asked, scarce believing her ears. She'd resigned herself to waiting weeks before hearing word.

"One of the footmen I set to watching Tregarren's home," Elizabeth explained, casting a quick glance over her shoulder to make sure they weren't being overheard. "He returned to the house yesterday afternoon with the news he'd seen the man going into the earl's home. He *is* staying there, just as you thought."

Kate sat back in her chair. "Is he certain?"

"Positive. He described him perfectly, right down to his beard, and said he'd seen them going into the house together." She shook her head in wonder. "There really are two of them, so it appears I owe his lordship an apology. I fear I still suspected him of playing some wicked trick on you."

"As did I," Kate replied, remembering her thoughts earlier that morning. All her doubts vanished and she felt gloriously free. "Oh Elizabeth, this is wonderful!" She cried, clasping the other woman's hands in hers. "How can I ever thank you?"

"I take it then that you are pleased?" Elizabeth

teased, smiling at the joyful expression on Kate's face.

"Pleased? I am ecstatic!" Kate exclaimed, then quickly lowered her voice. "But I must be practical. Now that I know Mickey is truly in London I can send him a message at his brother's."

"Do you think that wise?" Elizabeth asked, some of the laughter fading from her eyes. "I thought you didn't wish the earl involved in this."

"If Mickey is staying with him then he already is involved," Kate said, dismissing the danger with a wave of her hand. "He must know the whole of it anyway, and the fact he hasn't said anything must mean I can trust him . . . with my reputation if not my virtue," she added, hoping to tease her friend into better spirits.

Her ploy did not work as Elizabeth's face took on a somber cast. "You must not joke about such things, Kate," she said, and for a flash of a second Kate caught a glimpse of a terrible pain. "A reputation is a fragile thing, and once it has been broken there is no mending it. For your sake, I pray Lord Tregarren is as honorable as you say he is."

"This will never work," Peter muttered, his nose wrinkling at the sharp smelling glue. "She'll see through this disguise in a moment."

"No, she won't," James said, leaning closer as he added the final touches to Peter's beard. "Now stop pulling faces, or I'll never get the blasted thing straight. There," he gave it a final pat and then stepped back to admire his handiwork. "Not bad, if I do say so myself."

James leaned forward and anxiously surveyed his image in his dressing mirror. "How do I look?" he asked, running a hand over the beard's coarse hairs. It was far longer than the shortly cropped beard he had worn while with Kate, and he thought it made him look ridiculous.

· "Like a brigand," James assured him, pulling his brother's hands away from his face. "Your pretty widow will take one look at you and swoon with delight."

"I don't want her swooning," Peter grumbled, rising to slip his arms into the black jacket James was holding for him. "I just want her to keep quiet until we have Payton safely netted."

"Dreamer. I've never met a woman yet who'd hold her tongue when she could be wagging it," James replied with a cheerful laugh. "You would not believe all the questions Deidre asked of me when I went to her dressing room."

"What did you tell her?"

"Nothing much. I muttered something about jealous husbands and the pressing need to disappear for a wee bit, and she was more than happy to help me." James grinned at him. "Tale spinning must be a family trait."

Peter's cheeks reddened when he remembered the lies he had told Kate, and the lies he would be forced to tell her tonight. He turned away and scratched at his chin. "Damned thing itches," he grumbled, his eyes not quite meeting James's steady gaze.

James said nothing, his eyes continuing to survey his brother's strained face. "Are you sure this is the way you want to play it?" he asked quietly. "I can take her away to some place safe, and when all of this is over you can come for her. She'll understand."

"If there was a chance in hell I thought it would work I would say yes," Peter said bleakly, leaning against the window pane and staring out into the blackness of an April night. "But the trap is all but sprung, and I can't risk anything that might alert Payton."

James digested that for a moment. "Then let me go in your stead," he said, striving for a light tone. "A lovely woman with a fondness for Irish smugglers sounds most intriguing."

That did bring a smile to Peter's face, although the

effect was hidden by the thick beard. "Which is precisely why I shall be the one to go," he said, swinging around to face his brother. "Is everything set?"

"Aye. Your friend Giles has arranged for the underbutler to sneak you into Mrs. Delecourt's sitting room. When she returns from her fine party she'll be handed a note advising her where you are, and if the luck of the sprites are with us, she'll not say a word but go quietly up the stairs."

"What about her abigail?"

"Already taken care of," James answered soothingly. "The underbutler will tell her that Mrs. Delecourt told her not to wait up; something she often does, apparently, and so there will be no one about to witness your . . . er . . . reunion."

The thought of being alone with Kate again brought a flash of pleasure, and Peter pushed it firmly to the back of his mind. He couldn't afford the luxury of such emotions, and he forced himself to think of more mundane matters. "How do we know the underbutler won't spread this all over London once we are done? I'll not have her whispered about."

"Again, your friend Giles has seen to that. It seems the underbutler had a bit of a misunderstanding with the runners at his last position, and it could prove most awkward were they to learn of his location. We may rely on his complete discretion."

Peter nodded, implicitly trusting Giles's word. He glanced at the clock above his mantle. It was almost midnight. He straightened his shoulders and turned towards the door. "Let's go," he said, his voice already taking on the lilt he had affected as Mickey. "I'd not want to keep the lady waiting."

James winced. "Please, little brother, spare me your poor theatrics. Pray God my English accent is better than your Irish, or we'll never be pulling off the rest of this performance."

264

Kate accepted the footman's hand, her shoulders drooping with weariness as she stepped down from the carriage. It was almost two in the morning, and she was ready to fall asleep on the spot.

"I still don't see why we had to leave so early," Portia was complaining, frowning as she surrendered her wrap to the hovering servant. "The Fullertons are sure to be insulted."

"I told you Aunt, I have the headache. I'll send them a note tomorrow explaining everything," Kate said, handing her wrap over to the servant as well. She recognized him as the underbutler, and wondered what had happened to Johns, her aunt's formidable, but aging, majordomo. She hoped the poor man was already abed; he was far too old to keep up with Portia.

"Excuse me, Mrs. Delecourt," the servant stepped forward, offering Kate a note on a silver salver. "But this came for you while you were out. The lad said it was urgent."

Kate took the note, her eyebrows arching with interest. She broke the wax seal with her thumb and spread the sheet of paper open.

> *Kate,*
> *I am waiting for you in your sitting room. Come at once and tell no one.*
> *Mickey*

"Why, Katherine, whatever is the matter?" Portia exclaimed, alarmed at the expression on her niece's face. "You've gone white as a sheet!"

"I . . . it's nothing, Aunt," Kate stammered, forcing her mind to function as she folded the letter and slipped it into her reticule. "Just a letter from Lord Westley; he–he wants me to go riding with him on the morrow."

"Is that all?" Portia shot Kate a puzzled look. "But I

thought the footman who delivered it said it was urgent."

"And so it is, to Lord Westley," Kate lied, inventing her story as she went along. "He wants to know what color my habit shall be so that he might match it. I am to send word first thing in the morning."

"What?" Portia was thoroughly disgusted. "Well, of all the ninny-hammered excuses! How very like that silly fop to write such a thing! But that still doesn't explain why you looked such a fright," she added, her brows lowering in suspicion. "Are you quite sure that is all there was to it?"

"Quite sure," Kate answered, all but dancing from one foot to another in her haste to be gone. "I told you, I have a terrible headache, and the notion of spending an hour in the viscount's company overset me. I believe I shall write and refuse him."

"Well, I should say so," Portia said, reluctantly accepting Kate's story. The gal was scrupulously honest, and in any case she did look dreadful; her green eyes glittering in her white face.

"Poor dear, you do look all done in," she murmured soothingly giving her hand a maternal pat. "Mind you go straight to bed, and make sure you take a dose of laudanum as well. I know you do not like such things, but it is just what you need to help you sleep."

"Yes, I believe I shall do just that," Kate eagerly grasped the excuse she had been handed. "In fact, I'll probably sleep in late tomorrow as well. We haven't anything planned; have we?"

"Nothing that can't be postponed," Portia assured her with another pat. "Do go on up to bed now, while I stay down here. Would you like me to look in on you when I retire?"

"*No!* No," Kate repeated in a more moderate tone. "There's no need to do that. I'll be fast asleep, and won't even know you're there."

"If you say so," Portia said, eyeing Kate with concern. The poor child had to be truly suffering, for she'd never seen her so nervous and agitated. "Good night, dear."

"Good night, Aunt," Kate dutifully kissed Portia's cheek and then started up the stairs, forcing herself not to rush up them in a manner that would make fiction out of her indisposition.

What the devil was keeping her? Peter wondered, his lips thinning with growing impatience. He'd seen the carriage pull up over a quarter of an hour ago; surely it couldn't be taking her this long to read his note and rid herself of her aunt. He reached up and scratched his beard. The affixant James had used was making his face burn, and his respect for actors increased tenfold. He couldn't imagine subjecting himself to such discomfort on a nightly basis.

He moved from his hiding place behind the drapes to stand closer to the connecting door leading to her bedchamber. What was he going to say to her? He knew what he had rehearsed, but suddenly it sounded so ridiculous. Kate was no one's fool; a fact neither James nor Giles seemed to comprehend, and he knew she would never believe the implausible tale he had been ordered to tell. Damn! There had to be some way he could be honest without telling her the entire truth!

"Mickey!" The door flew open and Kate rushed in, her head turning from side to side as she searched the darkness for him.

His heart slammed into his ribs at the sight of her. Standing in the doorway, the light from the hall spilling over her in a golden halo she looked as ethereal as she had the first time he'd seen her, and for a moment a powerful emotion held him in check; unable to speak or move.

She must have sensed his presence for she whirled in

his direction; her movements stilling as she saw him standing in the shadows. She took a hesitant step forward. "Mickey?"

"Aye, Mrs. Delecourt," he stepped into the light, smiling as he saw her face. "We seem fated to meet in darkened rooms."

Kate stood as if frozen, a myriad of emotions washing over her as she struggled for control. Anger, consternation, confusion, and an inexplicable sense of joy filled her, and she didn't know if she should throw herself into his arms, or box his ears for the days of misery and self-doubt he had caused her. She took a steadying breath and cast him an icy look.

"So you do exist," she said coolly, deciding that of all her emotions, anger was by far the safest bet. "I must admit I was beginning to have my doubts."

Peter grinned at her prim tones. He'd steeled himself for anything from shrieks of rage to tears of recrimination, and he was both relieved and oddly proud of the cool way she confronted him. He might have known Kate's sense of dignity would never allow her to make a scene, he thought, moving towards her with a slow, deliberate stride.

"Oh, I exist, Mrs. Delecourt, make no mistake about that," he drawled, his eyes boldly taking in her elegant gown of rose silk. "Did you think it was a figment of your imagination you had tucked beneath your bed all those weeks ago?"

"A figment of somebody's imagination, mayhap," she returned darkly, ignoring his teasing implication. Now that he had stepped more into the light she could see he had gained some badly needed weight in the intervening weeks, and she thought he looked even more handsome than ever. The thought made her blush, and to hide her confusion she raised her chin another notch.

"Now, would you kindly tell me what you are doing here, or why you have seen fit to contact me in such a havey-cavey manner?" she demanded imperiously. "And while you're about it, you might also tell me what you have been doing since you left my home. You were able to contact Captain O'Rourake, I take it?"

"Indeed I did, ma'am," he answered with a mocking bow, his blue eyes twinkling with the mischief she remembered so well. "And as to what I have been doing, well, I'm sure you'll understand if I hold my tongue. As I recall, you've no patience for my stories of shooting fish."

For a long moment she glared at him, and then suddenly she was laughing, her anger forgotten as she rushed forward and threw herself against him. "You wretch!" she cried, tossing her arms about his neck. "I thought never to see you again, and you dare greet me with that old plumper?"

"Kate," Peter's eyes closed as he held her in a fierce embrace. He knew he would have to release her, but not now; not just now. She felt so good, so right in his arms, and he wanted to go on holding her until the danger was past and he could reveal his true self to her at long last.

"I've missed you," he whispered, his arms tightening about her as he realized the impossibility of his desire. "God, how I have missed you!"

"And I you," she returned, tipping back her head as she smiled up at him. His beard had grown since she had last seen him and she gave it a playful tug, noting its coarseness with a vague surprise. She remembered it as being quite soft.

Peter dragged her hands away from his face. "Why didn't you tell me you were coming to London?" he asked, resisting the urge to kiss each of her fingers before lowering them to her side. "You could have tipped me over with a feather when I heard you were here."

"I wanted to tell you," she admitted, studying his darkly handsome face and marveling how much he resembled his brother. "That—that last night I went to your room to tell you, but . . ." she shrugged then gave him a searching look. "Why didn't you tell me Lord Tregarren was your brother?"

He might have known she would start asking questions, he thought whimsically brushing a golden curl back from her neck with the tip of his finger. Her inquisitiveness was one of the things that most delighted him. "It was not just my secret to be sharing," he told her, deciding that was as close to the truth as he could get. "Believe me, sweet, had it been left to me I would have told you the whole of it from the start."

Kate accepted that silently, understanding his desire to protect his brother. He could not know that she wasn't a vicious gossip, and Tregarren's already shaky reputation could probably be even further destroyed if Mickey's existence was made public knowledge. Thoughts of reputations brought to mind what would become of hers should she be discovered in Mickey's embrace, and she took a hasty step backwards.

"How—how did you find me?" she asked, her voice trembling.

It took a few seconds for the question to penetrate the mists filling Peter's head, then it was he who was forced to take a steadying breath. "It was Peter," he said simply. "He mentioned meeting you at a party. And then there was that other business," he added, his lips twisting at the way he had insulted her.

"Does he know about me . . . about us?" she asked, touched by his evident anger on her behalf.

Peter hesitated before answering. Both Giles and James had urged him to keep Lord Tregarren far in the background, but he did not see how that was possible. Besides, he had strong reasons for wanting to give her a good opinion of his other self.

"Not at first," he admitted, "but after you cornered him at Almack's, I had no other choice but to tell him all. Whyever did you mention the wager to him? You must have known it would connect you to me."

"That is why I said it," she admitted, blushing as she recalled her forward behavior with the earl. "I wanted so much to see you that I hoped to shock him into revealing your location." She peeped up at him from beneath her lashes. "Was he very angry?"

"Shocked, more like, but not so very angry once I told him how you had saved my life," he said, remembering again his horrified reaction to her question. At the time he'd suspected her of trying to trap him. But now . . .

"Kate?"

"Hmm?" She was busy examining the elegant planes of his face, and comparing them to his brother's image.

Peter hesitated, and then asked the question that had been consuming him. "Why have you been looking for me, Kate? Why was it so important that you find me?"

Chapter Nineteen

"Why, Kate?" Peter pressed, his eyes moving over the
perfection of her pale features. "Why was it so important that you find me?"

"I–I don't know," she confessed in a stricken voice,
stunned to find it was so. The reasons she had given
Elizabeth had been genuine, but they had only been
part of the truth. Gazing into Mickey's stormy blue
gaze, she greatly feared what the rest of that truth
might be.

"But you must have had some explanation," he persisted, and it wasn't just the agent who was asking. It
was suddenly vitally important to him that he discover
the reasons behind her search, and to see if they
matched his own. "After the way we parted I thought
you'd never wish to be seeing me again, and yet you
looked—"

"I didn't look for you!" Kate interrupted, confused by
his dogged persistence. "At least, not at first," she
added, waving her hand in a frustrated gesture. "But I
kept seeing you everywhere, or *thinking* I saw you, and
it was driving me mad! I even chased after some man
thinking he was you, and—"

"You chased after me? Where?" This time it was Peter who interrupted, his brows meeting in a frown as he
remembered the incident on Strand Street. Perhaps he
hadn't been bosky after all, he thought.

"By a book shop near Ackerman's," Kate replied, blushing to recall the cake she had made of herself. "I was standing by the window when I saw him walking past, and I went tearing after him screeching like a mad woman. Thank God it was not you."

"And how do you know it was not?" he asked, forcing a teasing note in his voice even as he was thanking heaven that the Fates had been with him that day. If she had succeeded in catching him . . . he gave a mental shudder at the prospect.

"Because of this, you idiot," she laughed, giving his beard another pull. "The man hadn't a hair on his chin, else he might have been your twin. Was it Lord Tregarren?"

"Possibly, but I shouldn't think so," he answered quickly, hoping to distract her. " 'Tis hard to imagine a rakehell like him hanging about anything so respectful as a book shop."

"That is so," she agreed, amused by the obvious affection he bore his brother. They were still standing in the center of her room, so close to each other that she could feel the heat emanating from his hard body. A belated sense of propriety came over her, and she shifted nervously away from him.

Peter sensed her sudden uneasiness, and in a flash he wondered if she was remembering the brutal way he had forced that kiss on her the last time they'd stood in a moonlit room. That he had no choice at the time was of little comfort, and a bleakness stole over his face as he looked at her.

"Kate, I–I didn't hurt you, did I?" he asked in a strained voice. "God, I could not bear it if I did. I would rather cut off my own arm than ever cause you a moment's pain . . ."

The anguish evident on his harsh features melted Kate's usual reserve, and she moved back to rest her palm against his cheek. "Don't you think I know that?" she asked softly, her eyes meeting his. "From the moment I found you lying on that beach I think I've always known you would never willingly do me harm. I trust you, Mickey."

He closed his eyes, something inside him breaking at the gentle words. He wanted to tell her the truth of himself more than he wanted to draw his next breath, but he could not. He gave a heavy sigh and opened his eyes, his pulse racing as he drank his fill of her quiet beauty. This could well be the last time he would ever see her, and he wanted to imprint her image on his very soul.

"Ah, my Kate, you are so very beautiful," he whispered brokenly, his hands sliding down to cup the fragile curve of her shoulders. "Like a sweet angel sent down from heaven.

His words made Kate burn, as did the lambent glow in his sapphire eyes. She was vividly aware of the hard masculinity pressing against her, and knew he wanted to make love to her. The knowledge should have shocked her, but instead she was filled with a fierce, feminine pride. In an odd way she felt safe with Mickey, safer than she'd felt in years and she moved instinctively towards the source of that safety.

"But I'm not an angel," she said, her fingers tracing the hard line of his mouth. "I am a woman, Mickey."

"I'd have to be a dead man not to know that," he replied, the breath catching in his throat at the unspoken invitation in her misty green eyes. He could feel her sweet softness along every inch of his throbbing body, and his already shaky control dissolved. Against his will he lowered his head, his mouth covering hers in a kiss that blazed with need.

At the first touch of his lips on hers Kate was filled with an overwhelming sense of joy. She responded at once, her lips parting for the urgent thrust of his tongue even as her fingers were burying themselves in the ebony softness of his hair. She wanted him, she realized exultantly, and she revelled in the freedom the shocking admission gave her.

"Kate! God, I want you," Peter moaned, lost in desire as his hands sought the tempting fullness of her breasts. "You are a fire in my heart . . . in my blood," his thumb moved over her nipple in a tantalizing caress that made Kate arch with pleasure.

"Mickey!"

Peter heard the name she cried out, and it was as if a bucket of ice water had been thrown over him. He stilled at once, his body clamoring for more even as he was closing his eyes in painful denial. He couldn't do it, he realized grimly. He couldn't make love to her with this lie between them.

"Mickey?" Kate sensed his withdrawal and blinked up at him in confusion. "What is it, my love?"

No, *not* Mickey, he longed to say. It's *Peter*. He wanted his name to be the one she gasped out in pleasure; his the name she whispered in the dark when she was alone. He wanted her to know the true name of the man who was loving her, so that when he left it would be his face she saw in her dreams. He dipped his head and sucked in a deep breath to calm himself.

"I can not," he gritted between clenched teeth.

Kate continued staring up at him, confusion giving way to dismay. Her eyes involuntarily lowered to his still aroused body. "But . . ."

He grimaced in sweet pain. "A poor choice of words," he managed with a shaky laugh, his voice rough with passion. "Perhaps what I should have said is 'I must not.' "

Kate's face flamed at his words. Now that the heat of desire was fading she could feel her conscience stirring, and she was acutely aware of what had almost happened. She was still reeling from the dizzying affects of passion, and while part of her was eternally grateful he had been gentleman enough to call a halt, the other part of her was sighing in disappointment.

Peter was watching her closely, and when he saw the

humiliation stealing into her eyes he drew her back into his arms. "No, no shame now," he said gruffly pressing a soft kiss on her tousled hair. "This is the sweetest thing to ever happen to me, and I'll not have you regretting it. It will be all right, I promise you."

Kate burrowed against him, unable to speak as she remembered the uninhibited way she'd responded to Mickey's touch. Not even with Charles had she been so wanton, and she struggled to come to grips with what her passion might mean.

Peter was also silent, lost in the sweet memory of Kate's honest response. He'd always known her to be a woman of honor and compassion, but he was delighted to discover she was a creature of passion as well. She was his, he decided with a flash of possessive satisfaction, and he would kill any man who tried taking her from him.

The savage admission made him frown as thoughts of the real world began sifting into the sensual aftermath. He still hadn't won her promise to avoid him—Lord Tregarren—a promise he realized that would now be doubly hard to explain. His arms tightened protectively about her as if he would shield her from what he was about to say.

"I have to go away."

Kate flinched, wanting to scream a denial of his words. She closed her eyes and cuddled closer, savoring the smell and feel of him before asking quietly, "For how long?"

"I don't know," he admitted, twining his hands in the thick softness of her gilded hair. It had come loose in the heat of their embrace, and he'd been delighted to discover it fell past her shoulders.

She raised her head and gazed up into his troubled eyes. "Is it dangerous?" she asked worriedly, stroking the thin line of his mouth beneath his bushy moustache. "You're not going after any more of those shooting fish . . . are you?"

He gave a reluctant grin at that. "You never did believe that piece of moonshine, did you?" he teased, his tongue coming out to taste her finger.

"No more than I believed that accent of yours," she replied, anxious to know more of him. "I know you were born in Ireland, but you seem so . . . so English at times. Were you educated here?"

"Yes." At Oxford, to be exact.

"Are you really a smuggler, or was that another lie?"

Her blunt question caught him unaware, and it was several seconds before he could answer. "At times it has been the truth," he said honestly.

"Why?" she demanded angrily; furious that he should think so little of his own safety. "You are intelligent and strong. Surely there must be some other way for you to make your living! Why must you risk your life doing something as foolish as smuggling?"

"For the sport of it," he answered, borrowing the answer James had given him when he'd asked that very same question. "And to rub the English's nose in it."

Kate digested that for a long moment. "Do you hate the English so much?" She asked softly, studying him through worried eyes.

"Sometimes," he said, remembering James's black anger when they had first met.

"What about the earl?" she pressed. "He is English. Do you hate him as well?"

"I love my brother," he answered swiftly and with such honesty that Kate was instantly reassured. "We may not have been raised together, but never think that I don't regard Ja—regard Peter as my own true brother."

Kate was too distraught to notice his slip of the tongue. "Then why doesn't he do something?" she cried, vexed beyond all endurance. "He is your brother, how can he simply stand back and let you sail away never knowing if—"

Peter silenced her with a kiss, his tongue flicking at

hers until she returned his demanding caress. Only then did he lift his head to stare up into her stormy green eyes.

"He is doing something," he said roughly, his breathing growing ragged as he fought for control. "We–we may go into business together when I return." This was also the truth, for James had finally agreed to let him stake him in a ship-building business.

Kate was quiet another moment. "When will you be leaving?" she asked, blinking against tears.

"Tonight . . . or should I say, today," he admitted, aware of how rapidly time was slipping past him. He wanted to grasp it and hold it fast; making this night last forever, but he was far too much of a pragmatist to believe it could be. Each second brought him that much closer to the inevitable parting, and there was nothing he could do about it.

Kate swallowed her protest; unwilling to subject him to tearful recriminations. After Charles's death she'd learned to accept that life offered no guarantees, and she was determined to be content with what she had. It was enough to know that he cared for her, and that he'd come back to her . . . if he could. The realization brought a swift jab of pain, but she knew it was a possibility that had to be faced.

"If–if something should happen," she began, her voice breaking despite her resolve, "will you ask your brother to send me word? I–I couldn't bear never knowing."

"All right," he agreed softly, thinking of the letter he had left with James against just such a possibility. "Now there is something I would ask of you."

"Anything."

"I want you to leave London."

Kate stared at him in surprise, trying to fathom the unexpected request. "You wish me to leave the city?" she echoed. "But why?"

"For so many reasons, my love," he said, brushing his

278

finger back and forth across her kiss-swollen lips. "But mostly because I would worry about you. I want," he broke off and gave her an intent look, "I *need* to know that you are safe, and you will be safest at your home. Promise me that you will go there."

"But it is the middle of the Season!" she protested, thinking of Portia and the howl she would be certain to raise.

"And . . . that matters?" he asked softly.

She feared he thought she valued her social position above him and touched his cheek. "No," she said gently, tracing the skin above his beard. "No, it matters not at all."

"Then you'll do as I ask?"

"As soon as it can be arranged," she promised, trying not to wince at the thought of the coming scene with her aunt. The older lady would doubtlessly scream the roof down.

"Today?" he asked hopefully, scarcely believing that in the end, it should prove to be so amazingly simple.

"Well, not so soon as all that," she said, wondering at his eagerness. "But certainly I could set out by tomorrow or the next day at the very latest. There is much to be done," she added with a reproving frown.

"All right," Peter decided it advisable not to press his luck. "And there is one more thing I must ask."

"What?"

"I would prefer that you avoid Lord Tregarren. I know he is my brother," he said when she opened her lips to protest, "but things are . . . complicated, and until they can be resolved I want you to have no contact with him. Please, Kate . . . for my sake."

Kate hesitated a moment, and then relented. Despite their reconciliation . . . if such it could be called . . . she and the earl were hardly bosom beaus, and since she would be leaving London in a day or so she didn't think it would be that great of a hardship to do as he asked.

"Oh, very well," she agreed with a soft laugh, bending her head to brush a soft kiss on his nose. "But when all of this is over, I expect for the three of us to meet at long last. I am beginning to have my suspicions, you see," she added somewhat mischievously.

"What suspicions?" he asked, a frisson of alarm bringing him fully alert.

"Well, the two of you are much alike," she teased, delighting in what she took as incipient jealousy. "The first time I saw his lordship I thought he was you, and I didn't know what to do."

"We have the same father," he answered gruffly, trying not to think of how she would react once she learned the truth. "It is not so remarkable that we should resemble each other."

"Perhaps," she said, shrugging her shoulders in a gesture that made him groan. "But it is more than a simple matter of a family resemblance, you know. I was going half-mad trying to discern what was afoot. I shall be eternally grateful that Sir Geoffrey told me of you, else I think I would have thrown caution to the wind and gone up to the earl and demanded to know if he was the smuggler I had hidden in my house several weeks ago! Only think of the scandal that would have caused!"

Peter gave her a sickly smile. "Imagine," he echoed.

They stood quietly for a few more minutes each reluctant to be the one who broke the fragile spell that surrounded them, but in the end Peter gently released her. "I must go," he said, gazing down into her face as if committing it to memory.

"I know," she smiled up at him, caressing his cheeks once more. "Be careful."

"I will," he ducked his head and kissed her, his mouth soft and tender. "Now mind you go home and wait for me. I will come for you, and then we shall talk. All right?"

She nodded, unable to speak.

"Good." He gave her one final kiss. "Now, close your eyes, my sweet, for there is no way I can leave if you are watching me."

Kate did as he asked, holding back her tears as she listened to the sounds of him leaving. It was only after she heard the door closing quietly behind him that she gave vent to her despair. She staggered over to the nearest chair and collapsed, burying her face in her hands and sobbing until she was too exhausted to think. Finally she raised her hand to wipe the tears away and was surprised to find them sticky; the tips of her fingers covered with a substance that was much like glue. What on earth . . . she stared at them, but was unable to solve the mystery.

"I don't like it," Giles grumbled, folding his arms across his chest as he watched Peter add the finishing touches to his toilet. "It will never work. It's far too simple."

"Which is precisely why it will work," Peter replied, dismissing his valet with a flick of an eyebrow. When he was gone he turned to James and the disgruntled viscount. "Don't worry, Westley, Payton will never suspect anything so blatantly obvious."

"Aye," James agreed cheerfully, although he kept a careful eye on his brother. "Our rat will be too busy nibbling on the tempting morsel we're offering to see the traps, and by the time he does," he brought both his hands together in a graphic gesture.

"A very eloquent analogy, to be sure," Giles said, his brown eyes narrowing in disapproval as he studied James's indolent pose. "But you can not tell me the marquess can be so easily duped. The man's not an idiot!"

"No, but he is desperate; too desperate to play it safe," Peter said, hoping to avoid open bloodshed between his associate and his brother. He'd awakened from a much needed nap to find the two men waiting for him, and loudly squabbling over the final plans to trap Payton. He'd tried maintaining a careful neutrality, but it was growing increasingly difficult as all of their nerves were stretched to the breaking point.

"A copy of the War Offices orders to Wellington will bring a small fortune in France," he continued, hoping to soothe Giles's overset nerves. "Payton won't be able to resist it."

"Especially after last night," James said with relish, bringing both men's heads snapping around to look at him.

"Last night?" they echoed.

"His fastest ship was run aground last night just south of Portsmouth," James explained, his green eyes growing wide in mock dismay. "Do you mean you hadn't heard? 'Tis all the talk in the local taverns. They're saying it was the Wreckers that did it," he added in a confidential manner, "and most shocking I consider it."

"But this will ruin everything!" Giles howled, visibly dismayed. "Our entire plan hinges on his being intercepted on the high seas with those plans in his pocket!"

"Don't worry, your lordship, the good marquess has two other boats at his disposal," James responded calmly. "The Belinda was the fastest ship to be found in these waters, and she would have outrun anything we sent after her; she is better left floundering on the rocks."

"What of the other ships?" Peter asked, having learned now that his wiley brother left little to chance.

"Ah, sad I am to report that the Aurora has also met with a most unfortunate mishap. Nothing serious, mind, just a wee bit of damage to her rudder. She'll not be out of commission more than, oh, say a week?"

Peter grinned at James's theatrics. "That would leave the Manchester?" he asked, having already learned what he could of the marquess's small fleet.

"Aye, smaller and not quite so maneuverable, but with a fine stateroom aboard." A pious expression crossed his handsome features. "I'd not want his lordship to be uncomfortable."

"How do you intend letting him know you'll be carrying the orders?" Giles ignored Peter's amused chuckle.

"I'm meeting him at his club this afternoon, and I'll let it slip that I have been entrusted with 'highly sensitive documents' which I will then be passing at Swansby's masquerade."

Giles had heard the plan before; had even helped arrange it, but now that the time for implementation was approaching, he found a dozen things to object to. "Won't he think it odd *you* have been entrusted with documents vital to our nation's security?" he asked, all but wringing his hands. "Or why you'll be exchanging them at a masquerade . . . of all things? It sounds damned rum to me!"

"That is because you're thinking like an agent," Peter said patiently. "And Payton, for all he is is a greedy traitor, is still an amateur. Besides, the part involving the masquerade will appeal to the bastard's sense of drama; that is why I selected it. Trust me, it will all work out in the end."

"I do trust you," Giles's voice was surprisingly even. "It is Payton I do not trust. Now if you will excuse me, I must be on my way. The Minister will be expecting a full report." And he quietly left the elegant dressing room.

"I hate to be agreeing with a man who bathes in eau de cologne," James commented, turning his head to survey Peter, "but he does have the right of it. Payton is as devious as he is deadly, and I'd not be trusting him further than I could pitch him. Watch your back, brother."

"I will," Peter told him, slipping a pistol in the cuff of his boots. "Mind you watch yours as well; remember it is you who will be making the exchange in my stead."

"Aye, and a clever piece of chicanery on your part it was, too," James laughed, looking pleased. "That devil's spawn will never think to look for two of us! My compliments to you, sir!"

"I'm rather proud of it myself," Peter commented, remembering his inspiration to send James in his place while he remained close by, in costume, and watching every movement. It gave them an edge; a small edge albeit, but an edge nonetheless. In the nether world of espionage, he had already learned that such things could often mean the difference between life and death.

"How did it go with your widow?" James asked, watching Peter intently. "Am I to take it that she'll not be troubling us any longer?"

Peter gave him a black scowl, knowing it would do him no good to prevaricate. James knew precisely what time he had come in this morning. "She has agreed to return to the country," he said reluctantly. "And once this is all over I mean to go to her and explain everything. I only hope to God she will listen."

"She will," James gave his shoulder a reassuring squeeze. "As you told your fine friend, it will all work out in the end."

"I pray that you are right," Peter sighed, his expression bleak. "Because if it does not, I don't give a damn if I survive this mission or not."

"Hussy! Traitor!"

"Now, Aunt Portia . . ."

"You have deceived me all along! You never once meant to remain in London for the Season. Did you?"

Portia took the news of Kate's impending departure better than she'd dared hope; throwing only a single tea cup and two saucers before launching into her furious tirade.

"I have nursed an asp to my bosom!" she cried, one hand clasped dramatically to that particular portion of her anatomy. "Oh, how sharper than a serpent's tooth is

284

an ungrateful niece! Of all the conniving, deceitful—"

"Daughter."

"—creatures you are without doubt . . . what did you say?" Portia broke off her harangue long enough to cast Kate an angry scowl.

"Daughter," Kate corrected, trying not to laugh at her aunt's declaiming. " 'How sharper than a serpent's tooth is an ungrateful daughter.' I don't believe King Lear had any nieces."

"Well, if the poor man did, I daresay she used him as wickedly as you have used me," Portia grumbled, flinging herself back onto her chair. "What do you mean you are returning to the country?"

"I mean, I am returning to the country," Kate replied, no longer so intimidated by her aunt's noisy displays of emotions. "I hope to leave by tomorrow afternoon, if at all possible."

"But I still do not see why!" Portia complained, wondering if a claim to illness would work since tears and hysterics had failed. "I mean, it's not as if you haven't taken; both you and Louisa have succeeded beyond all expectations! Even if you weren't to receive another invitation, you'd still have enough social obligations to keep you busy until summer."

"Yes, and I am very grateful that everyone has been so kind," Kate said gently, "but it makes no difference. I am still leaving."

"But—"

"Aunt," Kate interrupted, leaning over to cover Portia's hand with her own, "I am not asking you your permission, I am telling you. I am returning to Rye."

Portia closed her mouth at once, staring at Kate with wide eyes. "So, it's like that, eh?" she said, her voice surprisingly soft. "You've grown up."

"I've grown up," Kate agreed, grateful her aunt finally understood. "It's been a long time coming, I grant you, but I am finally my own mistress. I know what it is I want, and I am not afraid to say it."

"Well, you certainly picked a devil of a time to say it," Portia was soon back to her old, grumbling self. "What about the Swansby's masquerade, hmm? That is tomorrow evening, you know, and we've already spent a fortune having my gown altered!"

Kate had completely forgotten about the silly party. She did some swift calculations and then decided that one more evening wouldn't matter one way or another. She would simply set out first thing Friday morning, and be there in time for dinner.

"Well, since we have gone to all that trouble, I suppose I had really ought to attend," she said, pretending to give in with the greatest reluctance. "And I would like to say goodbye to Elizabeth . . . and Louisa, of course."

"Of course," Portia smiled. "Will you mind if I come and pay you a visit after the Season is ended? I've grown rather attached to your house."

"You must know you will always be welcome in my home," Kate said, tears welling in her eyes. "I hope you will come and stay a very long while!"

"I might just do that," Portia told her, looking thoughtful. "Yes, indeed, I might just do that."

Lord, but it was hot, Kate thought, fanning herself vigorously as she refused the offer of a rather inebriated Roman senator to show her the rose gardens. Since the moment they had arrived she'd been caught up in the mad rush of people, and she was beginning to regret her decision to attend. This was one of her worst nightmares come to life, and it was all she could do not to run screaming from the room.

"Are you all right, Kate?" Elizabeth materialized out of the crowd to stand beside her. "You are looking rather flushed."

"It is this dreadful crush of people," she confessed, wiping a shaking hand across her forehead. "One can hardly breathe, and it is so stifling in here! I do not see how you can endure it in those heavy skirts."

Elizabeth stroked the somber gown she had affected as Juliet's nurse; a rather fitting costume, she'd explained with a twinkle in her hazel eyes, since Louisa had confounded them all by coming as Juliet. "One learns," she said simply, "and really, it's not so bad; only look at poor Henry over there, so stuffed with padding that he is about to sweat his beard off."

Kate glanced in the direction Elizabeth indicated, smiling in sympathy at the red-faced man whose scraggly beard was hanging from his chin by the merest thread. "Poor man," she said, feeling somewhat better to know she wasn't the only person who was affected by the heat. "Why doesn't he just pull the silly thing off? It looks like a rat hanging there."

"Oh, I'm sure he shall, unless he can borrow some glue from one of the other Henry's. There must be at least six of them by my count; one for each wife!" And she laughed at her own witticism

Kate was about to follow suit when something deep inside her sounded an alarm. "What do you mean?" she asked, going icy cold where only seconds before she was all but roasting.

"His wives," Elizabeth was still chuckling. "He had six of them you know."

"No," Kate demanded, shaking her head slowly. "I mean, what did you mean about glue?"

"What?" Elizabeth blinked at her in surprise. "Oh! I was referring to the glue our Henrys have used to fix their beards to their cheeks. It's very sticky, I gather, and whenever the person sweats it comes lose again."

Kate had a vivid image of Mickey as she idly stroked his cheeks. And later, she found the tips of her fingers to be covered with a sticky substance.

"Of course, it is the intrepid soul who came dressed as King Charles whom I most pity," Elizabeth continued with another laugh. "Have you seen him; all rigged out in his velvet and lace, with his head stuck beneath his arm? The poor man must be baking alive!"

Kate gave a polite murmur in response, but all the while her mind kept going back to Mickey and the beard that was not as she remembered it. What if . . .

"Is everything in place?" Peter asked, settling his black domino about his shoulders and adjusting his half-mask. "We don't want any mistakes this late in the game."

"All is in readiness," James assured him, giving his own mask a tug. "And may I say how relieved I am to know 'tis only this damned cloak I need to be wearing? I was terrified you were going to rig me out in a bed-sheet like that poor sot," he nodded at a Greek who wandered past them, a giggling Cleopatra on his arm.

"I considered it," Peter admitted, his teeth flashing in a teasing grin, "but as you are supposed to be me, I thought it better that I keep our costumes simple. When the time comes, I don't want to trail Payton across the country dressed like something out of a third-rate theatrical production."

"And you're sure he will make a try for the plans to-night?"

"Positive. He all but drooled when I let him steal a peek at them while I was at his club. You could see him counting his gold as he was sitting there."

"Good," James rubbed his hands together. "Well, let's get to it, then. You're remaining out here?"

Peter gave the small alcove he had claimed for himself a cursory study, and then nodded. "It's close enough for me to see into the ballroom, but it also affords me a view of the street. I'll be able to see anyone coming or going."

"All right, see you in a few hours, brother. Mind you don't get too cold!" And with that he gave a jaunty salute, walking purposefully into the laughing mass of people crowded into the duke's salon.

288

Chapter Twenty

The next two hours passed slowly for Peter as he kept his lonely vigil. This was the hardest part; the waiting, but as it composed the majority of his work he'd learned to endure it. Payton's coach had arrived some twenty minutes ago, and he was profoundly relieved the marquess had taken the bait. Despite his reassuring words to Giles, he had been more than a little apprehensive. It was nice to know one could still reply upon simple human avarice he mused, his lips twisting in a sardonic smile. With luck, they would now have him in irons by week's end.

The thought brought to mind what would happen once Payton's arrest was made public. It was certain to cause a scandal; possibly even a Parliamentary investigation, given the marquess's nebulous connection to the Privy Council, and once that happened he didn't see how the Home Office could keep his name out of it. Once that happened the cat would be well and truly out of the bag, and Kate would know just how badly she had been duped. He only hoped he'd have time to tell her first himself. That way they might have some chance of a future together. Provided he could get her to listen; she could be so damned stubborn . . .

" 'Tis a good thing I'm not Payton, else you may have found yourself looking for your head," James said, stepping out of the darkness to appear at Peter's side.

Peter gave a nervous start and then whirled around. "James! Don't sneak up on me like that," he said, returning his pistol to his pocket. "I might have shot you!"

"Not before I had you laid out like a goose for the cooking," James returned in kind, waggling an admonishing finger at his brother. " 'Tis a poor shepherd who lets the fox slip off with the sheep while he's busy stargazing."

There was no denying this, and Peter's cheeks were flushed with embarrassment as he glared at James. "What about you?" he asked defensively. "It would seem you have left the flock unguarded altogether! Aren't you supposed to be having your pockets picked by Payton?"

"Such a mouthful of P's," James teased, his eyes gleaming behind his mask. " 'Tis a wonder you didn't tie your poor tongue into a knot."

"James . . ."

"Don't fash yourself, brother. The marquess is too busy playing the courtier to a fat Marie Antoinette to be engaging in any pilfering just yet. Oh, and he's dressed as Admiral Nelson, if you please, right down to the patch over his eye and the sleeve pinned to his chest."

"Bastard," Peter muttered, infuriated that such a low traitor would dare dress as so noble a hero.

"Clever bastard," James corrected. "With the sleeve pinned up that way it will leave his hand free for other things. 'Tis an old beggar's trick, and highly effective I've found it, too."

Peter grinned at James's droll aside, but then he grew serious again. "That still doesn't explain what you are doing out here. What if someone sees you?"

"They won't, but even if they do it is of little account. As for why I'm out here, you'd not be asking that if you had to wear this blasted robe in that hot house."

"That bad, hmm?"

"Worse," James replied with alacrity. "I haven't come

290

so close to disgracing myself since the first time I saw a hog butchered. But that's not the only reason I've put our plan at risk."

"Oh?" Something in James's voice alerted Peter. "What is it?"

"I thought you told me your Mrs. Delecourt was tamely tucked away awaiting your return."

It took less than a second for his implication to become clear. "Do you mean she is *here?*"

"And waltzing with our noble host, the last I saw of her," James replied grimly. "I'd not have known her at all, if I hadn't heard an old cat speculating as to whether or not the duke will be making her an offer in form. He is said to be quite besotted with her, you see," he added in a confiding manner.

A flash of pure masculine possessiveness streaked through Peter. "The hell he is!" he growled, and in the next moment he was cursing. "Devil take that woman! What in Hades is she doing here?"

"As I said, dancing with the duke," James said, studying Peter worriedly. "Are you quite sure she is not involved with Payton? She always seems to be where he is."

A thrill of fear replaced Peter's jealous anger, then he was shaking his head. "No. No, she has naught to do with this. I would stake my life on it."

"You already are."

Peter glared at James again. "Where is she?"

"In the ballroom; near the minstrel's galley if that is any help." James said quietly. "I take it you're going to have a word with the lady?"

"You're damned right, I am," Peter answered in a grim voice. "Will you stay here and make sure no one comes out?"

"Gladly," James assured him. "Any suggestions as to what I should do if Payton decides to take a French leave?"

Peter considered that and then said, "He won't. He's

come for those orders, and I can't imagine him leaving without them. Just watch the streets. I'll be back within the quarter hour," and he slipped through the double doors, his jaw set with fury.

"And this is my great-aunt, Lady Bettina Merivale," Lord Swansby said, introducing Kate to an elderly lady dressed in gray silk. "Aunt Bette, allow me to make you known to Mrs. Delecourt."

There was no response, and Kate turned to the duke. "I believe she is asleep, your grace," she said, trying very hard not to laugh. This was the third person he had introduced her to this evening who was either dozing or deaf as a post. She wondered if he had any relations who were awake and in full possession of their faculties. Other than his shrew of a sister, that is, she thought, grimacing at the memory of the sharp-faced woman who had suffered through their introductions with ill-grace.

"Is she?" Lord Swansby bent forward to peer at his ancient relation. "Oh dear, so she is. With Aunt Bette it is sometimes difficult to tell. Well, no matter, my dear, we shall just have to introduce you on some other occasion."

Kate managed a polite reply and allowed the duke to drag her off to meet the next family antique. She had explained to his grace that she was leaving London because of pressing business with her estate, but he hadn't seemed to pay her any mind. He seemed to think it a foregone conclusion that she would accept his offer, should he make one, and none of her gentle hints seemed to have the slightest effect. She only hoped he didn't send an announcement of their engagement to the *Times* while she was away.

While she and the duke took their turn about the room she allowed her thoughts to turn to Mickey. She'd already decided to think no more of the glue and his odd beard. She trusted Mickey, she told herself sternly. If he had glued a beard to his face, she was certain he must have a very good explanation for it.

After introducing her to an elderly gentlemen who seemed more interested in ogling a young girl dressed as Persephone than in meeting his nephew's chosen bride, Lord Swansby led her back to the ballroom. "I rather think Uncle Alfred liked you," he commented, giving her hand a paternal pat. "He doesn't often deign to speak to most people."

"How lovely," Kate said, wondering how a curt request to "Move it, gal," could possibly be considered conversation.

"Indeed, why, when Georgianna brought her fiancé home, he—"

"Good evening, Swansby," Peter said, stepping out of the crowd to block their path. "A pleasure to see you again."

Kate jerked in shock, the blood draining from her face as she studied the tall man standing before them. He was covered in a black domino, his face half-hidden by a loo mask, but she would know that voice anywhere. At least, she thought she would recognize it, she thought, her eyes going to the man's smooth jaw.

"Ah, Lord Tregarren good to see you," the duke greeted Peter with every show of friendliness. "What do you think of my masquerade? Quite a little party, eh?"

Peter's eyes were fixed on Kate, noting with disapproval the low bodice of her white and gold polonaise. "Very charming," he said in a carefully controlled voice. "It should be the talk of London for weeks to come."

The duke beamed with pleasure. "Do you think so? I spared no expense, you know. Going to do a thing, you ought to do it right, that's my motto. Pity you didn't wear a costume, though. Most folks did," and he indicated the scarlet robes he had worn as Cardinal Wolsey.

"My apologies, your grace, but I couldn't think of a costume," Peter replied, his ill humor little improved by the way Kate was clinging to Swansby's arm.

"Ought to have come as a Roman soldier," the duke suggested with a laugh, not seeming to notice his companion's strained silence. "Give the ladies a peek at your knees, eh?"

Peter gave him a thin smile. "An excellent suggestion, my lord, and one I will be sure to keep in mind. Meanwhile, I was wondering if I could prevail upon Mrs. Delecourt to join me for a moment? There is something I should like to discuss with her."

"Oh." Swansby didn't care to turn his lady over to such a notorious rake, but he didn't see how he could decline without risking the earl's legendary temper. "Don't see why not. Mrs. Delecourt?" He gave her an anxious look, deciding that if she had any objection to Tregarren's company she would surely say so.

"I–I would be delighted," Kate stammered, still not certain if it was Mickey or the earl who was standing before her. He sounded so much like Mickey, but he had no beard . . .

"Thank you," Peter reached out and grasped her arm, pulling her away from the duke with a decided sense of satisfaction. "Come, Ma'am," and he led her away, ignoring the duke's demand that he bring her back directly when he was finished with her.

They walked in silence, Kate too confused and Peter too furious to attempt conversation. There was a set of double doors leading out on to a small balcony and he led her through them, closing the doors with a bang as he whirled around to face her.

"Just what the devil do you think you are doing?" he demanded harshly, his eyes flashing with the force of his anger. "I thought you had left!"

Kate's jaw dropped. "I–I beg your pardon?" she stammered, trying to make some sense of the increasingly bizarre situation.

"Damn it, Kate, you told me, you *promised* me that you would return to Rye," Peter raged, his voice pitched low and furious. "You shall leave at once, do you hear me? You are endangering—"

"Mickey!" She could not control her stunned gasp.

That brought Peter up shortly as he realized he had just exposed his true identity to her. He quickly began repairing what damage he could. "No, I am Lord Peter Wyndham. Mickey is my brother, and he told me you—"

"No," Kate interrupted, feeling as if her brain was about to fly apart in a hundred different directions. "You said 'me,' 'You promised *me.*'" She looked up at him, her voice trembling with the force of her emotions. "Who are you?"

Peter was vividly aware of everything unraveling beneath his hands. "I've told you, I'm Lord Peter Wyndham, Earl of Tregar—"

"Are you the man I hid beneath my bed?" It hurt to ask the question, but Kate knew she had to hear the answer, even if it destroyed her.

"Damn it, Kate, I—"

"He's got the papers!" A second man in a black domino stepped out onto the balcony, his appearance and accent familiar enough to make Kate give swooning careful consideration.

"Hell!" Peter grabbed Kate and thrust her into James's arms. "Which way did he go?"

"Out the south door; just as you predicted," James said, easily supporting a stiff and silent Kate. "Be careful; he's sure to be armed."

Peter nodded curtly, his mind already on the chase ahead. He spared Kate a last, desperate look and then turned to James. "Take care of her," he ordered in a clipped voice, pulling the pistol from his pocket as he rushed through the doors and after Payton.

There was a long, uncomfortable silence before Kate was finally able to find her voice. "Are you Mickey?" she asked, staring up into a face that was similar but not identical to the one she thought she knew so well.

A wide smile spread across the handsome features visible beneath his mask. "James Lynchton," he corrected amiably, green eyes dancing with merriment. "And now if you don't mind, there's a traitor that needs catching. You look like a sensible sort of woman to me; promise to keep your wits about you and I'll take you with me. All right?"

Kate was too stunned to do anything other than agree. "All right."

"Good." He gave her shoulder a quick squeeze. "Let's go."

Peter rushed into the night, glancing about for any signs of Payton or the man he'd left standing guard. There were none, and he was about to return to the ballroom to gather his forces when he heard a low groan coming from behind the bushes. He inched closer warily, his pistol held at the ready as he moved towards the sound.

He found the guard on the far side of the bushes, the back of his head covered with blood. He bent down and examined him, breathing a sigh of relief when he found he was still alive, if somewhat the worse for wear. Removing his domino he carefully covered the unconscious man and was about to rise when there was a rustle behind him, and the unmistakable sound of a pistol being cocked.

"One move, your lordship, and you will be quite dead," Payton said softly, pressing the muzzle of his pistol against Peter's neck. "Hand over your weapons carefully, there's the lad."

Peter bit back a furious oath as Payton plucked his gun from his fingers. Two other men had joined them, a variety of weapons held in their hands as they surrounded him. He rose cautiously to his feet, his mind working furiously as he forced himself to think. He reasoned if they were going to kill him or knock him unconscious as they had Fredericks they would have already done so, which left only one other explanation.

"I can't tell you how disappointed I am to find you've brought me such a useless document," Payton said, dropping the false orders on to the ground beside Fredericks. "No matter, I am sure my French *amis* will pay far more to have you in their hands . . . again."

"So it was you who arranged that little ambush; I wondered," Peter murmured, in a desperate bid for time. He knew help would be arriving momentarily, but in the event it did not arrive in time he knew that he would not allow himself to be taken alive.

"Of course," the marquess smirked. "Not that I knew it was you, mind. I merely thought I was removing another irritation; not unlike that first fellow you sent after me."

Peter knew a sudden thrill of hope. The other man apparently didn't know that James had survived the murderous assault, or that he was his brother. Perhaps he might survive this after all, he thought with renewed optimism, fixing Payton in a baleful look. "You'll hang for this."

"Will I? Possibly." Payton seemed remarkably unconcerned with his fate. "But even if I do, you won't be alive to see it." He turned to the other two men. "Take him, and mind you bind him tight. He's a slippery bastard."

"What about Fredericks?" Peter asked, backing away from the others as he readied himself to do what he knew he had to do. "He needs medical attention."

"Yes, it would be a shame to leave him there, wouldn't it?" Payton said solicitously, then pointed his pistol at the unconscious man, firing a single bullet into the back of his head.

"You son of a bitch!" Peter leapt for Payton, determined to kill him before he himself was killed. He managed to grab the front of his costume, tearing one of the medals from his chest before a blow was brought down

297

upon his head. He held on grimly, fighting the pain and swirling blackness until another blow was landed. He fell to the ground, and his last thoughts were of Kate.

"Where is he?" Kate looked all about her as she and James rushed down the staircase and towards the door that was standing open. "He couldn't have gotten that far!"

"He's not far off," James said, restraining her with his arm as he drew his own weapon from the voluminous folds of his domino. "Now mind you stay back until I know the coast is —" His words were cut off by the muted roar of a gunshot.

"Peter!" James shoved Kate roughly to one side and took the stairs in two leaps, running out into the darkness at full speed.

Kate stared after him blankly, and then she was picking up her skirts and dashing after him, her heart in her throat for fear of what she would find.

There was no trace of either man outside, and Kate stood at the entrance trying to decide what she should do when she heard a noise to her left. She dropped her skirts and rushed forward, dashing through the bushes with little regard for her costly gown. The sight of James bent over a still figure lying in the ground brought her to an abrupt halt.

"Mickey!" she cried, dropping on to her knees beside James. "No . . . oh my God, no!"

"I . . . I don't think it is Peter," James forced himself to remain calm as he examined the man. "He isn't tall enough."

"But the domino . . ." Kate said, fighting tears and nausea as she stared at the grizzly sight before her. "He—he was wearing the domino when he left."

"I know," an icy desolation filled James at the thought he'd lost his brother. "Look away now, I'm going to turn him over."

Kate did as ordered, her eyes closing as tears streamed down her face. The matter of Mickey's . . . of Peter's identity was no longer important, and she found herself praying as she waited for the verdict. "Is it . . . is it him?"

"No," James's head dropped forward for a moment as he closed his eyes in relief. "It is some other man . . . Fredericks, I think he was called."

Kate said another prayer, this one for the unknown man who had been so brutally killed. She opened her eyes, keeping them fixed at some distant point as James rolled the man over again, carefully covering him with the bloodstained domino.

"We'll have to assume they've taken Peter," he said, wiping his hands as he rose to his feet. "I'll need to find Giles and the others so they'll know to watch the roads. He'll head for Rye is what I'm thinking, and we'll have to move fast if we mean to catch him before he sails for France."

"Who? Who are you talking about?" Kate accepted James's help as she stood.

"Payton." James decided it was too late to try and keep the truth from her. "He's a traitor as well as a smuggler, and we've been trying to catch him for the last five months."

Kate was beyond shock at this point; hearing the news with a dull sense of acceptance. She watched as James bent again and picked up some papers that were lying beside the body. "What are those?"

"Evidence." He returned the orders to his pocket along with the medal he found lying not far away. "The Home Office may want it. Not that it matters."

"What do you mean, 'not that it matters'?" Kate cried, her hands clenching into fists as she glared at James. "He is a murderer, and he has kidnapped your brother!"

"I know that," he replied in a deadly soft voice. "What

I meant was that the crown will not have its chance with Payton."

"Why not?"

"Because I am going to kill him," James said, his eyes meeting hers with a total lack of emotion. "Can you find your own way back to the ballroom? Time is of the essence if I am to reach Rye in time."

Kate gave him an incredulous look. "You are mad if you think I mean to return meekly to the ballroom after this!" she informed him indignantly. "I'm going with you."

He gave an impatient sigh. "Look, Mrs. Delecourt, 'tis not a sedate ride in the country I'll be taking. This is a matter of the gravest urgency, and I've no time to be coddling a hysterical female who will only slow me down."

"I'm not a hysterical female, nor will I slow you down," Kate said coolly, meeting his glare with determination.

James took her measure and revised his argument. "It is too dangerous. Peter will kill me were I to endanger you in any way."

"Then let him. I am going with you."

James opened his mouth to argue some more, than he closed it again. "Very well," he said, deciding he would let her accompany him as far as her house before setting after Payton alone. "But we need to leave now."

"My carriage is out front," Kate answered, inclining her head proudly. "After you Mr. Lynchton."

Chapter Twenty-one

Less than an hour later they were in Kate's travelling coach, rolling southwards towards Rye. James had shed his domino for a many caped garrick, and his expression was grim as he studied Kate in the flickering lamp light.

"I'm mad to have let you come," he said, his arms crossed as he leaned back against the squabs.

"And madder still to think I would have remained behind," she returned, meeting his glare with a defiant lift of her chin. Like James she'd changed from her evening clothes to something more practical, and her neat travelling dress of green-checked merino was covered by a darker green artois cloak. "If you hadn't brought me with you, I would have followed on my own.

James had already surmised as much; another reason he had allowed her to accompany him. He knew he would soon have enough to worry about without wondering where and when the pretty widow would pop up. This way he would be able to keep his eye on her, and if his luck held, keep her from getting herself killed.

"How did you explain your sudden departure to your aunt?" he asked, leaning back against the cushions. "You did leave her a note, did you not?"

"Certainly." Kate sniffed. "I wouldn't want her to worry about me. I simply wrote that due to an emergency I was leaving tonight rather than tomorrow."

James lifted his eyebrows in surprise. "Then you were planning to return to the country?" he said, looking relieved. "Peter will be pleased. He was most annoyed to think that you had lied to him."

"*I* lied to *him!*" Kate exclaimed, her green eyes sparkling with indignation. "Ha! That is rich, when he has done nothing but spin one tale after the other since the moment we met." James had already explained the reasons behind the deceptions, but she was still feeling far from mollified.

James gave her a sharp look. "I've told you, he was an agent of his Majesty's operating under the most secret orders. Surely you wouldn't expect him to reveal his true identity to everyone?"

Kate could have told him she was hardly "everyone," having kissed him passionately, but she was far too modest to begin. Not to mention confused; extremely confused, she amended, rubbing her eyes wearily.

"Of course not," she said in answer to James's question. "At least, not in the beginning. But later I . . ." her voice trailed off as she thought of Mickey . . . Peter, and the bone-deep integrity she had sensed in him from the very first. "No. No, I wouldn't have expected him to break his word."

"Good." James nodded. "It was killing him, you know. He wanted to tell you the truth, more than anything in this world, but he could not. He had taken an oath, and he could not reveal his identity to you without violating that oath. He left you a letter."

"A letter?" Kate asked hopefully. "May I see it?"

To her surprise James shook his head. "Not just yet. He left it with me in case . . . in case something should happen to him. Mayhap it is my Irish blood, but if I showed it to you now and something *did* happen, I would always worry that I somehow caused it. As it is, this is all my fault anyway."

"How can this be your fault?" she asked, staring at

him in amazement. "You said you expected Payton to steal those plans; which he did. There is no way you could have known he would want to take Peter as well."

"No, but he told me to stay on the balcony until he returned, only I began getting restless. I thought to poke my head in the ballroom for a wee bit, but then I felt the papers being lifted, and . . ." he rolled his shoulders. "None of this would have happened if I had stayed on the balcony as he asked me to."

Kate could think of nothing to say, knowing full well that having one's feelings of guilt brushed aside as foolish was almost as painful as the feelings themselves. Following Charles's death she'd bitterly blamed herself for not being a better wife while he was alive, and being told by well-meaning persons that she was being silly had often maddened her to the point of screaming.

"What are your plans?" she asked instead. "I gather you have notified the navy?"

"Yes," James stirred himself, turning his mind from his brooding thoughts to more practical matters. "They have several sloops and a man-of-war anchored just off the coast waiting to give chase. For all the good they'll do," he added bitterly.

"What do you mean?" Kate asked, something in his cold tones filling her with dread.

James glanced up at her, his eyes filled with bleakness. "It means that if Payton succeeds in getting Peter on a ship he is as good as dead. At the first sign he is about to be boarded, Payton will have him killed."

Kate paled. "Very well, then," she said, her voice oddly calm. "We shall simply have to make sure he doesn't get taken on board a ship. Won't we?"

James stared at her blankly. "And how would you suggest we stop them, ma'am? We don't even know where they are holding him!"

She was silent as she considered the matter, then a slow smile softened her mouth. "I believe I know someone who may be able to help us," she said, raising her eyes to meet James's wary stare. "Tell me, Mr. Lynchton, have you ever heard of a small inn called The Mermaid?"

Peter had no idea how long he'd been unconscious, but if the pain shooting through his bound limbs was any indication, it had to have been hours. His mouth felt bruised and dry, so he assumed he must have been gagged at one point. That they'd removed the gag told him they must be holding him in an isolated area where they needn't worry about anyone overhearing him. If he had been blindfolded it had also been removed, and he opened one eye to peer cautiously about him.

He was in a small hut of some kind and judging from the noises coming from the far side of the room, he wasn't alone. He went instantly still, his ears straining to catch any sound that might help him learn his whereabouts.

"Stop yer whinin', Croft," one man said distinctly, impatience evident in his rough voice. "Ye got yer orders same as me, an' they'll be no discussin' it."

"But I still don't see why it should take two o' us to watch the cove," the second man, Croft, complained in a high, nasal voice. "He ain't stirred so much as a toe since ye brung him here."

" 'Cause his Nibbs told us to stay," the first man said menacingly. "An' ye knows what he does to them what won't follow orders."

"Who says I ain't followin' me orders?" Croft denied fearfully. "I was jus' askin', is all."

They soon fell silent, but the brief conversation had provided Peter with all the information he needed. Two guards, and possibly more, stationed nearby. He moved stealthily, testing the strength of his bonds and found those binding his ankles had loosened. If he could work his feet loose and then his hands there was a small chance he could escape. And if not escape, he could make damned sure his captors had no choice but to shoot him. He rolled on to his side and began to rub his bound ankles carefully together; rubbing one strand of rope against the other.

"I said, no!" James exclaimed, hands on his hips as he glared down into Katherine's set face. "Blast it, Mrs. Delecourt, have all of your wits gone begging? I'd not send the most hardened doxy into that place, let alone a lady like you! Peter would gut me for sure."

"Peter won't need to know," Kate replied coolly, facing James with unshakable confidence. "Besides, what other choice have we? You've already admitted you're likely to be recognized. There is no one else to go."

James let loose with a spate of Irish curses which would have curled Kate's hair had she understood them. She remained resolute, however, her chin lifting in the defiant gesture James was beginning to recognize. He stopped cursing and stared at her for a full sixty seconds. "Ten minutes," he said at last, holding both hands up in emphasis. "And if you're not out of there by then I'm coming in after you."

"Ten minutes," Kate agreed, her shoulders slumping with relief. She'd been so certain James would fight her; for he seemed much inclined to behave like his autocratic brother. "It will work, James, I know it will."

James's lips tightened, and he kept up a running monologue as he escorted her to the front of the old inn. "It's easy, the lass says. Captain O'Rourake is my friend, the lass says. Aye, a friend who's been known to slit the throat of more than one Excise man and pick his pocket clean in the bargain! And what if he's not there, eh? On a night like this any captain worth the name would be out running his luggers past the cutters. You'll get attacked for sure, and then I won't have to worry about what Peter will do to me because I'll blow out what's left of me own brains myself!"

"Nothing will happen," she soothed, ignoring his

muttered imprecations. There appeared to be a great deal of Mickey in him, and she wondered if Peter had used him as the pattern card for the likable rogue. The thought brought a sheen of tears to her eyes and she blinked them away. They would rescue him, she vowed silently; she wouldn't allow herself to believe anything else.

When they reached the inn James gave her a last minute round of instructions, some of which had her blushing in distress. "I will not tell anyone I have already been hired for the night!" she exclaimed, feeling decidedly flustered. "Whatever would people think of me?"

"That you're not available to them, because God help you if they should think otherwise," James answered bluntly, already regretting his decision to let her go in alone. If there was any other way he would never have allowed such a things but as she so succinctly put it; what other choice was there?

"Have you any other instructions, sir?" Kate asked, infusing a teasing note in her voice to hide her trepidation.

"Just one." He pulled the pistol from the waist band of his pants and pressed it into her hands. "Use it, if you have to."

Her fingers curled around the weapon's handle and her eyes met his. "I will," she promised softly, tucking it into her cloak.

"Good." He gazed down at her for a moment and then bent to brush the lightest of kisses across her cheek. "For luck," he said simply, then stepped back to fade into the shadows.

Kate stared after him, wishing for one moment that she wasn't quite so headstrong. Then she sighed, her shoulders straightening as she turned and pushed open the inn's door.

She was met by a virtual wall of smoke and noise, all seeming to come at her from every direction at once.

She could hear the rattle of cutlery, the roar of voices raised in anger as well as laughter, and the jaunty notes of a fiddle. There seemed to be large, roughly-dressed men everywhere, and the way they were eyeing her made her clutch the pistol in a protective grip. The few women she could see were either barmaids or prostitutes, and the sight of them did little to reassure her.

She spied a bar in the very back of the room and was making her way towards it when a burly arm snaked around her waist, dragging her back on to a laughing man's lap.

"Hey lads, look here, I found meself a gentry wench!" He stuck his face closer to Kate's, and the stench of his breath almost made her gag. "Who be ye lookin' for, me love?" he asked, giving her arm a hard pinch. "Yer lord gone a'strayin'?"

There was another outburst of laughter and catcalls, the nature of which Kate couldn't even begin to understand. Telling herself to remain calm, she held herself as far away from her captor as was possible. "No, I am not," she informed him with cool politeness. "I am looking for Captain O'Rourake. Would you be so good as to tell me where I might find him?"

"O'Rourake, is it now?" He gave another laugh, his arm closing so tightly about her she was certain her ribs would break. "What be ye wantin' with that old sea dog, eh? I can give ye a much better time o' it than him! Just ask Betty here," and he gave the slovenly bar maid a swat on her ample posterior with his free hand.

Kate managed a cool smile, beginning to think she would have to use her pistol against this lout if she was ever to win her freedom. "My business with the captain need not concern you, sir," she informed him frostily. "My name is Mrs. Delecourt, and I —"

She suddenly found herself deposited on her feet several feet from her amorous swain as a sudden hush descended on the tavern.

"M–Mrs. Delecourt?" He stammered, his complexion paling to an ashen hue. "O' the manor house near the bay?"

"Yes," Kate said slowly, wondering what on earth was going on. "Have you seen Captain O'Rourake, sir?" she asked the man. "It really is most urgent that I speak with him."

"Oh yes, miss . . . uh, ma'am . . . me lady," he pulled the greasy cap from his head and bobbed a hasty bow. "He be in the back. Joseph!" he gave the gawking lad sitting at his right a vicious kick. "Go an' fetch the Cap'n quick like! Tell 'im Mrs. Delecourt be here askin' to see 'im."

The lad was off in a flash, knocking over his chair in his haste to be gone. No sooner had he disappeared than the men began swarming about her, offering her their chairs, a plate of food, or anything else they thought a lady of quality might require. When Captain O'Rourake came striding into the main room, Kate was sitting on one of the inn's barrel chairs, cautiously sipping the cup of tea one of her newfound gallants had fetched for her.

"Mrs. Delecourt?" He gave her a polite little bow, his gray eyes studying her with wary curiosity. "What can I do for ye?"

She set her cup down and rose to her feet, aware of the need for secrecy as well as urgency. "Captain, do you recall the friend of yours we spoke of some weeks ago?"

"Aye," he answered after a thoughtful pause. "Reckon I do."

"Excellent," she gave him her brightest smile. "Well, it seems he is having a slight problem, and I was wondering if I might prevail upon you to help us assist him."

"Us?"

"His brother is outside."

He scratched his chin for a moment, and then he broke into a wide, gap-toothed smile. "In that case,

Mrs. Delecourt, reckon we ought to be takin' a stroll. Always happy to meet the brothers of me friends. Lead the way."

The hours passed with agonizing slowness for Peter. To keep his mind off his grim situation he allowed his thoughts to drift towards Kate, and the burning kisses they had shared. It had been like a dream, he mused, rotating his foot and breaking a few more precious strands of rope. She had been all that he had ever imagined a woman could be, and he was finally able to admit that he loved her. He had to survive, he told himself desperately; not just for his country's sake, but for Kate's as well.

"Quit yer squirimin' over there!" Croft called out, his tone more petulant than ever. "I'll not be tellin' ye again!"

Peter glared at the small, unkempt man. "If this damned pallet wasn't thick with vermin I shouldn't have to squirm. You may tell your master his sense of hospitality is sadly wanting."

Croft's pinched face turned a mottled red. "He ain't my master!" he spat out furiously. "Ain't no man *my* master!"

"Really?" Peter drawled, tucking his reaction away for future use. "Yet you follow his orders quickly enough."

"Arrogant, blackhearted devil," Croft muttered, and Peter knew he was referring to Payton. "Thinks all he has to do is snap them fingers o' his an' we'll snap to attention."

"Hush!" The other man, Dorn, cast an uneasy look at the bolted door. "He'll be here soon, and if he hears yer yappin' he'll slit both our throats!"

"Let 'im try!" Croft had been fortifying his courage and his resentment with sips of brandy from his leather flask, and was decidedly belligerent. "I'm tired o' doin' his biddin' like some gutless puppy!"

That set off another argument, and while his two guards were busy hurling insults at each other Peter managed to snap the last of the ropes binding his legs. The rush of sensation to his cramped limbs brought a muffled cry of pain to his lips, and he gave himself a moment to recover before turning his attention to the cords about his wrists. He'd been working on them as well, and although he had yet to snap them he had succeeded in loosening them somewhat. All he needed was a few more hours; just a few more precious hours and he would be free. He took another breath and then began the laborious process of flexing and unflexing his wrists.

"I don't like this," James muttered, pistols held in each hand as he circled around the large tree set in the clearing. "Why couldn't we have brought the rest of your men with us and then just rushed the building? You said there were only two of them guarding my brother."

"Aye, and the pair of them armed," O'Rourake answered, calmly pouring powder into his musket. "I don't think I need tell ye what they'd do to him was we to come burstin' through that door like ye suggest. Calm yerself, lad, 'twill work out fine."

James muttered an Irish curse beneath his breath, wondering how he had ever allowed himself to be talked into such an insane plan. That O'Rourake knew the location of Payton's secret hideaway had come as no surprise, as had the fact that he knew the marquess was making an important "shipment" that night. What did come as a shock was his inventive plan for rescuing Peter.

"Now remember," O'Rourake said, testing the sharpness of his knife against his thumb before tucking it into the waistband of his trousers, "we give her five minutes to distract them, and then we come burstin' in."

"But what if they use her as a hostage?" James asked, his stomach clenching in fear. "Or what if she gets cut down in the cross fire? God, she is a woman; she should not even be here, let alone in the very thick of things!"

"I'm fair sure they won't use her as ye say, else I'd not have allowed her to do it," O'Rourake answered calmly, understanding the younger man's distress. "An' there won't be no cross fire neither, if I knows the two what are inside. Once they knows the odds are against 'em, they'll have their hands in the air fast enough. As for the other, the lady has more bottom than two men. She'll do just fine."

"I know that," James argued worriedly, "but—"

"Shh!" O'Rourake shifted around until he had an unobstructed view of the crude hovel. "There she is. Get ready now, 'tis almost over."

The frantic pounding on the door made both men leap to their feet, pistols held in shaking hands as they aimed them at the door. "Who's out there?" Dorn called out, wetting his lips nervously.

"Help! Help!" A female voice called out in obvious hysteria. "There are murderers out here! For the love of God, let me inside!"

The two men exchanged puzzled looks but went to unlatch the door, not knowing what else they could do. The moment the door was open a small woman rushed inside, blond hair falling about her shoulders as she turned to face Dorn and Croft.

"Murderers!" she shrieked, waving her hands and pacing about like a madwoman. "An army of them! They ambushed our coach and are holding my husband! Do something!"

The two guards exchanged frightened expressions. "M—murderers ye say?" Croft asked, swallowing in fear. "In the marsh?"

"An army of them," Kate repeated, interposing herself between them and Peter. "Ten at least, perhaps

311

more, and all dressed in black," she cried, dropping a knife on to the pallet next to Peter's hips and then edging away again. "Well, why are you just standing there like moonlings?" she snapped. "Go after them!"

There was another exchange of confused looks. "Go after ten men? Alone?" Dorn stared at her as if she had clearly lost her mind.

"Maybe there were a hundred," Kate invented, wondering how much time had elapsed. O'Rourake had been emphatic about the timing. Five minutes, he had said, and then she was to make sure she was well away from the door, and on the ground if at all possible.

"It was horrible, too horrible to relate," she rambled on, keeping the men's eyes trained on her as she continued her mad pacing. "They came at us from nowhere, like ghosts. They shot our poor coachman and then drove us into that dreadful swamp. I escaped by the very grace of God, and found my way here. I dare not think what those devils are doing to my husband and companion. Oh," she laid a hand on her forehead and swayed dramatically, "I feel faint."

The two men paled at the thought of a female succumbing to the vapors and moved forward to assist her. The moment they had stepped free of the door she laid her hand over her heart and emitted a shriek, crumpling to the floor in what looked to be a dead faint.

The echoes of her screams were still echoing in the hut when the door flew open and James and O'Rourake burst inside, guns trained on the cowering men.

"Peace, sirs, peace!" Croft cried, flinging both his hands into the air. "Ye can take the wench, only don't hurt me!"

Kate was on her feet, her own gun in her hand, as she smiled at the stupefied pair. "You, sirs, are no gentlemen," she said sweetly, and then turned to Peter, who had used the knife to slash through his bindings.

"Are you all right?" she asked, rushing over to kneel beside him. "We have been so worried! We—"

"What the hell are you doing here?" Peter demanded savagely, feeling a terrible sense of urgency washing over him. He'd felt like this only once before, when the French dragoons had surrounded him, and he was frantic to get her out of there before all hell broke loose.

Such a lack of gratitude brought Kate's jaw thrusting forward. "What do you think we are doing, you—you liar!" she snapped, looking furious. "We are rescuing you! And that is another thing, how dare you —"

"Later, Mrs. Delecourt, later," Captain O'Rourake chided, keeping his musket trained on the disgruntled guards as James bound them tightly. "Right now I think 'tis best we quit this place before his lordship decides to honor us with a visit."

"His lordship," a cold voice sounded from the doorway, "is already here."

They all turned and stared in horror at the four men who had shouldered their way into the small hut; guns held in their hands. Kate glanced back at Peter, love and desperation in her eyes as she quickly slid her pistol into his hands.

"Ah, the lovely widow," Payton drawled, walking past James and O'Rourake as if they didn't exist. "What a delightful surprise; I had never thought to connect you to all this."

Kate gave Peter's knee a warning squeeze and then rose proudly to her feet. "Didn't you?" she asked coolly, using her body to shield Peter's furtive movements. "How odd, I had you pegged as a scoundrel the moment I clapped eyes on you."

Payton's blue eyes blazed with chilling fury at the deliberate insult. "Did you now?" he said mockingly when he had regained control of his temper. "Well, I will just have to see what I can do to change your estimation of me, won't I?" He turned to one of the men he had brought with her. "Tie her up."

"Damn you Payton, if you dare touch her I'll kill you!" Peter growled, keeping both hands behind as if they were still bound.

"I am sure you shall want to," Payton laughed, delighting in his power over the helpless man. "Mayhap I shall take my pleasure of her in front of you, and then let my men have their turns with her. Would you like that, my fine and noble lord?"

That was too much for Peter, he was on his feet in a flash, pushing Kate roughly to the ground as he pulled his pistol and trained it on Payton. At the very same moment five of O'Rourake's men came through the door, easily subduing the marquess's men, who seemed singularly disinclined to fight for their repellent master.

It was all over in seconds, and as Kate rose shakily to her feet she saw Peter's face white with strain as he kept his weapon aimed at Payton's chest. "I want to kill you," he said, his voice shaking with suppressed fury. "God, I want so much to kill you."

"But you won't, will you?" Payton taunted, his eyes flicking from Peter to the other men. "You are a *gentleman,* and you would never stoop to shooting an unarmed man."

"No," Peter admitted harshly, "as you say, I am a gentleman."

"As am I," Payton said with a languid sigh. "And I really do not think I should wish to end my life kicking and gasping at the end of a rope while the great unwashed look on and jeer." He was still a moment, and then he was leaping at Peter, grabbing the weapon and pulling it towards his chest. Peter sensed what he was about to do and tried to pull the gun back, but he was no match for the marquess's desperate strength. There was the muffled report of a shot and Payton slumped to the floor, a bright stain of blood spreading rapidly across his chest.

"Hell!" Peter knelt over him at once, but he could see at a glance there was nothing he could do to save the other man. He knelt back on his heels and gave the marquess a bitter look. "Damn your black soul, Payton," he said heavily. "Damn you to hell."

Payton's lips curled in a faint smile. "Undoubtedly," he said weakly, the pale blue of his eyes already fogging over with death. "But this way you shall have your honor, and I . . . I shall have mine," his lashes fluttered shut, and in a heartbeat he was gone.

"More tea, Mrs. Delecourt?" Mrs. Parks offered, hovering solicitously over her beloved mistress. "And some strawberry tarts, perhaps? Cook made them special for you when she heard you was coming home."

"What?" Kate stirred listlessly, blinking up at the housekeeper in confusion. "Oh, no thank you, Mrs. Parks, that will be all."

"My, my, such terrible doings these days," the older woman scolded, draping a shawl about Kate's shoulders. "First you coming home in the dead of night looking as if the dear Lord above only knows what happened, and then Lord Payton shooting himself while cleaning his pistol on top of it all. . . . Well, I just can not imagine what this poor old world is coming to, and that's the truth of it!"

Kate gave no answer, and after awhile Mrs. Parks departed, still muttering and shaking her head in disapproval. Kate leaned back against the overstuffed chair and let her eyes drift towards the window. It was early May, and the garden was alive with a profusion of colors and sweet scents. In the terrible months following Charles's death she had often wandered the cobbled path wending between the flowers, finding solace in the renewal of nature, but there could be no such solace for her now.

Five days, she thought unhappily. It had been five days since Peter had left her on her doorstep, giving her a fierce kiss and a clipped order to "stay put." Well, she had stayed put, for all the good it had done her, and her patience was at an end. She had had to face unpleasant facts in the past, and it looked as if she would have to face an even more unpleasant one now. Peter was not coming back.

The admission brought a sheen of tears to her eyes. She loved him, she thought miserably. He was a scoundrel, a liar without principle, and he had used her shamelessly. Never mind he had done so for the best of reasons, he had still used her, and she wished with all her heart she could hate him for it.

Suddenly she couldn't bear her small parlor another moment, and leapt to her feet, her only thought to get away. She thought of the beach, and dashed out of the door, ignoring Richards's frantic plea to know where she was going. Less than a quarter of an hour later she was walking on the hard-packed sand, listening to the soothing murmur of the incoming waves. This is where it had all begun, and it seemed fitting this is where it should end.

She walked until she came to the spit of land where she had first seen Mickey . . . Peter, she corrected herself for the dozenth time. At that time her life had also been in turmoil, and she could remember thinking how desperately she wanted for it to change. The memory brought a rueful smile to her face. The next time she made such a wish, she decided, she would have to be more specific as to how she wished it to change.

She continued walking, no particular destination in mind as she strolled. Perhaps she ought to return to London, she mused, but the thought of running into Peter put a swift end to that. Perhaps next year she could face him with some equanimity, but not now. After all, she told herself, she'd recovered from Charles's death. She would recover from Peter's betrayal as well.

She wasn't certain when the mist began rolling in, but by the time she became aware, it had already grown dangerously thick. She turned and began making her way back, when she saw a figure emerging out of the rolling mist. In a few seconds the figure became a tall man wearing a cape of some sorts, and a few seconds after that the man's features became clearly discernible. Kate's breath caught in her throat as she recognized Peter's face.

"A fine way you have of following orders," he greeted her with a scowl. "And what the devil are you doing out in this fog without a cloak? You'll catch your death of a cold."

Kate stood mutely as he took off his own cloak and draped it about her shoulders. For one moment she feared she had lost her reason, but then she felt the warmth of his body pressed to hers and she knew he was really there.

"You bastard!" Her hand lashed out as she slapped him on the cheek with all her might. "You lied to me!"

Peter stared down at her hungrily, making no move to defend himself, even when she struck him a second time. The past week had been a nightmare, and the only thing that kept him going was the thought of her. He knew she would be furious with him, but he also knew that she loved him. It was that knowledge that brought him here, prepared to face her tears and anger if it meant he would have her once the screaming had subsided. And he had to have her, he told himself with despair, because if she rejected him, he would turn and walk into the sea.

"I trusted you!" Kate continued, tears streaming down her face as she hit his chest with her fist. "I was willing to give up everything for you! And you couldn't even be bothered to tell me the truth!"

"Kate . . ."

"I know you're an agent," she raged, her breath coming in ragged sobs, "I know you couldn't tell me who you were. But you let me kiss you, you let me call you another man's name, and all the while you were someone else . . ."

"My love, please . . ."

317

"And then you have to go and risk your life! I thought you were dead, did you know that? James and I found that poor man wearing your domino and I thought I had lost you! I wanted to die too, because I love you, and—"

"I love you, Katherine. Marry me."

"And you let five days, *five days* go by without so much as a word, and. . . . What?'

Peter saw the confused look that passed across her scowling face, and he threw back his head and laughed. He gathered her up in his arms, swinging her in a wide circle before depositing her back on the sand. "I love you, Kate," he told her huskily, his arms remaining possessively about her. "And if you don't marry me, I swear to heaven that I will tell all of London that you sheltered the notorious Lord Tregarren in your bed for weeks."

"I . . . I didn't shelter you in my bed," Kate stammered, it was an odd protest to make at such a time, but it was the only thing she could think of to say. She had gone from such despair to such joy that she didn't know what was real and what was not.

"So you didn't," he agreed, pulling her even closer as he bent to taste her sweet lips. "And if one is to be utterly precise I wasn't in the bed, I was under it. I pray you never tell James the full details of that particular story, my love; he would never let me forget it."

"But . . ."

"No more," James kissed her again, this time using his tongue to tease her soft lips apart. "We are being married by special license this very afternoon, and that is the end of it."

Kate threw her arms about his neck, love and joy filling her as she returned his kiss with all the passion that was in her. In the next moment she was thrusting him away from her.

"I shall not marry a liar," she warned him, hands on her hips as she glared at him. "And I shall not marry an agent, either! I have already given one husband to England, I won't give another."

"I quite agree with you, my sweet," Peter pulled her back into his arms. "And I promise you I shall not lie to you any more than any other husband lies to his wife."

"And the spying?" She was still scowling up at him.

"Finished," he assured her, tracing the peaks of her breasts beneath the soft wool of the cloak. "Whitehall has decided my usefulness is at an end, and so I am free to pursue . . . other matters. Now, have you any other objections, or may we return to our lovemaking?"

Kate considered that a moment. "There is one more thing."

"What?" Peter pressed her against his burgeoning hardness. "Talk fast my love."

"I want to call our first born Mickey."

Peter stared down at her in disbelief, and then he was laughing. "Mickey it shall be, my sweet, and Michelle if it is a girl. Now, may we make love?"

She returned to his arms, snuggling contentedly against his chest. "Why yes, my Lord Tregarren, I believe we can," she said, smiling up at him with love shining in her eyes.

They kissed one last time and then turned and made their way back to the house, their figures disappearing into the mists.